HOLD HER CLOSE

CROWN OF PROMISE

HOLD
HER
CLOSE

HANNAH CURRIE

WhiteCrown
PUBLISHING

This is a work of fiction. All characters and events portrayed in this novel are either fictitious or used fictitiously.

HOLD HER CLOSE
Copyright © 2024, Hannah Currie

WhiteCrown Publishing, a division of WhiteFire Publishing
13607 Bedford Rd NE
Cumberland, MD 21502

ISBNs:
979-8-88709-077-1 (paperback)
979-8-88709-079-5 (hardcover)
979-8-88709-078-8 (digital)

To the silent warriors who battle unseen illnesses every single day.
You are stronger than you give yourself credit for
And more valued than you know.
Thank you for getting up again and again
And for being bringers of hope.

My precious daughter,
Beloved of mine
If only you could see yourself
As I do
You look in the mirror
And see yourself as less
Sometimes even without worth altogether
And it breaks my heart
Because never once has that been
The girl I see
You see weakness, I see strength
You see scars, I see courage
You see flaws, I see beauty
You see someone you'd rather not see
I see the daughter I created
The very best parts of me
My precious daughter,
Beloved of mine
I pray one day you'll see yourself
As I do

Raedonleith, 1424

*B*arren.

The word brought forth images of dry, empty fields. Blistering heat. Sun-bleached bones. Cracked soil. Devastation.

"Are you certain?"

"I'm sorry, my lady. Perhaps the Almighty may grant you a miracle, but—"

The healer tried to smile. Attempted to offer hope. But what hope was there to give?

Barren.

Unable to produce life.

That was the other meaning for the word. The one searing itself across Rose's heart. Her mind. Her soul.

She'd prayed, hoped, *begged* the Almighty for a different outcome. But he hadn't given it. Instead, the healer confirmed what Rose already suspected. She'd been bleeding too much. Too long.

Rose focused on the healer's hands as the woman clasped a dark gray cloak around her shoulders and picked up her satchel. She was leaving now. There was no reason for her to stay. Nothing she could do. Her services were better given elsewhere. To people whose bodies and maladies she could fix.

Unlike Rose.

"I'm sorry," the woman said one more time before walking out the door.

Barren.

Rose couldn't look at her parents. Couldn't bear to see the anguish she knew would be on their faces. Their oldest child. Heir to the throne of Raedonleith.

Barren.

"We'll have to tell Prince Aldon," her father said as he closed the door behind the healer. "'Tis not right to keep it from him."

Yes. Her betrothed. He needed to know.

And her sisters.

And the people of Raedonleith. The ones counting on her to one day lead them. To continue the royal line. They'd all find out soon enough. If only she could continue to keep the humiliation to herself. Hide it away as she'd done with the suspicions she'd harbored the past five years. But hiding had never been an option. Not when she was the princess.

"I can tell him, if you wish?"

"Yes," Rose told her father. "Please." She'd never get the words out herself.

Almighty. Why?

All she'd ever wanted was a family.

A husband.

A child to love. Even just one.

"Rose—" Her mother's voice cracked, stunting whatever comfort she hoped to offer.

Rose shook her head. "I'll be well. Truly. In time."

It was a lie. Time wouldn't change this, nor would she be well. Not now. Not ever. She hadn't been well for years.

CHAPTER 1

Chapels weren't created as a place to hide.

Nicholas pushed the condemning but accurate thought aside as he knelt on the stone steps before the altar and pleaded with the Almighty to understand. He shouldn't be here—at least, not to hide—but it was the only place Nicholas could think of where the scores of women vying for his attention wouldn't bother him.

Forgive me, Almighty One. They're your children, filled with worth and value, but I'd value them just as much if they weren't quite so eager.

This was all his younger brother's fault. The day the marriage agreement was signed between Belairisia and Raedonleith, officially betrothing Aldon to Lady Rose, every woman in the kingdom had set their sights on the stubbornly unbetrothed Nicholas.

They swarmed him in the marketplace. Threw tokens at his feet as he walked. Ogled him in the Great Hall as he ate his meals. Lined the edges of the training fields as he sparred. He'd even found three fighting over him at the door to his chamber last night. As if he would let any woman who wasn't his wife into his chamber. Surely they knew better.

Nicholas might have shown more interest had those exact same women not ignored him while trying to win Aldon's attention for the past ten years. Right up until the day Aldon left for Raedonleith to claim his bride. Nicholas had thought it amusing then, thankful to be the far less handsome, far more responsibility-laden older brother. He didn't find it so amusing now.

Even the library, his place of refuge, had been crowded the past few days.

"Choose one and the rest will leave you alone," his father had advised when Nicholas asked for his advice. *"I've been urging you for years to take a wife."*

Choose one. As if he might just roll a die or pick a name from a hat and claim the winner his wife for the rest of his days. It was the way of things, Nicholas knew. Affection and respect didn't matter so much as title and connections when you were next in line to a throne, but Nicholas wanted to at least care about the woman he chose. Not that he didn't care for the women throwing themselves at him day after day— they were his people, after all—but not one of them had captured his mind or heart, fickle as they were. He couldn't imagine any one of them standing by his side as queen one day, much less be interested in the fact that he would rather read a book than wield a sword. They wanted his crown and wealth but cared little about him as a man.

And so he hid. Like the brave knight he wasn't.

Anything for a moment of respite.

A cleric walked into the chapel. Nicholas bowed his head and closed his eyes before the man could make eye contact. The cleric would ask if he might intercede with the Almighty on Nicholas's behalf and if there was a particular reason Nicholas had come to worship today. Admitting he was scared of a crowd of women and had come to hide would at best get himself ridiculed and at worst thrown out along with a severe admonishment to respect the house of the Almighty as it deserved.

Nicholas let out a sigh that ruffled the ties of his blue tunic and bowed his head deeper. Perhaps if he prayed while he was here, the guilt churning his stomach over using the chapel for something other than worship might go away.

Almighty, thou art good and worthy. Thank you for the life you have given me. For health and wealth and my daily bread.

A waft of smoke tickled Nicholas's nose followed by the sweet scent of honey. The cleric must have lit a candle.

The judgments of the Lord are true and righteous, desirable more than gold, and sweeter than honey and honeycomb.

Nicholas had read that line just yesterday in the Holy Scriptures as he sat tucked under a table in the library. He'd been sitting *at* the table until the chatter of two women approaching the book-filled room sent him scurrying. Perhaps they'd come to extend their knowledge but Nicholas couldn't help but doubt their zeal given they'd walked in, looked around the library for less than a minute, and walked away again.

There was more to the psalm but Nicholas's mind had wandered after that, tumbling into an abyss of wondering. How did bees create honey? How hot did a fire have to be to melt gold? Why was gold the most desirable of metals? Where on the shelves before him was a book describing such processes?

His thoughts were wandering again. Prayer and worship. They were the reason he was here. Not bees and gold. Although there were many mentions of gold in the Scriptures. Gold statues, golden utensils in the holy temple, crowns of gold, streets of gold...

Forgive me.

A commotion sounded outside the building. Shouts. Cheers. Probably his father riding through the marketplace. The people were always thrilled to see their beloved king. Nicholas shuffled his knees to a more comfortable position and forced his thoughts back to prayer.

Bless my father and mother. Bless my brother and Lady Rose and their upcoming nuptials. Bless the people in our care. Give us wisdom to lead them and courage to do what's right. May we ever be your humble servants, worthy of the crown you have bestowed upon us.

The shouts grew louder, closer, the words clarifying.

"Prince Aldon! Prince Aldon!"

Aldon? But—

No. They must have been saying something else. Aldon was in Raedonleith, preparing for his wedding. There was no reason for him to have returned to Belairisia. Unless the circumstances had changed. But King Lior would have sent word had that happened. There had been no word.

To thy name be all glory, honor, and power, above and beyond all—

The door clattered open. Nicholas wondered if continuing to kneel with his back to whoever entered would make the person go away.

"Prince Nicholas, forgive me for disturbing you, but—"

Apparently not.

"—your brother has come home."

Nicholas opened his eyes and stared at the worn steps under his knees. Aldon *had* returned. But why? He wasn't supposed to marry for two more weeks. Nicholas, along with his father and mother, planned to depart for Raedonleith three days hence to arrive in time for the wedding.

Either they'd missed the wedding, or it wasn't happening.

Nicholas hoped for the former. Raedonleith needed them—their name and the strength of their army. King Lior had stated as much when he humbly requested the marriage alliance. Their kingdoms wouldn't join as one, but they'd fight together should the need arise. King Lior believed it would. Soon. A neighboring lord sought to overthrow him and his family.

"Sire?"

The messenger wasn't going away. Nicholas bowed his head a moment longer before standing. "Where is he now?"

"His chambers, I believe. He requested food be sent there."

Not to see Father then. Intriguing. Worrying.

But perhaps Nicholas was reading the situation incorrectly.

"Is Lady Rose with him?"

"No, sire. Only the men he traveled with."

And perhaps he wasn't. Nicholas rubbed a hand over his eyes. It was time Aldon took on some of the responsibility of the kingdom. There was so much more to being a prince than fine clothes, good food, and women swooning in the streets.

Forgive me.

That was cruel. Aldon was more than a figurehead, and while he enjoyed the attention his warrior's physique and skill with weapons gave him, he'd never once taken advantage of any of those women. He was young and arrogant, to be sure, but Nicholas would have been too if he'd been blessed with his brother's gifts. Weaponry came easy to Aldon. Women too. Nicholas knew better than to judge before hearing the whole story.

"Thank you," he told the messenger. "I shall meet him in his chambers shortly."

But not before he begged the Almighty—again—for wisdom. And a double portion of patience.

⋆·ᚺᚷᚺ·⋆

"Where's your wife?"

Nicholas didn't bother with niceties. The amount of food piled on the table before Aldon and the rainbow of fabric tokens discarded at the door indicated he'd already been well welcomed. The maidens of

Belairisia had wasted no time in transferring their affections back to the younger of their two princes.

"I don't have one."

Was he being purposely obtuse? "Your betrothed, then."

"I don't have a betrothed either."

"The papers Father signed with King Lior of Raedonleith say otherwise."

Aldon shrugged. "Agreements can be broken."

True, they could. But not without pain—and often bloodshed—on both sides. Nicholas pulled a second chair over to Aldon's table and sat. Though Aldon offered him a bunch of grapes, Nicholas shook his head. He'd come for answers, not food. Answers his brother was intent on holding hostage.

Nicholas looked down when a tiny movement caught his attention. Aldon was tapping his heel. Some of Nicholas's frustration melted away. Aldon only tapped his heel when he was upset. It was rare but a tick he'd had since childhood.

"What happened?" Nicholas asked quietly.

"Nothing. That is what happened." Another grape. More heel tapping. Nicholas hadn't seen his brother this agitated in years. Of course, he'd also not seen his brother in almost two months. He should have gone with Aldon to Raedonleith. He'd considered it. He'd even gone so far as to make plans, only to change them when Father had become ill. Whatever the malady was, it had only lasted a day, but it had been enough to remind Nicholas of his responsibilities. He was Belairisia's heir. He couldn't go traipsing off to another kingdom for months at a time to support his brother. Aldon was a man. He could look after himself.

Or so Nicholas believed.

"Something must have or you wouldn't be here. News of your arrival will have reached Father by now. He'll be calling for you and an explanation any moment, so you may as well tell me." And give Nicholas the chance to decide whether to defend his younger brother's decision before the king or march him straight back to the stables and on his way to Raedonleith. "You said Lady Rose was beautiful."

"Aye. The most stunning woman I've ever laid eyes upon. She was attractive as a girl but has truly grown into her beauty. Willowy and graceful, like an angel or spirit, with a smile so gentle you can't help but feel honored every time she bestows it. A man would be fortunate to have her by his side."

"Yet here you are. Without her."

Aldon's heel tapped faster. "It is for the best."

"For you? Or for the kingdom? Because being a prince doesn't come with—"

"The luxury of selfishness. I know. You've told me. Many times."

Still, here his little brother sat. Feasting in his chamber when he should have been in Raedonleith by Lady Rose's side. Aldon had always been somewhat vain, but most of it was justified. He was an exceptional warrior and a trusted strategist. He knew what to say to make any lady he came across swoon at his feet. At tournaments, it was almost impossible to tell his own colors from the scores of rainbow tokens tucked into his breastplate.

"I'm not here to judge you, Aldon. I can help you. I can stand with you as you explain to Father why you returned. But only if you tell—"

"Lady Rose is barren."

Nicholas blinked. Frowned. Watched as Aldon took a gulp of his ale and wiped a hand across his mouth before picking up a piece of bread. *Barren?*

"You know this for certain?" How could Aldon know when he and Lady Rose weren't married? Nicholas wasn't a healer nor a married man, but he would have assumed such a conclusion couldn't be proclaimed until a couple had been wed for several years at least. Unless she'd been married before, which he knew wasn't the case. Which only left—

An illness. Something devastating enough on Lady Rose's body to steal her future.

Aldon nodded. "A healer confirmed it. Three healers, actually. First Raedonleith's healer. Then the queen, who has trained in the healing arts. And then one who knows…uh…women's issues."

Poor Rose.

"How did Lady Rose take the news?"

Aldon shrugged and tore apart another piece of bread. "I don't know. The king told me the news."

"You left without speaking with her?" His brother was young—and a man—but surely Aldon had considered, at least in part, how devastating such a verdict could be. How had Rose dealt with the news? Had she had any idea prior to the news how her life was about to change?

Barren. Nicholas felt hope shriveling just thinking the word.

"King Lior said he wouldn't hold me to the betrothal, given the change in circumstances, and that he'd let Rose know my decision. As if there were a decision to make. I could hardly marry someone unable to bear children. Like you said, I have to consider the good of the kingdom. Once the betrothal was broken, there was no reason to stay."

"How could you?"

Aldon frowned. "You would have done the same."

"No, I wouldn't." Not with so little thought or care. He'd have waited. Spoken with the woman he'd pledged to marry. Given her the respect of that much, at least. After that, he'd have gone to the library, certain somewhere in the vast collection of tomes there would be an answer. Even now his fingers itched to hold a book. To search out stories and remedies and options.

"Then you're either a fool or a liar."

Perhaps he was both, but his heart ached for the woman who'd had her future stripped away from her in one fell swoop. No children. No husband. What good was a crown without a future? He'd never even met the woman yet he wanted to throttle his brother on her behalf. To walk away without even a word?

"How could you do that to her?" Nicholas asked.

Aldon's heel stilled. "What do you mean? Her father said she'd understand and that she wished me well."

Because, no doubt, she too had been taught since childhood to put the good of her kingdom above her own life. It was what a royal did. They cared for their people. But who would care for her?

Someone needed to go to Raedonleith and make amends. Someone being Nicholas. His father couldn't go. He was needed here. It should have been Aldon, but his brother wouldn't do so. Why would Aldon fight for a woman he didn't want when within a day every woman in Belairisia would be falling over herself to catch his attention? If Aldon had truly cared for Lady Rose or the alliance, he wouldn't have returned home at the first sign of trouble.

Forgive him, Lady Rose. His words are pretty, but his head is in need of maturity.

Though only two years lay between Nicholas and his younger brother, it had always felt like many more. Ten. Twenty. Nicholas had thought Aldon was finally maturing when he agreed to marry Lady Rose. Settling down. Supporting a wife and family. Realizing that there was more to life than feasts and frivolity and more to running a kingdom than keeping the people happy. It appeared that hope had been hasty.

Nicholas would go to her. Apologize on his brother's behalf. Beg her forgiveness. And that of the king. Before Raedonleith retaliated. Wars had been started over less.

He looked out the window. The sun hadn't yet reached its highest point. If he spoke with his father and left within the hour, he could ride six hours today before having to make camp. It would take a week to reach Raedonleith, if not more, but it was hardly the longest journey he'd ever made. He'd speak with King Lior. Confirm Aldon's news. Perhaps there had been a mistake. Or an answer they hadn't yet seen. Perhaps they could work out a different alliance. Not marriage but... something.

Belairisia had made a promise to Raedonleith, and Nicholas would give his own life before he saw his kingdom break that. It wasn't even a matter of family anymore. It was a case of honor.

CHAPTER 2

The chapel was quiet as Rose slipped through the doorway. She rarely came this early, but today she'd woken with a hunger to meet with the Almighty in the quiet reverence of this holy building.

Sometimes others came in—her father, Sir Darrek and Evangeline, one or two of the knights—but today she was alone. To her relief. Her emotions were too big to share. Too expansive to contain, overflowing into tears that dripped down her face and left dark spots on her gown. No matter. No one would see but the Almighty.

Aldon had left. Eight days already he'd been gone yet still her chest felt tight and her mind as stunned as when Father had first reported Aldon's decision. His leaving hadn't come as a surprise. A man wanted children to carry on his name, not a barren wife with more things wrong with her than right. Though she'd hoped he might stay, she'd expected him to leave. What she hadn't seen coming was how deeply his rejection had cut.

Once again, Rose had been the one left behind. Because she wasn't good enough.

Time held its breath as Rose walked to the front of the chapel and knelt at the altar. The pale pink of her gown spread out, floating down to settle on the cold stone. The sun wasn't yet high enough to reach the leaded glass of the windows nor light up the cross that reminded all who entered of their Lord's sacrifice.

Praise the Almighty, from whom all blessings flow.
Praise Father, Son, and—

She groaned as the prayer caught in a whorl of grief. She knew the words she should say as well now as when she'd learned them as a child, but sometimes the words weren't enough. Today, they were woefully lacking. She did praise the Almighty, but today, she also ached. For different answers. A different outcome. That the same Almighty One who created the world and painted stars across the sky would heal her. Even if it were just her heart.

Almighty, take away the ache. My dream of marrying and having a family too, if you must. You gave it to me. Please, take it away. I can't live with this pain.

Physical pain was different. Easier, in many ways, than the ache of her emotions. The wanting. The disappointment in her body. The disappointment in herself. The knowing that she'd never be enough and there was nothing she could do about it.

Almighty, help me. Heal me. Please.

Though she wept, she did so silently, the sobs as quiet as her pain. Her face, wet with tears, lifted, her attention catching on the cross. She'd never taken it, nor the sacrifice it represented, for granted, nor had she appreciated the depth of that sacrifice as deeply as she had this past week.

Her Lord had never borne children either. Nor married. He'd had family, friends, and a calling more than any other person on earth could claim but no wife or children.

Perhaps he was the one person who understood.

Almighty, make the pain stop. Please. I beg you. It hurts too much.

She'd once felt most able to be herself in her chamber, away from questioning eyes and people who cared. Lately, the chapel had been the one place she truly felt peace. No, not peace. Her heart still rankled, and her mind fought the injustice of it all, but here she felt seen.

Yes, that was it. Not peace, as such, but the knowledge that she was seen. By someone who wouldn't ask questions, or doubt her responses, nor walk away upon realizing she spoke the truth. Someone who felt her pain, her frustration, her wanting. Who knew the times she rejoiced. The times she failed. Here, in the chapel, before the Almighty alone, she was seen. And she was loved.

Here, she could rail and cry and weep and show every emotion she was too afraid to show anywhere else. The Almighty accepted her. Dirt, mess, and all.

If I could have had a calling, like Mykah, or a child to care for, like Evangeline, perhaps I wouldn't ache so much. But who am I if not my father's heir? What use is an heir who cannot pass on the crown to her own children?

A husband, Lord. Did you have to take that away too? If you won't give me a child, could you not at least have given me someone to share my days with? I know you're enough, and no man could ever compare but—

I wanted love.

Hot tears streaked Rose's cheeks, scalding their way down. She didn't bother to wipe them away. More would only follow. Sometimes the heart simply overflowed. Today was one of those days.

You filled my heart with so much love to give, and I have no one to give it to. No one to share it with. No way to share it even if I could. My body fights me at every turn. Evangeline worked as a servant for four years. Mykah trekked the forests and fights as well as any knight. And here I am, barely able to rise some days because of the pain. Stumbling as I walk because my legs won't hold me. Falling off a horse because my head spins and I have not the strength left to fight it. No one but you sees the true extent of it. None but you understands.

Almighty, I could deal with the pain if only I had a reason. Why? Why would you give this to me? There has to be a reason. Our Lord had one. A reason. A calling. A purpose to walk this earth.

Aiyana had found one. She'd lost her husband and never had children, but she'd found purpose in being Raedonleith's healer. But Rose wasn't strong like Aiyana. In faith, perhaps, but not body.

Almighty—

Rose dropped her head, curling in on herself as she knelt there at the altar. Words caught in her heart, the ache too much to bear. Hadn't it been enough to live without strength? To fight every day to stand? Did she have to lose her future too?

She hadn't loved Prince Aldon. Not yet. But she'd cared for him. Respected him. Been well on her way to giving her heart.

But he'd walked away. And she'd let him. She could have fought, but what would have been the point? He would have left anyway, and she would have lost. All over again. It was easier to let him go.

I have no one. No one but you, Almighty. I know you're enough but—

No. You are enough. You are.

Please. Please. Be enough.

Rose walked out of the chapel determined to make the best of what she'd been given. Determined that the Almighty would be enough. For her. For her future.

Her stomach churned with doubts and her heart with guilt. She should believe it. She always had in the past. But she'd never faced rejection like this before.

No. She would be strong. The Almighty would be enough. He had to be. Because Rose wasn't.

Not enough. Barren. Alone.

Mykah barreled around the corner, face flushed and emerald skirts dancing. Oh, what Rose would give for a portion of Mykah's strength. "Rose, there you are. Evangeline and I have been looking for you."

"I was in the chapel."

"Which was the next place I was going to look."

Rose doubted it. "Really?"

Mykah grinned. "No, but I would have gotten there eventually." She tugged Rose's arm. "Come on. Our gowns for the tournament have arrived, and Mother's making us wait to see them until we're all there. Father commissioned bracelets for us as well, though he won't say why. Mother and Father are being mysterious. Come on, Rose. Let's go."

Rose couldn't help smiling at her sister's enthusiasm. They were just gowns. And bracelets. Although she too was curious about the secrecy. This was to be a special tournament, being the start of Mykah and Finnian's wedding celebrations, but she and her sisters already had new gowns for the ceremony. They'd arrived several weeks ago. Even Arthur had a new tunic for the celebrations.

"Faster, Rose."

If Mykah tugged any harder on Rose's arm, they were going to fall. She pulled it free, gripped her skirts, and followed Mykah to her chamber. Evangeline, Mother, Father, and several maids were already there.

"*Now* can we see them?" Mykah begged Father. "I found Rose. We're all here."

"Almost but—"

"You're going to make a speech? Papa, can't it wait until after?"

Rose never would have spoken to her father in such a way, but Mykah was Mykah, and Father's laugh proved he wasn't offended. Though nor was he swayed.

"No, it can't. Patience, my warrior."

Mykah sat on the bed with an exaggerated sigh. "It was worth a try. Speak, Father, for your daughters are listening."

Even Rose laughed at that. Oh, how she adored her sisters. The three of them couldn't have been more different, but she'd never found better friends. Even if they had grown apart these past few years as worries and the pressure that came with growing up stole the carefree naivete of their childhood.

Father gestured for Rose to sit before beginning.

"Next week, Raedonleith shall hold a tournament. I told you it was to celebrate Mykah's marriage—and it is—but it is also to celebrate you, our precious daughters."

Rose blinked back emotion. It would have been her wedding too.

No. No more tears. She was determined to move forward. Her plans had changed, but the Almighty's faithfulness never would.

"The three of you are more valuable to us than all the jewels and gold in the kingdom, and we couldn't be prouder of you. You have been through so much, yet here you are. Our daughters. Our beautiful girls.

"I'll leave you to try on your gowns and sort out all that frippery, but I—*we*—wanted to give you these."

A maid passed the king a deep blue velvet bag from which he pulled out three gold bracelets. They were engraved, though Rose was too far away to see the details.

"Upon each of your births, we had a goldsmith create a crown for you in commemoration of the miracle of your lives. Though we never told anyone, your mother and I also had him design a matching bracelet engraved with a specific prayer we committed to pray for you every day henceforth. In recognition of the women you have become, and the way the Almighty has answered those prayers tenfold, today we wish to give them to you."

Rose twisted in her seat, uncertain whether to be worried or intrigued. When Mykah had said Father commissioned bracelets, Rose had assumed she meant recently. Not twenty years ago. To commemorate a prayer they'd prayed every day of those twenty years. What had they asked of the Almighty for her?

She glanced at her sisters, testing their reactions to better decide her own. Mykah grinned, eyes wide, her whole body leaning forward as if to hear their parents' words that tiniest portion of a second sooner. Any more excited and she'd fall off the bed she perched on. Evangeline too smiled like she'd already been given a prize. Rose tried a smile but couldn't hold it for long. Not when the memory of her crown and the circumstances under which Father had gifted it were still so raw.

I'm sorry, Rose. He's gone.

Already? It's only a few hours until sundown.

There was a group of minstrels leaving Raedonleith this afternoon. Prince Aldon decided it would be safer to travel in numbers so departed with them.

A nice way of saying Aldon had wanted to leave as soon as possible. Without even a goodbye.

I want you to have this, Father had said, holding out the gold crown. *We planned to give it to you on your wedding day but—*

But now there wasn't to be one.

We want you to know that your worth doesn't come from who stands beside you. You are as beautiful and valuable to us today as you ever have been or ever could be. Whether you marry or not, bear children or not, you are our Rose. Our beloved. Our treasured firstborn. Wear the crown and know every time you do how much we love you.

Rose had hidden it away as soon as she'd returned to her chamber. Though she wanted to believe this would be different, her heart clenched with uncertainty. She tucked her trembling hands beneath her skirt.

Be my strength, Almighty One. Keep me steady.

"Evangeline, since birth we have prayed that you would be a light to those around you. The messenger of truth and light you are named for. We see that in you. How you shine with the goodness of a life changed."

Father handed one of the bracelets to Evangeline. The smooth gold had a swirling design across it. When Evangeline held it up, Rose could just make out the word *light* etched into the middle. Two tiny white diamonds sat either side of the word.

Beautiful.

"Mykah, for you we prayed for courage. That the Almighty would use the strength he'd given you, even as a child, to do good. And you have. You have allowed the Almighty to use you to change hundreds of lives across Raedonleith and beyond. You have brought life and strength and hope to those who struggled to find all three. Though some days I wonder if we should have prayed for a little less courage—"

Mykah laughed at her father's chagrin.

"—we've seen in so many ways how the Almighty has answered that prayer."

Mykah's bracelet too had etchings around it and two jewels though this time they were green. Though Rose couldn't see the word, she assumed from what her father had said that it was *courage*.

"And Rose, our firstborn."

Rose tensed before forcing herself to calm. It was only a bracelet, not a prophesy over her life. She couldn't fail this. But words held power and prayers even more. What had her parents chosen for her?

"From the day you were born, we prayed you'd know love."

No. Why, Papa? Why?

Of all the words they could have chosen, all the prayers they could have prayed. Did her parents not realize how much Prince Aldon's leaving had crushed her? How tightly she held to the tiny piece of hope she had left? Had Aldon still been here, had the healer not proclaimed such disappointment over her future, Rose might have cherished such a gift. Now, the bracelet might as well have been a manacle on her wrist, reminding her every time she saw it of what she'd lost.

"We prayed that you'd be both overwhelmed and held close by the love of the Almighty. That you'd know your worth and how much we cherish you. And that the certainty of that love would overflow to those around you."

If anything was going to overflow right now, it would be Rose's stomach. *Love? Why, Father? Mother? Why would you do this to me?* Faith. Strength. Purpose. Hope. There were a million words they could have chosen and prayers as numerous as the stars they could have prayed. Instead, they'd taken the one thing Rose most wanted and turned it into a knife. Thrust it into Rose's chest.

"You are loved, Rose," Mother said.

Rose didn't stay to receive her bracelet nor stop at Father's anguished cry of her name. The hall was a blur of tears as she stumbled toward her room. She couldn't stay. Didn't he realize that? Why had he chosen to do this today? Of all days.

She knew she was loved by the Almighty, but that didn't change Aldon's choice to leave. Along with all hope held for her future.

She should have been married years ago. Would have, if the years hadn't passed her father by as he yearned to see his youngest daughter come home. Rose had waited patiently as other girls her age married and bore children. *He'll remember me*, she'd told herself, time and time again. *He loves me. He's just distracted. As soon as Evangeline comes home, all will be as it once was.*

But he hadn't remembered. Not in her eighteenth year. Nor her nineteenth. He'd been bedridden with worry about Evangeline through most of Rose's twentieth and away fighting for Evangeline for the start of her twenty-first. It wasn't until Evangeline had come home that her father had finally signed betrothals for Rose and Mykah. Not that either of the men he'd chosen had stayed.

Prince Aldon had left and Sir Colin, Mykah's betrothed, had been stripped of his knighthood and exiled after abducting Mykah and stealing from the castle. He was fortunate he'd been allowed to live.

Rose had been patient. Understanding. Was not Evangeline's life more important that a mere wedding? Rose wanted her sister home as much as anyone. She'd spent hours in the chapel begging the Almighty for her sister's return. But Evangeline was home, and Rose's patience had worn thin.

Love.

She slammed her chamber door closed and tried to calm her breathing as she walked to the window looking out over the hills surrounding the castle.

Love.

It was cruel. Too cruel. No doubt her parents meant well. No doubt she'd go to them later and apologize for walking away. But right now, the word only brought pain.

The one thing she wanted would never be hers.

Couldn't they have prayed for hope? That word she would have clung to with every bit of strength she had. Light? Courage? The same words they'd prayed over her sisters. She would have shared those. But love?

No. Not today. Not when her heart was already shattered.

CHAPTER 3

ive days from Belairisia. Two more to Raedonleith. If the weather held.

The clouds above threatened rain, but they'd been doing that since Nicholas left. They seemed as uncertain as he.

He'd set off to Raedonleith full of righteous anger over Aldon's treatment of Lady Rose. To leave her, break his promise to her, when she'd already been dealt such a blow was cruel and not as a prince should act. Their father had taught them better. Of course Aldon should have stayed in Raedonleith and honored the betrothal. Of course he should have married Lady Rose, even if she couldn't bear him children. A promise was a promise. A man's word should mean something, and if it didn't, what right did he have to give it?

He'd set out immediately to rectify his brother's wrong.

But was Nicholas the one in the wrong?

Five days traveling gave a man plenty of time to think. And regret. Perhaps he'd been hasty, both in his judgment and his reaction. Aldon was young, full of energy and big dreams. None of which involved a crippled wife. Or whatever stopped Lady Rose from bearing children.

Even if she'd been the one to break the betrothal, it didn't mean she'd wished to. Or that King Lior approved. Or had she wished to? Had they decided it was best for Raedonleith if Aldon simply left? Nicholas was riding to Lady Rose's rescue—to save her honor—when she might not even want him to do so. He'd arrive in Raedonleith and what? Make a painful situation worse?

Well planned, Nicholas.

"Trust me," Nicholas had told his father when he'd announced his immediate departure. Father had, of course, asking only how many guards Nicholas wished to take with him. Nicholas had been proving his wisdom and quick mind for years in meeting after meeting, he and his father discussing for hours what was best for Belairisia and its people.

Father could have been disappointed at his oldest son's lack when it came to weapons but, if he was, had never once shown it. "We've armies full of men who can fight but a man who can lead and keep them alive through his wisdom and wits is to be valued," he would say. Nicholas had been his chief advisor since the tender age of fourteen. He had yet to steer them wrong. But what if this was?

He glanced again at the clouds, heavy and dark. Humidity hung in the air, coating his throat. The sky had looked the same yesterday afternoon, and amounted to nothing. Nicholas had seen rain in the distance through a brief break in the forest but none had reached him and his companions. The day before that had been overcast from sunrise to sunset. The dismal lack of sun wasn't doing anything for his confidence.

Nicholas wasn't normally so impulsive. Quite the opposite. First-born of the king, heir to the kingdom, he knew what was expected of him and how vital he was to the future of Belairisia. His father had been training him since the day he was born.

Then why haven't you yet agreed to a betrothal? Why do you keep putting it off? It's not for lack of options.

Nicholas pushed his horse faster, wanting the journey over. He'd come because it had seemed like the right decision at the time. If he'd second-guessed it every day since, so be it. He'd made it this far. It was only logical that he'd complete the journey. For Belairisia.

A drop of water fell onto his hand, followed in quick succession by several more.

His two guards pulled their horses either side of his.

"Sire?" the one on the left asked.

The rain grew heavier, pasting Nicholas's hair to his forehead. His horse shook his mane. Milori had never liked the rain. He'd be a beast to control if this continued, putting them all in danger.

"Make camp," Nicholas ordered, praying it would be a short shower—or deluge, as it quickly became. Though they'd not planned to stop for another two hours, his stomach wouldn't protest an early meal nor his body a break from Milori's saddle.

Rose tugged a stitch free of the embroidery, knotting it in her frustration. It wasn't the needlework's fault she was angry. Or barren. Or alone. No, that blame lay purely on her body. If she could have left herself, she would have. Instead, she hid in the corner of her room, one pillow at her back, another across her lap, a blanket around her shoulders. Warm, comfortable, and safe from questioning eyes, if not at ease. She'd sent her maid away, promising she'd call if she required anything. Quin would check on her every hour regardless, and guards still stood outside the door, but she and Quin pretended at least that Rose was alone.

Thank you, Almighty, for Quin.

She thanked the Almighty often for the personal maid he'd gifted her with. Rose wouldn't have made it through this past five years without Quin. Through secrets kept, night-long vigils, tears, frustration and moments of understanding, Quin had become more than a personal maid. She'd become a friend. A confidante. The one person Rose's age who she could truly be honest with.

Blessed with sleek brown hair, brown eyes and an eternally optimistic outlook on life, Quin would have made some man a wonderful wife. Rose had given up trying to convince her.

Until the Almighty calls me elsewhere, my place is with you, my lady, Quin would say.

Rose alternated between hoping the Almighty would open men's eyes to the worth of her friend and guilt-ridden prayers that Quin would never leave.

"Rose?"

The door opened before Rose could answer, admitting Raedonleith's healer. Rose shook her head. Whatever Aiyana had brought, it wouldn't work. It might dull the physical pain, but nothing could fix her heart. But when Aiyana pulled over a low stool to sit, she held nothing in her hands nor was her healing satchel of herbs anywhere to be seen.

"It's time for you to leave this room. It's been four days. You can't stay in here forever."

No question of how Rose was feeling or greeting of any kind. Rose picked at the thread again,

"I went to dinner last night." She'd left right after, but she'd been there. Smiled, even. Talked with Mykah, enough to avoid speaking with her parents. She hadn't spoken with them since running from Mykah's chamber, but the bracelet had appeared in her room the next day. She'd wrapped it in a cloth and tucked it inside her clothes chest. Out of sight. If only she could get it from her mind too.

We prayed for love.

So had she. And the Almighty hadn't answered any of them. She'd accept the gift one day. When the disappointment wasn't quite so sharp, and her faith found the courage to trust again. She'd find a new normal, just as she'd done when the bleeding had first begun and when Evangeline had run away. It would take time, but she'd do it.

Just not today. Today, it hurt too much.

"You're moping," Aiyana said.

"Grieving." There was a difference. Small, though it may be. She'd learned long ago that the fastest way through the pain was to let herself feel it. Let it break her. Crush her. And then, from the broken pieces, rise. New, if different. Stronger, though still shaken. "I think I'm allowed." She picked at the thread with her thumbnail, trying to loosen the knot. It wasn't working. She'd have to cut it.

"Your life isn't over, Rose."

No? It certainly felt that way. The same chest that hid her bracelet hid her crown. The one created upon her birth to be given to her on her wedding day. Father had given it to her the day Aldon left instead. A consolation prize. Proof that he too thought her future set even if he didn't say the words aloud. Yet another reminder of what she didn't have. Far from the jewels and sparkling beauty of her sisters' crowns, Rose's was simple. Gold intertwined with round, white rocks so dull they barely shined at all. Elegant, her father had called it. Just like her.

Yes, beauty alongside ugliness. Just like her.

She should return the bracelet and crown to the jewel cabinet for their own safety. Otherwise she might toss them into the river in a fit of frustration.

"I can't have children. The man I was supposed to marry left me. No one else will want me. And my family looks at me with pity."

"Your life isn't easy, it's true. But that's no reason to give up."

"I'm not giving up."

"Aren't you?"

No. She wasn't. It wasn't selfishness that kept her to her room but kindness to the rest of her family. If she weren't there reminding them, life could go on as usual. Mykah could go riding without wondering if Rose would collapse off her horse beside her. Evangeline could laugh and play with her son without feeling guilty that Rose would never have one. Father wouldn't look at her like she was broken nor Mother like she'd failed her eldest daughter.

It was for the best. For their sake. A royal's role was to inspire. What hope could a broken, barren, un-betrothed princess give them?

"I need time." It wouldn't stop the pain, but it might dull the sharpness of it.

"Time will only make it more difficult," Aiyana said, empathy in her voice that Rose hadn't heard before. "I know. I hid too, when your father chose your mother instead of me. It was easier to hide my pain than to face people. But in doing so, I gave up my friends. I lost my family. It was a choice I made, and it made me who I am today, but I missed so much along the way. Things I would have changed if I'd had the courage."

Quin entered through the open doorway, a hot drink in her hand. She set down the mug beside Rose before walking out again and leaving the two women alone. Rose took a sip, wrinkling her nose at the bitter herbs.

"I want more for you, Rose. More than hiding or watching in the stands as the world happens around you. You're to be Raedonleith's queen one day, and you will be a wonder to see. Wise, compassionate—"

"Alone."

Bitterness clawed at Rose's throat. *Forgive me, Almighty.*

She wished she could pull back the word, accurate as it was. Especially when Aiyana narrowed her eyes. Rose sighed. She'd be fine. She really would. One day. Why did Aiyana have to come today, when resentment ate at Rose's heart like an open wound? She was fighting for faith. She was. But she was tired. And faith always came harder when she was tired. Faith in the goodness of the Almighty, at least. She'd never once doubted his existence or touch on her life. Only, sometimes, his purposes.

Rose sighed, exhaustion coating her weariness and what will she had left. "Maybe it would be better if Mykah was queen. She's strong and wise and passionate. Our people love her. Evangeline too. They don't need me."

"Of course they do. They love you, Rose."

"I'm weak, Aiyana. Weak. Barren. Rejected. You know my failures, and soon all of Raedonleith will too. They'll know that I can't give them an heir. That I wasn't good enough for Aldon. Maybe not anyone. I don't know if I can be the leader our people need, and I don't have the strength left to pretend I am."

Aiyana placed a hand on Rose's arm, stilling her fight with the thread. "Then stop pretending. Let them grieve with you. Let them love you and remind you that you have a purpose."

"Do I? Still?"

"The Almighty had a purpose for you long before you were born, and that doesn't change just because of some bad news."

"I wanted to be a wife and mother more than I ever wanted to be queen."

"I know." Aiyana took a deep breath and let it out. "So did I."

Of course she had. "Forgive me," Rose said quietly.

"Nothing to forgive. I made my choices. Though they brought pain, they also brought love, and I cannot regret having known both." Aiyana stood, offering her hand. "Come with me to the village. There's a family there in need of my care. Their youngest girl shares your name and thinks the world of you. I know it would bring a smile to her face, and that of her parents, to see you."

Rose shook her head. "Another day."

Today, if she saw the girl, she'd simply cry. She was no one's hero. She didn't even know if she wanted to be their queen anymore.

"I have your word on that?"

"Aye."

Not today. Not tomorrow. Perhaps not even this month but—

Soon. She'd rally again, as she'd done so many times already. She'd find a smile, and a purpose, and a new hope. Something to live for. As Aiyana had.

Just not today.

Lior stared through the darkness as if he could see beyond the castle's torchlit courtyard. He'd done the same for days, months, *years* on end, waiting for news of Evangeline. He gripped the weather-worn stone of the tower's half wall. The occasional shout came from below where men stood guard and servants laid one day to rest and prepared for the next. Only when a cloak was wrapped around his shoulders did he realize he wasn't alone.

"You're nigh on frozen, my love. Come inside."

He pulled his wife to his side, wrapping the cloak around them both as he battled his disappointments.

"I thought Cormac would come."

"He still may."

"The tournament is tomorrow." And the wedding not long after. For years Lior had tried to bridge the gap between them to no avail. He'd hoped, despite the past, that Finnian and Mykah's wedding would bring the families together again. He'd been wrong. Again. Cormac wouldn't even put aside his bitterness for his own brother. Why had Lior thought he might for a friend?

"I'm sorry, Lior. I know it means a lot to you."

"I've sent him gold, protected his borders, given him chance and chance again when he's been nothing but cruel to our family. He abused and held Evangeline captive for years and tried more than once to kill Mykah. I could have taken his life for far smaller a transgression, but I didn't because he was my friend once. My brother. But what more can I do? I can't change a decision I made more than two decades ago—nor would I want to. Marrying you was the best decision I've ever made."

"There's nothing you can do."

He was starting to believe she might be right. And he hated it. Cormac Cavendish, twenty years Lior's best friend, twenty years his enemy. If only they could begin again. Clear the record. What Lior wouldn't give to spend the next twenty years—likely their last—as brothers.

"I miss him, Cara."

"I know."

"I never meant to hurt him."

"I know, and so does he. You've told him. You've apologized. Many times."

"Then why— Why—" His voice cracked, a sob cutting it in half. He gripped the stone of the tower's ledge with a strength that would leave creases in his skin for hours. He couldn't change the past, but he'd done all he could to change their future. To no avail. No amount of gold could change a mind intent on holding on.

"I don't know."

CHAPTER
4

Rose closed her eyes, leaned back, and tipped her face toward the sun. The warmth felt wonderful on her cool skin. If she blocked out the noise of a few hundred people anticipating the next round of the tournament, she could almost imagine herself watching the sunrise from atop her favorite tower.

It was good to be here. Comforting as well, to know life went on and people could still find reasons to smile even if she couldn't. One day, she'd smile again. Aiyana was right. Rose still had a purpose. She'd find a way. Perhaps even marry, if by some miracle a man chose her. Not everyone married for love. There were other reasons too. Honor. Companionship. Convenience.

She fingered her bracelet through the fabric of her sleeve. She'd worn the piece to the tournament out of respect for her parents and the faithful prayers they'd prayed, but it hurt too much to display.

One day at a time.

"You can open your eyes. It's over," Mykah said. "Landon won."

Sir Landon must have been the knight raising his bow in the air while another knight clapped him on the shoulder. Rose didn't know the knights as well as her sisters did. Mykah spent a large portion of each day on the training field, and Evangeline had likely flirted with every one of them before marrying Sir Darrek. Rose recognized some of the men by name and sight, but many she'd not be able to pick enemy from friend.

She needed to spend more time among them. Not to flirt or fight but to come to know them. They'd pledge their allegiance to her one day. It would be helpful to distinguish whether they planned to protect her or kill her before the effect.

But the more time she spent with people, the more chance of them seeing her weakness. She could pull a cloak of strength around herself for an hour. Longer, on her good days, or during events like the tournament where she sat in the stands and watched. But to be among them for hours on end? Weeks? Months? They'd see. They'd wonder. Was their future queen strong enough to lead them?

Rose wondered that too. No. She didn't wonder. She knew. She wasn't. She could intercede for their hearts and provide for their bodies, but she was all too well acquainted with her weakness. She hadn't meant to admit to Aiyana that Mykah would make a better queen, but it had been on her mind for some weeks now. Ever since the revelation that Mykah was the Guardian of Raedonleith. The mysterious benefactor bringing food, care, and protection to the villages by night.

Rose had been as shocked as everyone else at the news. Shocked, immensely proud, and, though she hated to admit it, jealous. Mykah had courage, passion, and a selflessness that had changed the lives of countless families in Raedonleith. Mykah was exactly the kind of person they needed as their future queen.

If Rose were stronger—if she didn't fear the peoples' reactions—she'd hand her sister the crown today. But loving her people meant being the person they expected her to be. She couldn't walk away. Not from them. Not from herself.

The knights competing in the archery portion of the tournament lined up before the stands, and Sir Landon stepped forward to receive his winnings. Evangeline looked proud enough to burst when the king called over her son, Arthur, to present the prize money. Rose had to swallow back emotion of her own when Sir Landon knelt before young boy. Sired by Lord Cavendish and born out of wedlock, the king would have been well within his rights to send Evangeline's son away. Instead, he'd welcomed Arthur into their family with all the love and honor a proud grandfather—and king—could bestow.

It was as beautiful as it was heartbreaking. If Rose had married all those years ago, if her body hadn't given up before it had the chance to thrive, if circumstances had been different, that might have been her son standing there today.

Might have been, for who could know the hand of the Almighty? Perhaps her womb had been broken from birth only to manifest as she grew.

The pain had gotten worse these past two years. Since she was fifteen, it had been bad, but she'd taken it in stride. Every woman had pains. It was part of being female. But every year, Rose's pains increased. Nausea turned to excruciating pain that stole her breath and, on more than one occasion, her consciousness. There were days she crawled to bed because the pain was too much to walk.

It wasn't so bad today, but nausea still turned her stomach. Tomorrow might be better. Or it might be worse. Her illness might have been easier to deal with had it been predictable.

The unpredictability had forced her to speak with Aiyana two years ago. The special combination of herbs that Aiyana had prepared to mix with hot water when the pain became too bad had worked for a time, giving Rose the ability to hide it from everyone else. But these past six months, hiding it had become impossible.

Even with the herbs, some days agony stole her thoughts and left her curled in a ball of tears until she fainted from the pain. Quin had found her passed out in her chamber one too many times to keep it from the Rose's parents. They'd sent immediately for the special healer Mother had once studied under, hopeful she might have answers.

It had been an anxious six-week wait for news that wasn't good. Nothing could be done.

"Evangeline and I are going to see the knights before they begin the next round of competition," Mykah said, breaking through Rose's musings. "Come with us?"

By "the knights," Mykah no doubt meant Darrek and Finnian as well as a small—or potentially large—amount of kissing. To boost morale, of course. Give their men something to fight for. As much as Rose cared for Darrek and Finnian, she had no great desire to be in the room for that.

"Thank you, but no. You two can chaperone each other. And be sure you do."

Mykah reddened. Evangeline laughed. Rose sent them on their way with a swish of her hand and settled back into her seat.

Almighty, thank you for my sisters and the closeness we're finding again. Thank you for the good men you've blessed them with.

She'd thought once—many years ago—that Mykah would be the one to marry Darrek. Not because Mykah had shown any particular interest in him compared to any other knight but because of his strength, quietness, and fierce loyalty to his king and those around him. He and Mykah had that in common. Evangeline, at the time, had been far more interested in handsome squires, guards, and the occasional knight who toed the line of honor. Men who were thrilled when a young, beautiful princess flirted with them and happy to display their strength and finesse on the training field or the dance floor.

The last five years had changed Evangeline more than Rose ever could have imagined. Much of what had occurred during those years when Evangeline had been gone and Darrek and the other knights had searched for her Rose didn't know and probably never would. Not because she didn't care but because Evangeline held it close. The stories *and* her son, Arthur.

Evangeline had married Darrek, and Mykah would marry Finnian.

Rose was trying just to get through each day still standing.

She stifled a yawn. There were enough knights wandering about and interesting things happening on the field that she didn't think anyone would be watching her, but she didn't want anyone to think she was bored. She wasn't. Just tired. She could fall asleep here in the sun. The rays lulled her, making her eyelids heavy as she sat. She'd slept well enough last night but woken early.

For once, it wasn't her body wearying her but her emotions. They'd been overwhelming this past week. Hers *and* the emotions of those around her. Her parents' grief. Aiyana's hope. Her sisters trying to tamp down the ardor they had for their knights whenever she was around. Mykah doing her best in Rose's presence to minimize her excitement about her upcoming wedding. Rose's guilt that she was stirring such emotions in everyone else. And all that on top of her own grief. The loss. The pain. The exhaustion that came from clinging to hope when everything felt so hopeless. Of hours spent pouring her heart out in the chapel. Trying to find a reason. A purpose.

She wouldn't give in to the hopelessness. She'd be strong, like Aiyana. Like her Lord.

But it was hard. As if she hung from a precipice and a thin piece of fraying rope was all that kept her from falling. Every time her hand on the rope slipped, she'd grab it again. Hand over hand over hand. But she was tiring. She couldn't keep doing this forever. Sooner or later, something would give. A hand would reach out to save her. Or she'd fall, unable to hold on any longer.

She desperately wanted it to be the former.

Almighty, please. Please, save me. You alone know how close I am to falling. I don't want to fall, but I just don't have the strength to keep grasping. Hold me. Give me strength for today. I don't need tomorrow's yet, but please, Almighty, give me enough for today.

Evangeline and Mykah returned, their laughter preceding them. Rose straightened her spine and pushed back her shoulders. This was a day for celebration, not despair.

She clapped along with her sisters and parents as the knights competing in the jousting lined up beside their mounts and presented themselves. The horses stood as tall as their knights, well aware of the importance of the part they had to play. Rose prided herself in picking out Sir Edison with the predominantly orange flag, Sir Spencer with the lion on his, and Sir Finnian in black and green. She couldn't find Darrek but was too embarrassed to ask her sisters which one he was amid the several wearing Raedonleith's colors. Perhaps he wasn't competing in this event.

Servants brought the family refreshments as the event began. Rose took a drink eagerly, though only nibbled on a piece of bread. Her stomach wouldn't appreciate cheese or anything richer. She hoped her family would put her limited appetite down to nerves rather than physical weakness. They knew how nervous she got watching tournaments. She understood the importance of keeping knights occupied during periods of peace and the fun of healthy competition, but she couldn't get past the idea that it was an unnecessary risk. Knights were injured. Sometimes badly. All for the sake of entertainment.

Her sisters and the rest of the crowd might appreciate the thrill of the show, but Rose would be relieved when the day was over. She spent the better part of every tournament praying to the Almighty that the competitors would make it through the day alive.

She jolted when Mykah poked her side.

"It's Finnian!"

How her sister had the energy to bounce about in her seat with a twice-broken-still-healing collarbone, Rose didn't know. Mykah had been like a giddy child all day as she cheered on her betrothed and, it felt like, every other knight wearing Raedonleith colors.

The crowd cheered as Finnian and his opponent raised their lances. Rose hated jousting the most out of all the events, cringing every time the lances clashed. Mykah had long ago stopped trying to convince Rose that the knights wore armor for a reason and the glances off it didn't hurt. Rose didn't believe her. A hit was a hit, and most hits meant bruises or broken bones, if not worse. Armor couldn't cover a whole knight, and while it protected their skin, it did little for the muscles within.

Almighty, keep them safe. Put your protection around them. Guide their strikes. Intervene, if need be. If they must fight, let them fight, but please, please, bring them out alive. All of them.

She felt the pain of every hit as if she were the one on the horse, lance in hand. Every bruise. Every cringe. She sat here only because, as princess, she was obligated to. Her people expected it. She expected it of herself. She clutched the green stone on her necklace, running her thumb over its smooth surface.

Keep them safe. Please, Almighty, keep them safe.

"Is that—"

The knights' lances lowered, their run halted before it could begin when a man rode into the arena, flanked by two guards. He wore no armor, held no flag nor colors. His cloak was black, his tunic a pale green. Nothing to distinguish him from the many travelers who came through Raedonleith. Except his bearing. He rode like a knight. And he looked like—

No. But it couldn't be.

"Prince Aldon?"

Mykah stood, pulling Rose with her. Darrek, Manning, and several other knights strode out from the side of the stand to crowd around the man, blocking him from view. Rose pushed aside the urge to flee. What if it were Prince Aldon? What if he'd come to apologize? To renew his suit? Did she want that? Could she let him? Was it right?

Breathe, Rose. Center yourself. Find your anchor.

A bird called from somewhere above the tent's shade cloth.

The flowers tucked in Mykah's hair smelled like jasmine.

Three other women in the stand with Rose had worn blue gowns today. Four wore yellow. One wore purple. Mykah wore red and Evangeline green. The queen wore gold.

The knights still blocked the man who might be Prince Aldon.

Rose's palms grew slick. She rubbed them against her skirt. Finnian dismounted and joined the group. Mykah, either taking his action as permission or too impatient to wait for answers, strode down to join him. Rose fought again the urge to run in the opposite direction. What if it were Aldon? What if it weren't? How long did it take to discern a man's identity?

Think. Breathe. What else can you see? What can you feel? What can you smell?

Her slippers pinched her little toe.

There was a scuff of dirt on the hem of her dress.

The air smelled of dirt, dust, jasmine, and excitement.

The knights finally moved, making way for the man and his horse. He rode to the base of the stand, right before the king and queen. And, to their left, Rose.

It wasn't Prince Aldon. The man's look was similar, but his hair darker. His build slimmer. His manner more…reserved? Respectful? Unassuming?

He bowed his head. When he lifted it, it wasn't the king he looked at. It was Rose.

His eyes were blue. Blue like the sky on a clear day. Blue like the palest of sapphires. Blue like the sea she'd watched atop a cliff as a child. Before the pains had begun. Before her life had blown away piece by piece like sand across the cliff-face that day.

Blue like her lips were going to be soon if she didn't take a breath.

"Rose—"

It was a whisper on the man's lips. A mistake, no doubt, the way he blushed then dropped his gaze. He smoothed the front of his tunic before swallowing and raising his sights to the king and queen. This time, when he spoke, his voice was clear.

"Forgive me the intrusion, Your Majesties. I am Prince Nicholas of Belairisia, and I have come to wed your daughter."

CHAPTER 5

The feast was lasting forever. Not helped at all by the fact that Rose had been awake since long before the sun anointed the castle walls with its golden glow this morning. She stifled a yawn and tried to focus on the ballad the minstrel was singing instead of the whispers being passed from ear to ear. She couldn't hear them from her place on the podium with the rest of her family, but she didn't need to hear to know she was the topic. She and the prince who'd come to marry her.

Or so he claimed. In front of every royal, knight, lord, lady, and other influential person in the kingdom. And a hundred others happy to give their opinion. The whispers had started before she even left the stands.

It's so romantic.

Is he taking his brother's place? Can he do that?

A prince has come to save her. He must have ridden day and night to get here so fast.

What of Belairisia? Isn't he the heir?

Not as handsome as his brother, but he's got some charm.

Some charm. As if Rose's cheeks hadn't warmed the moment he looked at her. And kept looking.

Whether the people thought Prince Nicholas was a hero or a fool, everyone had something to say about him and his bold declaration.

I've come to wed your daughter.

Her parents welcomed him to Raedonleith Castle but had not given away any of their thoughts on his suit. Though the tournament had continued, Rose hadn't stayed to watch the rest, sequestering herself in her chamber for the rest of the day. Skipping tonight's feast would have been her preference also, but some responsibilities a future queen couldn't avoid.

I've come to wed your daughter.

There was no mistaking which daughter he meant, the way his blue gaze had seared hers.

Her heart had skipped a beat before bursting into joy at his declaration. Her. Married. To Prince Nicholas of Belairisia. Her delight had soared for all of three seconds before reality shredded its wings, crashing her back to earth. He'd renege the declaration as soon as he knew the truth. His brother had. She wasn't the woman he thought he wanted. She might have been beautiful, but it was only skin deep.

Prince Nicholas sat in a place of honor at her father's side, as befitting his royal title. Though she refused to meet his gaze, Rose was aware of every movement he made. Every time he bent his head to speak with the king, every time he lifted his cup. Every time he looked her way.

She couldn't marry him. Even if she had been willing and whole, Prince Nicholas was Belairisia's heir, as bound by responsibility and his kingdom's future as she was. Perhaps in a perfect world, the kingdoms might have come to a peace-filled agreement—a joining of the two lands alongside the marriage of their rulers—but what would be the point? Upon marrying Rose, Prince Nicholas would become as barren as her. His future along with it.

Rose took a sip from her goblet and tried to steady her shaking hands. Nausea swirled in her stomach—a common occurrence—though she suspected nerves made it worse than usual. What was Prince Nicholas thinking to have offered for her in such a way? They'd never spoken. Never even set eyes on each other before today.

She'd know his thoughts if she asked or even took a few moments to speak with him. Which was precisely why she'd spent the afternoon in her room and was intent on staring at the table in front of her. She didn't want to know. Didn't trust herself to meet his gaze again and find the strength to look away. It wasn't love or even infatuation, but there was something about him that made her feel more than she should. A spark of hope she couldn't afford to kindle. It would turn into a wildfire and burn them all.

"May I have the honor of this dance, Lady Rose?"

Determined to ignore one man, Rose hadn't even noticed Sir Spencer's approach. It was fortunate there were plenty of guards and knights about the place to protect her because she was doing a poor job of staying alert herself. Except to one man. Who wasn't the one asking her to dance. She didn't want to dance—she wanted to escape—but since it was too early to politely leave, dancing would use some time. And put some distance between her and Prince Nicholas.

"Of course, Sir Spencer. It would be my honor."

Rose's legs only wobbled a little as she stood. She ducked to pick up the folds of her gown's long gold skirt, hiding the moment of weakness. An arm on Sir Spencer's was enough to steady her as she rose. If she leaned heavier than decorum called for, he didn't mention it, promenading her across the dais to the cleared dance floor in the middle of the castle's Great Hall. Cleared of tables, not of people.

Mykah's laughter was louder than the music as she threw her head back and spun in Finnian's arms. Evangeline, too, glowed with happiness as she danced with Darrek. Rose's parents sat at the table, speaking with Prince Nicholas, but they'd likely take their turn in a dance soon too.

The last time the Great Hall had boasted such revelry was the night of Rose and Mykah's betrothal ball. That night, the dancing had been interrupted by the shock arrival of Sir Finnian Cavendish. He'd been the enemy then. Three days from now, he'd be Mykah's husband.

Rose couldn't help wishing someone would interrupt tonight's festivities so she could hide. Someone not purporting to be her groom. Guilt churned her already queasy stomach. She shouldn't think such things.

She gritted her teeth and did her best to ignore the swirling nausea. One word of how she was truly feeling and Sir Spencer would escort her all the way to the door of her chamber. Likely even carry her, apologizing for forcing her to dance. She would be tucked into bed, warm under her covers, far from gossip and speculation within minutes. Far from Prince Nicholas too. But that would mean admitting her weakness. And if she took to her bed every time she felt weak, she'd never live at all.

No. Better to grit her teeth, smile through the pain, and keep dancing. She could do this. It was only a dance.

One, two, three, four. Clap, two, three, hop.

Sir Spencer took her hand and raised it, walking around her as the music dictated. She took three steps to the left, then three to the right, mirroring his footwork. Her golden gown shimmered a thousand shades of royalty as it caught the light of the candelabras about the room. It was easily the most stunning gown she'd ever worn, a beautiful gift from her parents to mark the occasion. She'd kept on their bracelet too, knowing how much thought and care had gone into the gift even as she tried not to think of its significance.

"You look stunning this evening, my lady. Every inch our future queen."

"Th— Thank you."

Her drink threatened to reappear as she spun twice more. She blinked back the dizziness that arrived with the nausea. Infuriating weakness. Dancing wasn't helping. Neither was Prince Nicholas of Belairisia.

Breathe, Rose. Smile. Walk out the dance. Forward. Backward. Circle. Clap. Listen to the music. Pick out the harmony. Count the instruments.

A dagger of pain sliced her gut, sending fire down her left leg.

No. Not now.

Sir Spencer frowned as she gasped and bent forward before forcing herself upright again. She smiled and turned away, not waiting to see if he smiled back. The room became a cacophony of color, blinding her as a drum took up beating in her head. Her stomach. Her leg. She blinked and tried to steady her breathing.

It wasn't working. She had to stop. Brace herself. Sit.

Almighty, I can't— I can't—

"Lady Rose?"

Ignore the pain. Ignore the prince. Listen to Sir Spencer. Focus on his voice. What can you see? What can you hear? What do you know?

Sir Spencer was tall, maybe two inches taller than her. His reddish-brown hair—sun-lightened in parts and darker in others—skimmed his shoulders. Light freckles spattered his nose, as if he'd walked through a spray of them. His hands were strong, as one would expect of a man who spent his life wielding a sword and controlling the reins of a horse. His voice was kind. He wasn't rough like some of the other knights, but gentle. Reliable. There was a reason Sir Spencer was one of her favorites.

Slowly, her heart rate returned to normal. The pain in her gut eased to a throb. Not enough to ignore but enough that it wasn't bringing tears to her eyes.

Courage, Rose. You have breath in your lungs and strength in your legs yet. Stand, though you shake. Smile, though your heart breaks. They look to you. Show them someone worth looking to.

With one more stanza, the dance would be over. She could say her goodbyes and return to her chamber. Prince Nicholas might not understand why she left early, but he would soon enough.

"Oh."

Her foot hooked on a long piece of straw, her tenuous balance with it. Rose was falling before she could take a steadying step. Though Sir Spencer caught her arm before she hit the floor, the damage was done. Her legs wouldn't hold her any longer.

"Lady Rose?" He knelt by her side.

"I'm— Sorry. Forgive me. I—"

She bent forward. She was going to lose her dinner. Here, in front of everyone. They'd think her drunk.

Sir Spencer's hand was strong against her back, steadying both her body and her mind. "'Tis no worry, my lady. We all tire sooner or later. Let me call for Quin. We'll walk you to your chamber. Unless you'd like to stay?"

No. She didn't want to stay. She hadn't even wanted to come.

"There's no need for you to come. Quin will assist me. Look. There she is now." In truth, the maid had been waiting for an hour already, knowing how Rose liked to retire early. And how shaken she'd been by the prince's arrival. Quin had spent the afternoon stitching in Rose's chamber while Rose lay on her bed pretending the morning hadn't happened.

"Actually, you'd be doing me a service," Sir Spencer said with a wink as he helped her to her feet. "A horse kicked me in the leg this morning, and though I told the other knights it was nothing, it's paining me something fierce now. Much as I've enjoyed the festivities, I've been looking for an excuse to leave since I arrived."

He was being kind again. Perhaps his leg was bruised, but he'd hardly have asked her to dance if he'd been in excessive pain. He had too much honor to leave her when she was unwell but too much respect to point out her weakness.

Sir Spencer was a good man. She swallowed and smiled at him.

"Well then. I could hardly embarrass you in front of your friends.

Your assistance would be appreciated, though you need only walk me part of the way."

He walked her the whole way, his arm under hers. Quin walked on Rose's other side. Neither of them mentioned how heavily she leaned on them nor the number of times she stumbled.

"Thank you, my lady. You have done me a great honor," Sir Spencer said when they reached the door of her chamber. "I owe you a debt of gratitude for your service. If ever you require a knight, you need only call."

Rose thanked him again as he departed. Quin helped her inside, out of the beautiful gown and into bed. Tears mixed with the music drifting through the window from the feast as Rose wept. Wishes were naught, and dreams only brought heartache, but she couldn't harden her heart to them. The dream of a normal life. Where her legs didn't shake and her stomach didn't threaten to tear itself open with every movement. Where her head didn't spin and she didn't have to talk herself into breathing.

Where a good man, like Sir Spencer, walked her to her door not out of pity but because he cared so much he couldn't bear to say goodnight. And she let him, affection rather than guilt filling her heart.

"Can I get you something, my lady? A warm drink? Another blanket?"

"No, thank you. I'm well."

Crippled but well.

Rose rolled over and tucked her hands under her head.

Thank you, Almighty, for the breath I breathe. Thank you for my heart that beats. Thank you for my family and your care.

And thank you for getting me through another day.

--- ❦ ---

Hours later Rose was still awake. The feast had ended, the laughter and shouts from the Great Hall dimming to an occasional conversation passing through the doors. Rose didn't know why she bothered trying to sleep. Even if her body hadn't ached, her mind wouldn't stop.

Nicholas.

Barren.

Love.

Marriage.

The thoughts tumbled over each other in a terrifying dance, growing in size and fear as doubts attached themselves like fungi to a rock. Instead of answers, questions amounted until Rose felt as if any moment her head would explode.

Too much.

The chapel. She'd find focus in the chapel.

She crept out of bed, wrapping a cloak around her for warmth. Comfort too. There was something so reassuring about a downy, thick cloak. Quin had retired to the room next door an hour ago. Though she'd told Rose many times to wake her any time, Rose never once had. Quin needed her sleep as much as anyone and dealt with far more when caring for Rose than most personal maids should have to.

The guard at Rose's door stood to attention when she opened it.

"Is everything well, my lady? Can I call for someone?"

"No, thank you. I've a yearning for prayer."

"Of course."

Though he didn't move as she walked away, at some point he'd follow her. Or send someone else to do so if he'd been ordered to hold his position. There had been more guards in the castle since Mykah's abduction. Though at times it felt overbearing being watched in a constant manner, Rose couldn't fault her father. He'd been shaken by Mykah's injuries. They all had. But Rose had far more pressing things on her mind than the presence of a guard who'd do naught but watch over her from a distance.

Like the man who'd asked to marry her. And the yearning to agree, even knowing she couldn't. Was it wrong to want to marry? It was wrong to hide the truth of her situation from him, though she planned to hide it for as long as she could.

The way he'd looked at her. Like she was the answer to every one of his lifelong prayers. Like no one else existed, though she sat in the middle of a crowd. He'd stared outright, not even trying to hide his interest in her. *Her!* The broken one. Oh, how she wanted to be unbroken for him. To accept. To have him hold her and promise all would be well. That she was worthy of love. Her family loved her, of course. She'd never doubted that nor took their love for granted. She adored her parents and sisters and knew they'd do anything for her in return.

But to have a man *choose* her. Choose to love her when he could have anyone. Not because they were joined by blood but because he wanted to. Because he loved her. That was so different.

Beeswax mixed with a heady scent of incense met Rose as she pushed open the chapel door. Mykah fought on the battleground. Evangeline battled in her mind. But this… this was where Rose fought her battles. In the chapel. On her knees.

She took a deep breath, letting peace fill her lungs along with the familiar smell. There were only two places in the castle where she could truly breathe: the far east tower where hope rose each morning with the sun, and the chapel.

The tower, few people ever visited. At least, not as early each morning as she did. Her parents and the guards knew she went, but they never bothered her there. It was her refuge. Her shelter.

But the chapel, that was special. The moment she walked through the doorway, she felt accepted. Faults, fears, devastation, and all. Here she could weep. Smile. Argue. Worship. Laugh. Cry. Often a mixture of them all. She didn't have to wonder what the Almighty thought of her. Didn't have to wonder if his opinion of her would change "if only he knew" because he already did. Her best parts, her worst. Her disappointments and hopes. She never held anything back from the Almighty, good or bad. He accepted it all. Her greatest disappointments didn't surprise him. Her fears didn't overwhelm him. And her joys? He understood them. Without her even having to explain. Even when they were so inconsequential she'd have been embarrassed to admit to others how much they meant to her. Like the relief she felt each night as she lay down on her bed and thanked the Almighty for another day done.

He understood the mix of pain and joy when she saw her nephew every day. How thrilled she was for her sisters and the good men who cherished them even while jealousy tugged at her heart. How one didn't negate the other. The joy and the pain sat together. Each whole. Each all-encompassing.

The Almighty saw to the heart of her. The things she dared not admit even in the quietness of her mind but felt within her soul. The ache. The wishing.

If home was where your heart could breathe, then Rose's home was within the stone walls of this tiny chapel.

Almighty, here I am again. On my knees. At your feet.
Fill my heart. Direct my path.
Show me the way forward.
And help me not to be afraid.

CHAPTER 6

Nicholas stared at the roof of his chamber. It wasn't the lack of noise around him nor the unfamiliar lodgings that kept him awake but his declaration.

He'd told the king and queen and most of Raedonleith that he'd come to marry their princess. It had been as much a shock to him as to his rapt audience. The moment he'd seen Lady Rose sitting beside her parents, all reason had flown from his mind. She'd looked so fragile. So alone despite the crowd that surrounded her. He'd known in an instant it was her, the delicate beauty his brother had spoken of. He'd not meant to say the words, but by no means was he taking them back.

He wanted to marry Rose. Yearned to.

It made as much sense as him dropping everything the day Aldon had come home and traveling seven days to be here. Less sense, even. If visiting had been his only reason for coming, he might have spoken with King Lior, spent a few days as their guest, and returned home. But marriage changed everything. He and Lady Rose were heirs to their respective kingdoms. In order to marry, one of them would have to give up the claim to their throne. Society dictated, as the woman, it be Rose, especially given how unusual it was for a woman to inherit the crown already. But Nicholas would never ask it of her. Not after he watched her fall tonight, and the way her family had rallied around her.

Eyes downcast, Rose hadn't seen the way her sisters had run to her side, nor the way her parents had stopped mid-conversation to do the same. Sir Darrek and Sir Finnian had both stood guard at her back, blocking her from the crowd of dancers as much as they kept her from being trampled. The relief on their faces had been mirrored in the sighs of the king and queen beside Nicholas when Rose had found her feet again. They'd walked away only when Sir Spencer shook his head at their following. Even then, they'd not recommenced their dancing until Lady Rose, Sir Spencer and the maid were out of sight.

He couldn't take Lady Rose away from her family. He didn't know why she'd fallen, and perhaps neither did they, but they'd been there for her. As he wanted to be.

He should have been terrified at the thought of what he stood to lose. Terrified. Dismayed. Uncertain. He would be giving up his kingdom, his people, his family, and the future he'd planned to marry a woman he'd not even spoken to. His father would be disappointed that he'd trained Nicholas all these years to be king only for his eldest son to relinquish his role. He didn't know what Aldon would think. Probably that Nicholas had lost his mind.

Yet as Nicholas lay staring at the roof, peace continued to settle within him. This was right. Perhaps the most right thing he'd ever done. He'd wondered all these years if he was too picky, too bookish, too reserved to find a wife. Wondered if he'd have to put his own hopes and wishes aside and 'just pick one' as his father had counseled.

But…Rose. His heart thudded as he thought of her, his mind traveling to the future. To days of laughter and nights of warmth. To companionship and beauty and cherishing her in all the ways a woman should be. To growing old side by side and knowing that though the years grew short, their love grew stronger. He might be giving up everything, but he'd be gaining far more.

He'd hoped to speak with Lady Rose earlier, but she'd left the tournament not long after he'd arrived. He'd been introduced to knights— some of whom he remembered from when they'd come to Belairisia searching for Lady Evangeline—along with guards and Rose's family, but the woman he wished to marry was nowhere to be seen.

Raedonleith's royal family had been courteous despite the surprising nature of his arrival. They'd given him and his guards a room in the castle along with people to serve him, water to freshen up with, and food from the kitchen. He'd eaten the midday meal with the family though Rose had been noticeably missing. No one present had seemed surprised, so Nicholas had let it go. Perhaps Rose always rested in the afternoons. He could be patient. Lady Mykah must have noticed his disappointment, despite his attempt to hide it, because she assured him Rose would be at the feast this evening.

She had been. Only she'd arrived late. And left early.

Lady Rose hadn't glanced his way once during the entire meal, though he'd been all too aware of where she was. He could barely take his gaze off her. The gold of her gown made her seem ethereal, an angelic messenger masquerading as a princess. Her hair, braided into a crown before cascading around her shoulders in loose curls, was a few shades darker than her sisters'. Her features were finer than theirs too. Exquisite but fragile.

She'd smiled as she took Sir Spencer's arm when the knight had asked her to dance, but the expression had faltered several times as she spun around the room with him. Nicholas had barely heard a word of the king and queen's conversation as he watched her, jumping from his chair when she tripped, even knowing he was too far away to help. He'd been as relieved as he was jealous that Sir Spencer had caught her. When the knight returned to the hall, he'd walked directly to Nicholas's side.

"Treat her well," was all Sir Spencer had said before nodding and rejoining the other knights. Nicholas wasn't certain whether it was a threat or advice, but he'd taken it to heart all the same. He would treat Lady Rose well.

If he married her.

Almighty, let it be so.

King Lior hadn't given Nicholas an answer yet, though Nicholas could hardly blame the king for asking for time to consider. He'd put the king in quite a position, offering for her hand as he had.

Nicholas rolled onto his side. He was no sleepier now than when he'd gone to bed. If he were at home, he'd go to the library and lose himself in a book or lay on the castle's roof and watch the stars. He didn't know the way to either place within this castle, but walking anywhere would clear his mind. Or, at least, give it something else to focus on.

A guard stood two doors down the hall. Though he acknowledged Nicholas, the man did nothing to stop him. Nicholas passed another three guards before he reached the stairs at the end of the passage. Was the excess of guards due to the trouble King Lior mentioned Lord Cavendish had been causing? That was the reason the alliance between Belairisia and Raedonleith had been agreed upon, though Nicholas didn't realize it had escalated enough to require so many guards within the castle. Surely the man wouldn't attack the family within the palace. Would he? Aldon hadn't mentioned any attacks. Of course, Nicholas hadn't given Aldon much chance to mention anything but his broken betrothal before rushing off. Perhaps there was more to the story than simply a disgruntled neighbor threatening the peace.

A young maid passed Nicholas, bowing as she went, a piece of kindling falling from her full basket as she did. He stooped to pick it up and return it before she could drop more. With a squeak of a thank you, she scuttled away to whichever fire needed stoking.

Nicholas continued, walking through the empty Great Hall and the servers' room beside it. The castle's layout wasn't so different from his own, though he'd yet to find the stairs leading to the roof. Perhaps they were inside a room. As a guest wandering the halls long after most of the castle had retired, it would be inappropriate for him to open doors at random. Who knew what—or whom—might be behind them and whose privacy he might invade. Better to stick to the halls and rooms that were open.

Like the one at the end of the corridor. Nicholas looked around, reassuring himself of his bearings. He'd thought he'd reached the castle's southmost wall. Perhaps the door led to a small alcove outside. Feeble light flickered beyond the door, as if a candle struggled in a light breeze rather than a blazing torch. Curious, he opened the door farther, taking in the tall windows, the elegant swathes of fabric draping the table a lone lit candle sat on, and the rough-hewn wooden cross.

A chapel. That made sense. This must have been the family's entrance. He walked in, stopping when his gaze caught on upon the view in front of him. A woman in a blue cloak who looked remarkably like the one who'd captivated him at first glance knelt at the altar.

He paused in the doorway. Stay? Or go? He should give Lady Rose her privacy. The last thing he wanted was to intrude on her supplication. He could walk his thoughts away somewhere else. The hallways, perhaps. Or the courtyard. The guards seemed kind enough. They'd point him in the right direction. The Great Hall even. It had room enough to stretch his legs. He didn't know why she was here at this hour, but the fact that she was meant something.

He'd just turned to leave when he saw her shoulders shake and heard the unmistakable sound of weeping.

Oh, Rose…

Even from a distance, by the dim light of a candle, he could tell these were no ordinary tears but those wrenched from a soul torn in two.

What cut her now with pain so deep the heart leaks from the eyes?
For whence tears flow unguarded bright, soul's hurt cannot disguise.

Nicholas's hand stilled on the door, the words of the old ballad swirling through his thoughts.

Bear he the comfort that she sought, the peace to soothe her woes.
But knew he not what ailed her soul, nor fought she friend or foe.

Did Rose fight friend or foe? Why did she weep alone in the chapel when everyone else slept? Nicholas ached to comfort her as the man in the old ballad had his love. But the man in the ballad had been betrothed to the woman he held. Nicholas had no promises. He was a stranger to Rose. His well-meaning desire to comfort might do more harm than good.

With a gasp, she curled forward, her forehead touching her knees.

His feet moved of their own accord, his heart directing them rather than his brain. Nicholas was halfway to her side when reality broke in. They were alone. It was past midnight. He should leave. But to leave a woman sobbing—*any* woman—went against everything inside him.

"Rose?"

She tilted sideways in her hurry to turn, a knee tumbling off the stair. He rushed forward only to have her steady herself. He couldn't decipher the look she gave him. Couldn't tell if it was fear or surprise or if she even recognized him at all. She fled out a side door, gone before he could say another word. He wished he had the right to follow her. Instead, with slow steps he walked the rest of the way to the altar and knelt, right where she'd been.

There were tears on the stair. Rose's tears. Nicholas wiped them with his sleeve, the tiny drops of emotion more than his heart could bear.

Almighty—

Almighty—

When the words wouldn't come, he lowered his head and let his heart bleed.

"What are you thinking?"

Caralynne's question was quiet but clear in the stillness. Her fingers splayed across Lior's chest. Though they'd retired hours ago, neither of them slept. He'd tried to stay as still as possible to allow her to rest but knew when she touched his shoulder that it hadn't worked. Caralynne was as awake as he. Lior leaned over to light a candle before sitting. It didn't take a mind-reader to know what kept his wife awake. The same thing battled his mind.

I am Prince Nicholas of Belairisia. I've come to wed your daughter.

Even hours later, the words still echoed in Lior's thoughts. Prince Nicholas's bold declaration had thrilled him at first. As if, in an instant, all their problems had been solved. Rose's future secure. The alliance between Belairisia and Raedonleith also. No one need ever know the real reason Prince Aldon had left.

But relief gave way to doubt as reality reared its head. Rose was still barren. Her troubles hadn't changed because another prince showed up. If anything, they'd increased. Prince Nicholas was Belairisia's heir and had made his claim in front of a crowd of witnesses. There would be no quiet walking away if Lior chose to deny Prince Nicholas's request. Everyone would know. Everyone would wonder why.

Lior could spin the story, claim he'd denied the prince's request because Prince Nicholas was heir to his own kingdom and Rose needed to wed a second-born to one day rule this one, but it wouldn't be the truth. They could negotiate an alliance, blend the two kingdoms, change the line of succession—the options were there. But only the Almighty could heal Rose's womb.

Prince Nicholas. Oldest son of King William of Belairisia. Why was he really here? They all knew he had a duty to his own kingdom. It was why King William and Lior had chosen Aldon for Rose instead of the older of the two brothers. Yet here Prince Nicholas was, offering for her hand barely two weeks after Prince Aldon had left.

"Lior?" Caralynne asked again.

He sighed. "I wish I knew what to think." There was a good reason he was still awake, hours after he'd retired. "Two months ago, I would have accepted without thought. Prince Nicholas is known to be a good man. Reliable. Loyal. Respected. Quiet, but well-positioned to lead. It would be an honor to have him wed our Rose, even with the challenges that would create for the two kingdoms. But two months ago, we still believed Rose could bear children. Is it right to ask this of Prince Nicholas? Of any man?"

Lior would liked to have believed he would have married Caralynne regardless of whether she could give him children or not but the knowledge would have made him pause at the very least. There was something about fathering children, knowing your legacy and a part of you would live on through them, that proof of virility—vain as it sounded—that filled a man's pride.

Caralynne and her unfailing love and support were worth more to Lior than a hundred children, he knew that now, and if the Almighty had seen fit to hold children back from the two of them, he would still have cherished his wife. But to know *before* marriage that children wouldn't even be an option? A hope? Could he ask such a willing sacrifice of Nicholas? Would he have chosen it of himself?

"You don't think less of Rose, do you?" Caralynne asked.

Lior started, horrified she'd even consider such a thing. His precious Rose? "No, never."

Twenty-one years on and he could still remember the tears that had welled in his eyes the first time he held his tiny firstborn. Welled, and overflowed. Barely longer than his forearm, her rosebud lips had pursed and her little fist waved in protest when one of those tears dripped onto her cheek. He'd seen children before, held them too, but never one with his lifeblood coursing through her. He'd run a finger over her scruffy, dark hair and lost his heart completely.

As he raised Rose to his chest, so careful not to crush her in his strength, he'd finally understood the parable of the pearl and how a man might give everything for so precious a prize. Though he and Caralynne had put aside rubies for the crown they were commissioning for their heir, Lior decided in that moment to change the rubies to pearls. The purest and most perfect he could find. No matter the cost. Nothing was too much for his precious newborn daughter.

"Nothing in the world could change how much I care for our Rose nor her worth in my eyes. But I'm her father. I will always love her. Too much to marry her to someone who may not see her worth for her womb. I couldn't bear to see her spend her life unloved or left to the wayside when she deserves so much more."

"Maybe Prince Nicholas will love her."

"Perhaps."

But could Lior take that chance? He'd chosen husbands already for their three daughters, and all three had turned out to be poor choices. Evangeline's betrothed had planned to wed then kill her. Mykah's had almost killed her too, albeit out of misplaced affection. Rose's betrothed had left as soon as he found out about her illness.

Three men. All of whom Lior had believed were good choices. All of them disastrous. He rubbed a hand across his eyes. All his life, he'd prayed and begged for wisdom as he fathered his daughters. They were his greatest treasures, never once making him regret that he'd not fathered sons. He'd done his best to make choices that proved his love for them and their immense value. But when it came to providing husbands for them, he'd chosen wrong. Three times. What if this was a fourth mistake?

"I can't agree to Prince Nicholas's suit," he said, "not while I'm so uncertain, yet I can't help feeling we'd be fools to turn him away. A prince of such standing offering to marry Rose? Claiming her in such a public way? How can we say no?" There was the other reason too. The one that had played on his mind all too often since Prince Aldon left. Yet another of the compounding reasons he'd not slept well these past few weeks. "Raedonleith needs this, too."

It didn't take more than a few seconds for Caralynne to decipher his words. "There's been another raid?"

"Aye."

Two more girls taken from the village. Half their sheep killed, the other half taken. Theirs hadn't been a big flock, but the loss had been felt all the same. The girls' absence even more. His people were in danger, and there was little he could do to protect them. Not alone.

"Cavendish men?"

"Without a doubt. They left their colors behind to make sure we knew."

"Oh, Lior." Caralynne squeezed his hand. "Does Mykah know?"

"I hope not." He'd tried his best to keep it from her. This wasn't Mykah's battle, much as she'd fought it. She'd already come close to paying with her life. Twice. And had the broken bones to prove it.

"What are we going to do?"

"I wish I knew. Cormac wants a war, but I don't. I can't."

He put his head in his hands, the pressure of it all too much. It had been more than twenty years. Most people would say it was time to let the friendship go, especially as Cormac clearly wanted nothing to do with it. But Lior couldn't forget the boy he'd climbed trees with. The one he'd raced horses with and squired alongside and cried with when Cormac's favorite dog had died. They'd been the fiercest of competitors and best of friends. Brothers, in a way blood could never compare with. They'd talked of the day when Lior would be king and Cormac his right-hand man. Leading Raedonleith together. Of their wives being friends and their children as inseparable as the two of them had always been.

He couldn't give up on Cormac. Not when Lior had been the one to destroy that dream.

"He's my friend."

Caralynne touched Lior's jaw, sadness in her eyes. "He's hurting our people."

"I know." It was all he could think about. At least, it had been before Prince Nicholas had arrived. Now he had two impossible decisions to make. They pressed down on him like a physical weight. "I thought if Cormac knew Belairisia was on our side, he'd stop the raids. The might of two kingdoms against one man. I don't know if I can fight him. Not to the death."

"You fought him for Evangeline."

"I didn't have a choice."

"Do you now?"

Yes, though he didn't like it. He could go to war. It was what Cormac wanted. But people would die. Too many people. Innocents on both sides. There had to be another way.

Almighty, can't you change his heart?

It was a useless prayer. One Lior wasn't even sure he had faith left for anymore. He'd been overconfident in his faith the first few years he'd prayed it, certain the Almighty would answer. That Cormac would move on. Find a love of his own. Begin a family. Forgive. But when another ten years had passed with no end to Cormac's hate, Lior's prayer had grown tired. Not lacking in faith nor hope, but tired. As the years stretched further, and Caralynne and Lior marked twenty years of marriage, Lior began to wonder why he bothered praying it. Nothing had changed. If anything, Cormac had grown angrier. Though he still prayed the words, Lior had lost hope of them ever being answered.

"Perhaps the Almighty sent Prince Nicholas," Caralynne said. "Perhaps he is the answer."

The candle flickered before straightening. Lior watched the flame stretch. Some days he wished he had Caralynne's faith in the Almighty *and* in him. She always believed the best of him, even when he gave her no reason to.

"Perhaps."

"Do you think he knows?" Caralynne asked.

"That Rose is—" Lior couldn't say the word. It ate at him, the feeling that he'd failed his daughter, even though there was nothing he could have done differently. Or was there? These things happened. Illness abounded. Babies were born with imperfect bodies. It was part of life. But what if Rose's illness wasn't? What if it was something they'd done? Or they could have stopped it, if only— Something. Lior hated that life came with so few answers and even fewer certainties. "I don't know."

"We have to tell him, as we told Prince Aldon," Caralynne said.

"Aye. We will. Though I wish we didn't have to."

"Why?"

"Because if he walks away because of it, I fear we'll lose our Rose altogether. So much has been taken from her already."

"You think he'll leave too."

"I don't know."

There were so many things he didn't know. Far too many.

But could he do any differently? Could he really deny Prince Nicholas his daughter's hand when the prince had claimed it so publicly? With such ardor? There had been something in Prince Nicholas's gaze as he stared at Rose that reminded Lior of himself all those years ago. When he'd seen Caralynne for the first time.

Lior had been captivated. Certain, even as his mind tried to offer reason, that she was the woman he'd marry. Whether or not Prince Nicholas knew about Rose's weakness, Lior was almost certain he'd stay.

But could Lior trust *his* heart? After it had already led him astray?

Then again, had it? Though he'd chosen the wrong men for his daughters, those decisions had led them to where they were today. Evangeline's running from her betrothed had brought Darrek to her and forged a love between them that had changed Evangeline from a child to a woman and given her Arthur. In losing Colin, Mykah had found Finnian, a man who stood by her and saw the vulnerability behind Mykah's strength. A man who celebrated his daughter's unusual traits instead of trying to quell them.

What if meeting Aldon was merely the opening note of what would be Rose's true love story? A love that wouldn't run but would last a lifetime?

Almighty, let it be so.

"Come with me when I speak with Prince Nicholas in the morning," Lior said, twisting his fingers through Caralynne's. "We'll tell him the truth and ask for time. I don't believe that too great a request. If he's still willing to marry Rose knowing she is unable to bear children, and if he'll wait a month or two to do so, we'll take it as the Almighty's bidding."

"And if he leaves?"

"Then he leaves, and we accept that the Almighty has a greater plan for our oldest daughter than we do."

Caralynne nodded, her expression grave. Lior felt as if they were girding up for battle. A battle for their daughter. For her happiness, for her future. It went beyond a husband, though that was part of it. It went to her soul.

"We should try to sleep. Tomorrow will soon be here."

Lior fingered the ends of Caralynne's hair as they lay side by side under the blankets, and thanked the Almighty again for this woman whose love had both surprised and blessed him. He hadn't been looking for a wife when he'd met Caralynne but was so grateful they'd crossed paths. How different their lives would have been if he hadn't been distracted riding and cut his cheek that day, sending him to her for care.

"Lior, I don't think Nicholas will leave. I know we've only just met him, but I think he truly cares for our Rose."

"Aye. I believe it too."

CHAPTER 7

The sun's rising finally put an end to the night's torture. Rose's eyes were gritty and her head full as if she hadn't slept at all, though she knew she'd drifted a few times because she'd dreamed. She stretched her legs, the action tugging the blanket from under her chin. The cool air stole the warmth from her body but not so much she shivered. She pulled the blanket back up and tried to find the will to rise.

It was the fatigue which broke Rose. The shafts of agony came and went—the nausea along with it—but the fatigue stayed. It was overwhelming. Unending. And unlike the pain, she couldn't push through until it passed. It never did. She woke tired and went to sleep even more so. Sleep didn't help. The drain of it went beyond the physical, reaching into her soul. Baring it for the weakness it was.

Not enough.

Never enough.

She'd told herself all these years that it would be okay. She could still make a difference in this world, leave a mark to prove her worth, if only through her children. She wasn't strong, but her children would be. They'd have the strength she never did.

But now—

Hot tears trickled down her cheeks, her chest tight.

I'm sorry, my lady. I wish I had better news.

Her dreams had been torture. She'd dreamed of Prince Nicholas holding her too tightly to breathe. Of the betrayal in Aldon's eyes as he'd walked away. Of her sisters besting her in every way. Of the traveling healer proclaiming repeatedly that there was no hope. That she might as well have never been born.

No.

She was stronger than this. She was stronger than her pain. Wiser than the words that tried to pull her down. She wouldn't give in to them or the hopelessness they tried to drown her in. The Almighty had a reason. Rose might not know it yet. She might not agree with it. But he had one.

Even if—

She clenched the blanket in her fist and pushed the discouragement aside. Today was a new day. A new start. Another chance to praise.

Thank you, Almighty, for the breath I breathe. Thank you for my heart that beats. Thank you for the strength you share. Thank you for the family you have given me.

Forcing strength into her limbs, Rose left her bed. She would have enjoyed standing in the tower, watching as the sun reached its golden warmth across the land, but her window would have to do. She had neither the strength to manage the tower stairs nor the patience to let anyone see her fall. Twice in one week was plenty. And though it was still early, she couldn't risk Prince Nicholas being there.

Prince Nicholas.

She would have been better pressed to stay in the chapel rather than trying to sleep last night. Likely she would have, had the prince not come.

Prince Nicholas.

What had he been doing in the chapel?

He'd seen her. Pitied her. The tears in her eyes had magnified the sympathy in his. He'd caught her crying. Seen her fall before mortification gave her the strength to run. She'd fled only as far as the hall outside the chapel before her legs had given in and she'd collapsed against the wall, praying desperately that Prince Nicholas wouldn't follow her.

He hadn't. She'd told herself she wasn't disappointed. A pair of guards finishing their watch had found her and helped her back to her chamber. Quin hadn't even noticed Rose was gone, though she'd apologized so many times for her negligence that Rose had sent her away. Quin couldn't be expected to stay awake all day and night when there were guards about the palace. More than usual, given the threats—and recent happenings—to the royal family. Father was taking no chances.

A young maid knocked before entering Rose's chamber, a bowl of water in her hands. Rose accepted it with a word of gratitude, washing from her face the effects of her fitful night. She brushed her hair next, raising a prayer with every stroke of the brush. She'd done it since childhood, the repetitive action as soothing to her mind as the prayers were to her heart.

Almighty, calm my spirit.
Great One, hold my heart.
Let me serve you today, however that may be.

She prayed the same prayer every morning. Over and over, like a song. But this day, the words didn't stop there.

Lead me forward in your ways. Let my weakness not hinder your strength.
And whatever Father decrees—

Her brush stilled. *Whatever Father decrees.* Would he decree she marry Prince Nicholas? Could she obey? She had to. He was her father, her king, and the man she'd looked up to all her life. She owed him her obedience. But Prince Nicholas? She'd not even spoken with the man.

Not because he didn't want to.

Aye, she'd been the one to hide. But he'd seen her weakness once already. One time too many. Perhaps, after seeing her broken last night, he'd changed his mind and withdrawn his suit. Perhaps even left Raedonleith, as his brother had done. Rose would know as soon as she left her chamber. *If* she left her chamber today.

Almighty—

Could she pray the words she ached to pray? Would they be true? A lie? A hope she could never truly live up to? Did it matter? She wanted them to be true. No matter what her doubts claimed. At the heart of her, she wanted to serve the Almighty and do his will for as long or as short a time as she was given.

Almighty, your will be—

The door flung open. Rose dropped her hairbrush with a yelp. Mykah rushed in like the whirlwind she was.

"Have you talked to him yet?"

"Who? Prince Nicholas?"

"No, the stablemaster." Mykah rolled her eyes and pulled a stool over to sit beside Rose. "Of course Prince Nicholas."

He was still here then. Tangled as Rose's thoughts were concerning him, the knowledge shouldn't have given her such joy. She refused to look too deeply into what that might mean. "No."

"Why not?"

"Until Father makes a decision regarding the marriage Prince Nicholas proposed, I have no need to." Their breath of a moment last night in the chapel didn't count. It had been over so quickly Rose might have wondered if it were another of her many scattered dreams had embarrassment not still made her queasy.

"You're not even a little bit curious why he claimed in front of everyone that he was going to marry you? Have you even met him before?"

"No. And no." One of those answers was the truth. The other she wanted to be.

"He offered to marry you, Rose. Does that not make your heart flutter and your dreams come alive?"

Not in any way she was admitting, though there was some truth to the heart fluttering idea. Quin finished making the bed and came over to braid Rose's hair. Mykah greeted the maid before turning her attention back to Rose.

"Why aren't you more excited about this? Isn't being married what you always wanted?"

Aye, it was. But one didn't always get what they wanted.

Quin's fingers were nimble as they pulled and tugged and twined Rose's long, dark hair. The color she'd gotten from her father, along with her green eyes. Mykah and Evangeline had both inherited their mother's red hair, in varying stunning shades. Rose's was just brown, though Quin's skill made it beautiful. Did Prince Nicholas prefer red hair or brown? And why did she care so much? He'd hardly be marrying her for her hair. If he married her at all.

"Nothing has been decided yet, and even if it had, nothing has changed. I'm still barren. I have nothing more to offer Prince Nicholas than I did his brother. Less, even, given Prince Nicholas already has a crown and heirdom of his own."

"What if you aren't barren?"

Rose's hair wrenched in Quin's hand as she spun her head toward her sister. The tug of pain on her scalp wasn't anywhere near as painful as the shot to her heart. "Mykah—"

"No, listen. What if there was another answer?"

"The conclusion of three healers wasn't enough for you?"

Rose sighed, hating the bitterness that coated her words almost as much as the pain itself. Mykah could hope. Mykah could pray. Mykah could fight. But Rose was done. She'd held on to hope for so many years already that there might be a different answer. That her body might heal itself or the Almighty do it. But it hadn't. And he wasn't. It was time to let go of hope.

"Finnian said there's a plant—"

"No. Please no." She'd tried plants. Tried herbs. Tried leeches. Tried rest and exercise and sluggish concoctions that no human should ever have to ingest. At best, they'd had no effect. The worst, she hoped to one day forget.

Mykah was always like this with a new thing. She fought and pried and worked and persevered until a problem was solved. She'd learn soon enough what Rose had already discovered. Not everything could be fixed.

"You won't consider it? Not even for Prince Nicholas?"

Not even for herself. "Prince Nicholas will leave soon enough. Just like his brother." Everyone did. Everyone who had a choice.

"I think you're wrong. I think he's in love with you. Or well on his way to being so."

The thought had crossed Rose's mind, though she'd just as quickly thrown it aside. No one fell in love at first glance. And those who claimed they did couldn't be trusted. She'd decided that, and she was sticking to it.

Although, her parents had.

But no. This was different. She was different.

"All the more reason to stay away."

"Because you're scared?"

No. Because I can't bear to be hurt again. Whether Prince Nicholas went home as Aldon had or, more likely, married her out of honor, he'd pull away. He'd tire of her weakness, be disgusted by the blood, ashamed of her. He'd wish he hadn't married her. At best, he'd pity her. She'd seen it before. It was why she'd tried so hard to hide the truth all these years. She had to be practical about this. Being heir to a crown didn't come with the option for whimsy. For either of them.

Quin twisted the braids across the back of Rose's head, pinning them into place before brushing the hair she'd left to fall down Rose's back. With a final inspection and a nod of approval, she walked away, leaving the sisters to their discussion. She only went as far as the other side of the room, so she'd likely still hear their every word, but there was little Rose hid from her maid anyway.

And the woman already knew how confused Rose was over Prince Nicholas. Three times in the hours after the guards carried Rose back to her room, Quin had come to Rose's side to ask if there was anything she could get to help, not bothering after the second to go back to her own room. Quin had pulled out some blankets and made a bed on the floor at the edge of Rose's room, though she'd slept as little as Rose. Rose hated that her restlessness had cost Quin sleep, but Quin brushed the concern aside. "That's why I'm here, my lady," she'd said, her voice full of so much compassion that tears had welled in Rose's eyes.

It wasn't fear at the thought of marrying Prince Nicholas that churned Rose's insides but the guilt of being a burden to one more person. Like Mykah, he'd want to fix her. And, as Mykah too would have to accept, there was no way he could.

Rose stood and paced to the window, staring down at the scene below. People going about their daily business. Women with baskets in one hand and babes in their other. Guards walking in twos and threes, swords at their sides, armor on their chests. Children laughing as they played a game of chase. Travelers, their clothing worn and their steps weary, plodding through the castle gate. Though at this distance, she was removed from the dust and noise of it all, her senses still picked up every sound and smells like she was amongst them. The warm comfort of fresh baked bread peeking from the women's baskets. The tickle of dust in one's nose. The strength of the guards. The laughter of the children.

She would have been down there with them if she could. Loving them as Mykah did. Learning their names, their hopes, their needs.

She would have done a lot of things differently, if she could have.

One of the young children tripped, letting out a wail. A woman Rose assumed to be his mother was there within seconds, pulling him into her arms, drying his tears, loving him back to smiles. Rose turned away, her arms empty. As they'd always be.

"Why do you think he came, Mykah? Think. Aldon leaves me and less than a month later, his older, more responsible brother arrives? What other reason could Prince Nicholas have had but to fix Aldon's mess? Me, Mykah. I'm the mess. The broken promise. Belairisia can't afford to be at odds with Raedonleith. Broken betrothals lead to conflict, and conflict leads to war. Prince Nicholas didn't come because he cared. He came because he had no other choice but to wed the broken princess his brother discarded."

"You're wrong."

"You think the best of everyone and everything, but that's not reality. Sometimes life just hurts. There are no good choices, only painful ones." Tears clogged Rose's throat. She swallowed them back, refusing to give in. She wouldn't cry over her life. Mykah didn't understand, but it was better that way. Rose wouldn't have wished her pain on anyone, least of all her beloved sisters.

Mykah walked to Rose's side and squeezed her hand. "That doesn't mean there isn't good among the bad."

"I wish I still believed that."

"Rose—"

She pulled her hand free. "Let it go, Mykah. You can't fix me."

"I wasn't trying to."

"Weren't you?"

Mykah opened her mouth to argue the point before closing it again.

"I'm sorry, Mykah. I know you want to, but there's nothing you can do." There was nothing anyone could do. This was the life she'd been given, and she'd live it best she could. Even if it was a half-life. Devoid of the love of a husband. Devoid of the blessing of children. Devoid of the dreams she'd held onto since she was a child. She had her family. Her beating heart. The breath within her lungs. The care and acceptance of the Almighty.

Rose looked away before the pity in Mykah's eyes undid her. Pity. That's all anyone gave her anymore. If only she could have hidden her weakness from everyone for longer. She wanted to be Rose again. Just Rose. Beautiful. Quiet but respected. Betrothed.

Once, they saw who she was.

Now, they only saw who she wasn't.

"Finnian and I are riding into the village this morning," Mykah said. "Come with us."

Rose shook her head. "Thank you, but not today."

"You said that last week."

And she likely would next week too. Her sisters were trying to help, but they didn't understand. How could they? They were either married or, in Mykah's case, about to be married to men they adored and who adored them in return. Evangeline had a son, and no doubt more children would come along for both of her sisters soon. They'd carry them under their hearts and birth them and hold them close. Darrek and Finnian had fought for their loves. Put their lives at risk several times to save Evangeline and Mykah.

Faced with a choice to do the same, Prince Aldon had simply left. Rose couldn't help but expect his brother to do the same. Any man would. Prince or not.

"Come on, Rose. Give Prince Nicholas a chance. You gave his brother one."

Aye, and a lot of good that had done her. Aldon hadn't even come to say goodbye nor asked how she felt. Not that she'd have allowed it, but he might have at least tried. If Prince Nicholas thought he cared about Rose at all, it was because of her striking face and figure. But they merely masked the truth within. Beauty would fade with the years. Better to keep her distance.

"I'd only slow you down if I came."

"Rose, don't say that. You know we'd love to have you join us on our ride."

"I can't today." After a night as sleepless as her last had been, Rose wouldn't even have the strength to mount a horse, let alone ride one. Then there was her promise to Aiyana that she'd meet that family this afternoon. She couldn't do both.

Choices. Again. Everything was choices. Where to use her limited strength. When to push herself beyond it. When to rest. What was more important. What would it be like to have the strength to get through each day without having to choose?

Mykah's mouth opened before pity once again took over. "I'm so sorry. I didn't even think."

And why should she? Mykah didn't have to deal with a body that betrayed her at every turn. Mykah's collarbone was still healing from a break when she'd fallen on it, but it *was* healing. One day, it would be strong again. Rose didn't have that hope. Sure, there were good days and bad, but there always would be. And even the good days came with no guarantee. She could go from merely achy to curled into a ball of agony in minutes. Seconds, even, as had happened at the feast last night.

"It's a beautiful day. Enjoy your ride."

Mykah hesitated. "Are you certain…"

"I am. I'm going to stitch for a while. You're welcome to join me, but—"

"I'm going."

Rose smiled at Mykah's horror. Her sister would rather hold a sword than a needle and was far more proficient with a sword too. With a squeeze of Rose's hand, Mykah left, closing the door behind her.

CHAPTER 8

The pile of books discarded beside Nicholas threatened to topple over, yet he'd not found anything that might offer a cure for barrenness caused by illness. Nor any mention of it at all. Still, Raedonleith's library was large, and he refused to give up hope. Somewhere within these walls had to be the answer.

Perhaps he'd find it faster if he asked for assistance, but he didn't even know what he was searching for nor whether the details of Lady Rose's troubles were widely known. Nor, if he were honest, why he was so determined to find an answer.

He circled his neck and straightened his shoulders, feeling the stretch along his back. He should get up and move around. Perhaps return some of the pile of books to the shelves he'd acquired them from before they crushed him under their weight. How long had he been sitting at this table?

To write is to capture one's heart and soul, to read is to set it free.
More power there's in the written word than swords across the sea.

Nicholas allowed a small smile as the beloved words he'd once read swept across his mind. Aldon had thought them foolish when Nicholas memorized and shared them, claiming a book couldn't cut off someone's head like a sword, but Nicholas agreed with the ancient philosopher. Words held more power than most people dared to admit.

The familiar smell of books and ink had accosted and welcomed him as soon as he opened the door to Raedonleith's library. The sense of awe that always struck him in the presence of books followed. So much knowledge. So many ideas. So many hours of work and thought and consideration, all contained in the pages of the hundreds of tomes before him. History and hope and wisdom. He could spend his life reading and still not discover all that books had to offer.

His sword arm might be weak, but his mind was strong and his heart honed from hours spent curled around an open book. History was more than facts. It was stories. People's stories. What to do and what not to do. How to live. How to love.

Did Lady Rose read? Had she too searched these books in hope of an answer?

Nicholas turned another page of the healer's record open before him, his breath catching at the detailed sketch of a human body. He scanned the page, hope tugging with every word. But no. The healer only recorded the male form. Nicholas flipped forward several more pages before closing the book. It had been unlikely from the start, being written by a man, but Nicholas was determined not to leave any page unturned.

The door to the library opened, letting in Lady Evangeline, Arthur, and a guard. A second guard perused the room, his attention catching on Nicholas and assessing before he nodded and closed the door. Lady Evangeline was slower to notice him, her eyes widening when she did.

"Prince Nicholas. Forgive me. I didn't realize you were here, or I'd not have interrupted."

He shook his head. "It's no matter. If anyone is interrupting, it is me. This is your home, not mine."

Though, perhaps it would be his soon? How long before King Lior answered his request for Lady Rose's hand? His escape to the library this morning had been twofold: searching for answers for Lady Rose and keeping himself occupied while he bided his time waiting on the king's decision. Surely any moment now, the king would summon him. King Lior had to know how anxiously Nicholas waited.

"I don't suppose you came with a message from your father?" he asked.

"No, simply as a distraction for my son." She smiled down at the straw-haired wisp of a boy at her side. "He wants to be a knight, training morning to dusk with his father or riding to the village with Mykah and Finnian, but it's too dangerous."

"Because of the weapons?" Surely they had wooden swords, as he and Aldon had trained with as children. Arthur wandered to the window, his nose pressed to the glass as he stared outside.

"Because of the raids," Lady Evangeline said in a low voice. "Father thinks he's hiding them from us, but the people talk. At first, they were few—a skirmish here and there, the usual fights between neighbors for land and honor—but these past few weeks, they've increased in frequency and intensity. I don't know what Lord Cavendish means to achieve by them, but knowing him as I do, it's not good. For Raedonleith *or* Arthur."

"Arthur specifically?"

"The truth didn't spread to Belairisia?"

Nicholas shook his head. He knew of the raids and the threat to the family—it was why King Lior had requested the marriage alliance with Belairisia—but to target a child?

"Lord Cavendish sired him. He relinquished any claim on Arthur when my father bested him, but every day I worry—" Her voice broke. Though she didn't finish the thought, she didn't need to. The extra guards inside the palace made sense.

"The library is a good place for a boy his age."

"He'd rather be on the training field or in the stables but accepts that learning to read is a challenge worthy of a knight too."

"'Tis a skill which will serve him well no matter what comes of his future."

Arthur grew tired of the view and sat under the window instead, pulling three rocks from a pouch on his belt and balancing them atop each other. The third kept falling. Arthur's tongue stuck out the corner of his mouth as he concentrated. A lock of hair dropped over his forehead. Nicholas felt a surge of affection for the boy. His determination reminded Nicholas of Aldon as a child. Aldon had poked his tongue out when concentrating too. And been all too eager to join the knights, even as a toddler.

"You'll be good to my sister, won't you?" Lady Evangeline asked. "Not that I doubt you, of course, your highness, but she's been hurt before."

By Aldon. Lady Evangeline might not have named Nicholas's brother, but the narrowed eyes gave away her thoughts.

"My brother was wrong. He never should have left."

"Will you?"

Heat streaked across Lady Evangeline's cheeks, as if she'd not meant to be so bold. His respect for the woman grew when she didn't take the words back nor drop her gaze. She cared about her sister as fiercely as she did her son. Enough to confront him, a foreign prince with the power to annul the alliance between their kingdoms. Or start a war, should he choose to be offended.

He wasn't offended. Not at all. He wished he could promise her he'd not leave, but King Lior might send him away tomorrow. Today, even.

"Not if the choice is mine."

Arthur let out a cry of frustration before throwing the rocks. A quick glance at his mother sent him scurrying to collect them. Lady Evangeline smiled her approval and returned her attention to Nicholas.

"I believe you."

She looked at the books piled on and around the table. Nicholas grimaced at the sight of one open on the floor, its pages askew. It must have slid off the stack while Nicholas was too caught up in the hunt for answers to notice. He bent to right it, brushing a hand across the vivid hand-painted illustration embellished with gold before placing it carefully down.

"You're looking for answers?" Lady Evangeline asked, gesturing to the table.

"Trying to."

"Then you know."

"Not enough." Never enough. The answers had to be here. A woman didn't become barren for no reason. "I wish I could help her."

"Perhaps you will be the one who can." Evangeline smiled, though her expression held more sadness than joy. "The Almighty used the love of a good man to save my life. Perhaps he will do the same for Rose."

"I'm glad the knights found you. They came to Belairisia in their search, you know. I was sorry to have no answers for them but promised to join with them in beseeching the Almighty that you might come home. It was a good day when word arrived that you'd been found."

"Found. Fought for. Freed." She shook her head. "Darrek should have left me. I ordered him to do so enough times. But he stayed, convinced there was something in me worth saving."

"You doubt it?"

She tugged at the fabric of her sleeves. "Some days, though not nearly as many as I once did. The love of a man is a powerful thing. And the Almighty—" Her words caught, her gaze going to her hands as if she hadn't realized what she was doing. She dropped her hands to her sides and smiled again. "The Almighty is good. I know he will care for Rose too."

"That he will."

"She's more than her illness, you know. It's all she sees but it's not all she is."

"I—"

His words were cut off when the library door opened once more. A guard stepped through, his attention going straight to Nicholas.

"Your Highness, the king has requested your presence."

⸙

Nicholas's steps were far more confident than he felt as he followed the guard into the king's chamber. The room was similar to several he'd seen already within both this castle and his own. Richly colored tapestries, elaborate carved furniture, light streaming in through three large windows along one wall. A large fireplace, unlit candles lined up along its mantlepiece. He was surprised to see the queen sitting beside her husband. His father rarely involved his mother in matters of the kingdom. Though, Nicholas justified, it wasn't only Raedonleith the situation involved. Not if Lady Rose was truly barren.

"Prince Nicholas, thank you for coming."

Nicholas bowed and took the seat King Lior gestured to. Neither of Rose's parents smiled, but they didn't seem angry either. The guard who'd accompanied Nicholas bowed and departed, leaving only the king, queen and Nicholas in the room. Either they trusted him without fear, or they didn't want witnesses to what was about to occur. Having both heard and witnessed King Lior's affection for his family and people, Nicholas assumed the former.

"We wished to speak with you regarding your request for Rose's hand in marriage," King Lior began.

If the situation hadn't been so serious, Nicholas might have laughed. Did they think he'd expected anything else? One didn't make a claim like he had in front of such an audience without expecting a lively, if not heated, discussion in return.

"When your brother left, we thought that the end of a marriage alliance with your kingdom. Were we mistaken?"

Nicholas clasped his hands and laid them in his lap. "I apologize for the way my brother left. It was not right of him to do so. It is my hope, and that of Belairisia, that the marriage alliance will proceed."

Nicholas hadn't mentioned Rose's barrenness to his father when he'd confirmed the alliance still stood prior to leaving for Raedonleith. Instead, he'd stated only that Aldon had left because of a misunderstanding that needed to be rectified as soon as possible. Part of him wondered if his father would have been so quick to agree if he'd known. Nicholas pushed the thought aside. What's done was done and he had no intention of retracting his words.

"It's not your brother's hand you wish to pledge but your own."

Aye, it was. Nicholas swallowed, overwhelmed again not by what he'd done but by how much he wanted it. It was like an ache inside him, an emptiness in his belly. He'd never felt like this before—so bereft yet so certain he knew what would fill the hole. It wasn't even that Lady Rose was beautiful, though that made his attraction to her easier to understand. Something about her drew him in. Something deeper.

For light she brought to kith and kin, souls captive did she take.

Yes, that was it. The balladeer had known what he wrote of. It was as if, upon seeing Lady Rose, the Almighty had put his hand on her head and said, "This one. She's the one I've chosen for you." The knowledge was as humbling as it was exhilarating.

And could be short-lived if King Lior didn't agree.

"It is true, I wish to marry Lady Rose."

"Why?"

And there was the question that had kept him up most of the night. Why?

Nicholas looked beyond the king's shoulder to the tapestry on the wall behind. It depicted a battle, though not one he recognized. Unless, wait, was that a giant in the middle panel? With a child standing beside with a sling? Ah, he did recognize the battle. It wasn't a recent battle but one fought long ago. He knew the outcome. The child had won. No, not the child, the Almighty. That battle had made no sense either, but that hadn't stopped it from happening. And changing the course of history.

"May I be frank?" Nicholas asked.

"Of course."

"I didn't plan to offer for your daughter." He might as well admit that. Whether it made him more trustworthy or less, he didn't know, but Nicholas valued honesty above all. "When Aldon returned to Belairisia without Lady Rose, I was furious with him. Though he explained his reasons—reasons he thought more than justified—I couldn't agree. A promise is a promise, and the alliance between our kingdoms is too important to lose. I set out for Raedonleith with the intention of apologizing for my brother's self-centeredness and begging you for time in order to convince Aldon to return.

"But then I saw Lady Rose, and the words just came out."

"You wish to rescind them?" King Lior asked.

"No, sire. Not at all. I spent half the night in prayer and am even more certain today than I was yesterday. I know it seems hasty and perhaps even foolhardy, but I truly wish to make Lady Rose my wife. You don't know me, but I can assure you, I will treat her well, like the queen she will one day be. I will serve her, love her, support her, and protect her with my life. Should you agree to our marriage, I will renounce my claim to the throne of Belairisia and stand by her side all of her days."

"Bold words indeed."

"I mean every one of them."

Queen Caralynne put a hand on her husband's arm, turning her head to whisper into his ear when he leaned toward her. Nicholas couldn't hear what she said, nor did he feel it was his place to ask. The king nodded and several more quiet words were exchanged before they returned their attention to Nicholas. King Lior spoke first.

"You would give up your right to rule Belairisia in order to marry Rose and remain at Raedonleith? 'Tis no small sacrifice."

They didn't apologize for the interruption, nor did Nicholas ask for one. The situation was strange enough without adding distrust to the mix. His request was hardly a simple one. And they hadn't denied him. Not yet.

"I would. I realize it is unusual but I cannot help but believe her place is here. I would not seek to take her from her family. 'Tis little sacrifice for me when the prize is so worthy. For Lady Rose, I would give up everything."

"Including children of your own?" Queen Caralynne asked, speaking to him for the first time. A slight catch in her voice gave away the deep grief that lay behind the question.

Nicholas's gaze strayed to the tapestry again, picking out minute details but seeing little of it. If he married Rose, he'd never have a child of his own. Of *their* own. A kingdom was one thing, a small sacrifice in many ways given how easily Aldon would step into the role of heir, but was Nicholas truly willing to give up children? When he'd always thought them so certain? He shouldn't be. But he also couldn't help thinking how unfair it was that he be given the choice when no one had given the same to Rose.

He should tell the king and queen that he needed time to consider and truly take the offer. But nothing about his decision would change, and Rose needed him now. The knowledge bloomed deep in his heart, beyond logic and regulations and sense, in that place where only the voice of the Almighty could be heard. He and Rose were meant to wed. No matter what. He'd found the treasure he'd unknowingly spent his whole life searching for. The face he'd not seen in any of the crowds of women who'd vied for his attention.

He was captivated by her beauty but, more, he was drawn to her soul. Oh, how Aldon would laugh if Nicholas admitted that aloud. He would have done the same, had Aldon spoken the words to him. But that didn't make it any less true.

"Even then," he answered.

"You know then? Of Rose's troubles?"

"Aldon told me she is unable to bear children."

Silence stretched a moment too long. Uneasiness crept in.

"Is there more?" More than the princess being barren?

The king and queen looked at one another, a silent conversation Nicholas could never guess at happening within their gazes. *Almighty, what is this? Am I as big a fool as Aldon claims? What do I know of this woman apart from the certainty that we're meant to marry? Am I being too hasty?*

"Rose is..." King Lior looked again to his wife, lost for words. Angst pushed against Nicholas's lungs when Queen Caralynne laid a hand over her husband's before turning her attention back to Nicholas.

"Forgive my blunt words but you must understand," she said. "Rose's body is weak. She hides it well. Too well, one might argue. Until recently, we had no idea she'd become so ill. I wish I could tell you otherwise, just as I wish for her sake that it was different. The weakness affects her life far more than she cares to admit."

Weak. Oh. That wasn't as bad as he was expecting. The gravity in their voices—and the horror in Aldon's—had led Nicholas to believe Lady Rose was dying. He could be strong for her, take on whatever she couldn't. He'd never been one to desire hours of dancing or long days outdoors either. Perhaps they were better matched than even he had first thought. "I will care for her."

"She also has pains," Queen Caralynne continued. "More than most women."

King Lior's face was almost as red as the cloak clasped at his shoulder. It was the fact that he wouldn't meet Nicholas's eyes that communicated the reality behind his wife's carefully phrased words. Pains. *Oh*. Nicholas swallowed. And swallowed again. And then a third time. Thank the Almighty Rose wasn't part of this conversation. He could only imagine how mortified she'd be if she were. His neck grew warm on her behalf.

But it must have been important if her parents felt the need to tell Nicholas before they'd even agreed to a betrothal. Had Aldon been subjected to the same awkward conversation with Rose's parents? No wonder he'd run.

Pains. More than most women.

Nicholas would rather face a crazed swordsman than discuss such an intimate topic, with the king and queen of all people, but for Lady Rose, he would find the courage. Or fake it.

Perhaps it wasn't so bad. Nicholas's mother was ill—often bedridden—one or two days a month too, something that had confused Nicholas no end with its regularity until his father had spoken with him. It had been a horribly awkward conversation at the time—much as this had become—but he was thankful for it now. If not for that, he might have had to ask Rose's parents for more details. He didn't think he *or* the king could have survived the mortification of that.

"I see."

"She is strong in spirit, though, despite the weakness of her body," Queen Caralynne was quick to assure him. "Stronger than she knows. And perhaps one day the Almighty will grant her the miracle we pray for and not only heal her womb but fill it."

Thoughts tumbled over one another in Nicholas's mind, logic at war with hope, duty at war with dreams.

He cared for Rose. Wanted to marry her.

But Rose was weak. Not too weak to lead her people but ill enough that her parents thought knowing might change his mind. Short of a miracle of the Almighty, she wouldn't bear children.

From birth, he'd been Belairisia's heir. A prince. Being a prince didn't come with the luxury of selfishness.

But what was selfishness? Choosing to love and marry Lady Rose and stand by her side regardless of the cost? Or walking away. Choosing the good of Belairisia and its future, as Aldon had done. Perhaps Aldon was the wiser brother after all.

Unless they were wrong about Rose. Aldon had said that three healers—including the queen before him—had confirmed Rose's barrenness, but there could still be hope. Healers were trained but not all-knowing. Somewhere there was an answer. He'd go back to the library. Search again. If he didn't find it there, he'd try another. And another. He'd search in every library he knew, ask every healer who crossed his path and every wise woman who might hold a clue. He'd find the answer they'd stopped searching for.

But it might be years before he found it. If he chose Rose, that decision had to be based on the woman she was today. Unhealed. Imperfect.

Just as he was. As they all were.

Life never promised certainties. The future could change quickly. A war could begin, a stray arrow find an innocent victim, a plague break out. The only moment they were promised was the one they were in. His decision was made.

"Lady Rose is an exceptional woman, and my only hope is to be worthy of her. My request for her hand is unchanged."

A knock sounded on the door. King Lior excused himself and opened it, speaking quietly with a person out of Nicholas's view. The two conversed for less than a minute before the door closed again and the king returned to sit beside his wife. The short reprieve eased some of the tension in Lior's face.

"Prince Nicholas, you've been honest with us, and I wish to be the same with you."

Nicholas swallowed hard, though no amount of swallowing was

making his mouth any less dry. *More* honest? He knew intimate details of Rose's body and he'd still not even spoken with her. How much more honesty could he deal with?

Whatever it takes.

Yes. Peace settled over him. *Whatever it takes.*

"We're honored you would seek our daughter's hand and pledge your kingdom's support as our ally, but the path forward will not be an easy one. You must consider your own future as well as the good of your kingdom. It is not too late to withdraw your suit and return to Belairisia as your brother did. No one will think less of you for doing so. Especially once details are…more widely known."

More widely known. When the truth of Rose's illness and what it meant was announced to the kingdom. Nicholas couldn't imagine the amount of strength it would take for a woman to face her people after that. Not alone. He wouldn't make her.

They were giving him a way out. But he had no wish to take it.

"I understand and thank you, but I assure you my request is unchanged. I still wish to marry Lady Rose."

"You're certain?"

"I am."

"Will you still be certain in a month?"

"Sire?"

"I want to see Rose married but, more than that, I want to see her happy. Though I believe you want that too, it would be unwise of me to decide without giving us both time to consider all that will mean. I cannot give you the answer you want today, but I would be a fool to send you away when you may be my daughter's best chance at happiness and the future we've prayed for. Instead, I ask for time. A month. Maybe two. Long enough to be certain. Send word to your father of your intent and stay as our guest. Use the time to court Rose, if you will, so that you may be more certain of your decision also, whichever it may be."

His decision wouldn't change. Nicholas knew that already. But if the king needed time, then so be it.

"Of course, Your Majesty. I hope to prove in that month that I am a man of honor."

King Lior stood and offered the smallest of smiles. "I hope you do too."

CHAPTER 9

Rose pressed her back against the wall of the cottage and tried to pay attention to the young girl bouncing about in front of her. Little Rose. Her namesake, though the family called their daughter Rosie.

"I love your necklace. Is it an emerald? And the stitching on your gown. It's so beautiful. Mother says I can have a beautiful gown one day but only when I'm grown up because I like running around too much and when I run around I get dirt on my clothes and it's hard to get it out. Sometimes I climb trees too with my friend Jack. You must not run around or climb trees very often because your gown is still very clean. I can't see dirt on it anywhere."

The bench Rose sat on tilted each time she moved, as if one of the four legs was shorter than the rest. A splinter bit into the palm of her right hand in the soft pad below her little finger, a gift the first time she'd put a hand down to steady herself. The setting sun glaring directly into her eyes wasn't making her stay any more comfortable either. Though she'd still choose the rickety bench over a steady, shaded chair inside. At least Rosie's chatter blocked out the conversation within the cottage.

We're to have another baby!

Aiyana had only just finished introducing Rose to the family when the mother had made the delight-filled exclamation. Rose had stumbled backward, the words an arrow dipped in devastation. Aiyana's clear surprise turned to apology as she helped Rose outside. "I didn't know," she'd told Rose quietly. "I wouldn't have suggested you come if I'd known. Not so soon."

"Do you have lots of gowns?" Rosie asked, running a finger down Rose's deep blue sleeve, oblivious to the emotional angst swirling about them. "Which one is your favorite? This one is really beautiful but I think I like the one you were wearing at the tournament best. Yellow is my favorite color. What's your favorite color? Can you braid my hair like yours? I have some flowers you could put in it. I found them this morning by the river. Mother says I can't go too close by myself but I was with Jack and he can swim and I didn't go that close because the flowers were closer to the tree than the river and—"

A baby. The woman held a child not yet six months old and already she was expecting another. Life wasn't fair.

Rose pushed the thought aside. It wasn't the woman's fault. This was a joyous occasion. New birth. New life. New hope.

Thank you, Almighty, for the child that grows within her and the one she holds and the young one playing on the pallet by her side and this beautiful girl beside me and... and...

A sob caught in her throat, tears pricking her eyes.

Hold me together. Please, please, Almighty. Hold me together. I can't break down in front of them.

"Are you going to marry Prince Nicholas? Where did Prince Aldon go? I thought you were going to marry him. But then at the tournament, Prince Nicholas came and said *he* wanted to and I was confused but Mother put a hand to her chest and started crying and said it was the most romantic declaration she'd ever seen. Did you think it was romantic? Prince Nicholas isn't quite as handsome as Sir Finnian or Sir Darrek but he's still very nice to look at. Does he bring you flowers?"

Rosie's brown braids turned gold as she danced through a streak of sunlight before sitting beside Rose, her feet swinging beneath her skirt. She was up again seconds later, darting off to pick a flower she'd spotted at the edge of a nearby fencepost and presenting it to Rose. How did her mother ever keep up with her? Or perhaps the mother didn't, and that was why the girl had such an adventurous spirit. What had she asked again? Oh. Flowers. Rose spun the tiny bloom in her hand, marveling at the perfect white petals.

"He hasn't given me flowers, but then I've yet to spend any time with the prince."

"Father brings Mother flowers. Not every night but most nights. She likes the purple ones best but says they're all beautiful. One day a man is going to bring me flowers. I know it. Because I'll tell him how much

I like them and he'll like me so much he wants to make me happy and, oh look! A bird!"

A tiny brown bird hopped along a nearby roof before flying to the ground, chirping its arrival. Another followed. Rose watched the two of them hop about, pecking in the dirt.

"They're my favorite, the tiny little ones. They're no good for hunting because they don't have enough meat to make the effort worth it but doesn't their happy chirp make you smile?"

"They're beautiful," Rose agreed.

"Mother says they must be the ones the Almighty sends to remind us he cares because they're not good for much else."

A crash sounded from inside the cottage followed by a woman's shout and a child's wailing. No. Two children. The high pitched mewl of the baby and the louder screech of the toddler.

"No, don't—" Rose heard Aiyana say seconds before the mother rushed out of the cottage, the swaddled newborn screaming in her arms. The babe's arms flailed out of the blankets as she held the child out to Rose.

"Take him, please. He's just scared, 'is all. Hold him tight. He'll calm soon enough. It's his brother who's hurt. Good thing the healer's here to stop the bleeding. Never was good with blood meself. Here."

Take the baby.

The world seemed to close in on Rose, swirling around her. She couldn't hear, couldn't breathe, couldn't think.

Take the baby.

Her throat closed, regret punching the air from her lungs.

It was just a baby. She'd seen plenty of them before. Held them too. Snuggled their warm bodies against her chest, their downy heads tucked into her shoulder as she marveled at the miracle of life. How the Almighty could make something so delicate and perfect from nothing. Her heart had smiled every time, knowing that one day, the babe she held would be hers. *She'd* be the mother who could calm the child's cries with a hug, who'd be the one the babe looked to for love, food and nurture.

This would be the first time she'd held one knowing how unlikely that would ever be.

I'm sorry, my lady. I wish I had better news.

"I—I—"

Can't.

⸺◦◦◦◦⸺

He should've gone back to the library, searched more texts for answers. They were there. He was certain of it. But Nicholas's mind was too restless to sit. Instead, he'd wandered. Though the halls. Out one of the castle's side doors. Through the marketplace. Around the ballgame a group of children Arthur's age were playing. They'd asked him to play. He'd kicked the ball, rescued it from a nearby market stall's shade cloth with profuse apologies to the market-holder, held in his laugh as the children very kindly suggested he might be better at other things, and kept walking. He might have continued on if he hadn't seen Lady Rose. His heart tripped along with his feet.

A woman was trying to hand Lady Rose a crying baby. Had the woman been watching Rose instead of talking with the girl beside them, she would have seen how much Rose didn't want to hold the tiny baby. The princess took a step backward, her hands out not in acceptance but to push away, and her face... Was that a tear that sparkled in the late afternoon sunlight?

Oh Rose.

Five steps and he was by her side.

"Allow me."

The woman didn't even look at him before thrusting the child into Nicholas's arms and disappearing through the cottage door.

"Prince Nicholas, I—you—"

He shook his head at Rose, a smile and a gentle touch on her arm enough to assure her he wasn't at all put out by the child or her reaction to it. He didn't hold babies as small as this one very often but it wasn't the first. One of the clerics who frequented Belairisia's castle library had a passion for teaching children to read. Word had gotten around and it had become a common occurrence to find rooms of the library filled with children hoping to learn. Several of them carried the responsibility of caring for their younger siblings.

Nicholas had been called in to hold one or two of them on occasion. His father would have argued that it wasn't a prince's job to look after babies so peasants could learn skills they might never use but Nicholas didn't mind. While he didn't share the same passion for teaching as his friend, he truly believed that every person, no matter their age or status, should be welcome in the wondrous world of reading.

"Now, what's got you so upset, young squire?" he murmured to the boy. "Belly full of air?"

"There was a crash," Rose said, her hands fluttering in front of her as if she wasn't certain what to do with them. "His mother said he was fine, just scared."

"Ah, I see." The blanket wrapped around Nicholas's arm, catching on his belt as the boy continued to writhe and scream. "Those are some strong lungs you've got there."

He sat on the bench, lurching to the side when the seat tipped. Rose carefully balanced herself on the other side of it, far enough away from him and his wriggly charge that two adults could have fit between them. Was it him she was avoiding or the child? The young girl who'd been with Rose must have gone inside.

"Scared, huh?" The baby's screams turned to whimpers as Nicholas tucked the blanket back around the child best he could. It wasn't neat, nor did the baby's left leg want to stay covered, but at least the blanket wasn't likely to choke the poor child anymore. Or cut off the blood flow to Nicholas's arm. When the whimpers threatened to turn loud again, Nicholas stood. The one thing he'd learned from the children at the library was that babies liked being walked. Around in circles, across a room and back again, through a forest, it didn't seem to matter where, just that they were moving. This little one must have agreed. His cries lessened as Nicholas walked the length of the short cottage and back again.

"Hush, dear sweet babe. Dry now your tears.
You're safe in my arms, there's no need to fear.
Though your hands are small, my arms are strong.
I'll hold you and cradle you all the night long."

The lullaby came to him, the same one he'd heard his mother sing to him and Aldon every night for years. He didn't dare destroy any hope he had of winning Rose by singing but the words were lyrical enough that the baby soothed. He hoped the Almighty would forgive the lie that he'd hold the child all night long. He certainly hoped it wouldn't come to that. Though, he supposed, if it helped Rose, he'd be here.

"Dream now, sweet babe, of angels above,
And know that you're cared for and safe in my love."

❖

Prince Nicholas had never before looked so appealing. What was it about a strong man holding a tiny baby in their arms that made a woman swoon?

Rose had to get out of here. Go home. Away. Anywhere. But it would be rude to leave without Aiyana or saying goodbye to the family, especially Rosie. Though, perhaps they'd understand?

She scuffed her slipper across the dirt. No, of course they wouldn't understand. In order to understand, she'd have to explain why a tiny baby had her fleeing, and why she'd run outside to a rickety bench in the glaring sunlight instead of taking the chair the mother had offered. Why she'd not even stayed long enough to find out the mother's name. Why the news of an upcoming birth had her fighting back tears rather than delight, and the sight of the man who might one day be her husband holding a baby had her wishing she'd never left her chamber.

A shadow fell across her face.

"Rose?"

The child was silent, either asleep or just content. Rose couldn't see from her position. She wished she couldn't see the compassion on Prince Nicholas's face. It would be her undoing.

"I'm well," she lied.

He nodded. Whether he believed her or not.

"We've not spoken since I announced that I wished to marry you."

"We'd not spoken before that either," she said. What was he doing here? Was this truly where he wished to have this conversation? When her nerves were scattered about her and he held a baby and any moment the cottage door might open again to release the whirlwind that was young Rosie?

"Forgive me for not seeking you out earlier."

His apology was almost as startling as his presence here. They both knew she was the one who'd been hiding.

"I know it must have come as a surprise but I meant what I said. I do wish to marry you. I realize you don't know me but then, you didn't know Aldon any better when you agreed to marry him so I hope I have a chance."

Breathe, Rose.

She'd known already that he wished to marry her. A woman little more than a stranger to him.

A stranger with a secret.

It had to still be a secret. He would have taken the offer back by now if he'd known about her… problems. Aldon mustn't have said anything. Perhaps he was too ashamed. She understood all too well. Though she knew in her head that none of this was her fault, the shame was still there. Battering at her heart. Pressing guilt against her lungs. Making her want to hide. It took more courage than it should have to walk out of her chamber some mornings.

She should tell Nicholas now. About the bleeding. About what it had taken from her future. He'd never look at her the same, but maybe that was best. Better to get it over with now before he made any more promises he'd regret.

"Prince Nicholas, there's something—"

Her attempt caught when the door to the cottage opened and Aiyana, Rosie and the mother stepped outside.

"Well aren't you a wonder," the mother told Nicholas, taking the child from his arms. "Me own husband can't get him to calm most days."

"Prince Nicholas?" Rosie's eyes were wide with wonder. "I take it back. You're definitely as handsome as Sir Darrek and Sir Finnian up close. Why are you at my house? Oh, did you come to see Lady Rose? That's so romantic. You could take her to see the flowers! There are some beautiful yellow ones at the river. I could come with you, if you want. To show you where to go. I promise I won't go near the water. We could go right now. The baby's asleep and my little brother happy so I can—"

Nicholas put a hand on the young girl's shoulder before she could rush away. "No." Rosie's smile dropped and he tried again. "That is, thank you for your generous offer. I'm certain the flowers are lovely and that you would be an exceptional guide, but we've not the time today." Nicholas looked at Rose. She couldn't help but wonder if he saw right through the smile she held in place. If he saw the weakness she tried so hard to hide. "It's time I be getting these two ladies back to the castle."

"Where you're getting married?"

The expression on Nicholas's face changed, though Rose couldn't even begin to guess his thoughts as he considered her. His eyes seemed darker, his smile not as bright, though more... something. Loving? Caring? Hopeful?

"Today, I simply wish to take her home."

CHAPTER
10

For the third night in a row, Rose found herself at the chapel. Sleep wouldn't come. She'd made it through dinner and even managed full conversation with Nicholas. Steering clear of more emotion-filled topics, she'd asked him about his journey to Raedonleith, which had morphed to him telling her about his horse. The one with more attitude than most squires. She'd been captivated by his story and almost forgotten her pain and the awkwardness of their earlier meeting.

Then she'd reached for her cup and the movement had tugged something within her to the point that she'd gasped. Nicholas had noticed. Though he'd not said a word, she'd seen the narrowing of his eyes. He'd watched her for the rest of the meal, anticipating her every move.

She'd felt cherished. And guilty. And ill.

Because, for a moment, she'd forgotten how much Aldon's leaving had hurt, and how right Nicholas looked with a child in his arms, and dared to dream that this could be real. Sharing meals, him caring, her being cared for.

He'd offered to escort her and Quin to her chamber when she stood to leave. The denial Rose had forced had been quick. As if she hadn't just rebuffed his attempt at chivalry, he'd bowed and said he hoped she would sleep well and wondered aloud if he might see her on the morrow.

Perhaps if he'd not said such things, she'd have slept better. Her heart had been fluttering—and her mind along with it—since she'd lain down.

She was attracted to him against her better judgement. Or, at the very least, attracted to his kindness. Nicholas treated her like a treasure, as if he'd known her for years as Spencer and Darrek had, rather than days.

How he'd found her this afternoon, she didn't know. He'd taken the baby as if it was nothing for a prince to do so. As if he'd somehow known that holding the child would break something in her beyond repair. Had he seen the tear that escaped before she'd had the chance to brush it aside? He hadn't said a word. Had just kept on, talking like they'd spoken every day for years instead of for the first time.

Neither had he made any mention of their earlier meeting at dinner, nor asked anything of her when they'd returned to the castle. He'd simply escorted her and Aiyana to the castle door, said he'd see her at dinner, and walked away.

No questions. No expectations. Nothing but kindness.

Almighty, what am I to do? He's still here, so Father hasn't denied his suit, but neither he nor Father mentioned our marriage. I should have asked during dinner, but I could hardly do so when Nicholas was looking at me like that and so many people could overhear. I'll ask Father on the morrow. Though that will hardly help me sleep tonight.

She sighed, her breath foggy in the brisk night air. It was so different being here at night. The only light in the chapel was the candle Rose had brought with her, which brought a glow to the area but not warmth. She wrapped her cloak tighter around her arms. She should return to her chamber. Try to sleep even if she didn't succeed. Her body craved the rest.

But there was peace here.

Candle in hand, she moved to the side of the chapel, sat on the stone floor, and leaned her head against the bricks behind her. Rose closed her eyes and let the coolness of the chapel wash over her. She'd just stay a few more minutes. Bask in the peace. The knowledge that she was loved. Accepted. Held.

It would all work out. Somehow. The Almighty would have a plan. Perhaps it wasn't what she'd once thought or even what she hoped, but if there was one in this world she could trust, it was the Almighty. He knew all. Held all. And never failed. Her body did. Frequently. Those around her also, though she knew they meant well. It wasn't their fault they didn't understand. Sometimes her faith was shaky too. But never the Almighty. He could be trusted. No matter what.

Rose sighed as doubts pushed their way back in.

She was doing her best to be strong and pretend nothing had changed, but everything had. It wasn't just her future she grieved but her worth. Who was she anymore? She'd set her heart to grieve and move on. Trust that the Almighty still had a purpose for her. But then Prince Nicholas had come.

Her world was tumbling too fast to keep up with. Years of nothing, as if the entirety of Raedonleith were in waiting, and now, everything all at once.

Almighty, you've said you care for the birds. I wish I felt like you cared for me.

She gasped at the words, trying to take them back. Sometimes she became so comfortable in the presence of the Almighty that she forgot who she was speaking with. But then—

It was the truth. She knew in her mind that he cared. Knew it in her heart too. But beyond the words and knowledge and her faith in his might were the feelings. The ache. The wondering. If he truly cared, why would he do this? Was it a test? A commendation? Did he think she could handle it?

I can't. You know that better than anyone. You've seen how many times I've cried myself to sleep. How many times I've crawled from bed because the pain is too much to walk. I'm not strong. I want to be, but I'm not.

I wish—

No. No wishes. No dreams. Only trust. Faith. The kind that glowed ever brighter in the dark. Especially in the dark. She didn't know the way forward. She didn't know if she even had the strength to take a step in any direction. But she would try. She would trust. She would believe.

Whatever that looked like.

Her eyes grew heavy as she stared at the candle's flame. Though her stomach still gurgled, it was easier sitting. She stretched out her legs and tilted up her head. The dark obscured the picture windows, but she knew they were there. Same as she knew there was a way forward, even if she couldn't see it.

Thank you for the air I breathe.

Thank you for my heart that beats.

Thank you for the strength you give.

Thank you that it is enough.

Thank you for Prince Nicholas of Belairisia and for bringing him to this place.

And please, one day, let me mean that.

She might have continued to pray. Her heart did, though the words grew fuzzy as sleep pulled at her mind.

"Rose?"

Rose startled, eyes blinking in the dim light as she tried to orient herself.

"There you are. What are you—? No. Never mind. Thank the Almighty you were here."

Stone walls. Stone floor. Colored glass reflecting the dancing of Father's lantern.

The chapel. She was still in the chapel. She must have fallen asleep where she sat. Her father would have something to say about that. Quin too. And Aiyana, who'd told her it wasn't good for her humors to sit on the hard stone floor for hours at a time. She blinked again. Her father rushed over. Pulled her up and into his arms. It had been a long time since she'd felt his tight embrace.

"Thank the Almighty, oh thank the Almighty," he whispered into her hair. She stumbled when he released her, her lower limbs feeling the effects of hours on the floor. She grabbed at the wall behind her, bracing herself before she fell.

"Father. What is it? What happened?"

His hair was mussed, and his eyes wild. Though he was dressed, he'd left his cloak and boots behind. He breathed like he'd run all the way here. The chapel grew brighter as guards filed in behind their king, lamps held aloft. Though their concern eased when they spotted her, their alertness didn't. Two stayed by the door, and four others spread across the chapel, checking behind pillars and lighting every shadow.

"Come, Rose. Your mother and sisters are waiting."

"Mother and—" She blinked again and rubbed a hand across her eyes. What had she missed? None of this was making any sense. Alertness coursed through her body, but maybe she was still dreaming. Though why she would dream such a strange scenario, she had no idea.

"I don't understand. It's not even morning."

"They'll help you prepare."

He tugged at her arm. She winced at his tight grip. Definitely not dreaming. "Prepare for what?"

"Your wedding."

"My—" She stumbled.

"Forgive me. I thought we had more time. I wanted to give you more time but I can't see another way. He's a good man. He'll care for you. He'll keep you safe."

"Father—"

"I've decided you're to marry Prince Nicholas. Today."

❦

Someone was pounding on Nicholas's door. No. Wait. Were they trying to knock it down? It was loud enough. It was too dark to be morning, though the muted light straining through the room's window proved it was close. Whoever it was, they were intent on speaking with him. Or killing him. One or the other. Where were his guards? They'd been debating which of them took the first watch in the hall outside his chamber when he retired. They weren't dead, were they? He grabbed his sword from the floor, thankful he'd grown accustomed to sleeping clothed.

The door opened before Nicholas could reach it. His sword rose then quickly fell when he saw who stood there.

"King Lior?"

With a nod to Nicholas's guard, still at his post, the king and two Raedonleith guards walked inside the chamber. Even at this hour—whatever hour it was—the king was dressed, if not to his usual impeccable standard.

"I need you to marry Rose."

And the king had thought waking Nicholas in the predawn hours a good time to tell him? Nicholas bit back a yawn and tried to discern how many hours of sleep he'd claimed. Three? Four?

"Of course, sire. 'Tis why I came." More or less. It had become his reason the instant he caught Rose's gaze at the tournament that first day. "It would be an honor. When will the ceremony be held?"

"As soon as you are dressed."

All thoughts of sleep fled from Nicholas's mind, along with guards, and the time, and the feel of the cold stone against his bare feet. Nothing remained except the king's words. Or what Nicholas thought the king's words were. All of a sudden, he doubted he'd heard them correctly. Marry Rose? Today?

King Lior stalked to the curtains, peering behind them as if he might find something there. He checked behind the dressing screen next and crouched to look in the fireplace. And out the window. His two guards remained at the door. To keep Nicholas in? Or someone else out?

"Sire?"

"You have something appropriate to wear, I hope? Or shall I have something sent?"

"I—" Nicholas hadn't been expecting a wedding when he hurriedly packed for his trip to Raedonleith, but the clothes he'd worn to meet with the king would be appropriate. He would have liked to wear the crown his father had given him the day he came of age, but he hadn't brought that either. "I have clothing."

"Good. The chapel then. As soon as you're dressed."

He was marrying Rose. Today. It still didn't seem real, no matter how many times the words played over in his mind.

"Lady Rose is in agreement?"

"She accepts it."

Not the same as agreeing but at least she wasn't being forced to marry him against her will.

"If you don't mind, sire, why the change of heart? Yesterday, you told me you wished to wait a month, if not two, before accepting my suit. Now, we're not only to marry, but we're to marry immediately? Did something happen?"

Finally, the king stilled. His gaze caught Nicholas's and held. Nicholas was shocked at the amount of fear he saw there. Fear and...determination?

"Sire? What is it?"

"Someone tried to kill Rose. Had she been in her chamber rather than the chapel, he would have succeeded."

⁕ ⋯⋗❦⋖⋯ ⁕

I've decided you're to marry Prince Nicholas.

It hadn't been a request but an order. Rose hadn't seen her father so shaken since the morning they all woke to find Evangeline gone. Something had happened, but no one was telling her. For her safety? Or because it was too much for her to handle?

A wedding was too much for her to handle, but that hadn't stopped her father from foisting one on her this morning. Finnian and Mykah weren't to marry until tomorrow. It would have been Aldon and Rose's wedding day too—a joint wedding for the king's two daughters—until Aldon left. Invitations had been sent, a wedding feast was being prepared, nobles were arriving from all over the country. Rose understood her father's decision to have her wed Prince Nicholas but not the timing of it.

The sun hadn't even graced the day yet. Rose would usually be creeping up the stairs to the tower at this time to watch the day come alive, not preparing for a wedding.

"There. Perfect."

Mykah patted the elaborate braids she and Quin had spent the past hour twisting into Rose's hair. The gold ropes that wound through them matched the gold rimming Rose's pale blue gown. She'd been thrilled the first time she'd seen it, imagining how Aldon would think her beautiful. Of course, that had been before. Before the healer's news. Before Aldon left. Before his brother had come to take his place. As if any man would do.

No, that was it exactly. Any man would do. Any man who would take a broken wife and promise to provide for her as long as she lived. However long that may be. Aldon had once told Rose that his brother's implacable sense of honor would get him in trouble one day. Rose was that trouble. This was the day.

Prince Nicholas had offered for her, Father had accepted, and now the prince would be burdened with her for the rest of his life.

The unmistakable weight of a crown rested on Rose's head. Evangeline clapped her hands with delight. "Beautiful." The other women agreed. Rose tried to smile, but unlike her gown, she'd hated her crown on sight.

No. Not hated. Hate was too strong a word. Saddened was closer to what she'd felt, though even that didn't sum up the emotions flooding her as she held it. It was beautiful, in its own way, but not what she'd expected. Certainly not what she'd hoped for.

Exactly like her life then. Beautiful. Full of potential. And disappointing.

Enough brooding. It is what it is. Find a smile. Find the light.

Rose slipped her feet into the shoes Quin held out. Her mother and sisters departed for the chapel, all smiles and cheer. Minutes from now,

Rose would be married. Her lifelong dream come true. Even if it now felt like a nightmare.

What was Prince Nicholas thinking? He hadn't said a thing last night though he must have agreed, or she wouldn't be walking to the chapel in a wedding gown. He'd shown her kindness. Proclaimed his intentions publicly. Called her beautiful more than once. He'd said and done all the right things, but she couldn't help thinking he'd run, just like his brother had, if he knew the truth about the bride he was getting. She should have spoken with him when she had the chance. Before her father had decreed they wed. But that chance was gone now.

The blue of her gown swept the floor as she walked out of her chamber. Bleary-eyed servants looked at her and her wedding-day finery in surprise as she passed, whispers crossing their lips. She set her gaze ahead and did her best to ignore them. She'd walked the path to the chapel a thousand times but never in a wedding gown. Dread mixed with excitement in her gut, making for an interesting, and nauseating, dance.

The chapel doors loomed, closed as usual. Her parents waited outside. Prince Nicholas wasn't with them, though she had no doubt he waited nearby. The speed at which the wedding was taking place played with Rose's mind. Why so early? Why in the chapel with only a few people to witness? Why not tomorrow when a wedding and feast were already planned? Why hadn't Father told her last night? Or Nicholas? They'd both had the chance.

As you had the chance to tell Nicholas the truth.

"You look beautiful, my daughter."

Emotion made her father's voice wobble. Rose smiled her thanks before raising her chin and looking at the door. She should ask questions. Now, before it was too late.

Why Prince Nicholas?

Why now?

Why the rush?

Had a new alliance been made? Would she walk away from her birthright? Would he walk away from his?

Why did Father hold her so tight?

But the questions stuck in her throat, fear holding them captive.

One breath. Two. Three.

Almighty, hold me. Be my courage and make me strong. Stay the marriage, if it be your will. And if it not—

If it not—

She didn't have words to pray more.

"Ready?"

Her heartbeat was a flutter in her chest, batting at the lungs that couldn't take a full breath. No, she wasn't ready, but neither did it matter. Prince Nicholas had offered for her, and Father had accepted. He wouldn't have done so if he didn't believe this was best for her and for Raedonleith. She would be obedient. She would be grateful. She would trust him.

She would protect her heart. Somehow.

The doors opened. Prince Nicholas stood just inside, resplendent in a dark blue velvet cloak and white tunic. He opened his mouth, but when no words came, closed it again and offered his arm. Rose took it. She had no words either. He was perfect, from the dark brown hair that curved around his ears to the cleanliness of his boots. Even his fingernails were clean.

Wait. No. Not perfect. A tiny scar ran along his jaw under his left ear. Barely the length of her little finger and so fine it only showed at certain angles but there. Seeing it made her feel better. Minimally but better.

It was strange to think she'd been here little more than an hour ago, sitting in the dark with her one candle. The chapel looked so different now, filled with family, several knights, clergy, and enough candles to make it feel almost like daytime.

Almost. Nothing could quite make this feel real.

She glanced left as she and Nicholas began the walk to the front of the chapel. Her parents followed the two of them. Mykah, Finnian, Evangeline, Darrek, and Sir Manning waited near the altar. Arthur hadn't come, but then, the sun had yet to rise. Mykah's face twitched as she tried to stifle a yawn. Finnian grinned and poked her in the side before whispering something in her ear that made her blush and his grin stretch wider.

Nicholas squeezed Rose's arm gently, pulling her attention away from her family and doubts. She looked up to find his face close, his gaze gentle as he smiled. "Shall we?"

Rose took another deep breath. The wedding. That's why she'd come. That's why they were here. She nodded. Standing beside Nicholas at the altar, Rose breathed in fear and breathed out prayer.

Hold me. Be my courage. Make me strong. I don't understand. I don't like this. I don't even know him. But you do. You understand. You know him. I don't understand my father's reasoning, but I trust Father. And I trust you. You'll hold me, won't you? Please, please. Hold me. Keep my fear and frailty at bay.

And don't let me faint. Not this time.

CHAPTER 11

Nicholas stared at the flawless woman before him, hardly believing she was about to be his wife. Her light blue gown couldn't hide the delicacy of her wrists, her neck. She was fragile, like the blown glass his mother collected. But strong too, as Queen Caralynne had said. Though Rose didn't smile as they stood before the cleric, neither did she cower.

It was fitting that the gold crown she wore was adorned with pearls—weakness molded layer by layer into something so beautiful, so rare, so unique that no mined jewel could compare. She wore it well, standing tall, shoulders back, every bit a queen. The only glimpse of any uncertainty was her cheeks. They were rosier than usual, lending a spark of color to her pale face.

He felt every one of her breaths as she stood beside him, listening as the cleric spoke of love and commitment and promises. He should listen, but his mind was far too occupied thanking the Almighty for the woman he was marrying. Anyone who claimed Lady Rose was weak hadn't seen the courage in her heart as she stood here today.

A ceremony that could just as easily have been her funeral.

An intruder had been in her chamber last night. An intruder with a knife. If not for whatever it was that sent her to the chapel, she would have been killed while she slept. The man had jumped out the window and escaped before the startled maid waking to check on Rose could call for help. Guards had searched the grounds but not found the man. Rose had been missing too, sparking fear upon fear until she was found asleep in the chapel.

If he can get to her in her chamber, he can get to her anywhere. She's not safe here in Raedonleith. It wouldn't be appropriate nor easy for Rose to have a guard by her side at all times, but a husband—

A husband could sleep beside her and protect her. And a husband from another kingdom could take her to his home until the threat passed with few questions asked. King Lior wasn't only entrusting Rose's future to Nicholas this morning, he was entrusting her life. It was a sobering thought. One Nicholas determined to be worthy of.

The cleric wrapped a gold rope around their hands, binding them together. Nicholas squeezed Rose's hand, making his own promises to her. She caught his gaze before looking away. He longed to turn her face back to him but kept his unbound hand by his side. There would be time for wooing. Time to convince her of his sincerity. His care.

Almighty, let it be love. I know it's not the way of arranged marriages, but it could be. I commit today to love Rose and cherish her, no matter what, but please, let her love me too.

"Prince Nicholas, do you take this woman to be your wife?"

"I do."

"Lady Rose, do you take this man to be your husband?"

"I do."

"What the Almighty has joined here today, let no man tear asunder."

The cleric said a few more words, but Nicholas didn't hear them, too stunned by the fact that he was now married. Married! To this striking woman. How Aldon could have ever walked away from her, Nicholas didn't know, but he'd forever be grateful.

· ⚬◍⚬ ·

There were two strands of stitching poking from Nicholas's tunic. Three tiny holes beside them. His tunic was dark. Not black today, but—Blue? Yes, blue. Very dark blue. Four candles flickered on the wall beyond him. Seven stained glass windows bordered the chapel. Rose would see them all if she turned her head.

"Will you seal the marriage with a kiss?"

Rose started, wrenched from the careful litany of facts she listed to calm her heart.

Kiss?

She stared at Prince Nicholas. He squeezed her hand again, his gaze seeming to promise something, though she didn't know what. She'd all but married a stranger. She closed her eyes and tried to stay as still as possible. The wedding was almost over. Then they could break the fast, and she could hide in—

Wait. Was it still her chamber? She was married. It was his too. Or would she move to another? A larger one to share with her new husband? That's what she'd planned when her groom had been Prince Aldon.

Nicholas moved closer. She flinched as his warm hand touched her cheek but it was her forehead he kissed. Softly. Gently. All too quickly. By the time she opened her eyes, he was standing a respectable distance away again. Still too close but also, impossibly, too far. Her heart thudded with guilt at the shock realization of how much she yearned to pull him in again.

Mykah let out a cheer. Darrek clapped Nicholas on the back. Rose colored as red as her name. Her legs threatened to dump her on the ground, though it was nothing to do with her weakness and everything to do with the way Nicholas put his arm around her back. He didn't need to do that—everyone here knew their marriage was arranged, and quickly at that—but it was nice. Very nice.

Her father clasped her shoulder.

"You've done well, child."

He kissed her cheek, as he'd done so many times over the years. She thought he'd step away but instead he pulled her into an embrace. Nicholas's arm fell as Finnian and Darrek pulled him aside to offer their best wishes. Along with some chortles that made Nicholas redden and Rose thankful she couldn't hear.

"I love you, my beautiful Rose."

"I love you too, Father."

She looked up in time to see his throat bob as he swallowed once, then again. She pulled back. Was he crying? No. He couldn't be. But there was no mistaking the wetness in his eyes nor the tear that dripped down his roughened cheek into his beard. His beard had been dark brown once. The past four years had speckled it with gray to the point that it was almost difficult to see the brown anymore. Age? Or worry over his wayward daughters?

"I'm going to miss you," Father said.

"I'm not going anywhere."

His sigh ruffled Rose's hair and tugged at her heart.

"Your place is with your husband."

"Of course, but I can't leave. These are my people. This is my home." Panic welled, compressing Rose's lungs. She'd been sleepy when he told her about the wedding and as she prepared but not so much that she would have missed that. Leave Raedonleith? It was the only home she'd ever known.

"I fear war is coming. You're not safe here."

What can you see? What can you hear?

Tears continued to drip down Father's cheeks. One left a dark spot on his red doublet. Mother spoke with Nicholas, hands clasped together as if in prayer. She couldn't see Nicholas's face or the tiny scar that had calmed her. Mykah and Finnian held hands, faces close as if they'd forgotten everyone else in the room. Darrek and Evangeline were gone. To return before Arthur woke?

She couldn't hear anything but her father's pleas and the thudding of her heartbeat in her ears.

"If war is coming, none of us are safe. Don't send me away."

"Rose, please. Don't make this difficult. You're married now. It is only right that you spend time with your husband."

Married. Husband. Prince Nicholas.

She'd spoken with the man twice. Run from him twice too. She'd begged the Almighty last night to show her the way forward but was this truly his answer? To marry a near stranger and leave the only home she'd ever known the same day?

"Mykah is to be married. Will you send her away also?"

"Mykah can—" He stopped. Looked down. It was the looking down as much as the unfinished thought that told Rose what he really meant.

Mykah can look after herself.

Evangeline too.

Even little Arthur could hold a knife or run a message or make himself useful. They weren't crippled by weakness like Rose. That was why her father had changed his mind about her marrying Nicholas. It wasn't the alliance nor even Nicholas himself. The prince was merely a means to an end. The end being getting Rose out of Raedonleith.

"'Tis not forever. Only until it is safe to return."

The candles smelled of warmed honeysuckle. Father's cloak smelled like the lavender he was so fond of gifting Mother. Sometimes he used it to carry the blooms in when he didn't take a basket. Rose clasped the stone of her necklace in her hand, running her thumb along its smooth contours as she'd done a thousand times in the years since Mother had given it to her.

Not forever. She'd return to be queen one day.

Almighty, give me strength.

"When do I leave?" she asked. There was no use in fighting. Not when it was already decided. She was Nicholas's wife now, pledged to go wherever he did. She'd had her chance to ask questions. She should have taken it.

"The horses are saddled and waiting along with provisions. There are extra blankets and straw and enough food to fill you."

He kept talking, but Rose stopped listening. *Saddled and waiting.* She was leaving now. Leaving the only home she'd ever known. The only place she'd felt safe. With a man who was a stranger in every way but name. A man who was now her husband.

"Mykah's wedding?"

Her father shook his head. "I'm sorry."

She was going to miss her sister's wedding.

Mykah leaned forward to hug Rose. Evangeline took her turn next, Arthur snuggled against her side. Then their mother. Darrek said something. Finnian too. Nicholas. The cleric. Rose might have smiled and thanked them, but the chapel had become a blur of sound and noise and tightly controlled emotions.

Don't cry. Be strong. Hold it in. Don't let them see. It's because they care.

Because they care.

Because they care.

Because she was weak.

No.

With a shake of her head, Rose banished the thought. Not one of her family had ever loved her less because of her weakness.

They want you safe. They're not sending you away. They're protecting you.

Protecting you.

Not smothering you.

Protecting you.

She held her head high. Took Nicholas's arm when he offered it. Determined to be strong. She could do this. It was just another frustration to work through. Just another day.

One day at a time, she'd take it. One hour at a time. One minute at a time if that's what it came to.

Almighty, thank you for the air I breathe. Thank you for my heart that beats. Thank you for the strength you give. Thank you for another day to serve you best I can.

She turned away from her father before the tears now streaming down his face undid her altogether.

⚬⚬⚬

They left through the back gate like criminals. Nicholas, Rose, Quin, Sir Spencer, Sir Adam, and the two Belairisian guards. A small party. Smaller to track, no doubt. They'd move faster too. Make it to Belairisia and the safety her father claimed it offered.

In all her imaginings of her wedding over the past six years, Rose had never imagined it beginning in shame.

No. Not shame. This wasn't shame. It was protection. Care. Love. Or so she tried again to convince herself. It felt like shame the way they walked their horses through the back gate of the castle, no crowd of well-wishers to see them on their journey.

Tears blurred Rose's vision. She closed her eyes and lifted her chin, determined to make the most of her new life. It wasn't what she'd expected, but that didn't mean it was over. Quite the opposite. This was a new beginning.

Almighty, you're with me here. This is no surprise to you. Thank you for the air I breathe. Thank you for the strength I have. Thank you that you hold me close.

And thank you for this man I now call my husband. I don't know what to do with him—I don't know what to do with me—but I trust you do, and you'll lead me, the same as you always have. Because even if this turns out to be a complete disaster and the worst decision of my father's life, I know you will be with me. You will not change. You will be faithful. No matter what.

CHAPTER 12

A noise sounded in the trees. It was barely loud enough to be called a rustle, but Nicholas looked over his shoulder all the same, scanning the forest for anything that might be out of place. He'd been jumping at noises ever since they left the shelter of Raedonleith's walls, certain they were being followed or that any moment they'd be set upon. He'd ridden these same roads and slept in these same forests day and night for a week and never once balked nor considered he might be in danger. But he hadn't had such precious cargo with him last week. Now, every sound made him flinch—every rustle of a tree branch, every call of a bird, every neigh of a horse.

Someone had tried to kill Rose as she slept. A man who might be following them even now.

Marry her and take her to Belairisia, the king had said. *I'm trusting you to keep her safe.*

The pressure of expectation was enough to fell a man, but Nicholas was determined to be worthy of the king's faith in him.

The trees held no danger Nicholas could see, though it was the unseen that unnerved him. If someone was following them, intent on trying again to eliminate King Lior's heir, he'd hardly advertise his position. Nicholas and the men would have to be alert, night and day.

"A word, sire?"

Sir Spencer drew his horse close to Nicholas's. Milori shook his head, but Nicholas pulled him back. If he'd known he'd be spending fourteen days on a horse, with nary three days in between, Nicholas would have brought a different one. One not quite so strong-willed. Spencer waited until Nicholas had Milori under control before speaking again.

"I need you to send your guards ahead to Belairisia." Spencer's words were quiet, and though he leaned in enough that Nicholas could hear, he kept his face to the front. His smile was nowhere to be seen.

"You've a reason?" Nicholas asked.

"Aye, because we won't be."

Nicholas moved to slow his horse, but Spencer stopped him with a shake of his head. Nicholas looked at the knight and raised his eyebrows. "Explain."

A quick glance at the rest of their group showed no one paying them any attention, but still Spencer kept his voice quiet.

"Adam and I, we've been ordered by the king to escort you and the women to a small village part way between Raedonleith and Belairisia. Lady Aiyana, Sir Finnian's sister, owns a house there."

That made no sense. The king's orders to Nicholas had been clear. *Marry Rose and take her to Belairisia.* "The king told me to take her to Belairisia."

"King Lior believes there's a spy at Raedonleith Castle. Someone loyal to Lord Cavendish. It was too much of a risk to tell you the real destination. Home would be the logical place for a prince to take his new wife, and one day I hope you shall. But it's not the safest place for her right now."

"And Sir Finnian's sister's house is?"

"A man got inside Lady Rose's chamber, sire. With two guards at her door and three more in the halls. Until he is caught—and Lord Cavendish stopped—nowhere is safe. But the house is unexpected, and only a few know of its link to Raedonleith's healer."

"Lord Cavendish must."

Though Nicholas had only been in Raedonleith a few days, it had been long enough to hear the whispers that Healer Aiyana and Lord Cavendish's sister, Lady Sunny, were one and the same.

"He knew where his sister was married but not that her husband, Christopher, willed the house to her when he passed. Aiyana didn't wish to live there without her beloved husband, so she left it in the hands of the village's healer on the condition that the door be opened to anyone who may have need."

"Lady Rose has need."

"Aye."

"And my guards?"

"We'll be faster and less conspicuous as a small group. Harder to track if our party goes in two directions. Adam and I will protect you and the women. I know you would prefer your own guards but—"

"I trust you." Nicholas had met the two knights for the first time several years ago, when they'd been searching for Lady Evangeline. He'd been impressed with their loyalty then. That respect had grown as word came that King Lior's band of knights had continued that search—traveling sparsely, sleeping in the dirt, being beaten and left for dead only to rise again and keep going—until the day they brought the king's youngest daughter home. The fact that they were the knights the king chose to protect Lady Rose spoke of a loyalty and strength beyond their years.

Nicholas allowed his gaze to move to Lady Rose, her back straight as she rode in front of him, her maid by her side. Much as he'd have liked to converse with his new wife, he didn't mind too much riding behind her. It was easier to keep watch from behind. Adam took the front, one of Nicholas's men with him. The other Belairisian guard took the rear.

The maid had pulled back the sides of Rose's hair in two thin braids to keep it out of her face as she rode, but the thickness of it still flowed down her dark gray cloak, brushing the saddlebag set behind her. There were no adornments in her hair—no ropes or flowers or beads. The crown she'd worn at the wedding was gone, either for comfort's sake or its protection. He'd heard rumors of the Raedonleith crowns and their significance. Upon each of the princesses' births, a crown had been commissioned to be given to her on her wedding day. He'd thought the tradition sweet the first time he'd heard of it, never guessing he might one day wed one of the Raedonleith daughters.

Nor that they'd spend the first week of that marriage running for their lives.

Rose straightened her back and shoulders again. Her maid, Quin, said Rose hadn't been to bed last night. Though Nicholas was grateful the choice to seek the Almighty in the chapel had saved her life, she must be exhausted. Rose should have spent the day sleeping, not marrying in the predawn hours and spending the day on a horse. Sympathy warred with a fierce need to protect her. They hadn't gone far enough. But would anywhere be far enough? Changing course was a good choice.

"I'll send the guards to Belairisia with word of my nuptials and official statement renouncing my claim to the throne," he told Spencer.

Nicholas pried the signet ring off his finger, wincing as it caught on his knuckle before sliding free. His finger was pale beneath it. He clasped the ring in his fist, a sense of loss coming over him immediately. He would have been king one day. He'd prepared his whole life for the role. Known since he could walk that a crown was his destiny. He might not have been as strong as Aldon or his father, but books had made him wise, and his reserved nature given him the chance to listen to what his people needed. A king's strength could be found in the people one surrounded themselves with, but wisdom could only ever come from within.

For the first time since seeing Lady Rose at the tournament, the weight of what he was giving up settled upon Nicholas's shoulders. No. What he'd already given up. The plans he'd made for Belairisia's future—opening learning to anyone who wished to read and not only those who could afford it, training more and better healers, having less excess at his table that those who needed food might have more. He wouldn't be in a position to make those changes. His people wouldn't suffer any more than they already were once he gave up his claim to the crown, but neither would their situations improve.

He'd made the right choice in marrying Lady Rose, hadn't he?

A flash of light caught Nicholas's attention. Rose had raised a hand to brush hair from her face, sunlight catching on the gold bracelet she wore. His grip on the ring loosened as he recalled how delicate her hand had felt in his. Yes. He'd made the right choice. Aldon would lead their people. Aldon would be a good king, albeit a different one than Nicholas would have been. Nicholas's place was with Rose.

He turned at a noise in the trees to their left. From the corner of his eye, he saw Spencer touch his sword. A glimmer of red, low down in the brush, was there for a moment and gone just as fast. A fox. Just a fox. Likely startled by the horses. Nicholas let out a breath, tucked the ring into the pouch at his belt, and returned both hands to his reins. The danger had been imagined this time, but Nicholas couldn't help noticing that the knight stayed a little closer to him—and Adam to Lady Rose—as they continued.

◦•◦◉◦◉•◦•

"Another hour and we'll make camp for the night. Will that be acceptable?"

Rose nodded, though her body screamed that it was a lie. Everything hurt. Everything ached. She'd wrapped Strider's reins around her fingers an hour ago when her fingers had refused to hold them anymore. She thanked the Almighty again for a pliant horse who followed the others without any direction from her. Strider's gait was smooth, but Rose's bones moved as if they'd been jolted out of alignment.

They'd made four stops throughout the day—two short ones to see to their needs, one slightly longer to break for a midday meal, and another for Prince Nicholas to speak with his two guards and send them on ahead. Every time it had been more difficult to remount her horse.

Quin kept glancing her way, a frown on her face. Rose had given up trying to find a smile for the maid after the third stop. Yes, she was in pain. Yes, she was pushing herself beyond what she should. No, she refused to slow the party down any more than she already had. She'd never ridden so quickly in her life.

She would have asked to slow the pace if Prince Nicholas hadn't been so determined to push them. Father had said a war was coming, but Rose couldn't help wondering if something else was at play.

She filled her lungs to capacity and counted five heartbeats before releasing the breath.

What can you smell? What can you hear?

One of the horses had either recently relieved itself or stepped in manure. The smell didn't hit one in the face out here like it did when walking into the stable at home but it still made its presence known. The trees had a scent to them too, though Rose couldn't quite put words to it. Perhaps if she hadn't been so tired. The thoughts were there but making sense of them was like slogging through thick mud. Every step forward was a battle.

A bird tweeted somewhere to her left. Spencer and Nicholas spoke in low tones behind her. Quin sneezed. Twice.

It was a silly game, listing off inconsequential sights and sounds, but one that had saved her composure more times than she could count. The distraction helped. Most of the time.

Her toes were numb inside her boots, her fingers close to the same, but at least she was only dealing with fatigue and dull pain today. Rose dreaded what a day in the saddle would be like if the agony hit.

The hour passed in a blur of telling herself to sit straight, remain alert, and stay on the horse. She couldn't have told anyone what the foliage around them was like or whether they passed any animals. Nor whether they were even going in the right direction. She didn't know and, more, didn't care.

Almost there, Rose. Almost there. Then you can sleep.

She didn't even think she'd have the strength to eat. Nor the desire. Just sleep.

Sleep. Oh no. Rose's cheeks pinked as a burst of alarm woke her sluggish brain. She cast a glance in Nicholas's direction. He smiled just as she looked away.

Oh Almighty, no. Please no. I can't. I just can't.

This was her wedding day, which meant tonight was her wedding night.

But we're traveling. And we're hardly alone. So perhaps Nicholas won't expect...

But what if he does? Could I?

She could barely walk. Perhaps he'd understand. If she could find the courage to speak. Which, given the way her cheeks had changed from merely pink to feeling as if they were on fire, was unlikely. She didn't even know the man. What if he angered easily? He'd been nothing but kind so far but she barely knew the man.

Almighty, give me strength for whatever comes.

⁂

Nicholas watched Lady Rose. Her shoulders were drooping despite how many times he'd seen her straighten them today. She did that a lot. He'd tried not to notice, to give her the space she no doubt needed after such a momentous day, but it was impossible to keep his gaze off her for long.

She was beautiful.

And complex.

She smiled when she caught his gaze, but more often than not, she didn't notice it. Nor did she look left or right as her horse followed the others. She barely said a word the first two times they stopped other than to thank him for the bread he handed her and the water bag he shared. He might have been offended except she didn't speak to anyone else, including her maid.

Who was she, this spark of light which stirred his heart to ring?
'A princess,' came the quick reply, 'the daughter of the king.'

Was Rose pleased to have married him? He wasn't as handsome or boisterous or strong as Aldon, the latter two of which she'd discover all too soon if Aldon hadn't told her already. Still, Nicholas would do his best to protect and be worthy of her. He would care for her and be loyal only to her for as long as he lived. Their wedding might have been rushed, but he'd meant every one of the vows he'd said.

A clearing came into view. Spencer slowed his horse, signaling for the others to do the same. It wasn't a large clearing, but it had a large fallen log that would make for a good seat and brace the wind while they slept. The clearing was close enough to the river to give the horses fresh water and allow the group to wash as well. The river also barricaded them on one side, should anyone be following them. It wouldn't stop an intruder, but it would slow them enough to give warning.

Dismounting, he walked over to Rose. She startled when he touched her waist. Had she not realized they'd stopped? Or that he stood beside her? She put her hands on his shoulders as he lifted her down. Her legs buckled. He pulled her into his arms before she could fall and carried her to the log Quin had cushioned with a folded blanket. With a whispered word of thanks, she turned to her maid. The two of them talked in low tones, not inviting him into their conversation. When Rose's cheeks colored almost purple and her eyes widened, he walked away. Best leave the women to their conversation while he helped Spencer and Adam set up camp.

Though he did wonder what had made Rose blush.

"Adam and I will go with Quin to the river," Spencer said. "Refill our water bags, let the horses drink, wash."

Nicholas grabbed one of the water bags. "I'll come. Let me ask Lady Rose if she'd like to wash off too." He'd carry her again if she didn't wish to walk. He knew well how painful one's legs could be after a day on a horse.

"Oh." The knights looked at each other. Adam's eyes crinkled as if he was trying to hold back a laugh. Spencer frowned.

"Oh?" Nicholas asked.

"We thought you may wish for some time alone. With your wife. To..." Spencer studied his toes. "Get to know each other. I know it's customary to have a witness but..."

Get to know—

Oh. His eyes widened. *Oh.* Was that what Rose's maid had been speaking of too? No wonder the woman had blushed. Heat crept up his neck and he shook his head, glad for the cloak that hid his embarrassment. And the thudding of his heart.

"No. No, that's— That is, I don't plan to— She's tired already and I... uh..."

Adam laughed while Spencer rubbed a hand across his neck. "Right. I'll, uh, speak with Quin about the food." He cringed and fled as if he'd rather be anywhere but in this conversation. Nicholas knew the feeling. With the amount of mortification around this campsite, they'd have no need for a fire soon.

Nicholas grabbed the reins of three horses and stalked through the forest to the river.

Feed the horses. Fill the water bags. Cool your emotions.

The last thing his exhausted new wife needed was his attention in that way. Not tonight.

CHAPTER 13

She was married. *Married.* At some point that was going to have to sink through her disbelief and settle in her mind.

Rose moved food around her plate. Though she'd smiled and nodded at everything Nicholas had offered her, she'd not eaten more than a few mouthfuls of it. Fear was far too busy reminding her of the husband sitting beside her for Rose to think of much else. She'd been aware of her wifely duties before Quin had asked what she planned to do about them. Rose was very, *very* glad Nicholas had walked away before overhearing that question. And the stammer of a reply she'd stumbled over.

"A toast to the newly married couple," Spencer said, raising his cup. "May the Almighty bless you and fill your hearts with joy as you begin this new life together."

Rose raised her cup and ducked her head in gratitude before setting it down again on the ground in front of her.

"You're not hungry?" Nicholas asked.

She put a piece of fruit in her mouth and passed her plate Nicholas's way. Did he always eat so much? Or was he equally as nervous but ate his nerves instead? She wasn't the only one who'd married a stranger today.

What came next? Obviously she knew what normally would, but nothing about their situation was normal. What did he expect this night to hold?

Needing something to occupy her shaking hands, she reached again for her cup. It tumbled, and liquid spilled onto the ground. Rose's cheeks reddened as she tried to right it. She should have put her hands in her lap and left them there. She was far too shaken to do something as basic as drinking.

"If you're worried about tonight, you needn't be," Nicholas said quietly as he leaned forward to right the cup and hand it to her. It was empty now, save for a few drops in the bottom, but perhaps he understood how much she needed something to occupy her hands.

No. That would be ridiculous. How could he know that?

"Tonight?" Her voice squeaked. She cleared her throat and tried to ignore the pulsing heat in her cheeks.

"I'll sleep by your side for protection, but I have no more plans than sleep. You need not fear."

Did he mean that? Was he only saying it for her sake?

Of course he was saying it for her sake. What able-bodied newly married man planned to sleep on his wedding night? Nicholas was being kind. He sat so close to her that, undoubtedly, he could feel her body shaking with the effort to stay upright.

"Also, your maid has been glaring at me all day. As much as I'm sure she appreciates tradition, I think she'd happily stab me if I dared even look at you the wrong way tonight."

Yes, she probably would. Quin always had been protective of Rose. "She's been my maid a long time."

"I'm glad she's on your side."

Nicholas twisted to face Rose. Her heart pounded as he took her hand and squeezed it. He lifted it to his lips and placed a gentle kiss on her fingers. She couldn't breathe.

"I'm also glad I am," he said.

His eyes looked almost gray tonight. She could see the reflection of the fire in them. And something else. Something deeper. She could barely hear over the drum in her chest. He opened his mouth to say something before shaking his head and closing it. She should speak. Thank him. Agree with him. Anything. But to speak required words. And they were lost somewhere in the confusion of her emotions. He squeezed her hand again before letting it go and standing. "I'll lay out your blankets. Get some sleep, my beautiful Rose."

⁘

Rose lay on the blanket and tried to sleep as Nicholas had directed. But though her body craved rest, her mind wouldn't stop. Images of the day flickered through, beset with worries, fears, and hopes. She'd survived one day on the road. How many more were to come? One week? Two?

Nicholas lay beside her, close enough to touch if she stretched out her arm but far enough that she'd not do so by accident while she slept. If she slept. She rolled onto her back and stared at the smoke from the fire, drifting toward the treetops. The men had debated for some time about the wisdom of lighting a fire, Adam arguing that it would give away their position to brigands and other unsavory characters, Nicholas that the temperature dropped too much at night to sleep without one. In the end, they'd decided to take the chance, the knights more confident in their ability to protect Rose against intruders than the weather. She had to agree.

It was quieter than she'd expected out here. She'd never slept outdoors before but found it wasn't as bad as she'd thought it would be. The air was cool but her blankets warm, helped by Nicholas on one side of her and Adam on the other. She'd been confused by the sleeping arrangements, namely why the men flanked her sides rather than Quin taking one, but tiredness overcame her need for understanding.

An occasional bug flickered past as it caught the light of the fire. Adam snored. Spencer hummed on and off to himself as he sat against a tree at the edge of the camp keeping the first watch. Nicholas would take the next, and Spencer would take Nicholas's place beside her.

Protection. That was all it was. Though she doubted her face would be so red when Spencer lay there.

Her heart yearned to pray, but for the second time today, she couldn't find the words.

Sharp pain in her side woke Rose before the sun had risen. She clutched a hand to her stomach and begged the pain to stop. Her begging was ineffectual, of course. She had as much control over her body as she did over the sun that rose each day. Bile welled in her throat. Sweat covered her forehead despite the morning's chill. Shivers wracked her insides. She was going to be sick.

She sat up. Too fast. Her head spun.

"Rose?"

Nicholas stepped over Spencer and was by her side in seconds. He must have been watching her to have noticed the movement so quickly.

"Do you need something?" he whispered, careful not to wake the rest of the group. "Are you hungry? Thirsty? Cold? I can—"

Rose lurched forward and vomited onto the grass, barely missing her stockings. Tears poured down her face as her stomach clenched over and over again with the pain.

As if through a fog, she heard others stirring around her, felt Quin's hand pulling back her hair, heard one of the knights gag, saw Nicholas's boots walk away.

Yes. Walk away. I would too.

Her throat was as raw as her head was pounding by the time she stopped. She pressed her hands to her cheeks, closed her eyes, and willed the colors behind her eyelids to stop swirling.

Focus, Rose. What can you hear? What do you know?

Spencer was telling someone—probably Adam—to ready the horses.

Quin was braiding her hair. She could feel the tugging. It must have been a simple braid today because the maid was almost at the end.

Someone knelt beside Rose and started rubbing her back. Quin? No. The hand was too large, and Quin was still tugging on Rose's hair. Nicholas then? He'd come back?

"Here. Drink."

She opened her eyes. Lifted her head the smallest bit. Nicholas knelt beside her, a cup in his hand. As gently as if she were a tiny babe, he held it to her mouth and tilted it. Icy water dribbled across her lips. She opened her mouth and drank more, slowly, so as not to upset her stomach again. When she pushed the cup away, he wiped her face with a damp cloth. More of her tears fell at his gentleness. He hadn't left her. He'd only gone for help. For water for her to drink. A cloth to wipe her face.

"Thank you," she whispered, her shoulders sagging. The pain still ruled her stomach, but the intensity of it had passed. For now. She'd lived with it too long to hope it would be gone for long.

"What can I do?" Nicholas asked.

Rose shook her head. "Nothing." She sighed. If only he could help. If only anyone could. But though the herbs Aiyana gave her sometimes lessened the pain they never took it away. Didn't stop it from returning.

"Please, Rose. There must be something. Food? Another blanket?

More water? A cool cloth. I can wet it again. The river is close and the water icy."

"I'll be well."

"You're not well."

No. She wasn't. But she would be. For a time. Long enough to rally. Find her strength again. Enough to get through another day.

"Quin?"

Nicholas must have given up on waiting for an answer from her.

"There are some herbs in her saddle bag, sire. If you could heat some water—"

Nicholas was gone before Quin could finish her sentence. Not that it mattered. Quin had only said it to give the prince something to do. The herbs wouldn't help. Not when the pain was like this. Quin knew it as well as Rose.

"Can you walk?" Quin asked quietly. Rose nodded, pushing herself upright. She'd walk. She'd ride. She'd even run if asked. Anything to prove she wasn't the invalid she daily felt like. She'd known Nicholas for three days, and he'd seen her fall twice and vomit once. She was determined this would be the last. She'd give him no reason to pity her. She'd had enough of that in her life already.

Half an hour later, having seen to her needs, she told Nicholas she was ready to go. Though he frowned, he didn't stop her. She wished he had. She wasn't ready at all.

Some days, Rose hated being strong.

CHAPTER
14

Two nights sleeping under the stars. Three days in the saddle. Rose was growing worse, and Nicholas didn't know what to do about it. He hated feeling so helpless. The illness should have passed by now. Earlier today, he'd been so sure it had. She'd talked more. Teased Adam about his voracious appetite, smiled and argued her defense when Spencer told Nicholas stories about her as a child. Stories Nicholas wouldn't have believed a word of even if Spencer hadn't been laughing so hard at times he couldn't speak. Rose was still quieter than any woman he'd ever known, but she was brighter than she had been. He'd thanked the Almighty for healing her.

Now he wondered if his relief had been hasty.

She hadn't had the strength to stand when he'd helped her off her horse tonight. Assuming it the product of three days in the saddle, he'd joked about making a knight of her yet and carried her to the blanket Quin had placed atop a large, flat rock. Rose hadn't moved until he placed a plate of food in her hands almost an hour later. Even then, she didn't eat.

She pretended to, and might have even gotten away with it if Nicholas hadn't been watching her. She'd put a piece of meat to her closed mouth, swallow, and hide it beneath a scrap of fabric that resembled the scarf she'd worn yesterday.

If she hadn't also looked like she was going to vomit—or faint—he might have questioned her about it. She needed proper rest. In a bed, not on the hard dirt. He'd offer to let her sleep in his arms if he thought she'd agree.

She wouldn't. He didn't have to ask to know. She was too proud. She wouldn't even admit she was unwell. Every time he asked, she denied it. Or, perhaps, avoided it was more accurate. She'd say she would be well, or that she was well enough, or ask an inane question about their journey. If not for the king and queen's mentioning her weakness, he'd not even have known she was in pain. She hid it well. Too well.

But the tells were there if one watched close enough. A hitch in her breath. The prolonged pauses between answers. The grip on her reins. The way she leaned against Strider for a few moments whenever she dismounted and held on to Nicholas's arm a whisper longer than required.

And now this.

She had to eat.

Nicholas brought the fire-roasted rabbit to his nose, its greasy smell catching his attention for the first time. On his fingers. In his nostrils. No wonder she was queasy. If she were feeling unwell already, the meat wouldn't help. Some water from the river might, so long as he first warmed it over the fire. Or the last hand-sized loaf of bread in his saddlebag. It was a little stale after three days but dry enough that it would fill her stomach. Or, at least, put something in it.

But how to suggest such a thing without being rejected. Her stubborn pride was going to be the death of her. Literally.

Not on his watch.

Striding to his saddlebag, Nicholas pulled out the bread, walked over to Rose, and dumped it in her lap. It rolled right off into the dirt. She picked it up, dusted it off, looked up at him, and burst into tears. Not the reaction he'd been expecting but at least she hadn't thrown it at his head.

No, she held it between her clasped hands as if that stale bread was a priceless jewel. Maybe they were tears of gratitude? He didn't wait to see, sitting down again before he made any more of a scene than he already had. Adam was still telling a story, the trees still rustled their leaves as they danced with the breeze, the fire still crackled. Nicholas tried not to look at Rose, but it was impossible. She broke off a piece of the bread and put it in her mouth. Chewed.

Good.

It was small, but it was something. She chewed long enough that the tiny piece surely liquified before she bothered to swallow, but then she took another. And another. By the time Adam finished his longwinded story about the larger-than-life rabbit he'd missed hitting by less than a hands' breadth while he and Spencer were hunting earlier, half of the bread was gone.

Rose caught his gaze, placed a hand over her heart, and nodded.

⁕

The empty place at Mykah and Finnian's wedding feast last night haunted Lior. It had been a day filled with love and laughter, with so many people wishing to celebrate the newly married couple that the festivities had overflowed the Great Hall and danced through the streets. Poor and rich, young and old alike had brought gifts for the Guardian of Raedonleith and the man who'd captured her heart. Speeches and well wishes had gone long into the night.

But with every speech, every gift, every laughter-filled kiss between Mykah and her beloved new husband, he'd been reminded of Rose.

When Mykah, far more skilled on the training grounds than dance-floor, tripped and fell part way through a spin and teasingly berated Finnian for not catching her, Lior couldn't help but remember how Rose had fallen the night of the tournament.

When Arthur attempted to sort the villagers' wedding gifts into order and accidentally set loose two squawking chickens and a temperamental duck in the Great Hall, Lior had laughed along with everyone else before guilt stabbed his joy. Rose would have loved it.

When a balladeer held them all captive with his words, when the kitchens served Rose's favorite lemon jelly, when Finnian thanked Lior for the honor of joining his family, when Caralynne caught his gaze straying to where Rose would usually sit and caught his hand. Rose might not have been present but she was in every moment.

He wished she had been.

Had he done the right thing sending his oldest daughter away? The intruder was long gone, and the spy Lior sent to Cavendish Castle had returned home with nothing more to report on the war front. Not when Cormac would strike nor how. Only that it was coming.

Soon.

Ominous, at best. Raedonleith was prepared, of course, at least as far as a kingdom who'd been at peace for two and a half decades could be. Preparation was only perfect until the fighting began.

He couldn't help feeling he'd acted in haste when it came to his oldest daughter. In the moment, he'd been so certain the only way to keep her safe was to give her the protection of Prince Nicholas's name and send her away, but the intruder was gone and war still more threat than reality. For all Cormac's taunts, it might not even come.

The two girls taken in the raid last week had returned home today. Battered and bruised but alive and otherwise unharmed. Someone at Cavendish Castle had a heart.

Lior should have waited. Looked to the Almighty rather than his fears. Perhaps he still would have done the same and wed Rose to Prince Nicholas, but perhaps he would have seen another way. Now, he'd never know.

Almighty, guide my daughter. Keep her safe. Show her love.

Forgive me for rushing ahead in my desire to protect her.

He'd seen the questions in their people's gazes when they noticed Rose's absence at her sister's wedding feast. Nicholas's absence too, no doubt. Lior would have to answer their questions at some point, likely sooner rather than later the way rumors abounded, but for now, the fewer people who knew where she was, the better. Cormac couldn't target Rose if he didn't know where she was.

Or so Lior told himself.

He still wondered if he were a coward.

No. Wise or foolish, the decision had been made. There was nothing for it now but to go on. He might have made the decision for Rose to marry in haste, but that didn't mean it was the wrong one. Prince Nicholas would do well by her.

Wouldn't he?

Lior sighed. He'd done what was best for his daughter. To protect her. To save her life. So why did he feel so guilty?

CHAPTER 15

Rose did her best to ignore Prince Nicholas, but he was making it incredibly difficult. He smiled whenever she looked his way, which was far more often than she planned. He helped her off her horse every time they stopped, and back on when they set off. He spoke kindly to her maid and with respect to the knights. He took longer watches overnight than was fair.

He'd caught her once, watching when she should have been asleep. Tilted his head as if to invite her over or ask if she was well. She'd rolled onto her other side and pretended not to see the gesture. She'd counted almost to a thousand before peeking a glance over her shoulder. He'd smiled. She'd thanked the Almighty that the darkness hid her blush. And the tears that dripped off her cheeks into the blanket he'd given her to bunch under her head.

Was there any man better than Prince Nicholas of Belairisia?

He had the honor of her father, the respect of Sir Finnian, the kindness of Sir Spencer, and a love all his own. She told herself it didn't matter, but it was a lie. The more she tried to push him away and guard her heart against the knowledge that he'd leave, the closer he came.

And the more she liked it. It was a heady feeling to be noticed. To be the center of someone's world.

But it didn't matter. Couldn't matter. Because she was broken. Barren. Nicholas deserved more. The longer she spent with him, the more she was certain of it. She'd go with him to Belairisia and stay there as long as her father wished, but she'd request an annulment as soon as they arrived. If Prince Nicholas didn't first.

It was the right thing to do. The fair thing. She respected him too much to tie him to a future cut off before it even begun. He would go on. Find a better wife. Father a castle full of children and make every one of them feel like the most cherished person in his world. Recite them lullabies and hold them close when they cried, as he'd done with Rosie's newborn brother that day. Some men were born to be fathers, and Prince Nicholas was one of them. She wouldn't take that from him.

Yes. Leaving would be best.

Nevertheless, Rose found herself speaking with Nicholas. A little here, a little there. Not full conversations, certainly nothing deep, but something every day. He asked about her favorite flower. Whether she preferred cold weather or warm. Who'd named her horse Strider. What books she liked to read. She might have been offended he'd assumed she sat for hours reading except he admitted he did the same—and proceeded to prove it by listing several of his favorite books and why he loved them. He asked her to call him Nicholas, rather than Sire as she had been.

"Are you warm enough?" he asked as they rode. He'd asked that at least once a day since she'd mentioned she preferred warmer weather. She should have kept her mouth shut and not given him more reason to care, but she liked it.

"Yes, thank you."

He didn't say anything else for several miles, content to walk his horse beside hers. Every time they stopped, he helped her off Strider, and he lifted her atop the horse again when they continued. They stopped more often than she suspected he and the knights would have if she'd not been there. She'd become accustomed to the guilt of slowing the journey.

"We've found a cave ahead, sire," Adam said, pulling his horse up alongside Nicholas's. "It's small but sheltered and has no sign of an animal living in it. We've another hour at least of daylight, so we could continue, but the wind is picking up."

Nicholas nodded. "Make camp."

Rose let out a breath. Another day done.

Thank you, Almighty.

⁕

"You care for her."

Spencer sat beside Nicholas at the mouth of the cave, the night's stillness a relief after the constant movement of travel. Four days in the saddle, though they weren't even two days' journey from Raedonleith. They could have moved faster and taken fewer—and shorter—stops, but Nicholas refused to ask it of Rose. Neither she nor her maid were accustomed to long days traveling, and Rose wasn't sleeping well. She'd roll from her back to her side for an hour or more before drifting off. Even then, her rest was fitful.

She'd kept him awake several nights. Partly because of her restlessness but just as much because she was there. His wife. Lying beside him. Close enough to feel the brush of her hair against his face when the wind caught it, but in every way that mattered, out of reach.

Because as much as he wanted her, she had to want him too. She didn't trust him. Not yet. Not that he could blame her given they'd known each other for less than a week.

Spencer had joined him a few minutes ago, relieving Nicholas of his watch. A wise man would have gone right to bed, but the night was clear, the company welcome, and his mind too distracted by other things to sleep. Namely, his wife.

"Aye, I do care for her," he told Spencer. "More than I thought possible in so short a time."

"You seem surprised."

Surprised. Confused. Guilt-ridden. Certain. His thoughts on the matter changed as often as the weather. "I came to Raedonleith to convince King Lior to give Aldon time. I thought my brother had run like a fool. But then I saw Lady Rose and—"

Nicholas snapped the twig he'd been playing with, once then again. "And?"

He let out a rueful laugh. "And I was grateful Aldon had run because the thought of her being with anyone but me was too painful to consider."

"She's beautiful."

"That she is, but it was more than her beauty. It was just *her*. I don't know how to explain it apart from that. As if, in that split second of a moment, my eyes were open, and everything made sense. Lady Rose was the woman I'd been waiting for. The reason I'd come. The reason I'd been born, even. To protect her." He laughed quietly. "I sound like a fool."

"You sound like a man in love."

In love. Was he? Nicholas looked over his shoulder at Rose, curled beneath two blankets, naught but the top of her head to be seen. Was she warm enough? Resting deeply enough? She needed to sleep in a real bed, but she wouldn't. Not until she was safe. And he'd be right beside her. Not because he had to but because— .

Yes.

He loved her. The feeling went beyond attraction. If it had only been attraction, he would have left the first time he saw her fall. But it wasn't pity either. His heart had been moved by pity before as he'd watched the plight of those less fortunate than himself, but he'd never dreamed of holding them.

"Can it really happen so quickly?" he asked.

"Aye, I believe it can."

"You speak as if you know."

For a long time, Nicholas thought Spencer wouldn't answer. The knight let the silence stretch, content to let it go. It wasn't Nicholas's place to intrude. He'd become so comfortable in Spencer's presence that he'd forgotten for a moment that they weren't brothers.

With a nod, he picked up his cloak and stood. He should lie down. Claim a few hours' sleep before dawn.

"I do." Spencer's quiet words stopped Nicholas. He turned back. Waited. Spencer's sigh mixed with the soft breeze playing around the cave's entrance. "There is a woman. I saw her and I knew..."

Spencer was in love? And he'd come anyway? King Lior hadn't said anything about Spencer having a sweetheart in Raedonleith. Of course, neither had there been need for him to. A knight did what his king ordered, no matter who it took him from.

Though Nicholas suspected he already knew the answer, he still asked, "Does she know?"

The night air pulled around them, punctuated by the distant call of an owl as Nicholas waited again for Spencer to answer. For a long time, he wondered if the man would. Then, so quietly Nicholas almost didn't hear, he spoke. "No."

"Is it Rose?"

⁕ ⸱❀⸱ ⁕

Rose barely breathed as she waited for Spencer's reply. The men must have thought her asleep or they never would have spoken so openly. Did Spencer care for her? He'd always been so kind to her, asking her to dance, walking her to her room, keeping her spirits up with his ridiculous stories when she'd started to flail. Had she mistaken his friendship for love?

Spencer.

"No. It's not Rose."

She exhaled. Not that she didn't care for Sir Spencer. She would even go so far as to call him a good friend, but she'd never felt more than affection for him. Not that she'd ever felt more than affection for any man—before Nicholas.

It was more than her beauty, it was just her. Lady Rose was the woman I'd been waiting for.

Waiting for. As if… as if…

As if I was worth *waiting for.*

As if the Almighty held Father back from seeking a husband for her all those years not because Rose was forgotten but because she was treasured. Saved. Set aside for something more. For Nicholas. Did he truly care so much?

A rush of emotion too overwhelming to consider washed over Rose as she lay in the dark cave. Of love. Of acceptance. Of purpose.

She pushed it aside, unable to deal with such deep thoughts when she was already so tired, and set her mind to another mystery.

Who did Spencer care for? Did Rose know the woman? Mykah likely did. Mykah knew everyone—guards, knights, servants, villagers, and nobles alike.

"Will you tell her?" Nicholas asked.

A sigh loud enough to be heard over the sound of the crickets came from the knight at the mouth of the cave. "I can't. Not yet. One day, I pray."

"I'll pray too."

"Thank you."

Adam let out a loud snore, startling himself before he rolled over and steadied his breathing again. Footsteps approached. Rose closed her eyes and focused on steadying her own breathing. A hand touched her forehead. So gentle. So soft. Seconds later, a blanket settled over her. She snuggled into its weight and warmth, feeling instantly more at peace with Nicholas so close. Perhaps she'd sleep this night after all.

"Good night, my love."

Nicholas's words were so quiet they wouldn't have scared a rabbit. But they terrified her.

My love.

Lady Rose was the woman I'd been waiting for.

She wasn't the woman Spencer had fallen for, but she was the one Nicholas had.

Fear crashed against her mind as his words played over again. Why did the thought of him loving her scare her so much? She'd not been afraid of Aldon. But then, Aldon hadn't made her heart pound like Nicholas. Aldon hadn't made her wish that she was courageous like Mykah, or wise like Mother, or strong like Evangeline. Aldon hadn't made her ache to be more. To be enough.

She prayed as she lay there. For Spencer and the woman he loved. For Quin. For Adam. For the guards on their way to Belairisia. For her family at home. For the new family she had yet to meet.

For Nicholas.

And then, for herself. That the Almighty might give her strength. That he'd get her through the days to come. That he'd heal her and make her whole. That one day, she might be more.

CHAPTER 16

"What is this?"

The furious maid's arrival distracted Cormac's opponent just long enough for Cormac to disarm the man. It was hardly fair, but little was in a real battle. With a scowl and a bow of defeat, the man walked away. Cormac wasn't even sweating. He needed a better opponent. That was the problem with being the best: Few could challenge him.

He swung his sword a few more times, loosening his shoulder, before sheathing the weapon and turning to Maeve. She was almost purple as she waved a piece of paper in the air. His spy's report. He couldn't read it from here, especially not moving about as it was, but he recognized the handwriting. He snatched the paper from her hand, tucking it into his belt.

"*This* is none of your business." He stalked away, not surprised at all when she trailed him. Maeve might have the title of servant, but she'd never been one to back down from a fight. Nor be intimidated by his bluster. Her mother had been his nurse as a child and Maeve like a sister to him before life had taken them in different directions. She'd taught him to read and never told a soul that she'd done so, nor had she laughed at how long it had taken him to achieve the task.

He turned left. Her footsteps followed, her incrimination along with them.

"You've gone too far."

"You shouldn't be intercepting my messages," he tossed behind him. "I could have you thrown in the dungeon."

"Not without me telling everyone that you tried to have the king's daughter killed."

He slowed at her words. *Tried to.* Then the man hadn't succeeded. Rose was still alive.

Foiled again.

"You're better than this, Cormac."

What would Maeve know? She might have been his friend once, but these days she was just a maid. She worked in the kitchens. Or wherever Cormac sent her. He could make her clean the stables if he saw fit. At least, he could tell her to. Whether she'd obey or not was still to be decided.

He stopped at the door to his chamber, turning to face her. "That's Lord Cavendish to you. And right you'd be to respect me."

She frowned at him. "I'll give you the respect you ask for when you earn it. Which is not by attempting to murder your friend *and* king's daughter. I've known you since you were a boy. Your parents taught you right. You're the one who chose this path."

He chose it? Hardly. "No. Lior did."

Maeve's expression softened into pity.

Eyes narrowed, Cormac turned and walked into the room. He would have slammed the door if Maeve hadn't already followed him inside. Pity. *Pity.* He was Lord Cormac Cavendish. The best swordsman in the land. People feared him. They obeyed him. He refused to be pitied by a mere maid.

"Leave me before I call a guard and make you," he threatened.

She crossed her arms, the faded fabric of her apron straining across her chest. Her mother had worn that apron once. The tiny russet smudge on the corner was his blood. Faded, like the fabric, but still there if one knew where to look. He looked away. That had been a long time ago. He wasn't that boy anymore. One look at his chamber proved that. There was glass in his windows, bright colored rugs on the floor, a small pile of books on the carved wooden table by the wall, a fire always burning in his fireplace. It was the chamber of a lord. One who'd taken what he was owed time and again.

"Is this truly what you want?" Maeve asked. "Two families destroyed because you're too stubborn to let go of a grudge?"

"I wanted Cara."

"And she chose Lior."

"I loved her."

"Then care for her family. *Care* for Rose. Stop trying to destroy Queen Caralynne's family and make amends. This isn't you, Cormac."

"How would you know?" He threw his cloak onto the bed, pulled out his sword, and swung it. Maeve didn't flinch.

"Because I remember. I remember the man you were before all this happened. When your parents were alive, and you knew how to smile. You and Lior were inseparable then. One would have thought you were brothers the way you cared for each other and joked together."

"Lior betrayed me."

"He married the woman he loved not knowing you cared for her too. If he'd had any idea you cared for Caralynne, I have no doubt he would have stayed away from her. He lost his best friend that day too."

"We're not friends." Hadn't been for more than two decades.

Her hands moved to her sides, her eyes narrowing. "Make it right."

"I am."

"No. You're making it worse. And if you don't stop, you're going to destroy more than Lior's life. Don't think I haven't seen how little you sleep."

She was judging his sleep now? Was there anything this woman wouldn't meddle in? "What would you know, woman?"

"A lot more than you think. I know this bitterness is keeping you awake at night. I know you've called the healer more than once for something to dull the pain in your head. I know your hand shakes sometimes when you hold your sword, and—"

"I'm fine."

"Cormac—"

"Guards!"

Two men burst through his door, a third close behind them. One nod in Maeve's direction, and they escorted her away. She'd pulled her arms free of them before she was out of his sight, head held high as she walked away without a trace of regret. Brave woman. Brave, stubborn—and wrong.

Lior was the one who needed to make this right. He'd taken everything from Cormac. And Cormac was determined to take everything from Lior in return.

Sitting at the table, he smoothed the spy's message.

Foiled but escaped. Rose alive. Married in secret and on route to Be-

lairisia with husband, Prince Nicholas. Finnian and Mykah married also.
Finnian sworn allegiance to King Lior. Await orders.

Finnian marrying Mykah and remaining loyal to the king wasn't a
surprise. His brother had made no secret of where his loyalty lay when
he'd refused to heed Cormac's orders and harm the Guardian of Raedonleith. Lior had sent an invitation to Cormac to attend the wedding.
Cormac had sent a man to kill Rose instead.

But Rose marrying Prince Nicholas? That was a surprise. By his spy's
earlier account, the woman was barren. And dying. Lior truly must have
been shaken by the attempt on Rose's life to have her quickly marry the
prince. How close had Cormac's man come to killing the woman?

She'd left though. Because Lior thought marriage would protect her
where a castle fortress hadn't? The king was a fool. On the road they'd
be vulnerable, no matter how many guards the king sent. The road to
Belairisia took them past Cavendish Castle.

If Cormac had anything to say about it, they'd not reach Belairisia
at all.

He pulled the lid off his ink bottle and dipped in a pen. Four words.
That's all it would take.

Bring her to me.

CHAPTER 17

Rose hated to ask to stop again. This would be the fourth time since lunch. Four times. In less than two hours. But what had begun as a twinge of pain in her back upon rising had intensified as the day wore on. Waves of pain shot along her shoulders and hips and made her stomach lurch with every step Strider took. She was unravelling and didn't know how much longer she could keep herself from coming apart altogether.

No. You can do this. No one else is complaining. It's not even as if you're doing any of the work. You're just sitting atop a horse. Sitting. All day.

You're fine.

You're well.

You're going to cover your gown and *horse in vomit if you don't stop right now.*

She pulled back on the reins, willing Strider to ignore the other horses plodding ahead and stop. She should have told him verbally too, but that would involve opening her mouth, and if she opened her mouth—

"Rose?"

Strider stopped. Nicholas dismounted, coming to her side before she'd even decided whether to wait for assistance or climb down herself.

"Let me," he said. His hands clasped her waist to help her. The instant he held her, she knew she'd made the wrong decision. His grasp was light, guiding more than squeezing, but even that smallest pressure on her stomach was too much.

"Oh— I—"

No. Oh no.

She should have slid off herself. She would have fallen in a heap on the ground and been mortified for the rest of her life, but her husband wouldn't now be covered in vomit.

"Rose—"

"I'm sorry. I'm sorry. I'm so sorry." The tears came then—part pain, part fury, part mortification. Her stomach lurched again and again as she stumbled her way to the river's edge until there was nothing left to expel. Nothing left of her pride either. She curled into a ball of misery, hating herself, her weakness, and that there was nowhere to hide. No chamber with a door, no chapel with its privacy, no tower far above the ground. Just one prince, two knights, and one maid watching their esteemed lady fall into pieces.

A hand rubbed her back. Rose refused to look up but knew from the waft of vomit coming her way that it was Nicholas. Of course it was. He was too good to be true. And right now, she really wished he wasn't. His unending patience and strength only made it worse.

Wasn't I weak enough already, Almighty? Did you have to take every-thing?

The hand on her back lifted. Good. He was leaving.

Wait, no. He wasn't. In place of his hand came his arms, wrapped around her. Lifting her. Carrying her.

No. No. Please, Almighty, no. Just let me ache in peace. I can't let him see. I can't—don't—I just want to be alone. I don't have the strength to be a good wife right now. Or even a good person. I don't even have the strength to be grateful.

"I'm sorry, Rose. So sorry."

He was sorry? For what? He wasn't the one who'd regurgitated lunch all over her. Or cried like a babe. Or hid in shame.

Make him go away, Almighty. Please.

"I should have realized. Should have known. Should have seen."

She didn't dare open her eyes but could tell from the rush of water that they were following the line of the river. Shadows danced across her eyelids. Where was he taking her? Something pressed against her hair. A kiss? Surely not. She was disgusting.

They stopped. The water grew louder as he sat, still holding her. She wanted to squirm away but worried the pulling would upset her stomach again. She gasped, eyes wide as something cold touched her face. What—?

A wet cloth. Nicholas was cleaning her face. Again. She turned her head. "Don't. Please, don't." She couldn't take any more of his kindness.

"There's no shame in being unwell. Or letting someone help."

No. Not when an illness lasted a day or two. But when it lasted a lifetime? When she was in constant need, like a helpless babe? Yes. There was shame. There was guilt. There was anger. At herself. At her body. Even, though she tried to remember his goodness, at the Almighty.

Forgive me, Almighty. I know you have a purpose. I know you have a plan. I want to be faithful no matter what, but—

You ask too much.

If not for her weakness, they would have been close to Belairisia already. If not for her weakness, Nicholas never would have been forced to marry her. If not for her weakness, he'd be clean rather than reeking of vomit.

Scalding tears mixed with the icy water Nicholas continued to brush across her cheeks. She scrambled out of his lap, out of his reach, and forced strength into her voice. "I'm well now. Thank you." Her back screamed with the movement but she refused to cower.

"Rose—"

"If you'll give me ten minutes alone to wash, I'll be ready to ride again."

"Rose—"

She lowered her head. "Please." She hated to beg, but she needed this. Ten minutes alone. Just ten minutes to clean herself up and pull herself together. To find her faith again. And her courage. They were there. Hiding behind the shame but there. She could do this.

"It's okay," Nicholas said. "There's no need to rush."

"Ten minutes. I promise."

Though he sighed, he also nodded, handing her the cloth. "I'll wait on the other side of those trees. Call if you need me. I won't be far." She watched as he walked away then dropped onto her knees, hands sinking into the sand at the river's edge. It felt good. The coarseness of the sand. The iciness of the water. She stayed like that for a few minutes before cleaning her hands. Her face. Smoothing her hair, wrapping the long braid around itself and tying it with a ribbon. Then she scooped water into her hand and washed out her mouth.

Nicholas was waiting right where he said he would be, far enough to give her privacy but close enough to hear if she called. She wrinkled her nose. He still smelled of vomit.

He must have noticed her reaction. "Forgive me. I'll change before we depart. I didn't want to leave you." He brushed a hand down her cheek. "Better?"

"Much," she lied.

Nicholas held her hand as they walked to the rest of the group. Quin took his place at Rose's side the moment they stopped, pushing a drink into her hands. Nicholas spoke with Spencer briefly before disappearing into the thick of the trees to change. Rose sipped the drink, hoping it would settle her stomach further. She wasn't certain whether the pain was from hunger or nausea anymore. To put more in her stomach might make her ill again, but empty it made her ill too. The thought of getting back on a horse didn't help. At all.

But she'd do it. Because she had to. Because it was what was best. Because she refused to be the one who held them back. Again.

The drink rolled her stomach before she could finish it, so she tipped the rest out and handed the cup back to Quin, who packed it away in one of the bags.

"Ready?" Nicholas asked.

No. Not at all. "Yes."

Nicholas's head tilted as he looked at her. Placed the back of his hand against her forehead. She flinched, closing her eyes lest he see the truth in them.

"Rose—"

"I'm fine. Let's go."

"Is that really what you want? To leave again so soon? Forgive my disbelief but I don't think you do. Nor would I if I had just been ill. In fact, I can't help but think that the last thing you feel like doing right now is getting back on a horse."

"But—"

"What do you want, Rose?"

To roll back the years before all this started. The pain, the guilt, the doubts. To be that person again, quiet but whole. Certain of herself. Certain of her faith. As excited for an adventure as Mykah and Evangeline. Dreaming of a future full of love and life and happiness. Oblivious to what was to come. She would have been proud to meet Nicholas back then, thrilled to begin a life with him. Oh, how she missed that Rose.

But she couldn't go back nor was that what Nicholas was asking.

"It's still light. We could travel another hour or two before dark," she answered instead. "We've barely made ground today."

"No."

"No?"

"Not what do *I* want. What do you want?"

Rose looked to where Adam and Spencer stood speaking with Quin. "Not them either."

Anger reared as quickly as the illness had. "Am I not supposed to care? I can't do that. Their opinions matter. What if they're tired of being on the road and just want to be in a warm bed again? That's never going to happen if I keep slowing us down."

"They'll understand."

"I won't."

She should have moved. Should have mounted Strider. Proven to Nicholas and everyone present, herself included, that she meant what she said. She *could* pull herself together. She *could* ride another hour or two before making camp. But she was tired and Strider's back looked as high as a mountain. Just the thought of having to move again had tears of exhaustion pricking the corners of her eyes.

Nicholas's voice was quiet as he laid a hand on her arm.

"Perhaps it's time you give yourself the grace you so freely offer us. It's good to care for the needs of others, sweet Rose, but you have to think about what you want too. Take your place in this world. Let us care for you as well as you care for us." Nicholas grasped Strider's reins, running a hand down the horse's neck before meeting Rose's gaze again. "What do you want?"

She wanted to stop. To lie down. To be warm, and well, and sit on something that wasn't moving. But that was selfish. She was only one of five people in their party. One person's opinion shouldn't matter that much.

Nicholas moved his hand on her wrist, his thumb grazing a pattern across her skin. "Rose?"

"To rest." She shouldn't have said it, but she couldn't hold it back, nor the accompanying sob of dismay and shame that came with it. Nicholas nodded.

"Then we'll make camp and set out again tomorrow."

"Just like that?"

"Just like that."

Guilt buffeted Rose so hard she flinched. It was physical, battering her mind, her stomach, especially when she saw the look of dismay on Adam's face, though he quickly hid it.

Nicholas smiled as he tugged the blankets off Strider's back. "Don't worry, Rose. All will be well. We'll get there."

"It'll take longer."

"More time to enjoy the wonders of the Almighty all around us. Another night to study the stars and stand in awe of his greatness. More time with you before the pressures of responsibility bring us both back to earth."

"You can't mean that."

His expression was serious when he turned to face her, the bright blue of his gaze searing hers. "I absolutely do. Rose, if this journey takes weeks, I would only thank the Almighty for the privilege."

"I don't believe you."

He tucked a piece of hair behind her ear. "That doesn't make it untrue."

CHAPTER 18

N icholas stared into the darkness and wished, not for the first time, that he'd been able to pack Belairisia's entire library into his saddlebag. It was a ridiculous notion. Bulky as the books were, he wouldn't have even been able to fit one in his bag. Precious as they were, he wouldn't have dared. Poor weather could destroy in seconds what had taken a scribe years to write. He wished for one all the same. He felt lost without a book in his hand, as if he'd left an important part of himself behind. But beyond the comfort the written word brought him, Nicholas couldn't help holding on to hope that in a book somewhere, he'd find the answers he sought.

Rose had been truly ill this afternoon. And he'd had no idea. Not until she vomited on him. She'd been smiling. Talking to Spencer less than five minutes before. Sitting high on her horse as if she could ride another few hours. They'd stopped several times so she and her maid could see to their needs, but had appeared well again when they remounted.

Then she'd stopped. And collapsed, too ill to stand.

How had he not known? What had he missed?

The dying fire glowed, casting just enough light for him to see Rose, blankets tucked to her chin. She was sleeping, for which he was grateful. But tomorrow would come soon enough with its hours of travel. Would one night's sleep be enough to refresh her? Perhaps they should stay another.

But staying in one place brought a host of other dangers. King Lior trusted Nicholas to keep his daughter safe. Here, on the road, she wasn't, and the longer they tarried in one place, the better chance they had of being found. He shouldn't even have allowed a fire to be built tonight except he couldn't bear the shivers wracking his wife's shoulders.

In all the times he'd imagined marriage, never once had he imagined it tearing his heart out. He cared for Rose already, but he had no idea how to love her as she needed. He was supposed to be on her side, and he couldn't even tell when she was sick.

A symphony of bugs played in the distance, but otherwise the night was quiet. If not for the stars and the soft waning of the fire, he'd have wondered if time stood still. Nicholas ran both hands through his hair, his head in his hands.

A book. A philosophy. A scripture. Something. Anything. He needed answers.

But he had none. No book, no words. Not one of the tens of scriptures or ballads or quotes he'd memorized came close to the answers he sought. Even the Almighty was silent tonight.

He jumped when someone touched his shoulder.

"Forgive me," Quin whispered. "I thought you saw me."

Nicholas shook his head in apology. "Seems it's I who needs beg forgiveness. I was lost in my thoughts. Do you need something?"

"I thought you might." She held out a cup. "Rose has trouble sleeping sometimes too. Aiyana taught me to make this drink for her. It's just herbs, but they may help you too."

He took the cup from her, swirling the liquid.

"It's better warm," Quin said. "A few minutes over the fire should do it."

"Thank you."

She moved to leave, stopping when he said her name.

"Was there something else, Your Highness?"

"Aye." He took a sip of the drink, wrinkling his nose at the bitterness before taking the maid's advice and sitting the cup over some coals. There were so many questions in his mind he didn't know where to begin. "How's Rose?"

"Sleeping soundly."

"No. I mean…how is she finding the travel?"

Quin tilted her head, her rich brown hair muted in the moonlight. "As well as can be expected, sire."

"In truth?"

She hesitated.

"Please, Quin. She's my wife. I want to help her, but I don't know how."

"If I may, you're only newly married. You can hardly expect to know everything about each other in a matter of days."

She was right, of course. And perhaps his expectations were too high, especially of himself. But he couldn't help feeling as if time would be more of a hindrance than a help in this case. Nicholas wanted Rose to trust him, and the only way for that to happen was for her to know he cared. If he gave her space now, it might grow in the future.

"Be patient with her."

"That's it? That's all the advice you have? I can't tell when she's sick. I don't know what she needs or what she wants or how to make her smile. I thought she was happy today, but then she collapsed. She tells me she's well then loses her lunch. I try to talk to her, to get her to trust me, but she's holding back, and I don't know why."

"She's always sick. Sometimes just more than others."

"That's hardly helpful. Please, Quin. She's my wife. I've seen you anticipate her needs. She trusts you. All I want is to be there for her."

"Then do it."

"I don't know how!"

Quin flinched at his anger. He was losing his temper in front of a maid. More, if he didn't quiet his tone, he'd wake the woman who so desperately needed rest.

"Forgive me."

"I didn't know she was ill today either," Quin conceded. "Some days, though I've served her for ten years, her strength fools even me."

"But other times, you've known. The warm drink you have ready. The times you've asked us to stop."

"Ten years of watching my lady fall, and clench her teeth against the pain, and cry herself to sleep. Ten years of hiding the vomit and blood. Of washing her gowns before the other maids see them. Of assuring her she isn't the burden she feels."

"She doesn't trust me." That much was clear.

"She doesn't trust anyone."

But he was her husband. A wife should trust her husband.

"If there's one thing that may help..." Quin's gaze met his for the first time. She wrung her hands, hesitance written across her heart-shaped face as clearly as it sounded in her voice.

"Please. Anything."

"Stay with her. I know 'tis not always easy or pleasant, but neither is it for her."

CHAPTER 19

Rose was fading. Fast. The cramps had begun in her stomach, but shot pain down her legs, through her chest, across her shoulders. The backache yesterday made sense now. Intense nausea combined with an ache in her back was how many of her courses started. If she'd not been so flustered by the marriage and travel and madness of the past week, she would have seen it coming.

Her head pounded with the concentration it took to keep herself from fainting. She should get off her horse before she fell, but they'd only just stopped for a break—at her request—ten minutes ago. And, again, thirty minutes before that. After getting a late start this morning because of her and stopping twice not long after. Because of her.

She couldn't stop them again. Not after she'd lost them several hours of travel already yesterday. It was too mortifying. Nicholas could claim all he liked that her needs mattered, but four other people were in their group, and none of them had started on this journey so they could wait for her to be well enough to ride. As if she ever would be.

She wrapped the reins around her hands and twisted her feet into the ropes of the saddle. There. That was the best she could do. If she fainted, she'd not fall. At least, not quickly.

She bit back a groan and wiped the sweat prickling her forehead on her sleeve.

Look ahead. Don't think about it. Focus, Rose. Straight ahead.

What can you see? What can you hear? What can you smell?

She could see herself falling, tumbling to the ground and being trampled.

She could hear pounding in her ears, louder than the rhythm of five horses' hooves.

She could smell fear.

Bile rose in her throat. The rocking of her horse wasn't helping. She had to stop. But she could just imagine the expression on Nicholas's face if she asked to stop again. Frustration. Disbelief. Irritation. Not that he wouldn't cover them with concern. He was good at showing concern.

Too good. She felt smothered. Quin would do as she said, not acknowledging anything was amiss. Rose didn't need to explain her predicament to her maid. Neither did she feel the need to impress Quin. Unlike Prince Nicholas and the two knights. If they hadn't been here, she would have stopped. If they hadn't been here, she'd still be back at the place they'd camped their first night. If she'd even made it that far.

Instead, she was pushing herself to continue, mortified that they see how weak she truly was. They were knights, and she couldn't even ride a horse for ten minutes.

Focus. Find your backbone. It has to be in there somewhere. Stare the path down. Every step forward is one step closer to the goal. And one second less you have to be on this horse.

Forgive me, Strider. You're a wonderful horse.

Sweat stung her eyes. She closed them. Strider would follow the others.

"Rose? Are you—"

No. Closing her eyes made the pain worse. With her eyes closed, it was all she could see. Feel. Was her head spinning? Her stomach split open? The dagger. The invisible, scorching dagger. It was ripping through her spine. Her side. She bent forward, hands clutched to her stomach. The bile wouldn't stay. The pounding in her head wouldn't stop. The dizziness pressed in. The dagger moved to her chest, jabbing at her heart. She couldn't breathe.

"Rose. Talk to me."

She blinked. Gasped for air. Slid sideways. She tried to grasp the reins to pull herself back, but her fingers wouldn't work.

"Rose!" A hand clamped on her leg, hard enough to bruise. Hard enough to slow her fall. Slow but not stop. "Spencer. Adam. Help."

Someone came up on her other side, arriving just in time for her to retch onto his saddle. Her face pounded now. In time with her head and heart. Her horse stopped.

Someone unwound the reins from her hands and boots. Someone lifted her down and carried her away from the horses. Someone's arms wrapped around her as he sat, not letting go. Though his whispers were calming, she couldn't make out the words.

She slumped against…Nicholas? Spencer? She didn't even know who held her. Not that it mattered. She never wanted to see either of them again.

She never wanted to see anyone.

＊＊＊＊＊＊

He shouldn't have allowed Rose on the horse this morning. He'd known she was too weak. But where was the line between respecting her strength and coddling her weakness? She'd said she was fine. He could hardly call the princess a liar. He still didn't believe she was one. Fine was a relative term. Perhaps she'd thought she was.

Then.

She wasn't now.

Nicholas brushed hair off Rose's wet forehead and tugged her in closer as he leaned against the tree's thick trunk. He'd hold her all day and all night if that's how long it took her to wake. Needless to say, he wasn't letting her back on her horse. Not alone. And there was no reason for them both to ride Strider when Milori was larger. Rose would ride with him. Whether she wanted to or not. His heart couldn't take seeing her fall again. Not when next time, he might be too far away to catch her.

He'd glanced at Rose earlier to see her staring. At nothing. She'd not reacted when he'd called her name. Not the first time. Not the second. And then—his heart had stuttered when she began to slide. If he'd been any further away, she would have fallen.

Her gown was dusty. Her face and hair too. Nicholas picked a leaf from her braid and used his sleeve to wipe a smudge from her cheek. Even dusty, she took his breath away.

Though your hands are weak, my arms are strong. I'll hold you and keep you safe, all the day long.

They weren't quite the words of the lullaby he'd heard his mother sing so many times but they fit. A promise for the woman who'd captured his heart. He didn't know if he could protect her, not like Spencer or Aldon or even Darrek and Finnian would have, but he'd not leave. He'd be there to catch her when she fell. He'd stay by her side and fight with every bit of strength and proficiency he had until the option was taken from him.

Quin brought over Rose's water skin. Nicholas took it but didn't try to wake her. Not yet. She couldn't fight him when she was asleep, and she needed sleep. The shadows beneath her eyes grew darker with every day.

They should never have left Raedonleith.

CHAPTER 20

It was past sundown when Rose woke. Nicholas could hardly believe she'd slept four hours but was grateful for it all the same. His left arm had gone numb hours ago, his backside also, but he'd refused to let her go. His arms had to be more comfortable for her than the rocky ground. That, and he wanted—needed—to be close enough to assure himself she was still breathing. Seeing her fall had been the most terrifying moment of his life.

Rose stretched, hitting his face with her arm before freezing and opening her eyes. And closing them again. A blush started at her neck and raced across her cheeks before turning her ears a deep red. Nicholas could feel the heat of the one that lay against his arm. When she tried to move away, he let her, though only to sit beside him.

The fire sent sparks spinning into the sky when he kicked a log toward it. Spencer and Quin had retired for the night. Adam sat on a fallen log on the other side of the fire, ever alert for danger. He and Spencer had accepted no arguments from Nicholas when they told him they'd split the watch between the two of them tonight. "The lady needs you more," Adam had decreed. They might as well have said he was distracted and therefore useless but Nicholas didn't mind. There was truth to the statement.

It had taken some convincing for Quin to leave her lady. She'd agreed to sleep only when Spencer reminded her that Nicholas was Rose's husband and had already spent four hours with Rose in his arms. And if that wasn't proof he'd take care of her, Spencer didn't know what was. Quin must have believed the knight because she'd followed the others and lay down on the other side of the fire. But not before giving Nicholas strict instructions to feed Rose and give her the dried herb-laden drink Quin left her. Along with a thick wad of fabric the maid had awkwardly passed over.

When he'd asked what that was for, Quin had told him Rose would know then quickly walked away. Relief had washed over Nicholas when he'd guessed what it must be. If it was the time of month when Rose needed that then—

She would be fine. Sick for a day, maybe even two, but it would pass. She wasn't dying in his arms. Though right now, red as her face was, she probably wished she had. He gave her the drink and, with it, time. He'd spent the past hour trying to figure out how to approach the subject with her. It would be awkward at best for both of them, but they were married. It would have come up sooner or later. Better to broach it now while the two of them were still finding their footing in this new relationship than later when it might be a stumbling block too big to conquer.

Rose finished her drink but didn't put the empty cup aside, holding it with both hands in her lap. Moving it around in a circle. Tapping an unsteady rhythm against it with her fingers. The rhythm was a close match to his heartbeat.

"Why didn't you tell me you were ill?" he asked, his voice low so as not to wake the others. He would have taken her somewhere more private to speak if not for the warmth of the fire they both needed. It wasn't a cold night, but there was a bite to the air. Although if Rose's cheeks got any redder, she'd likely start a fire of her own. His finger twitched with the need to touch the softness of her blushing skin, but he held it still. She was skittish enough already.

When the silence stretched from seconds to minutes, Nicholas wondered if he should have clarified, though couldn't help but think she knew exactly what he was asking. She stared at the cup in her hands if it held the secrets of eternity rather than a few remaining drops of river water.

"Rose?"

"Because I didn't want you to know."

That much was obvious.

"Why? Being a woman is just part of...being a woman." *Wonderful, Nicholas. She'll really feel comforted with that exceptional explanation.* "I mean, you don't need to be embarrassed. I realize this relationship is new to us both, but surely I've proved by now that I'm not afraid of a little mess."

"If only a little mess was all it was."

Though she whispered the words to herself, he still caught them. Considered them, trying to understand what she meant. Why she was so afraid to admit that she was ill? She'd fainted while riding a horse. She could have fallen. Could have been seriously injured or even killed if she'd landed the wrong way. If he hadn't been close enough to catch her. And all for the sake of avoiding the embarrassment made worse when she hid the weakness? It made no sense. "I don't—"

"Because for once in my life, I just wanted to be normal. Just a woman. Without all the mess and pain and disappointment. Because I wanted you to think I was strong and beautiful and desirable and whole."

"But I do." He turned his whole body to face her and took her hand in his, desperate for some connection. He would have kept her in his arms if she'd allowed it. Held her all night, all day. Kissed the cheeks and neck growing redder by the minute. The lips that denied his love while making him ache with a yearning to cover them with his own until she knew, without a doubt, that he was here. And she was more than merely desirable. He leaned forward. She pulled away.

"I don't know how you could. My body is broken. I can't ride for more than an hour at a time, can barely sleep for the pain. I'll never dance for hours on end like my sisters, or feast long into the night, or even go for a simple walk without the risk of pain crippling me minutes into it. I can't even…" She stopped, a hitch in her breath. Her fingers were white around the cup as she gripped it. "I can't even have…"

"A child," Nicholas said softly, finishing the words she couldn't. "I know. I'm so sorry, Rose. I can't imagine how difficult that must have been for you to hear such news. And then to have Aldon leave the same day."

"It was—" She dropped the cup, her eyes wide as she stared at him. "You know? That I'm…"

Barren. That was the word Aldon had used. Her parents had been kinder with their words. Was he not supposed to know? Had she thought it a secret all this time? Was that why she'd put up such a wall between them? Because she thought that would change his mind about her? "Aldon told me. And your parents confirmed it." Although he still hoped for another outcome. His mother had the same pains, yet she'd delivered two healthy sons. Perhaps she would have a different answer. After all, how could one declare a person barren when they'd not even attempted to have child?

"Aldon? But then, you knew...before..."

Before he'd met her. Before he'd spoken for her at the tournament. Before he'd stood in the chapel and promised himself body, heart, soul, and future to this remarkable woman.

"Aye."

"Why?" she asked. "Why would you do that?"

"Because I care about you."

She was shaking her head even before he finished speaking. "No. No, I can't accept that. There has to be another reason. Was it pity? Penance? Did my father offer you more gold than you could walk away from?"

"Penance? How would marriage to a beautiful woman be penance?"

"A broken woman."

"Rose—"

"I speak only the truth. You can't deny it."

He squeezed her hand gently. "Your body may be broken, but you, my love, are not. And if it takes a lifetime to convince you of that fact, I would pledge every day of it to doing so."

She opened her mouth before closing it again. Twice. Good. He'd given her something to think about. Hopefully planted a seed that would grow and prove as hardy as the trees that filled the forest around them.

"You're like the crown you wore at our wedding," he said, remembering how well it suited her.

She scoffed. "Ugly?"

How could she ever think that? "Your crown isn't ugly."

"Evangeline's has diamonds on it. Mykah's has emeralds and onyx. Mine's just dull. The stones don't even shine. Like me."

"I'm going to ignore that foolishness you tacked on the end about not shining because we both know that's far from the case, no matter how you may feel today. But I can tell you why the stones don't shine. It's because they're not stones. They're pearls."

"Pearls?"

"'It shone with light, its luster clear. Color stalked its sheen. White, then

rose, then turquoise blue, as round he'd ever seen." She frowned again. He smiled. "Lines from a ballad I love and the reason pearls are my most favorite jewel. Forgive me. Aldon likely told you I'm forever lost in a story, even without a book in my hand." He ran his thumb across the back of her wrist.

"Did you know that pearls are one of the most valuable gems you can find? They're beauty borne of pain, created deep under water inside an oyster shell when an irritant gets inside. They're incredibly rare. And made all the more valuable because of it. Your crown isn't ugly, Rose. It's priceless, rare, and infinitely beautiful just like you."

"You think I'm beautiful?"

She doubted it? He leaned forward, placing a gentle kiss on her heated cheek before forcing himself to pull back. "I think you're the most beautiful woman I have ever seen. No book, nor jewel, nor child of my loins, could ever be more precious to me than you."

Her eyes filled with tears. "I need to go. See to…personal…"

Nicholas stood, holding out a hand to help her. She'd gone back to avoiding his gaze, hiding the wad of fabric behind her skirt.

"Do you need Quin?"

Rose shook her head. "Don't wake her. I won't be long."

His mind roared as a battle waged between giving her the privacy she requested—and deserved—and the fear of letting her out of his sight.

"Don't go far," he conceded.

She walked five steps before, with a gasp, she fell to the ground.

"Quin! Spencer!" Nicholas called, rushing to her side. Hang sleep. Hang privacy. He should never have let Rose leave his arms.

※

"You are not getting on that horse."

Nicholas couldn't believe Rose was even standing. Not after she'd collapsed twice yesterday. Though Quin had assured him this was normal for Rose, all the assurances in the world couldn't have convinced Nicholas she was well. If not for the steadiness of her breathing last night, he'd have wondered if she were still alive. Checking on her—and no small amount of anxiety-fueled prayer—had kept him awake most of the night.

"Of course I am."

"You're too weak."

Hurt slashed across Rose's face. Nicholas wished he could pull the words back. They were true, but he shouldn't have said them aloud.

"I'm sorry. I didn't mean—"

"Yes, you did. And it's true. I am. But Strider isn't. He can carry me."

"Please, Rose. Rest until you're well. We can wait another day."

"And what if I'm not well tomorrow? Or the next day? What if it's a week before you deem me well? What if you never do? We'll never make it to Belairisia if you wait on me. You've done that enough already. Five days' travel and we're still on Raedonleith land. Because of me. I won't hold you back another day."

He didn't want to wait. She was right in saying they'd barely made ground. They should have been at the healer's cottage by now, but he wasn't going to risk her life to make up time.

"We wait until you're well."

"Nicholas..."

"Or you ride with me."

"With— No. I can't."

"Then we wait. The choice is yours, but you'll not ride alone."

The way his chest had constricted when he'd watched her start to fall yesterday, he wouldn't survive her actually falling. His heart wouldn't just hitch, it would stop altogether. Sharing a horse had the potential to be awkward and slow them further, but at least she'd be safe.

"I'm not a child that you must coddle me."

Nicholas sighed. Is that what she thought? That he was coddling her? Perhaps he was. But he didn't do it because he thought her a child. Quite the opposite. He coddled her because he couldn't bear the thought of her in peril and him being too far away to help. Because he loved her. Already. Because the more precious something was, the closer you kept it. A jewel. A prize. This woman he still couldn't believe was his wife.

He didn't coddle her because he thought her weak. He did it because he was.

He stepped closer to Rose and cupped her shoulder. She let out a tiny gasp of a breath when his thumb skittered across her bare collarbone. Her skin was softer than the finest leather book he'd ever held. Warmer too. Like—

Focus, Nicholas. This can't be about you.

"I've never once thought you a child. Nothing could be further from the truth." He leaned in, unable to resist kissing her cheek. Spencer was preparing their horses. Quin and Adam had gone to get more water. Nicholas and Rose were as alone as they could be. Not as alone as he'd like, but given the weariness on his wife's face, that was for the best.

"I care about you more than I would have thought possible in so short a time. But even if I didn't, you're my wife, sweet Rose. Please, let me help you. It would kill me to see you fall again."

Tears welled in the corner of her eyes. She stepped back before he could brush them away, taking Strider's rope in her hand. She wasn't going to try to mount her horse alone, against his wishes, was she?

Almighty, please. If you care about me at all, stop her from getting on that horse.

"I don't know if I can."

Her voice was barely a whisper, but it cut through bone and marrow all the same. He'd thought they'd gained ground last night but here in the light of day, her defenses were as high as ever. He told himself it didn't matter, that trust would come with time alongside love and respect, but it still hurt.

"With Spencer, then?"

She blinked at that then finally met his gaze, a touch of amusement in the crinkle of her eyes. "You hated offering that, didn't you."

Yes, he really had. If they were going to make this marriage work—and arrive at the healer's house before this time next year—he was going to have to make some compromises. It didn't mean he had to like them.

"Spencer's a good man, but you're *my* wife."

There it was, a turn of her lips. The tiniest of smiles. Nicholas could have won every event in a tournament and not felt as much of a sense of achievement as he did in this moment. He'd made Rose smile.

"I'll ride with you."

"You'll—" *Thank you, Almighty One.* "Thank you."

He pulled Rose into an embrace, one she pushed away from almost as quickly, but she was still smiling when she did.

CHAPTER 21

The rain started just before midday. First it was a drizzle, then a shower, then a downpour so heavy Nicholas could barely see Adam's horse in front of him. He pulled his cloak tight around himself and Rose. His wife slept in his arms. He tucked her head in under his chin to keep her warm, though he knew it did little. His cloak might keep in some of her warmth, but the two of them were already soaked. The drops that fell were like ice against his skin. It was a wonder the rain hadn't woken her.

He moved his horse closer to the shelter of the trees, grateful to see the others had done the same.

"We can't ride in this," Adam said, mirroring Nicholas's thoughts. "We won't be able to start a fire either."

Which meant a long time before any of them would be warm or dry. If he'd been traveling alone, he'd have waited it out. Put up with being wet for a few days if need be. Wrapped himself in a blanket, perhaps used some fallen boughs to make a shelter. But they were responsible for the lives of two women, the weight of which sat heavy on Nicholas's shoulders.

He couldn't do that to them.

"There's a … shelter. Not far from here," Adam said, hesitation in his voice. "A cottage. Or most of it."

Nicholas wondered why the man hadn't suggested it earlier. They could have stayed there last night. Rose could have been warm.

"It's close?"

"Less than a half hour's ride, I'd guess."

Nicholas flicked dripping hair out of his eyes and cringed as stream of icy water found its way down his back. He hated being wet. At least he hadn't risked bringing a book. It would have been destroyed in this deluge. "Let's go."

"It's not safe," Spencer said, frowning at Adam.

"Better than here," Adam argued. The two men faced each other, frowns arguing a silent debate Nicholas had no chance of joining. Rose shivered in her sleep. They were wasting time. Whether it was a cottage or a cave, they needed shelter. Now.

"Well?" he asked the knights. "Why isn't the cottage safe?"

"It's exposed," Adam said.

"To the elements?" Adam had said *most* of a cottage, though three walls and a roof was still better than the tree they were currently sheltering under.

"No," Spencer bit out. "To Castle Cavendish."

They'd been skirting Cavendish land for two days now—riding close enough to the road to stay on course but far enough to evade Cavendish patrols. Nicholas and his guards had done the same on their way to Raedonleith. Though Lord Cavendish held no particular animosity toward Belairisia, his patrols were known to cause trouble for anyone who came across their path.

"But Cavendish may not know about the cottage," Adam argued. "It's on his land but far enough away from the castle that it's all but forgotten. We sheltered there on several occasions when we were searching for Lady Evangeline. We were never spotted."

That didn't mean they wouldn't be this time.

"Cavendish abused Lady Evangeline and tried to have Lady Mykah killed twice," Spencer argued again. "I have no doubt he's behind the attempt on Lady Rose's life too. If he finds us, he won't care that you and Rose are married or that you're a prince. He'll kill us all. Trespassing on his land, he'll be within his rights to do so."

"We don't have another option," Adam said. "Lady Rose is ill. She can't stay out here. I think it worth the risk."

Nicholas looked to Rose's maid. "Quin?"

"He's right," she said. "We're all in more danger sitting here."

"No," Spencer gasped, his gaze capturing the maid's. Was he begging her to change her mind? Nicholas didn't know. Right in this moment, he didn't care. Though the knights were stronger, as prince, the decision was his.

He swept another dripping piece of hair out of his eyes and looked down to where Rose still, mercifully, slept. The cottage could be an answer to prayer in this deluge or it could mean danger. He didn't know which. Couldn't know which. Adam and Quin were willing to try. Spencer held back.

A distant rumble of thunder made his choice for him. They couldn't stay out here in a storm. They'd deal with whatever else happened when they got there.

"We'll go to the cottage. Lead the way."

⁓ ⁀⁀⁀ ⁓

Rose stretched her arms above her head and hit a wall. Her eyes sprung open.

A wall. In a room. A simple room but definitely a room.

There was a mat on the floor. Two un-glassed windows. A wooden door. A wooden table. Two wooden chairs. A bucket. No, four buckets. One beside the door, two near the wall to Rose's left, and another beside the blanket she lay on.

Who had need of four buckets? Who lives here? Where am I?

And how had she gotten here?

That was the question which set her heart pounding. She was sleeping in someone's cottage, and she hadn't walked there herself. Last she remembered she'd—

Been atop Nicholas's horse, pretending to be asleep lest he start a conversation and the breathiness of her voice give away how much his closeness affected her. She must have fallen asleep for real.

But that didn't explain where she was now. Or why she was alone. She hadn't been alone in more than a week.

The door flung open and she skittered back against the wall, pulling the blanket with her. A squeak stuck in her throat when she realized it was Quin.

"Oh good, you're awake." Quin stuck her head outside the door, calling to someone. "She's awake. You can stop your fretting."

Nicholas was through the door and by Rose's side before Rose could take a full breath. He ignored the chairs and sat beside her on the floor, hands reaching toward her before he seemed to think better of it and clasped them in his lap.

"You're awake."

Yes, they'd established that. Rose was more concerned about what came next—and what had come before.

"Where are we? Where are the horses? And the others?"

"Outside. They're hunting and seeing what provisions they can find while the rain is stopped."

It had been raining?

"You slept through it. The rain, the storm, the ride here."

"Rain? But my clothes are dry." She peeked under the blanket still tucked up around her chin. Her eyes widened. That wasn't the gown she'd been dressed in this morning. Oh no. He hadn't—

"Quin changed you into dry clothing. You slept through that too."

Rose would have thought he was lying except she couldn't deny the proof in front of her. She pulled at a thread on the blanket, only now noticing the pile of wet clothing in one of the corners of the cottage. They'd need to hang them before they started to smell. Perhaps one of the men would have a rope among their things. They could string it between the two chairs. Rose clutched her necklace and ran her thumb over the stone.

"Who lives here?"

"No one, we hope."

"You don't know?"

Nicholas sighed. "We're on Cavendish land. Spencer and Adam knew of the cottage, having sheltered here while watching over your sister. When the rain grew too heavy and the thunder began, the choice was made for us. We had to stop."

Cavendish land. Her father wouldn't like that.

"I'm sorry," Rose said.

Nicholas's mouth quirked at one side. "For the rain? Neither of us control the weather."

"For putting you in danger. You would have been safe at home, sitting warm in your library, lost in the pages of a book if not for me."

"Though the picture you paint is delightful, I would only wish it if you were there beside me."

His gaze was gentle, loving and... fierce, pulling to the fore every emotion she'd pushed aside earlier cradled in his embrace. She'd fought so hard to ride alone, and known instantly the battle had been well justified as soon as Nicholas put his arms around her. She'd been lost. Lost to his warmth, his shelter, his care. She'd stopped fighting and simply breathed, knowing she was safe. He'd protect her. He'd love her. He'd keep every one of those vows he'd made no matter what.

When he'd looked down at her, his face so close she'd seen herself reflected in his brilliant blue gaze, the urge to close the distance had been as fierce as the expression on his face now. One of hunger. Of need. She'd yearned to surrender to his care and lose herself in his love.

But she couldn't. Because part of herself would never be enough. Not for her. Not for him. Nicholas didn't wield a sword like a warrior but he had the heart of one. He'd fight for her, stand by her.

And, in doing so, lose himself forever.

Pull back. Now. If you let yourself be drawn in by his care now, it'll only hurt more later.

"You don't want me," she said.

Rose's breath caught as he brought her hand to his lips and kissed it. "You, my love, are all I want."

⁕ ⁕ ⁕

The day stretched Nicholas's patience. He was accustomed to long days indoors but not this—five people attempting to keep their emotions under control within a tiny cottage.

Spencer wouldn't leave the doorway, one hand on his sword as his gaze searched out every noise, certain any second they'd be found.

Adam sharpened his arrows until they could cut through stone, sullen over his failure to find dinner before the rain returned and sent animals large and small to ground.

Quin and Rose had sequestered themselves in one of the corners of the cottage, heads bent together, backs to the men. Though Quin sent the occasional glance over her shoulder to check on the rest of them, there was little mistaking Rose's reticence to be there.

You don't want me.

Her words had lit an anger-fueled fire inside him. It had taken all the strength he had to control it and answer her with words rather than the guttural scream he wanted to send skyward. That a woman as kind and desirable as Rose would think herself not worthy. Just because her body was weak. Fury burnt his insides as her words played again in his mind.

Yes, he wanted her.

He craved her smile. The amused one she'd given Spencer that night he'd told stories about her as a child. The soft one that had played along her lips when she spoke of Arthur and the rock-balancing game of his that Rose was determined to conquer. The one Nicholas had finally won himself when he'd admitted how much he hated the thought of her sharing a horse with anyone but him.

He ached for her trust. For her to believe in his care enough to stop hurting herself in an attempt to please him. He hadn't lied that night when he told her it didn't matter how long the journey took. Though he could have done without the angst of wondering if they were being followed, the confusion about his wife, the discomfort of the ground each night, and his perpetually sore backside from hours spent on a horse, he was enjoying the journey. Adam and Spencer had become friends, and Quin cared for her mistress with unparalleled devotion. He couldn't have chosen better companions to travel with.

He yearned for her touch. Every night when Nicholas kissed her cheek goodnight, he wondered what it would feel like for her to do the same. Every time he held her hand to help her up, he hoped she'd hold on tight and not let go. Every time he lay beside her, he prayed the day would come soon when she'd close the distance and be his in every way.

His breath caught as Rose stood and walked toward him, then rushed out as she veered toward the door instead, brushing past Spencer to go outside. She must be seeing to her needs again. They'd moved one of the buckets outside the cottage under the overhang of the roof and hung up a blanket to hide it from view. It wasn't perfect, but it was the most privacy they could offer while still being on high alert.

"She'll come around."

Nicholas sighed at Quin's words. "Will she?" He wasn't so certain anymore. He'd been so sure Rose would learn to love him in return and yearn as he did for their marriage to be real. A few times, he'd thought he saw a spark of something in her gaze or felt her sway toward him, but it would be gone as soon as he recognized it, hope along with it.

"If there's one thing I've learnt serving Lady Rose, it's that there are different kinds of strength. It takes one to face an enemy with a sword but another entirely to get out of bed, day after day, and face oneself. She is strong, our lady, and she cares for you," Quin said.

He didn't deny she was strong. He'd seen Rose get back on her horse too many times to deny that. But caring? Quin must have seen something he didn't.

"How do you know?"

"She wouldn't be fighting it if she didn't."

Fighting it? Was that what Quin thought Rose was doing? Nicholas didn't see fight. He barely saw anything. Whatever thoughts or emotions flared inside her, nothing showed on her face. At least when speaking with him. He'd thought they'd grown closer the night they'd talked of her barrenness, but she'd gone straight back to hiding everything the next day. The only reason she'd ridden with him was because she had to. "You're seeing things."

Quin shook her head. "I don't think I am. She's different with you than anyone else."

"Because she hates me."

"No, because she's afraid."

"Of me? How could she possibly be afraid of me? I've treated her with nothing but care. I bring her food and water and make sure she's comfortable each night. I ask after her wellness every morning."

He'd done everything he could think of bar shouting his love to the hills.

"She knows you care. No one could doubt how much you care. I think it's that which has her running. She's afraid you'll leave."

"I won't."

"I know—or, at least, I hope you won't—but Prince Aldon did. Friends too, when she was too tired to keep up with them. And when they married and had families and she didn't. Maids also. Even her sisters, in part."

So many. But that didn't mean he would. "I'm not leaving her."

"Prove it. Be patient."

He'd thought he was. "For how long?"

"As long as it takes."

As long as it takes. Nicholas mulled that over as Quin helped Rose back to their little corner.

CHAPTER
22

It rained all night and all the next day. And the next. Rose would have been grateful for the time to rest away from their horses if not for two things: She wasn't getting any rest, and the men were nervous. They wouldn't admit as much to her, but the cottage walls were thin, and their hushed conversations outside were not as hushed as they assumed.

They didn't like to stay in one place for so long. They were too close to Cavendish Castle. The horses would give away their position. They needed to move on, but the ground was too muddy and the river too fast. Nicholas worried about her health and what might happen if she grew ill again. Spencer worried they'd not see an intruder through the rain before it was too late. Adam worried they'd not have food enough to wait out the rain.

It was a wonder they'd not hurt each other, restless as they were.

Yesterday afternoon Quin had handed Rose a needle, thread, and a pale blue square of fabric the length of Rose's arm. Why the maid had packed them or when she'd thought they'd be useful while traveling for days on end, Rose didn't know. Neither did she think Quin had any idea *what* that square of fabric was. If she had, she never would have packed it.

Rose had taken the unexpected gift with shaking hands, grateful for something to keep her busy while they waited for the rain to stop but aching inside. Quin could have chosen any one of the many projects Rose was working on, but in her haste to depart, she'd picked this one. The baby blanket. Rose hadn't worked on this project since before the healer had come.

For two years, she'd poured her heart into the intricate design. She'd stitched forget-me-nots around the border, intertwined with bursts of lavender and ivy. Tucked in around the flowers were prayers. Words of hope. Words of blessing. Words of encouragement. The prayers she'd prayed for the child she'd hoped to one day carry. The child she no longer would.

She could still see the slight stain where a tear had fallen when she'd packed it away after the healer had departed.

Tempted as she was to give the blanket to Adam to use for the horses, she refrained. There was little else to do and, though it broke her, she couldn't let it go. There was a reason she'd packed the blanket away after the healer left rather than tearing it to pieces or throwing it into the fire. Perhaps one day in the future she'd give it to Evangeline or Mykah for their child. Let the prayers be for a niece or nephew. If her heart could take it.

She threaded the needle with black cotton and started another word. Another prayer.

Strength.

Almighty, give the child who sleeps under this blanket strength. Strength of body, strength of will, strength of heart. And may they know your strength most of all. May they know that though their strength may fail, yours never will.

Whoever that child may be.

Her mind strayed to home. Mykah and Finnian were married now. She'd missed their wedding. Were they safe? Had the threat of war become reality? Were they even now girding up for battle?

Let it not be so. Let them live long and happy lives together. With children and grandchildren and—

A tear dribbled down her cheek, the ache always so close to the surface. She wiped it away. She needed to get past this. Let it go. She wasn't going to have a child. That didn't make her worthless. Just…broken. And sad.

Almighty, I hate this. I want to be faithful. I want to tell you that whatever you give me is good because you are good, but it hurts. So much. Perhaps it's good that I'm going to Belairisia for a time. I won't have to figure out how to find a smile when my sisters tell me they're expecting. Not yet.

They would one day, filling the castle with more red-haired children. Or would their hair be dark, like their fathers'? Perhaps…

Ouch!

Rose shook her head and blinked a few times before rubbing at her finger. No blood, thank goodness, but she really shouldn't doze off with a needle in her hand. She hadn't even realized she had dozed off, which was even worse. She would have stood and walked around the cottage if there had been room. Restless as she was, she would have even taken a walk in the rain if Nicholas had allowed it. He wouldn't. She'd asked. He'd looked at her as if she were out of her mind. Perhaps she was. Close to it, at least. With a sigh, she went back to her stitching—and tried not to think too hard about what it was she was making.

She'd almost completed the word when Nicholas sat beside her. His hair and clothing smelled damp, like the forest at dawn, but he was warm. He was also making her nervous. Could he tell?

He nodded toward the fabric in her hand. "Will you teach me?"

Rose fumbled with the needle. "To stitch?"

"Unless you think it beyond me."

"No. Of course not." She had no doubt Nicholas was the type of man to excel at anything he put his mind to, though she'd not in a million years considered the delicate art of needlework one of those things. "But...why?"

"Why not?"

"You're a prince." Had he somehow forgotten? They had been stuck in this cottage for two days. Perhaps the confined space was getting to him too.

"A bored one. There are only so many times I can check on the horses. The rain doesn't look like it'll let up anytime soon, the room is too crowded to exercise, and I don't have anything to read." He shrugged. It was the most adorable thing Rose had ever seen. "Also, I snagged my cloak on a branch and tore a hole in it." He held up the cloak, pointing to a tear the size of his hand that was far too even to have been made by a branch. Had Nicholas used his knife to cut a hole just so he could ask Rose to help him fix it?

"I can sew it for you." She reached out a hand to take the cloak from him, but he pulled it away.

"Of that I have no doubt, and you'll do a far better job than me doing it, but I'd like to try. If you don't mind teaching me."

Rose shook her head. "I don't mind." Teaching Nicholas to sew, even nervous as she was, was far more preferable to crying over lost dreams.

She handed him her needle, amazed at how small it looked in his hand. Were his hands so much larger than hers? Suddenly she wanted to know.

"Rose?"

Teaching. Right. Focus, Rose.

"Forgive me, I— That is—" She took a breath and started again. "The first thing you need to do is thread your needle."

She had no idea how long the two of them sat there, her explaining each step as Nicholas held the delicate needle between his fingers and tried to make simple, even stitches on his cloak. It was peaceful. Far more so than she'd expected.

"Oh."

Rose looked over at Nicholas. "What is it?"

He tilted the fabric toward her. "I don't think I'm very good at this."

A giggle bubbled up Rose's throat and escaped before she could think to hold it back. She wasn't even sure what had her laughing the most—the pitiful expression on Nicholas's face or the pitiful mess of his stitching. Even calling it a mess was kind. Threads were going every which way, the fabric was tangled over itself, and Nicholas seemed to have sewn one of his fingers into it. Not through the skin but knotted around it enough that they'd have to cut him out.

"You laughed," he said.

"I'm sorry. It was rude of me. I shouldn't have."

"I've never heard you laugh before."

Nicholas brushed his free hand across her cheek, his gaze full of wonder and—something else.

Oh.

He wasn't angry at her. He was captivated.

"Do it again."

"What, laugh?" She couldn't laugh on command. Laughter didn't work that way. Although, if she let her gaze stray to the thread attached to his hand she might be tempted. A smile tugged at her lips.

"Beautiful."

The thumb of his free hand touched her lips before stopping at the corner of her mouth. Her breath caught. This was— This was—

Needlework. That's what it was. Not romance. Not courtship. Certainly not love. There was no reason at all for her heart to be pounding like it was or his pulse to be doing the same. She could feel it where his thumb still rested against her lips.

"I—"

Don't know what to say. Go away. Stay. Pull me closer.

Kiss me.

She flinched backward. His hand dropped to her shoulder. "You're afraid of me. Why?"

"I'm not." Afraid of the strength of her own emotions, certainly. But him? He'd done nothing wrong since the day she'd met him. He was kind, strong, endlessly patient. Even now, he moved back when another man might have pressed his advantage. Simply because she'd flinched.

"I won't hurt you," he said.

"I know." That was what made her so afraid. He would love her, protect her, care for her, fight for her as long as he lived, just as he'd promised the day they'd wed. And he'd lose another piece of himself every time he did until he was a shell of the vibrant prince she knew today.

From her place in the doorway, Quin laughed at something one of the knights said. The sound mixed with the pounding of the rain on the roof. Rose couldn't hear their conversation and hoped they couldn't hear hers. She pulled her shawl tighter around her shoulders. The half-finished baby blanket mocked her, poking like a needle at her failings. Nicholas waited, silent as Rose gathered her thoughts. She shook her head, unable to meet his gaze as she gave him the only truth she could.

"You deserve better. You deserve someone whole, who can give you children and a future and a reason to live."

"You're my reason."

"I'm no one's reason."

"You're mine." He dropped his hand but didn't move away. "Did you ever wonder that I never married before?" His words were quiet, meant only for her. "I wondered. My friends married. My younger brother was betrothed. My father advised me to marry, and plenty of women offered themselves as my bride. But never once was I tempted by any of them. Until you. You are all I can think of. The moment I saw you sitting in the stands at the tournament, I fell."

He'd said the same thing to Spencer that night she overheard them talking. She believed it as little now as she did then. "The sun was probably in your eyes," she muttered.

"The sun was behind me, lighting up your countenance as if the fingertip of the Almighty singled you out. I don't want a kingdom or a crown, Rose. Aldon can have them. I only want you."

"You'll want children." Every man did. A child to lavish affection on, to work by his side, to carry on his name and pass on his wisdom to future generations.

"Not if it means having them without you."

"You don't mean that."

"Aye, I do. I know you don't believe it, not yet, because you see yourself as less than you are. But I believe it. I know it. I've never been more certain. You are all I want."

All I want. Had Rose ever been that for anyone? She hadn't been enough for Aldon. Hadn't been brave enough or strong enough for her father to let her stay when danger came. She desperately wanted to believe it of Nicholas now but how could she when she'd only known him so short a time? Others who'd deserted her, she'd known for years. Some, all her life.

She'd had friends once, beyond her sisters. Girls she'd giggled with and dreamed with, learning dances and swooning over men far too old for them. They'd chatted about beautiful clothes and whiled the days away at picnics and twittered over the knights at tournaments.

And then, Rose had gotten sick, and laughter turned to brittle smiles as she tried—and failed—to keep up with her friends and their boundless energy. Long strolls and nights dancing turned to making excuses to disguise the hours spent curled up in her room in pain, hiding from them all. She wasn't there when they fell in love and, thinking she no longer cared, left her out of their lives. She cared. She just didn't have the strength to show it. They danced. It took all of her energy to merely stand.

Then they started marrying. And having children. And moving on without her.

She was the princess, she reminded herself, again and again. She'd never had the freedom they had, even without her illness. Mykah and Evangeline were all the friends she needed. But now Mykah and Evangeline were married too.

They hadn't deserted her, but it still felt as if, once again, she'd been left behind.

No. I won't let myself think that. They'd be horrified if they knew I'd thought such things. Thank you, Almighty, for the gift of my sisters' friendship. I don't know when I'll see them again, but I pray you bless them.

And that you'd bless this man beside me, whose charm is so infuriating. It's not right or wise for me to want to keep him when he deserves so much more, but there's no use in hiding the truth you already know.

She gestured to the fabric still attached to Nicholas's hand. "Let me free you and then, perhaps, if you still wish to learn, you could try on something smaller? I have a piece of cloth you might use."

He paused a moment longer before allowing the change of topic and nodding. "That might be best."

Rose forced her hands to remain steady as she cut the thread from his hand and undid each of the stitches he'd made. The tear in his cloak was even bigger now but she could fix it. Unless one was looking, they wouldn't even know the hole was there by the time she was done.

"Thank you," he said, his quiet voice skimming through her ears to rest in her heart.

She walked away before temptation could make her stay. Quin was more than happy to fetch the handkerchief from Rose's bag, and if she wondered why Nicholas needed it, didn't ask. Rose sat on one of the chairs by the window and let the sound of the steady rain bring peace. She didn't move again until the sun set.

When sleepy limbs forced her to rise, she was surprised to see Nicholas hadn't moved from his place, nor set aside his stitching. Gathering far more courage than it should have required, she sat back beside him.

"You're still trying?"

"Did you think I would give up because I made a mess of my first attempt?"

Yes. Though it appeared she was wrong. He was improving too. For one, his hand wasn't attached to the fabric, but his stitches were becoming more uniform too. Though still oversized like a child had created them, they were straight and even.

"What do you think?"

He handed her the square of fabric. She took her time examining the stitching around the edges—more to calm her thoughts than because she needed to. A grown man with a needle in his hand shouldn't make anyone swoon but her heart was having trouble staying unmoved.

"It's—"

And then she saw it. Her name. Sewn into one corner. Again, childish, but the four letters unmistakable.

"You did this for me?" Her voice caught on the emotion clogging her throat.

His thumb brushed her lip again, his hand cradling her jaw before he leaned in and kissed the top of her cheek. His words were a whisper in her ear.

"I would do anything for you. One day, you'll realize that."

CHAPTER
23

Cormac's sword clattered on the cobbled stone, the sound like an anvil to his head. His heart raced with a beat that had nothing to do with the sparring he'd been doing. Trying to do. This was the third time his sword had fallen from his hand. The first time, he'd blamed the slickness of the weapon's grip in the early morning dew and ordered a squire to fetch him a pair of gloves. The second time it had fallen, his opponent's weapon had been close enough to Cormac's arm that he'd acceded the loss before anyone questioned it.

There was no explaining away a third. Not when his opponent hadn't even taken his stance. If they'd been in a true battle, Cormac would be dead.

I know your hand shakes sometimes when you hold your sword.

His hand was beyond shaking today. It was too weak to even grip the sword.

Curse you, Maeve.

He'd been fine before she came along and started putting thoughts in his mind.

His vision faded in and out in time with the pounding of his head. If he didn't sit, he was going to fall. A sword on the ground could be explained. The lord of the castle on the ground would be far more difficult.

"Enough," he told the guard. "Train with the others. I've business to attend to."

The guard tilted his head in acquiescence and departed. Cormac didn't waste words telling the man to keep his mouth shut about what he'd seen. He'd punished enough men for far less to worry about rumors spreading.

He picked up his sword, thrusting it, his gloves and his helmet into the hands of a waiting squire. "Clean that. I expect to see them sparkling and back in my chamber within the hour."

The boy nodded and rushed away. Cormac kept the pounding of his head at bay until he reached his chamber. "Out. Now," he ordered the servants waiting there.

"My lord, you're early. Do you wish for—"

"No." It didn't matter what they were offering. All he wished for was silence.

I know you've called the healer more than once for something to dull the pain in your head.

He reached for a cup of ale, swigging it down in one large gulp. The cup slipped from his hand. Empty, but a death knell on his already shaken composure.

I know this bitterness is keeping you awake at night.

No. Maeve was wrong. His sleeplessness was due to eager anticipation, not bitterness. Any moment, news would come from his spy. News that Rose was dead, Raedonleith's future along with her. Or that Lior had finally given into Cormac's taunting raids and declared war. Either way, Cormac would be ready.

He poured another cup of ale, using his left hand this time to bring it to his mouth. Already the pounding in his head was easing.

See, Maeve? Nothing the matter with me.

A knock sounded.

"Cah…mmm."

The word caught on his tongue, sliding when it should have shouted. Was he drunk? No. He couldn't be. He'd only had two cups of ale this morning. Hardly enough to incapacitate him. He wasn't fool enough to imbibe while waging battle against his greatest enemy. He shook his head and tried again.

"Come in."

There. That was better.

A man entered, the dirt on his face a perfect match to the openings of the helmet he carried. Blood streaked his right arm from elbow to wrist, the accompanying bruise on his cheek hinting at a story. His boots left muddy footprints across the floor. His news must be important to have come directly here from patrol without taking the time to clean up first.

"My lord, there's something you'll wish to see."

"Is it Rose?"

"No but almost as good."

Cormac doubted it. He'd been close plenty of times already. No one gave a prize to second place. His vision clouded. He took a breath and blinked it back to clarity.

"Two Belairisian guards."

Belairisia? He had no quarrel with them. Unless—

"They claim they were traveling with Lady Rose and her new husband."

"Were?"

"The prince sent them on ahead. It appears the rest of the party are traveling slower to account for the two women with them."

Slower. Between Raedonleith castle and Belairisia lay all the land Lior had bestowed Cormac. A lot of land. Lady Rose might be closer than he'd expected.

"Where are the guards now?"

"In the dungeon, my lord. They didn't wish to be captured."

They'd put up a fight then. That accounted for the blood and muck. No doubt his men were taking their revenge on the guards seriously.

"Don't kill them before I have the chance to speak with them. They might be useful."

"Aye, my lord."

His vision blurred again, slower this time to clear. The pounding returned with a vengeance. He was going to do some killing of his own if this blasted headache didn't ease.

"Leave me," he ordered.

"I thought to accompany you."

"I know where my own dungeons are," Cormac spat out. "Take your stench and get out of my chamber."

The man bowed and left.

At least, Cormac assumed he did. He was too busy clutching the table behind him and trying not to fall to either notice or care.

CHAPTER
24

Rose rolled over for a sixth time. Since Nicholas had started counting.

"What can I do?"

Though the light was dim, he saw her startle at his whisper.

"Nothing," came the quiet, and predictable, reply. "Go to sleep."

"How can I when you aren't? Are you cold?"

"No."

"Hungry?"

"No."

"Uncomfortable?"

Her silence was answer enough. Nicholas wrestled his options for only a moment before rising. There was space enough beside her for what he planned. He folded his blanket over several times before sitting on it. Her eyes were wide in the darkness as she watched him. He held out his hands in invitation.

"Sit with me."

She didn't move. He didn't either.

"Please. Let me help you."

"Just sit?"

"Aye. Unless there's another way I can help. I'm hardly a bed but I thought, perhaps if you lay against me, let me hold you, you might, well…" He shook his head. His words wouldn't come out straight. Perhaps if he just told the truth. "You need rest and I care, Rose. Please let me care."

"How will you sleep?"

"It wouldn't be the first time I've slept sitting upright."

"If you're certain."

Nicholas's heart thudded as Rose took his hands, using them to pull herself to her knees. The three steps it took for her to stand before him might as well have been a mountain climb for the way she breathed. He tugged her closer, heart thrilling when she came and sat within the circle of his arms, her back against his chest. Just as they'd done while riding, except this felt different. There was no horse beneath them. Nor was it daylight.

"Am I hurting you?"

Nicholas held back a laugh, not wanting to offend Rose. She, his wisp of a wife, hurt him? "No. Are you still uncomfortable?"

Again, that silence. It stretched, pulling at his nerves and spirit, making him wonder if she was going to answer. It was a personal question. Far more personal than she'd been sharing to this point. But darkness had a way of tearing down barriers. As did exhaustion. He wrapped his arms more tightly around her, bracing the trembling which wracked her body. Never in his life had he felt as helpless as he'd felt each day since meeting Rose. She was in pain but never complained, and he knew she was exhausted.

"No."

Good. He let his eyes close. Held himself as still as possible. He could tell she was doing the same, though her stillness was likely out of fear rather than a desperate yearning to be found worthy. He counted the minutes of silence until her body relaxed against his and her breathing evened out. Her hair was soft against his lips as he kissed her head.

"Sleep, my love. I've got you."

⁕ ⁕ ⁕ ⁕ ⁕

Rose couldn't remember the last time she'd been so befuddled around a man. Had she ever? She'd certainly never felt this way around Aldon. Nicholas made her forget her own name. Forget she was broken. Forget the reasons she kept him at arm's length.

He'd brought her a cup of water this morning, warmed by a fire she had no idea how he'd started, wet as everything was. He'd not said a word about how she'd woken, arms wrapped around his waist, cheek nuzzled against the warmth of his tunic-clad chest. She'd breathed out a happy sigh she knew he must have heard before remembering where she was and stammering something about needing to see to some personal needs. As if her face hadn't been burning with mortification already.

He'd helped her with her cloak, his hands pausing on the clasp a second longer than required, a look of contentment on his face as his blue gaze caught hers. Contentment which changed to something far more intense when their gazes held. She'd leaned forward before a catch in his breath had cleared her foggy mind and forced her backward. What had she planned to do, kiss him? *That* she would never recover from.

When the rain lightened to a drizzle, Nicholas and Adam went hunting. Rose had breathed another sigh, this time with relief. And stubbornly refused to acknowledge Quin's silent questions. And Spencer's knowing smile. Had Spencer been the one to suggest Nicholas go with Adam, somehow understanding how much Rose needed space from the man who confused her so?

No. She was reading too far into it. Spencer had taken two of the three watches last night. Rose knew, because Nicholas had been with her. It had been a logical choice for Nicholas to go hunting, not an emotional one.

Definitely not an emotional one.

Spencer let out a snore. Quin muffled a laugh. Rose leaned her head against the wall and listened to the rain. It was almost as soothing as the silence of the chapel.

Almighty, I don't know what to do with Nicholas. He says he cares for me and proves it daily, but I know it can't last. It's one thing to care for someone for a week or two when they're ill, but quite another when that illness never goes away. When I'm always weak. Always a burden. Broken beyond fixing. I could be the most loving wife in the world, and I still wouldn't be enough. I don't have the strength to stand by his side, nor can I bear his children. What do I have to offer him?

Nothing. That's what I have. Nothing but pain.

I can't do that to him. I care too much already to watch his ardor die. And it will. When weeks turn to months and then to decades. When he realizes this isn't going away. That the woman he married isn't the woman he hoped for. When I grow so weak he has to carry me or make excuse after excuse to his friends and people for why I'm not beside him, or I'm too ill to give him any joy at all. When love fades to bitterness and a wish that he'd never taken his brother's place. The burden his brother had been right to flee.

A burden is all I'll ever be. No matter how much I wish it could be different.

A tear escaped Rose's closed eyes, scalding down her cheek. She let it fall. What point was there in wiping it away when more would follow?

"My lady?"

Rose startled at Quin's words. She'd fallen asleep praying.

"Forgive me. I only wanted to tell you they're back. And the rain has ceased."

They're—oh. Nicholas and Adam. She could hear them chatting outside. Spencer too. Rose wrinkled her nose at a new smell before breathing deeply of it. Roast meat. Pheasant? Partridge? Quail? Her stomach rumbled. Whatever bird it was, it smelled good. Not like the rabbit they'd cooked last time.

"Prince Nicholas plans to sleep here tonight and, if the rain stays away, leave at first light tomorrow."

"Another night? We'll not leave now?"

"The paths are still too wet." Quin grinned. "I also suspect he quite enjoyed helping you sleep last night and hopes to repeat it tonight."

Rose flushed red all over again. "Nothing happened. I only sat with him."

"There's no need to apologize or be embarrassed, my lady. He is your husband, after all."

"I couldn't sleep, and—"

"He held you so you could. I know. And I'm grateful. You ask for so little, even when you should. It did my heart good to see you accept his care. If only you let more people in."

"I let people in."

Quin raised her eyebrows. "Do you?"

Spencer's arrival in the cottage saved Rose from answering. Their feast was ready. Rose took his offered arm and allowed him to help her along the slippery paths to where Nicholas and Adam had set up a meal.

See, Quin? I let people help me.

She dropped Spencer's arm as soon as they arrived, making her wonder if she protested more than she should, but assured herself that such thoughts were foolish. A grown woman, even a weak one, didn't need a man's assistance to sit on a rock and eat. Especially when her husband sat so close beside her that she couldn't have fallen if she tried. Or take a full breath.

A beam of sunlight broke through the trees, throwing warmth across

Rose's shoulder. She looked up in time to see several water drops fall through it, glistening in a moment of gold before fading.

Beautiful.

She might have preferred staying inside the castle to galivanting about outside as Mykah did, but there was something about sunlight after rain. It filled the air with freshness and warmth and made the whole world glow. As if the Almighty broke the bounds between heaven and earth and reached down with whispers of hope.

It never rains forever.

I am Light. I am Hope. I am Life.

I'm holding you.

I won't let go.

Trust Me.

Oblivious to her epiphany, Nicholas handed her a plate full of meat. It smelled even more appetizing up close than it had from inside.

"Thank you."

She ate in silence until her plate was empty, content to listen to the men talk around her. They spoke as if they'd been friends their whole lives, teasing and trying to outdo each other with stories which grew more and more outrageous with each telling. Rose wasn't sure whether to be envious or grateful.

Grateful, she decided, smiling as Adam clapped Nicholas on the back. She was glad Nicholas had made friends. Grateful he was happy. Grateful, even, in this moment, that she was here with them to share it.

Spencer announced he was going to the river to clean up and water the horses. Quin offered to go with him, claiming she had clothing to wash while they had the chance. Adam, too, found a reason to rise saying he was going on patrol now the rain had cleared and would be back in an hour or two, leaving Nicholas and Rose alone.

Very, alone. For the first time since they'd married.

"Thank you for the food."

"Would you like to accompany me on a walk?"

Their words tumbled over one another. Though Rose made sense of Nicholas's question, she wished he hadn't asked it. Certainly not with such hope in his gaze. Because she wanted to say yes, but she had to say no.

"Thank you, but I'm not sure that would be wise."

"Why not?"

A bird hopped near the other side of the fire, poking its beak at the ground as it searched for food. A friend joined it, basking in the post-rain beauty.

Nicholas touched her hair. "Rose, why wouldn't it be wise? Are you unwell?"

No. For the first time in over a month, she was feeling well enough to take a walk. The food had helped, as did the few hours of solid rest she'd found last night, and two days doing little more than sit. It wasn't her physical health but her emotions holding her back. She couldn't let herself love Nicholas.

Even if he was everything she'd ever hoped for in a husband.

Because he was everything she'd ever hoped for in a husband.

"Why do you run?" he asked quietly.

CHAPTER
25

Sunlight danced around the treetops, lighting them with a golden glow too bright for the turmoil swirling Rose's stomach. The beauty she'd treasured only moments ago grated against her spiraling emotions. It should have been raining still. Storming. Great clatters of thunder. White streaks of lightning. Wind so strong every thought was blown from a person's mind. Instead, the clearing was quiet. As if even the weather held its breath.

"I've never run in my life," she told Nicholas. He shook his head.

"You know what I'm asking. You run from me. Every time I come close, you flee. Perhaps not in reality but I see it in your expression. You close yourself off. You smile with Adam and laugh with Spencer and your maid, but with me, you run."

She wanted to run right now. If she could have, she would have fled to the other side of the ocean. Away from Nicholas. Away from his piercing gaze. Away from the love that betrayed her every time she almost convinced herself to leave.

"Please, Rose. Help me understand."

Please, Rose.

His words were her undoing. They always were. That and the fact that he saw her.

The bread that time she couldn't stomach the thought of rabbit.

The extra blanket each night.

The fire he'd kept stoked despite the rain so that she might have warm water to settle her stomach.

It was as humbling as it was endearing.

She rubbed the stone on her necklace between her fingers, finding comfort as she always did in the stone's solidness, so little like her own life, blown about by the whims of pain. She ran because Nicholas terrified her. Because if she stayed, if she let him in—his love, his care, his understanding—she'd never be able to take her heart back. And she cared too much to hurt him.

"I can't."

"I love you."

"You can't."

He laughed as if that was amusing. "You're my wife, Lady Rose of Raedonleith. Of course I do."

"Then you shouldn't. You deserve better."

"How can you still say that? You're the kindest, most beautiful, faith-filled person I know. You intimidate me."

"Me? Hardly."

"You're closer to the Almighty than anyone I know, clerics included. If people spent half as much time in the chapel as you, the world would be a very different place. Your faith is great."

Rose shook her head.

"Not great enough. He hasn't healed me." The moment the quiet words escaped her throat, she wished she could pull them back. She'd never admitted that to anyone. Not even herself. It made her faith seem weak. As if faith depended on what the Almighty did for her rather than who he was. "Forgive me. I should be grateful. I'm trying to be. I know the Almighty has his reasons and is good and true but—" She sighed. "I hate this. I want to be more. I'm always tired. Always in pain. Always slowing people down, frustrating them. I'm so sick of always being the weak one. For once, I just want to be strong."

"You are."

"No, I'm not. Walking with me these past eight days has shown you that. I've fainted. Fallen off my horse. Vomited on you. Stumbled over every root and pebble. We could have been at Belairisia by now. Instead, we're barely off Raedonleith land. All because of me."

"If not for you, I wouldn't have even come."

"I told you not to," she said.

"And I didn't listen. Because walking with you these past eight days has shown me not your weakness but your strength. You fell of your horse and got right back up. You rise with the sun, pack your things, help Quin, even though I know you sleep little. You let me carry you, each time you fainted."

"I was unconscious. I could hardly complain."

"I might have taken advantage of that. But the rest, they show your strength. It takes courage to be weak."

"Then I must be the bravest person in all the land."

She said it as a joke but one look at Nicholas's face proved he didn't take it as one.

"Yes. Yes you are."

She dropped her head into her hands. It was too much—his words, his care, his love. She wasn't worthy of the love he was so determined to lavish on her. The Almighty loved and accepted her but it was easy to trust someone who both created and sustained her. He saw everything—her doubts and fears, tears and hurt—and loved her still.

But he was the Almighty. Nicholas was simply a man. A good one, but one who would tire of her weakness soon enough. When the rest of the royals feasted and danced and Rose was too ill to leave her bed. When his friends had sons and daughters enough to fill their homes and hearts in their older years and he had simply her.

"You deserve more," she said quietly. "Someone to share your life with, rather than someone you have to keep rescuing, who'll slow you down day after day. I want to be that person you deserve but I never will be. I'll never be strong like Mykah, or a mother like Evangeline, or a strong queen my people can count on."

Nicholas growled. "Rose, look at me." He waited until she met his gaze. "Now listen and listen well. You are not your sisters."

She scoffed. "Believe me, I know." They were far better people than she'd ever be.

"You're not listening. You're not your sisters, and that's good. The world already has an Evangeline and a Mykah. The Almighty gave them their purposes and journeys. They're different from you, but that doesn't mean you're inferior."

"I feel as if I am."

"Because you compare rather than relishing." He knelt in front of her, taking her hand in his. "I know what it's like to want what someone else has. For years, I was jealous of Aldon's ease with weapons and people. He excelled at everything he did. People loved him and he loved them back. Aldon fought so well the first time he picked up a sword that the knight training him sweat through his tunic. The first time I picked up a sword, I sliced my own face." He gestured to the scar under his left ear, the one that had given Rose such comfort at their wedding. So that's where it had come from.

"Are you still?" she asked.

"Jealous?"

Rose nodded.

"No. I realized one day that, as much as I admired Aldon, I didn't want to be him. I had no desire to spend hour upon hour on the training fields honing my skills, nor feast long into the night, nor be fawned wherever I went. I determined instead to be the best version of myself I could. I read books, I studied history and maps, I walked about the kingdom and listened to my people and their needs.

"That, and I have you. If anyone should be jealous, it's Aldon."

Rose shook her head. Such foolishness, that anyone would be jealous of her.

"We are more suited than you realize, beautiful Rose. I, too, like the quiet and hide from people more often than a royal should. I don't need to be entertained or outdoors with a weapon in my hand or feel the applause of a crowd to know my worth. And, as much as I care for Milori, if I never ride a horse again, I'll be very happy.

"You would be an incredible mother, Rose, of that I have no doubt, but your worth doesn't lie in your children any more than mine does in my skill with a sword. I don't want your sisters. I want you. Just as you are. Illness and all."

"I can't—"

"It's not me you're afraid to trust, it's yourself. You don't want to believe that someone might love you when you won't love yourself."

Rose pulled her hand from Nicholas's. He didn't understand. It wasn't his fault, but it still hurt.

"Only someone who doesn't live with an illness every day could say that. It might not be all of who I am, but it *is* part of me. A very big part. It's never going away. Every decision I make is impacted by it. I choose my clothing based on how painful my stomach is and how tight a belt I can stand. I choose what I eat and drink, and how much, depending on my nausea. When someone asks me to go with them—even just for a short walk—I have to consider whether I have the strength, whether I can walk back again, who might be there to help me if I fall, if the time spent with that person is worth the amount of energy it may take.

"What I do, where I sit, the people I speak with, the places I go— when you only have a scant amount of strength, everything becomes a choice not of whether I *want* to do something or not but whether I *can*. I don't hide because I want to. I hide because it's the only way."

He reached to take her hand again. She hid both in her skirts and looked away. Quin would say she was acting childish and perhaps she was, but perhaps she'd earned the right after dealing with matters beyond her age most of her life. He wanted honesty? He wanted to know her? There it was. The bitter truth.

"You don't have to hide from me."

"Of course I do." He hadn't run yet but he would. Even Father had left the room when the healer began to speak of blood and the pains Rose had.

"Why? Because you're ashamed? Because you're afraid? You can trust me, Rose. Haven't I proven that already?" Nicholas ran a hand through his hair. "How many times do I have to show you that I'm staying? Stop pushing me away."

"You don't understand."

"Because you won't tell me! I'm trying, Rose. But you have to too."

She met his gaze then, fury bubbling out in scalding words.

"You think I'm not trying? Do you have any idea how hard it is to sit on a horse when your body is so weary you can feel every bone in your spine working to hold you up? Or to force yourself to eat, because you know you must, when your gut roils with every bite? Do you know what it's like to hold a conversation when your head is spinning? Or smile though agony that wrenches your insides like a sword thrust through your side? To bleed for days or weeks on end and have to hide the fact because it's uncomfortable for those around you? To do everything you can to keep *them* comfortable when you're dying inside?"

Anger forced tears from her eyes and made her voice shake as pain, held too long inside, burst free.

"Do you know what it's like to have friends leave because your life is dull? To doubt your own legs will hold you when you stand? To wake every day more tired than when you went to bed? Do you have *any* idea what it is to feel like a burden to those closest to you, and wonder what the Almighty was thinking when he brought you to life, so broken?

"How dare you claim I'm not trying or that I'm more than my illness as if I can somehow forget it exists. It's not going away. And it's not going to get any easier. No matter how hard I *try*."

She swiped tears off her face with her sleeve, furious at the words that had escaped her carefully curated speech. They were the bitter ones. The hidden ones. The ones she fought against and prayed against and hated. Only the Almighty saw those. And the shame that came with them.

She flinched when Nicholas's hand touched her shoulder.

"I'm sorry. I shouldn't have—didn't—" His sigh ruffled her hair and made her heart ache. "I'm sorry. I only—I'm your husband, Rose. Let me help you."

"And what if I do? I let you in. I trust you. I let myself care and rely on you, only to have you walk away. What then? I can't accept your rejection."

"I'm not leaving."

"Aldon did."

"I'm not Aldon." He sighed before moving back to sit beside her on the log. "I know you're scared but I'm not leaving. How could I leave the most beautiful woman I've ever known? We're wed, you and I, and that means something. Everything. I'm not the strongest or most handsome man you'll ever meet nor, as you've said, do I have even the smallest understanding what it is you face, but I am a man of honor. I keep my commitments. You are the one I love, my beautiful Rose. The one I choose. I want this marriage to be real. I want to spend my life with you. Every minute the Almighty grants us."

Because she was beautiful. She wouldn't always be. Time would steal that too. "You don't mean that."

"You're very, very wrong, my love." He leaned close, his warm breath on her ear sending tingles all the way down to her littlest toe. "I mean every word."

He tilted his head. His thumb stroked its way across her cheek. Was he even aware he was doing that? His gaze hadn't left hers.

"Walk with me?" he asked again.

"I can't." She pulled back, almost falling off the log in her haste to put space between them. "That is. I should— I have—" *What? A touch in the head? A sudden stutter? An intense desire to curl into a ball of misery and never face this man again?* "I told Quin I'd work on my needlework this afternoon. We won't have much time once we start out again."

Did her excuse sound as flimsy in his mind as it did in hers? Needle-work? Truly? Unless someone was bleeding out, she could think of no situation that would warrant needlework being urgent.

"You're running again."

Yes. She was. She absolutely was. Because as well as being weak, she was afraid. He was ignoring her walls. No, he was breaking them down.

Almighty, I despise Nicholas right now for making me admit all that but I'm far angrier with myself. Is it true what he said? Am I afraid not because I don't trust Nicholas but because I don't trust myself? I thought sending him away was the right thing to do, to protect us both, but what if, in doing that, I've sent away a gift you've given me? Did you send him to my side to love me? Is Nicholas the answer to my prayer?

She fingered the bracelet on her wrist. The one she couldn't bear to remove. *Love.* Her parents had prayed she'd know love. She had too. The love of the Almighty. The love of friends. The love of a man.

When the healer said I was barren, I thought your answer was no.

No, Rose, you can't have a husband.

No, Rose, you won't have children.

No, Rose, I another purpose for you.

But what if I was wrong? What if your answer was yes? And I was so afraid of the answer that I pushed him away?

I don't want that. I don't want to be afraid.

But Almighty, the honest truth of it is, I'm terrified.

CHAPTER 26

Rose couldn't get comfortable. Nicholas had offered to let her sleep in his arms again, but she'd been too embarrassed—and proud—to accept. Sleeping wasn't supposed to be so difficult, and she'd already let him see far more than she wanted today. She'd spent the hours before bed alternating between wanting to erase every word she'd said, and wishing she'd stayed. Given in to the yearning she saw in his eyes. The same yearning mirrored in her heart.

She rolled over again, wincing as a pebble bit at her hip. If she stayed atop it, she'd be bruised black by morning. If she rolled back over, Nicholas would know. He'd taken the middle watch tonight. He was supposed to be surveying outside the cottage, but she had no doubt he'd be keeping watch over her too. She sighed and tried to wriggle just far enough that the pebble would move.

It didn't. Tiny as it was, the pain was one thing too much when she'd not yet been to sleep. She faced barrenness and blood and agony which forced her to the ground on a regular basis and a rock no bigger than her fingernail was what broke her. She gritted her teeth and tried to stop the tears. They'd do no good. Crying never did. But she was just so tired. And so tired of the pain. Of everything causing pain.

Nicholas's steps as they approached were light but might as well have been the clodhopping of a giant. He'd noticed. Of course he had.

"Rose."

She could pretend she was asleep but couldn't handle the lie. Not on top of everything else. Nicholas crouched beside her, taking her hand.

"Come and see the stars," he whispered.

Rose shook her head. "I can see them from here." One or two perhaps, out the open door, if she angled her neck just right. If her eyes weren't so blurry with tears.

"The view is better outside and—" He stopped.

"And what?" Her voice was as quiet as his, scared by what he might say. More, by what she might feel. Every hour it grew harder to resist the way his care knocked at her heart. This afternoon had almost undone her.

"I want to share them with you."

"Nicholas—"

Spencer sat up, rubbing his eyes. Their whispers must have woken him. Or it was time for his watch. Likely the latter, given the way he nodded to them both before picking up his sword and walking outside. Maybe now Nicholas would rescind his invite and choose sleep.

He didn't. Of course.

"We're married, Rose. For better or worse. I know you think this is a mistake and you want to run from it—and me—as fast as you can, but I don't. I chose to marry you. I chose knowing who you were and what that would mean."

"You can't have known."

"Perhaps not every detail as you do, but I didn't marry expecting to run. This isn't a mistake, Rose. I'm not going to leave. I want to share my life with you, and share your life, and right now, the sky is clear and the night beautiful and I want to share the stars with you."

It was more than an invitation to look at stars and they both knew it. Nicholas was asking more. For her to trust him. For her to consider loving him. Consider being his wife, for real. Forever.

He waited, patient as always. She wished he'd rail occasionally. Get angry at her even. His calmness made her feel as if she was the only one fighting this. Why couldn't he understand how badly this would end? He kept hoping to change her mind, but she'd seen too many people walk away to believe he wouldn't do the same. She had to keep her distance.

"Please, Rose?"

But, maybe just for this one night, would it hurt too much to sit and watch the stars? To remember their beauty. Their hope. Their promise of the Almighty's faithfulness. To accept the love Nicholas offered and pretend it wouldn't fade like the stars when light shone across the world again.

Rose put her hand in Nicholas's, letting him pull her to her feet. He

waited for her to steady herself before tucking her hand into the crook
of his arm and walking outside.

Nicholas led her to the same large log she'd sat on at dinner. Placing
a folded blanket on it, he gestured for her to sit.

A blanket. For her. He was so thoughtful. Rose swallowed a lump
of emotion as he sat beside her and tilted his head back to look at the
sky above.

It was full of clouds. There were stars beyond them, without a doubt,
but Rose couldn't spot a single one of them.

"The clouds will clear. See how fast they move?"

She didn't mind if they stayed. She hadn't come to see the stars. She'd
come for Nicholas. Because of his kindness, and care. Because he treated
her like a treasure too precious to comprehend. Because she was tired,
and he was strength. Because though she knew it would hurt all the
more later, she selfishly craved this one night. One night to accept the
love he offered, to forget her shame, ignore the brokenness, and feel as if
she truly were the most cherished person in someone's world.

One night to imagine that this could all be real.

Tonight, the invitation was there, and she had no will left to resist.

Time stretched as they sat under the cloudy sky. Nicholas didn't
speak so neither did Rose. Seconds turned to minutes and minutes to
an hour. Though Rose grew sleepy, she was too content to move. There
was something so nice about sitting here together in the silence. No
questions asked. No expectations disillusioned. She'd have to retire to
her blanket in the run down cottage at some point, but she was in no
rush. Neither, it seemed, was Nicholas. He was so quiet and still that
Rose wondered if he had fallen asleep. She chanced a glance his way to
find him looking at her. When she would have turned away, he took
her hand.

"Do you miss the chapel?" he asked.

"What?"

"Raedonleith's chapel. The quiet tonight. It reminds me of the chapel. You spend a lot of time there, or were you only hiding from me?"

Rose smiled as she shook her head. "Chapels aren't made to hide in,
as well you know since you found me there. I do, *did*, go there often."

"Why?"

"Because there I can breathe."

"Do you wish you were at the chapel now? I'd take you, if I could."

"No."

"Why not?"

"Because when I'm near you, I can't."

The admission slipped out before she could think better of it. She might have hedged and tried to take it back if not for Nicholas's delight. Though he tried to tamp it down, pulling in his cheeks to lessen the smile that threatened to break them, his gasp had already given it away. That and the softness of his gaze. A girl could drown in the affection she saw there. And be so happy she didn't even care.

"Dance with me?"

Rose tilted her head. "There's no music."

"I'll sing."

"You sing?"

"Poorly. But I'd do it if you'll dance. Unless you'd rather a ballad. I could recite one if you like."

She couldn't imagine Nicholas doing anything poorly. Though he was quieter than any man she'd ever known he was observant and a quick study. He noticed things others didn't. Likely because he wasn't rushing in to save the day sword raised, heart pounding, the instant he saw trouble as most men were wont to do.

"You've entire ballads memorized?"

"A few, though I hope to learn many more. Their words have a beauty to them. Lyrical, like a song, but a ballad's music is found in its story."

His voice was gentle, as quiet as the night around them.

"What if I fall?" It was dark, and the ground rocky. Dancing was simply asking for trouble.

"I'll catch you. Same as always."

Yes. He would. "Don't you ever tire of saving me?"

He took her hand, running his thumb along the edge of her wrist. "You underestimate the pride I feel when I do. I'm not a knight and I'll never be as quick a swordsman or accurate an archer as others, but I can be there for you. I count it an honor. Every time."

"I wish there weren't so many times."

"And I wish you'd dance with me. Your weakness doesn't frighten me, Rose, so you can stop using it as a weapon."

It was too clear and perfect a night to delve into whether or not he was correct. Especially when Quin had said something similar.

"What does frighten you?" she asked, desperate to find a chink in his armor as he'd found so many in hers.

"Losing you." He stood, her hand still in his, and waited. "Dance with me, my love. I'll go slow. I'll sing. I just—I want to hold you."

The night air was cool against Rose's blushing cheeks as she nodded and let him help her to her feet. When she wobbled, Nicholas steadied her, his arm strong across her back. He didn't let go, pulling her in against his chest. True to his word, he started to hum. Also true to his word, he was terrible, but Rose loved it all the same. Her fears didn't seem so loud within the shelter of his arms.

Or perhaps it was the intimacy of the night tucked around them.

His humming faded, replaced by the quiet words of a ballad.

"The day was bleak when first he saw the girl whose heart rang true.
Her hair was gold, her spirit bright, her smile like hope renewed.
He watched her walk yon market fair, no frown left in her wake.
For light she brought to kith and kin, souls captive did she take."

Nicholas's chin rested on Rose's hair as she lay her head against his chest, letting the rumble of his voice soak into her heart. Was this what marriage was? Shared moments amid the daily journey?

Nothing had happened today that Rose would recall a year from now as significant, and yet she cherished this moment—standing in Nicholas's embrace as the crickets joined his recital and the brisk air bit their skin. It mirrored the feeling she got when she walked inside the chapel. Of acceptance. And all being right with the world, because she was loved. Pain would come again tomorrow, dragging frustration and enough regret with it to send her running but this moment, she would treasure.

"But who was she, this spark of light which stirred his heart to ring?
'A princess,' came the quick reply. 'The daughter of the king.'
He bowed his head, his worth brought low for he was but a man.
Not fair of face nor fleet of foot before the king to stand.
'Long all the kingdom's paths he searched, rough oceans did he part,
Certain nigh he'd find the gift to win his lady's heart.
But naught he found could bear the weight of expectation high,
For what to give a maid like she who owned all gold could buy?"

Their dance slowed to a sway and then to a stop. Nicholas's voice faded as well. Rose looked up to find her gaze captured. She couldn't make out the brilliance of his blue eyes in the darkness, but she could see the yearning in them. For her. It was all at once humbling, terrifying and thrilling. And yet, he held back. Ever the gentleman. He might not have been a knight, but he was as noble as one. If not more so.

She lifted her hand to his cheek with a boldness she knew would mortify her tomorrow and skimmed her finger along the dimple of his cheek. He swallowed, his neck bobbing. She was almost certain he was holding his breath.

She leaned closer. He sucked in a gasp. His hands tightened around her waist.

CHAPTER 27

ose wanted to kiss Nicholas.

The thought pounded her mind in time with her heart, eclipsing every reason she should walk away. Her fingers trembled against his cheek, not from fear but ache. To be closer. To be his. He wouldn't make the first move out of honor, but she could. If she dared.

Did she dare?

This moment wouldn't come again. The chance to give him something in return and gratitude for all he'd lavished on her. Morning would bring its own wagon-load of problems but tonight?

Tonight...

His breath caught as she stretched up and kissed him. Once, then again, before pulling back. Her heart raced so fast she was certain he could hear it. What now? She didn't know. She'd never kissed a man before, much less one she was married to. Nicholas stared at her for an endless breath of a moment before curling his hand around her cheek, fingers lost in her hair as he kissed her back.

Her heart stuttered with emotion, her mind unable to land on a single word to describe what she felt, held so tightly in his arms. It was acceptance. And fear. And humility. And overwhelm. And yearning. And ache. And love. So much love.

His kiss was as gentle as the man himself, and over far too soon when Rose lost her balance. True to his word, Nicholas caught her. He held her close for a few seconds more before setting her on her feet with a wry smile.

"You're tired. I should let you sleep."

She nodded but didn't make any move to leave. Sleeping would be the wise thing to do, given the sun would be rising soon, and their group setting out again for a long day of travel. But she didn't want to leave. Not this place. Not his side. When the sun rose, so would her doubts and the fears.

For once, Rose didn't want to be wise. She wanted to hold on to this moment with no thought or care for the morrow. Be reckless instead of second-guessing every single decision she made and how it would affect her health and future and the good of those around her.

To just be.

With Nicholas.

Her husband.

"We could stay," she whispered. She could have cursed the gust of wind that brushed past them right as she whispered and made her visibly shiver. Cursed it because even as the words left her mouth, she knew Nicholas wouldn't accept them. He was too honorable to keep her out in the cold when she could be warm under a blanket in the shelter of the cottage. The cottage where they'd no longer be alone. "You could recite the rest of the ballad. I've not heard that one." Not that ballads were what she most wanted right now.

"I would like that, more than you know, but we shouldn't. Not tonight." With a final lingering kiss on her forehead, he lifted her into his arms. "Come. You need rest."

Nicholas carried Rose all the way to the cottage, his steps far more certain in the darkness than hers had ever been in the light, and lay her on her blanket, tucking another blanket—and then his warm cloak—around her. When he moved to leave, Rose caught his fingers, stilling him.

"Nicholas?"

"Aye, my love?"

"Thank you for showing me the stars."

His frown turned to a smile at her words. They hadn't seen a single star, but what they'd shared was so much better.

"Any time, sweet Rose."

⁂

Nicholas couldn't have slept if he tried. Rose had kissed him. Twice. Of her own accord. And melted in his arms to the point of losing her balance when he'd kissed her back. He grinned at that. He shouldn't be so thrilled by her stumble, but he'd never been more so. It was so much more than he could have dreamed. He really had just been planning to show her the stars when he'd invited her, though the dancing had been far more enjoyable. And the kissing—

The kissing had made Nicholas understand for the first time in his life why wars were started over women.

"Patience paying off?"

Nicholas didn't even bother to try to wipe the foolish grin off his face as he looked up at Spencer. "I sure hope so."

"That looked like a lot more than hope to me."

"You were watching?"

"You, our surroundings. Someone had to. You weren't doing a very good job."

Nicholas winced. Spencer wasn't wrong. The world could have blown to pieces while Nicholas had been holding Rose in his arms and he wouldn't have even cared. If he noticed at all.

"Thanks for taking the rest of my watch," he said. "I know I should have—"

Spencer brushed his gratitude away, nodding toward the cottage. "Rose needed you. I was awake anyway. Get some sleep, if you can."

"You're certain? I—"

"Am so distracted by the memory of kissing your wife that you'll make a terrible lookout. Go. I'll wake you at dawn."

There was some truth in that, much as Nicholas didn't like to admit it.

"Thank you. Again."

"Go, before I change my mind."

With a laugh, Nicholas turned to walk away. An arrow whizzed past his ear, landing in the cottage wall. He stared at it.

"Nicholas, go!"

Spencer's words were still registering in Nicholas's mind when another arrow joined the first, this one taking skin off Nicholas's arm on its way through.

Arm. Arrow. *Rose.*

"Nicholas, move!"

Spencer shoved him to the ground, sword raised as more arrows struck the cottage.

"I'm here. How many?" Adam said.

"Two. In the trees," Spencer answered.

"I'll take the left."

The knights ran. Swords clashed. Horses neighed. A shout. Groan. Thud.

The attack was over as quickly as it had begun. If not for the arrows still sticking out of the cottage wall and the sting in his arm, Nicholas might have thought he dreamed it.

Adam and Spencer were tying ropes around two unconscious men when Nicholas joined them by the dying fire.

"Are they—"

"They're alive. Though they might wish they weren't when they wake."

"Nicholas?" A soft hand touched his arm. "You're bleeding. You too, Spencer."

Rose. Nicholas would have preferred she sleep through this. He opened his mouth to tell her to return to the cottage but she was already stalking away. She was in the cottage for less than twenty seconds before walking out again, bandages in hand, Quin close behind.

"Sit," she ordered Spencer. He shook his head.

"I'm fine, Rose."

"You're not fine." She pointed to the blood blotching the fabric of his left leg and raised her eyebrows.

"He nicked my leg. It's stopped bleeding already."

"It could fester."

"And there could be more assailants in the trees. Let me protect you, princess, and *then* I'll let you bandage me up."

Though Rose frowned, she did as she was told, turning her attention to Nicholas. His sleeve was already torn from the arrow, but she tore it further, pulling pieces of thread from the wound before winding a bandage around it.

"Quin." Adam gestured for the maid to join him before pointing to the men bound and unconscious on the ground. "Are either of them him? The man who was in Rose's chamber that night?"

"What?" Rose's protest was loud. Shocked. Quin cringed, guilt written across her face, but held Adam's gaze.

"I don't know." She nodded at one of the men. "He might be. He's the right build. But so are many men. I never saw the man's face. He had a scarf over it."

"Then she could still be in danger."

Rose jerked Nicholas's arm, tying the bandage tight enough to make him wince. "Explain," Rose demanded. "Now."

There was silence around the circle of friends as they all looked from one to another, hoping someone else might speak. Or perhaps that was only Nicholas. Gone was the woman who'd sighed into his kiss and thanked him for the stars only minutes ago. In her place stood a woman who was every bit a queen. Her hands fisted as her glare turned fierce, disapproval curdling the memory of their kiss.

"That's why you married me. Why Father was so eager to see me gone. It had nothing to do with the war. Someone tried to kill me."

No, that wasn't it at all. The impetus, but not the reason. "Rose—"

"And none of you planned to tell me."

"Rose—"

"Because I'm weak? Is that what it is? Rose is too weak to handle the information that someone tried to kill her so we'll just marry her off to a stranger and send her away. I should have known."

Her voice shook with fury. Or was it betrayal? Nicholas looked at the other three. Quin played with a strip of bandage, first winding then unwinding it around her fingers. Spencer and Adam faced away from the fire, their attention on their surroundings, though Nicholas knew they had to be listening. He'd get no help from any of them.

"Rose—"

She flung her hands out, the move throwing her balance before she caught herself. She glared when he moved to assist. He sat down again.

"What? I'm wrong? No one tried to kill me? My father didn't rush our wedding because he was scared? You're going to tell me our wedding was real and truly what you wanted?"

"Yes, it was."

Rose shook her head. "You're more noble than Aldon, I'll concur, and perhaps when I've had some sleep I'll thank you for that, but I don't need someone to save me. Least of all the man I thought cared." She called Spencer's name, ignoring Nicholas. "We're leaving, I assume?" Spencer nodded. "I'll pack our things."

CHAPTER 28

"The spies have returned, Your Majesty."

Lior nodded. He'd seen them arrive from the tower. He could have gone right to them to demand answers but refrained. It wouldn't help their anonymity any to have the king meet them at the castle gate. He'd known their news would reach him soon enough.

"And?"

Manning surveyed the grounds below them as Lior had been doing for the past hour. The knight was unhurried with his report. Whether that was because there wasn't much to report or simply because the man was gathering his thoughts was still to be discovered. Lior had always appreciated Manning's calmness and wisdom in times of upheaval. Of which there had been a number in the past five years.

"There are Cavendish men in the forest."

"How many?"

"Not an army."

"But?" There was something in his friend's tone that made Lior certain there was more to the story.

"Enough to cause trouble."

How much trouble remained the question playing on Lior's mind. "Don't engage them but set men to keep watch over them."

"Aye."

War felt more inevitable by the day, but Lior wouldn't be the one to start it. War meant death. Lives altered. Boys becoming men before their time. If Cormac started it, Raedonleith would have to engage but the longer Lior could put it off, the better.

"What of the man who tried to attack Rose?"

"Nothing to report, sire. It was like he vanished into the night."

"I wish I knew who sent him."

"You know who did."

Aye. Cormac. "I don't want it to be him."

"But you can't deny it is."

Though it felt like a lance through Lior's heart to condemn the man he'd once called friend, Manning was right. Lior spun around, stalking toward the stairs, hating that it had come to this. Twenty years. Twenty years he'd offered peace when Cormac wanted war. Twenty years he'd offered forgiveness when Cormac hurt him. Twenty years he'd prayed. That Cormac's heart would change. That he'd let the pain go. The bitterness.

Lior should give up on his once friend. He knew that. Twenty years was a long time to hold on to hope when no hope was to be found. It was foolish, even weak, by some people's—many people's—definition. No doubt they thought Lior should have killed the man when he had the chance. There had been plenty of chances.

But he couldn't. Wouldn't. Not while there was still hope.

"There's something else, too." Manning said. "Rose and Nicholas never made it to Aiyana's cottage."

CHAPTER
29

The break in the rhythm of Milori's hooves was what woke Rose, Spencer's shout coming a second later. A second too late to brace herself. She was falling. Nicholas along with her.

Wind rushed past her ears. Her mind hadn't even processed the screams around her when she hit the ground. Hard. She couldn't breathe. Couldn't move. A whinny rent the air. Piercing. Pained.

"Rose, no—"

A body rolled atop of hers. Her vision grew blurry. Air. She needed air.

Then, weight. Too much weight. And screams. Quin. Spencer.

Where was Nicholas? She wanted Nicholas. She was furious at him and the secrets he'd kept but as darkness clawed at her vision and she fought to figure out which way was up, he was all she wanted. He would help her breathe. He would become her breath.

If only she could find him.

﹡﹡﹡

"Rose. Rose, you have to wake."

The air felt foggy. Wet, against her face.

"Please. Please. Rose, please. Wake."

A hand brushed over her hair. Small. Female, to match the voice. Quin?

Her eyelids flickered, the light too bright to keep them open for long. Was it morning? It had been... Had been...

"Please, Rose. I beg you."

Night. It had been night. Images came rushing back through her mind. Adam lifting her onto Nicholas's horse. Nicholas's arms bracing her. The taste of blood when she bit her lip too hard in an attempt to keep furious tears at bay. His whispered words she'd tried to ignore. Being tossed through the air. Struggling to breathe. Pressure. In her head. On her chest. She must have fainted. But for it to now be daylight. She had just fainted, hadn't she?

"I'm awake."

"Oh, praise be the Almighty."

Quin's cheeks were wet with unchecked tears. Rose put a hand against the grass and tried to pull herself up. An army of aches made her wince. It was her back this time, and elbow. Hip? Not her stomach, thank the Almighty. Her head hurt too. Quin put a hand behind Rose's back, assisting her to sit. Though Rose's head spun, she managed to stay upright.

"What happened?"

"Your horse stumbled in a hole and threw you and the prince. You landed hard. The horse would have fallen on you if Prince Nicholas hadn't protected you. The man was injured already and still put himself between you and the horse."

"Where is he?" She looked around.

"Prince Nicholas?"

"Yes, Nicholas." Who else would she be asking after?

"He hasn't woken."

"What?"

"He...hit a rock. When he fell. It gashed his side. Then the horse..."

The horse fell on him. Because he'd moved to save her. Of course he had. Her husband was going to kill himself trying to protect her.

"We cleaned him up best we could but—"

"Take me to him."

"You're not well either."

"I need to see him." Her voice broke, emotion clogging her throat. He'd thrown himself in front of a horse for her. Taken the wounds which should have been hers. Even after she'd thrown his words and love back in his face. She owed him so much more than her life.

When Quin continued to hesitate, Rose struggled to her feet. Higher now, she could see where Nicholas lay several yards away at the base of a tree, a blanket attached to sticks forming a shelter above him. She stumbled to his side, a hand going to her mouth as she fell to her knees.

"Tell me," she begged Spencer, praying he understood her terse words. She couldn't have pushed out anymore, not without collapsing into a mess of tears. Nicholas looked terrible.

There was a bruise across the left side of his face and, though his nose was still straight, it too was swollen and red. His tunic had been removed and a thick bandage wrapped around his chest and arm. In any other circumstance, Rose might have appreciated the sight of his muscled shoulders, but his face was too pale and his breathing too shallow for her to do anything but beg the Almighty to spare his life.

"He's bad," Spencer said, "but don't doubt his strength."

"Quin said he hadn't woken."

"He hasn't."

"Then how do you know he doesn't have worse injuries? His head? His mind? Inside him?"

"We don't."

Rose heard what Spencer refused to say. Nicholas could die. Perhaps he already was dying.

This was too much. Rose's heart thudded, pounding in her ears. Her fingers. Her stomach. She wanted to curl up into a ball, or scream, or—

The panic welled, rushing through her mind, blocking everything but its cry.

No, no, no, no, no. Don't take him. Don't take him. Please, Almighty. Don't take him.

Fear pressed like a stone against her chest.

Breathe, Rose. Count—something.

There were three strands of hair brushing Nicholas's forehead. Three specks of dirt beside them. The cloak he lay upon was a blue so dark it looked black in the shade. Thirty-two stitches closed the hole he'd torn in the bottom of it. She knew. She'd sewed every one of them.

"Lady Rose?"

His name had eight letters. Two the same as hers. His title gave him another six.

An ant crawled near his bandage. She brushed it away, hating the way her hand shook.

"Rose."

He could die. This man who'd promised he'd never leave her. The one she'd just begun to believe.

No.

She wasn't going to let that happen. Not when it was within her power to do something about it. He'd picked her up more times than she cared to count. Now it was her turn.

"We're going back to Raedonleith."

"No. Your father—"

"We can and we will. You'll take Nicholas on your horse. I'll ride with Quin. Adam can go ahead to warn them of our arrival. We'll ride through the night if need be. Nicholas needs a healer. We're closest to Raedonleith." Thanks to how slow a traveler she'd turned out to be. "Aiyana will be able to help him. My mother too. You know I'm right."

"We can't move him. Not yet. Not until we know more. 'Tis too dangerous. We left those men tied up, but they'll find their way out. They could be on our tail even now. Neither Adam nor I are leaving you."

"So you'll just let him die?"

"My lady—"

She was not going to lose this. She couldn't. Wouldn't. Though her stomach quailed at the thought of getting back on a horse, she could do it. For Nicholas.

"This is not a discussion, nor will you talk me out of it. Nicholas needs help and Raedonleith is the closest town with healers I trust. We leave now."

"No."

"No? *No?* You can't tell me no. I won't have it. I am your future queen. You will do what I say."

Spencer shook his head, the sympathy on his face pressing tears to Rose's eyes. She didn't want his kindness or his understanding. She wanted his action. Adam and Spencer had fought and won against those two assailants, however many hours ago it had been, but what was the point in winning if they were just going to lay down and die now?

"I know you want to help him, Rose. I do too. But he could die if we move him."

"He could die if we don't." She brushed a hand across Nicholas's forehead. He was so pale. "Please, Spencer. I have to do something. I can't—can't—"

"I'm sorry. I know it's not what you want but when I pledged my loyalty to your father, I promised to do all in my power to protect his people. I'll send Adam for help but the rest of us stay. I can't hold an unconscious man on a horse and protect you at the same time."

"You don't need to protect me."

"Nicholas would have my head if I didn't."

"He won't know."

"He will if you die too."

But—

"We stay, Lady Rose. And if your father revokes my knighthood for going against your wishes, then so be it. At least I will have done all in my power to keep you and the prince alive."

"Spencer—"

"If his condition doesn't change overnight, we'll ride for Raedonleith at dawn tomorrow."

"You promise?"

"I do."

                       ❧

Nicholas hadn't woken. Neither had the fever which started late in the afternoon abated. He was restless in his sleep—a sure sign that he was alive but not that he was well. Rose wished she had some herbs to give him or that there was something she could do to help but she couldn't have gotten the herbs into him even if she had known which to use. Once again, she was completely useless.

No. Not useless. She was praying. Over and over, the same two words.

Heal him.

Heal him.

Heal him.

With every breath she breathed, every beat of her heart.

Heal him.

She had to believe the Almighty would. Because if she didn't? Then this whole week had been nothing but a waste. Their marriage, their leaving Raedonleith, the days in the cottage, the journey at all. A waste of time and...lives. Nicholas's life. Because he wouldn't have been in danger without her. He wouldn't have even left Belairisia. A home he might never see again.

Nicholas moaned. Rose brushed a hand across his forehead. Still burning. How long could one burn with fever before it caused permanent damage? A boy in the village had raged with fever once. It had lasted three days and left him blind. Rose knew of too many others who'd died from theirs.

Heal him. Please, Almighty, heal him.

And if you won't, at least break the fever.

Hours passed as Rose lay beside Nicholas, begging the Almighty to spare his life. And with every hour that passed, Rose grew more impatient. He wasn't getting better, and he wouldn't *get* better without a healer. If she were Mykah, she would have left already. Saddled her own horse, ridden through the night.

She wasn't Mykah.

She put a hand to Nicholas's forehead, his skin scalding her as she brushed back his hair. What she wouldn't give to see his blue gaze again.

"Nicholas, please. Wake up. I need you."

She shivered as a brace of a breeze flew over them. She'd given all her blankets to Nicholas, to make him a comfortable bed. He would have argued had he known, told her he wanted none of them if it took them from her. She laid her hand against his cheek. From the day she met Nicholas, he'd been giving everything for her. Blankets, food, affection, time, patience. And she'd thrown it all right back in his face.

"You should see the stars. I wish you would. Open your eyes, put your arm around me. We could share a blanket again and look at the stars. There are so many of them tonight, and not a cloud in sight." Perhaps they'd even see a shooting star. A glimpse of the eternal in the unfathomable expanse of the night sky. "You could tell me the rest of the ballad about the man so unworthy and the woman he loved."

It had to be close to dawn, surely, and yet the sky was as black as ever. Not even a hint of blue or purple peeked through the trees. Would this night never end? How could the others sleep? Spencer had kept watch for hours before succumbing to exhaustion. Rose should have woken him but hadn't seen the need. She was awake, with no chance of sleeping. She could alert Spencer and Quin if there was danger.

As if anything that came could be worse that what they already faced.

"Don't die, Nicholas. Please. I want to stay with you. I want to stand beside you as you lead your people. Be your wife, for as long as the Almighty gives us. I shouldn't. I know. It's not fair to you. But it turns out

I'm selfish. I want you. I want to believe you won't leave me. That you'll catch me each time I fall, just like you promised." Her fingers caught on his ear as she stroked a hand over his hair. His hair was soft. Softer than she'd expected. Like the heart that lay behind Belairisia's crown prince. The one who gave and gave and gave some more, asking for nothing in return but that she accept it. "I love you."

"Sweet Rose."

Her hand dropped at Nicholas's whisper, wondering a second later if she imagined it. He'd not moved, not opened his eyes.

"Nicholas? Nicholas? Can you hear me?"

No more sound came. No more movement either. If his chest hadn't been moving under her hand, she would have worried he'd passed. She couldn't bear that.

Couldn't bear this. The waiting. The wondering. The helplessness. Nicholas might be dying, and here she simply sat and watched.

No more.

There was another castle, closer than Raedonleith. Rose had never been there, but Evangeline had. And, in the castle full of enemies, Evangeline had found a friend.

Maeve. A servant, but a kind one. Evangeline spoke often of her loyalty and friendship. Maeve would help Rose. Help Nicholas. Spencer was brave and wise and strong, but as he'd said, he was just one man. They needed help, and they needed it now.

It was dangerous. Evangeline had gone into the castle one person and come out very different. If not for Darrek and her father, she might not have come out at all. But Rose was desperate. And determined. This enmity between Lord Cavendish and her father had gone on too long.

If Mykah could be brave, so could Rose.

But first—

Rose crept over to the saddlebags, pulling free a scrap of parchment and ink, scratching out a message. It was messy, barely legible in her rush to get the message down while nervous energy made her hand tremble, but clear enough. Her crown was next, catching on the fabric as she tugged it free of its velvet bag. They'd brought it to prove her title. A title she no longer had need of. A lump lodged in her throat as she held it. She was leaving behind more than a simple gold crown, but it was right. It had to be done. And she was the only one who could do it.

Almighty, give me strength. Be with me as I ride. Let my life not be in vain.

Her slippers were silent in the grass as she left the note on the blanket still bunched from her wrestling thoughts. Rose wrapped a cloak around her shoulders, pulling the clasp tight. She wore her thickest gown, but even so, she shivered. It wasn't the temperature that plagued her but fear. That Spencer would wake and stop her. That she'd lose her way. That Nicholas would die before she saw him again. That she wouldn't be enough.

But she wouldn't let fear stop her. Mykah didn't. Evangeline hadn't either. They were strong. Courageous.

Everything Rose wasn't.

Usually.

Emotion welled in Rose's chest as she stared down at the man who'd so wholly and quickly stolen her heart. She could do this for him.

It was proof of how exhausted Spencer and Quin were that neither of them woke as Rose saddled and mounted Strider, grateful to find a steady rock high enough for her to use.

Almighty, lead me to the castle. Give me strength to get there. And please, Almighty please, let this not be a fool's errand.

Sleep bit at her eyes. Fear pressed against her sides. The chill of the night had her shivering. But she refused to look back. Forward was the only way. She had to do something.

She rode for what felt like hours, back aching from the strain but her heart hurting far more. She couldn't lose Nicholas. Not when it was her fault he was injured.

Almighty, guard my steps. Lead me on. Show me the way.

The sky changed from black to purple, streaks of orange peeked through the gaps in the trees. Paths grew wider. Through the morning haze she could just make out the top of a stone tower in the distance. Rose breathed a sigh of relief. She was going the right way. Now, if she could just—

A dagger of pain shot through her stomach. She gasped. Curled in on herself before forcing her back to straighten. One deep breath. Another. She was almost there. Stone walls joined the tower, marking their place. A few more minutes. She could hold the pain at bay that long.

Almighty, hold me tight. Keep me safe. Make me strong.

Her head swirled with the strength it took to hold herself upright. Her stomach throbbed. A shout came from her left. Or was it her right? Horse hooves clattered on the hardened path, growing louder the closer they came. Spencer must have caught up with her. Good. He could—could—

She blinked. Swayed.

"You there—"

Oh. Oh no. Strider's reins slipped from Rose's trembling hands. Her breath caught in her throat. That wasn't Spencer.

A glove clamped on her arm.

"What have we here?"

CHAPTER 30

It was the ache in Rose's shoulder that woke her. The dank, cold room before her made her wish she hadn't. A thin blanket lay beside her, as if someone had had enough compassion to want her to be warm but not enough to lay it over her. A cup of tepid water sat nearby. Though her throat begged for something wet, the dirt floating atop the liquid stayed her hand. She'd take a dry throat over death. Though, looking around her, that option may have been taken from her.

She leaned against the wall, wrapping the blanket around her legs. She shouldn't let herself cry. Who knew when she might be fed again? Or given something decent to drink. A tear dripped down her cheek anyway.

Almighty?

What had she been thinking? She couldn't save Nicholas. She couldn't even save herself. She wasn't Mykah. Wasn't Evangeline either. Evangeline would have charmed her way out. Mykah wouldn't have been fool enough to be caught in the first place. But Rose?

Rose was too weak to fight. Too weak to ride a horse. Too weak to stand or lead or love. She could pray, of course, but what was the point? None of her prayers had been answered. She should thank the Almighty for the breath in her lungs, the strength for today, the goodness of his love. But it felt like a lie. Hope felt too far. The Almighty too. All her life, she'd believed in his goodness, his faithfulness. He'd stayed by her side when others had walked away. Understood her, when no one else had. Flooded her heart with hope when despair tried to pull her under.

She should believe. She should hold onto those moments. Those certainties. If the Almighty could save her once, he could save her again. But—

I can't. I'm sorry.

Her strength had finally given out. The hand over hand of holding on had become too much. She'd slipped. Fallen. Failed.

How long had she been in here? Hours? A day? It was impossible to know with no windows or doors to let in light. Sconces on the walls held torches, with just enough of them lit to illuminate the hopelessness around her.

Sound echoed down the hallway. Footsteps, the clanking of a door, voices. Rose pulled herself upright, ignoring the protests of her aching body. But the voices faded away, the footsteps receded. No one came to the depths of the dungeon. Rose's stomach lurched, sending bile up her throat. She just made it to the bucket in the corner in time to lose what little there was in her stomach. She clutched her sides as the retching went on and on despite nothing coming out. Tears burned her cheeks. Her lungs burned too. When at last her stomach stilled, Rose bunched the blanket into a lump, lay her head on it, and curled into a ball of misery.

─ ⋆⋆⋆ ─

"Rose. Rose."

Nicholas's voice whispered through the darkness. Rose opened her eyes before closing them again. A dream. Just another dream. There had been so many of them since Rose woke to find herself in the dungeon. She drifted in and out of sleep, in and out of dreams, so weak in both body and spirit that she couldn't tell anymore which were real and which weren't. Sometimes he was kind. Sometimes he betrayed her. Sometimes she tried to stay asleep just so he would stay, and she wouldn't feel so alone.

Even the Almighty felt far down here.

"Lady Rose."

Not Nicholas's voice. A woman's. Soft, like Mother's. Oh how Rose wished she were at home, wrapped in her Mother's quilts, snuggled in a chair by the fire. Warm. Loved. Safe.

"Lady Rose!"

Someone was shaking her shoulder. Rose gasped as a streak of pain ripped across it, waking her fully. Sudden brightness had her shading her eyes. Not a dream.

"Move the torch."

The brightness dimmed.

"Can you stand?"

Stand? She could barely breathe. Who was this woman? Friend? Foe? Another person who'd dared to oppose Lord Cavendish? Rose squinted through the fingers she held over her eyes. The woman was older, dressed in simple servants' garb, a once-white apron tied about her ample middle. Her brown hair was threaded with gray. Rose couldn't make out any details of the shadow of a man behind the lantern except his height.

"I know you're in pain, but we need to leave. Now. I don't know why you came to Cavendish Castle, but you can't be here. You're in danger. Cormac is not thinking clearly."

"Who are you?" The words felt strange on her lips, the voice dry like her throat.

"Maeve. And this is George," the woman said with a nod to the man with the torch. "A friend of Darrek's."

Which immediately made him a friend of Rose's too, as Maeve must have known. Maeve. Rose had found her. Or rather, Maeve had found Rose.

"You're helping me escape?"

"Well I'm certainly not helping Cormac kill you. I was silent once when I should have spoken, and your sister paid the price. I won't do that again."

"Thank you."

"Thank me when you're free. Come on. We don't have much time."

Her first step almost sent her to the floor. George frowned, sending a wave of shame through Rose's already weary body. How she hated being so weak. She looked away. Let the man judge her. He wouldn't be the first. But no condemnation came from the tall man. Instead, George handed the torch to Maeve and put an arm around Rose's waist, offering his shoulder for her to lean on.

"This way."

Stone walls passed in a blur of keeping herself upright as Rose followed Maeve along a passageway, up a flight of stairs, through several doors, up another flight of stairs and—finally—through a heavy, wooden door. Dark sky filled with a million stars greeted Rose along with a burst of brisk air that sent a shiver through her body. She would have paused to breathe in the freedom if Maeve hadn't tugged them onward.

"Don't stop. You're not safe yet. Far from it."

"Maeve—"

"Shh. Not here."

The castle grounds were as silent as they were empty, like Raedon-leith when Rose looked down on it from the tower just before dawn. Rose couldn't see who they were hiding from, she didn't doubt that there would be guards around, and that Maeve knew who and where they were. Evangeline had said her friend had been a servant at Cavendish Castle for more than twenty years.

Though she stumbled several more times, Rose made it to the stable door George held open without falling. Maeve followed her through, closing it behind them. Rose collapsed onto a bale of straw, lungs burning as if she'd fought with a sword for hours.

"Here."

A piece of cloth hit Rose's face. Dust motes danced around it making her sneeze. She picked up the cloth. A black cloak. Completely un-adorned.

"It'll be big on you but it's warm and dry," Maeve said.

"Thank you."

"And here's some bread. It's not much but—" Her voice trembled, her smile with it. With a gasp of a sob, she knelt and wrapped Rose in an embrace. "Lady Rose. I can't believe it's really you. I haven't seen you since you were a babe."

"You know me?"

"Your father and mother came to visit Cavendish Castle not long after you were born. They brought you with them. I'd never seen a child so perfect. Your lips were like little rosebuds and your eyes— Even as a babe, your gaze slayed hearts."

"I didn't know—"

"When I heard Cormac had you in the dungeon, it was all I could do to wait until night to set you free. You must have been so scared. I'm sorry, Lady Rose. So sorry I didn't come earlier. I knew it was best that I wait until he slept—Cormac isn't himself and I couldn't risk him or any of his guards hurting you out of spite—but I hated to leave you there. The dungeon is no place for a lady. It's no place for anyone.

"You can rest here for a few hours. George will protect you but I think it's best you—"

"I can't stay." Rose shook her head. "Thank you for rescuing me but I can't stay. I came to ask for help. Yours and—" She looked at George, silent as he watched the two of them. "—anyone else willing to help. I came to Cavendish Castle to find you, Maeve. I knew it was dangerous, but I had to—" Had to try. She took a steadying breath. "Nicholas, my h-husband, he was thrown from a horse. He's hurt badly and Raedonleith was too far. Spencer wouldn't let us move him and—"

"Sir Spencer? Darrek's friend?" George asked.

"Yes." Of course. Spencer had been one of the knights Father had sent to bring Evangeline home. Adam too. George would have known them. "Someone tried to—" Her voice caught, the truth still difficult to believe. "Someone tried to kill me. Spencer, Adam and Nicholas were taking me to safety. But our horse stepped wrong, and we were thrown, and Nicholas rolled to save me and it's my fault. He wouldn't be hurt if not for me. I have to get him to a healer, but Spencer can't protect us on his own and carry Nicholas too and Adam went to get help, but he'll be gone too long, and I don't know what to do so I came to you for help but was caught before I could reach you." Tears clogged her throat. "I don't even know if he's still alive."

The stable door flung open, clattering against the wall. A man stepped through, sword in hand, fury on his face.

"Cormac." Maeve moved to stand in front of Rose, blocking her view, though not her hearing. George faded into the shadows.

"You thought you could take her from me?"

"You're drunk, Cormac."

"Not so much that I don't know what you did. You took her. Just like that fool took Cara. And Eva. But not this time. Not this time. She's mine. Rose is *mine*."

"She's not yours. She never has been."

The crack of a hand against skin made Rose's eyes water, though it was Maeve who Cavendish hit. The maid reared sideways but held her ground.

"Don't do this," Maeve begged. "You're better than this. I know you are."

Cavendish paused in an endless moment of hope before wrenching Rose's arm and throwing her into one his guards. "Take her to my chamber. The maid goes to the dungeon."

CHAPTER
31

I have Rose.

The paper shook in Lior's hands, the words too blurred by fear to read anymore. The missive had arrived two hours ago, only minutes after Spencer had arrived at the healer's cottage with an unconscious Prince Nicholas in tow. The castle was in uproar.

It was Evangeline all over again. The fear, the helplessness, the failure. He'd sent Rose away to protect her. She should have been safe. Not locked up in Cavendish Castle. Or worse. Held within Cormac Cavendish's clutches.

I have Rose.

Lior should have stayed to hear Spencer's report but he'd come to the chapel instead. Laid down his sword and knelt before the altar. Begged the Almighty for wisdom. He didn't want to start a war, but did he have a choice? Cormac had Rose.

Almighty, she's my daughter. My heir. My love.

I tried so hard to protect her. But everything—

A sob gripped his chest, crumbling him forward.

Everything I do goes wrong. Cormac, Evangeline, Mykah, Rose. I tried to save them. Asked for wisdom and walked forward in faith but—

It wasn't enough. They still got hurt.

Night pulled around Lior, candles growing low as he prayed. Wept. Begged.

For his family. His people. His friend.

For forgiveness. For wisdom. For strength.

That he might be the king *his* King had called him to be.

That he might be the father his daughters needed, and the husband he'd promised his wife he'd be.

But mostly, that he'd be a man of honor, remembered not for his power or might but for his heart.

As the sun poked fingers of light through the stained-glass windows above him marking a new day, Lior finally rose, brushed off his knees, sheathed his sword, and walked outside. He didn't know what this day would hold, or if he'd live to see another but there was one thing he did know.

The time had come to fight.

CHAPTER
32

There were noises around him. Not birds or horses or wind rustling the trees but women's voices, something being stirred in a metal cup, a door closing? Was he indoors? Nicholas twitched the fingers by his side just enough to feel. Cotton-covered straw. Rough wooden frame. Not the blanket over grass or dirt he'd become accustomed to but a bed. He was lying in a bed. Why? How?

A shadow loomed, giving him a three second warning before a hand touched his forehead.

"Shouldn't he be waking by now?"

A woman's voice. She was the shadow, the hand on his forehead. Rose? No. The hand was too rough, the voice similar but not right.

"Patience, Mykah. He'll wake when he wakes. You know that."

"But it's been four days."

Four days?

Nicholas opened his eyes, startling the woman still leaning over him.

"Prince Nicholas! Thank the Almighty."

"Where am I? Where's Rose?" he asked, trying to rise. To remember. Rose had been thrown. The horse had been falling, right toward her. He'd rolled. Pushed her aside. And— Nothing.

"You're in Raedonleith."

"Raedonleith? No. We have to leave. It's not safe."

"You're not going anywhere," a second voice said.

"I have to. We can't be here." King Lior had specifically tasked him with taking Rose far from the dangers at Raedonleith. Nicholas's head spun as he tried again to rise.

"I'll get Spencer," Lady Mykah said, walking out of Nicholas's line of sight. Another woman stepped forward to take Lady Mykah's place. This one was older, his parents' age, Nicholas would guess. Her clothing was plain, but well-made and clean. She carried a definite air of authority and knowledge in the way she rattled off questions, completely ignoring his own.

"How's your head? Fever's finally gone so that's good. Arms? Ribs? I'll wager you cracked a few when you were thrown, or when the horse landed on you. Mercy of the Almighty you weren't awake for the ride here with the way you were bouncing about atop Sir Spencer's horse when you arrived. Pain anywhere else I need to know about?"

How the woman thought he'd get an answer in amid her muttering, he didn't know. With her assistance, he sat in the bed, hating that he needed the help. He gasped and clutched a hand to his chest. She was right about the ribs. They hurt. A lot. His head pounded too, though it was a dull ache. There, painful, but not so demanding of his attention as the rest of his body.

For the first time in his life, Nicholas wished he'd been a knight, or at least trained and kept his body at peak performance like one. Maybe then he wouldn't be in so much pain. He felt like he'd slogged his way up a mountain, and then fallen off the top, catching every stone and tree branch and cliff face on the way down. And then the mountain had fallen on him. For good measure. He couldn't decide what was worse—the burning behind his eyes, the fire in his ribs, or the overwhelming urge to dispel everything from his stomach. Which he was trying his best to quell because it would set every nerve and muscle ablaze if he gave in to it.

Pain. Pain. More pain. It was all he knew. It was enough to make a man want to surrender back into the oblivion he'd tried so hard to fight his way out of.

"I'm fine." He might have laughed at the absurdity of such a comment given the way his body screamed the opposite but it wasn't a lie. For the first time he fully appreciated the vagueness of Rose's favorite answer. He'd live. Right now that was the line by which he judged his pain. There were far more important things on his mind. One more than the rest. "Where's Rose?"

"Drink this," the healer said, handing him a steaming cup which smelled similar to the concoctions Quin made for Rose.

He pushed it aside. "Not until you answer me."

"You need your strength."

"I need my wife."

The door opened to admit Spencer. He looked as broken as Nicholas felt and a far cry from his usual steady confidence. Worry added a churning stomach to the rest of Nicholas's injuries.

"Nicholas," Spencer said, trying a smile that faltered as fast as it formed. "I'm sorry. It's my fault."

No.

"Where's Rose?"

The knight hesitated only a second before answering. "Cavendish Castle."

"What?"

"I fell asleep. I should have been watching. She was gone when I woke. She left—She left—" His voice caught. His head dropped, shame coating him. He pushed something into Nicholas's hands. Rose's crown. And a note.

> *My dearest Nicholas,*
> *Forgive me. I know you'd try to stop me if you could, and you'd be right to, but I have to do this. I have to save you. At the very least, I have to try.*
> *Give my crown to Mykah. She's a far better queen than I could ever be. I hereby relinquish my claim to the throne of Raedonleith. Should we both come through this alive, the only king I wish to stand beside is you.*
> *Rose*

He read the short note several times, heart thudding more with each reading. It read like a goodbye, and yet, that last line. *The only king I wish to stand beside is you.*

"We have to rescue her."

"You're too weak," the healer argued.

Nicholas shook his head, wondering how many times his wife had been told the same. How many times she'd believed it of herself. Not today. It took strength to write a note like the one he held, strength to walk into the unknown, strength to walk away for the sake of someone you loved. And she did love him. It was written in every word of the letter he held. In every action he'd witnessed. She was strong, without a doubt. And now it was his turn.

"I'm strong enough."

The healer didn't agree.

"You've several broken ribs, the remnants of a concussion, a split in your head, and are clearly not thinking straight if you're considering getting back on a horse so soon. The king left for Cavendish Castle this morning with every man able to wield a weapon. When the battle's done, he'll bring her home. You're to rest and that's all there is to it."

"No."

"You don't believe me?"

"I believe you but I made my wife a promise to stay, no matter what. If Rose is at Cavendish Castle, then that's where I need to be. King Lior has a war to wage and I'll not be resting while he does so."

"You've no fear of Lord Cavendish?" the healer asked.

"He's only one man."

"Yes," she replied. "He is." She considered Nicholas for a few moments before walking to the other side of the cottage and staring out the window. Nicholas turned to Spencer.

"Come with me."

"You still trust me?"

"There's no knight I trust more."

Spencer bowed his head. "Thank you, sire. It would be my honor to accompany you. I will not let you down a second time."

Nicholas wanted to assure the knight that he'd not let Nicholas down a first time but knew Spencer wouldn't accept it. Nicholas wouldn't have either had their situations been reversed. Instead, he simply nodded.

"I'm coming too."

Nicholas looked in surprise at the healer. "I thought—"

"You're going to need me to remove those stitches in your head in a week and who knows what other trouble you'll encounter along the way. You shouldn't be traveling at all in your state but if you're going to be all noble and insist, I will at the very least be there to patch you up when you fall apart. And there's no saying what state Rose will be in when you—" She swallowed. "When you find her."

A pain that went far beyond the physical clutched at Nicholas's lungs, pressing breath from them. *What state Rose will be in.* Spencer, Adam and the king all believed Lord Cavendish had sent the man to kill Rose, and now she was within his clutches. Was she already dead?

No.

He couldn't think that. This wasn't the end of their story. Until he saw with his eyes that hope was gone, he'd cling to it with all the strength the Almighty gave him. As Rose did. Every day.

"And as you said, Cormac Cavendish is just one man. One man I've allowed to rule through fear for far too long. No more." The woman rubbed her hands on her apron and gave a decisive nod. "No more."

Nicholas turned to Spencer. His confusion must have shown because Spencer smiled and moved to stand beside the older woman. "Prince Nicholas, may I present to you Lady Aiyana Cavendish, once known as Lady Sunny. Lord Cormac Cavendish's older sister."

The noble lady turned healer. The one whose house had been their destination. In his pain-induced fog, Nicholas had forgotten the connection. "You're his sister."

"Aye, for what it's worth. I'm not sure I deserve the title, but someone once told me it's never too late to start again."

"I'm coming too," Lady Mykah said, walking back inside. Her black cloak did little to hide the weapons she wore, nor the determination on her face. "I was going to give you privacy but—"

"You've never given anyone privacy in your life," Aiyana said, her voice wry.

"How can I help people if I don't know what they need?" Mykah said with a grin. "I heard it all. You're going to Cavendish Castle and I'm coming too. Enough of this nonsense about me being not allowed to fight because I'm a woman and newly married and all. My husband is there, my sister and father too. I'm coming."

"Me too, if you'll have me," Quin said.

"No," Spencer was quick to argue, fear on his face that wasn't there before. "You're safer here."

Quin quirked her eyebrow but didn't back down. "We all are, but staying won't help Rose. She'll need me."

"She'll need us all," Nicholas said quietly, silencing Spencer before he could argue further.

He looked around the circle of people. One knight, one injured prince, one well-armed princess, one healer and one maid. Hardly the fear-inducing army they should have been taking to storm the castle and rescue their princess, but this group had something stronger. Without even asking, Nicholas knew that every one of them would give their life to rescue Rose. They would fight, as long as it took. They wouldn't come home without her. Nicholas couldn't think of anyone better to have by his side.

He nodded and dropped his feet over the edge of the bed, waiting for the dizziness to clear his head before standing. "Then let's go."

CHAPTER 33

Warmth crept through the chamber's mottled glass window, throwing gold across the floor and making the woven floor mat where Rose knelt glow. With its glassed windows, bold tapestries and high four post bed, the room might have been more opulent than any she'd ever been in, but Lord Cavendish's room was no less a prison than the dungeon had been.

Her knees ached from hours spent in prayer but not as deeply as her heart. She'd failed them. Nicholas. Her father. Maeve. Why had she thought she could save them? Love had spurred her hope only to have reality splinter it to pieces.

She was no savior, only a broken woman.

She clasped her hands together and prayed, heart crying out to the only one who could hear.

Here I am again, on my knees before you. I've nothing to offer, no reason you should listen and yet, I know you do.

Forgive me. For my stubbornness. For doubting your goodness. For throwing back at you every gift you've given me. My family, my faith, my home, Quin.

Nicholas.

If I die in this room, let him live. Let him move on. Bring him love, someone to care. Someone who won't hold back as I did, until it's too late.

Was it too late? *Almighty, let it not be too late. I'm sorry. So sorry for doubting you. For not realizing what a gift he was.* A man comfortable with quiet, who didn't run in disgust when she was ill but wiped her face, held her close. A man more at peace in books and chapels than at tournaments, who couldn't sing any better than her but would do it, just for the chance to dance with her. Who spoke in ballads and beauty and taught her to hope again.

She touched the gold bracelet on her wrist, running her finger over the engraved word. *I love him. I do. I thought I was protecting myself from hurt by pushing him away, but I was hurting us both. Forgive me, Almighty, for doubting. For fearing when I should have believed. I don't know if I'll ever leave this room, nor see Nicholas again, but if I do, I promise I'll do better.*

Rose's stomach grumbled, hunger battling her churning nerves for supremacy.

Three days she'd been here. Three days she'd been alone, having seen no other person. Servant, guard, or master. Some fruit in a bowl on the side table and a half-jug of ale had replenished some of her strength, though she'd finished the last of them last night. She'd had nothing to eat or drink today.

She'd not slept the first night, certain any moment Lord Cavendish would burst through the door and follow through with his threat. *Mine,* he'd said. Rose knew too much of Evangeline's story to mistake Lord Cavendish's meaning.

He hadn't come. Not that night, not the next day when she'd finally succumbed to a restless sleep, not the next. There were guards at the door—she'd heard them speak, wondering when their master would claim the prize he so carefully kept—but the door didn't open.

A wave of dizziness tipped Rose forward. Her courses had ended, thank the Almighty, but the weariness and nausea remained. She'd been ill thrice. The room stank of it, no maids having come to empty the large chamber pot. Rose had covered the shameful mess with a cloth she'd found but it did little to mask the smell.

The only reprieve she found from the welling panic and shame was on this mat, on her knees. With her eyes closed and her head bowed, she could imagine she was in Raedonleith's chapel again, wrapped in the presence of the Almighty.

Free Maeve, please. She doesn't deserve to be in the dungeon. It's not right. She was only trying to protect me. And George. He went for help, didn't he? Please, Almighty, let him have gone for help. Save me. Protect me. Bring Father.

Her courage was slipping in the waiting. Soon, it would disappear altogether.

No. I can do this. For Nicholas. For my father. For myself.

Hold me tight. Keep me safe. Make me strong.

She didn't know where Lord Cavendish had been these past three days but it wasn't his chamber. In one part of her mind, she was grateful for that. Another part railed the unfairness.

Almighty, help me.

Loneliness wasn't a new sensation to Rose. It had become a companion in itself the past five years, but though she'd been lonely, she hadn't been alone. Not truly. Quin had been there. And Mykah. Aiyana. Her parents. Later Evangeline, Darrek and Arthur. Servants. Workers. Townspeople.

The silence in this room was an altogether different torture.

And so she prayed, turning Cavendish's chamber into a chapel as she fought on her knees.

Change his heart, Almighty. I know you can. Show Cavendish how to love again. How to let go of the bitterness. Make him brave. Make him new.

Heal Nicholas. Keep him safe. Show him your way that he may walk in your steps. Give him an undivided heart that he may serve you.

Bless Evangeline and Darrek and Arthur. May they know your goodness in their lives. Bless Mykah and Finnian and their marriage. May they—

The door burst open.

"Submissive. That's how I like my women."

Rose braced a hand on the window's ledge and pulled herself to her feet, covering her gown's stain with her hand. Lord Cavendish closed the door behind him and leaned against it. The thirty steps from the door to the window shrunk to ten. He frowned and looked about the room, likely searching for the putrid smell, before turning his attention on Rose. She gulped a breath too big for the panic compressing her lungs. Sunlight caught on the knife in his hand.

Almighty.

Help.

She'd wanted him to come, asked the Almighty to send him even, but now he was here. And she was terrified. Why hadn't she searched the room for weapons? Not that she would have known how to use them but holding something in her hand would have given her a measure of comfort.

"Quiet too. Nothing to say to me, Lady Rose?" He closed the distance between them. Rose's heart pounded in her chest as he ran a hand down her arm, grasping her wrist and bringing it to his lips. His breath smelled of ale. Perhaps that was why the smell of vomit and excrement didn't bother him as much as it did her. "My spy's report said nothing of your beauty. I should have him hanged. To think I might have deprived the world of such loveliness." He sheathed the knife in his belt and returned his free hand to the back of her neck. His fingers burned her terror-cooled skin as he played with the hair at her nape. "No matter. You're mine now."

"Help," she whispered.

"Help?" Lord Cavendish laughed again, though there was no mirth in the sound. "I admire your attempt, lovely Rose, but no one is here to hear you. Certainly no one is coming to save you."

"No. You. Help." She could barely get the words out past the fear lodged in her throat.

"Me?"

She forced a breath into her lungs and tried again. "My husband fell. He's hurt. He needs help."

"And you came to me? How touching. But you're mistaken if you think I care."

"Please."

"No."

Rose's legs trembled with the effort it took to stand. The hand she used to grip the windowsill did little to help. She needed food, water, and rest. But at least she was standing. It was more than could be said for Nicholas last she'd seen him.

"You would let him die?"

"Yes."

"Please." It was the only word she had left.

Cavendish's hands on her face forced her gaze to his. "I owe you nothing, Rose of Raedonleith. Your father took everything from me— the woman I loved, my sister's happiness, my brother's loyalty, my only friends. He made me a laughingstock when he fought me for your sister, and then took my son to ensure every person present knew his power over me. I won't be made a fool again.

"Your husband is dying? Good. Let him die. Let it break your heart. Then, maybe, you and your father will know a portion of the pain the good King Lior has caused me."

"Don't do this."

"Clean yourself up. You smell worse than refuse."

He stalked away, a sneer on his face, but the barb didn't stick. Rose knew she smelled. It could hardly be helped when she'd been locked in a room without even a washcloth. What she hadn't known, hadn't seen before, was the hurt behind Lord Cavendish's bluster. She'd known the enemy all her life, but never the man.

"I'm sorry," she called before he could open the door.

"Right you should be. You're a disgrace."

"No, I'm sorry you were hurt. I'm sorry that made you feel a need to control everyone around you. I'm sorry you don't know how loved you are."

He stared at the closed door.

Boldened by her realization, Rose took a tentative step toward him. Then two more.

Almighty, forgive me. I should have thought. All these years, he's been in pain. Is that why I'm here? Me instead of Mykah? Because Lord Cavendish didn't need someone to fight him but someone to understand his pain?

"I'm sorry I never realized how lonely you were," she said. "I—We have that in common."

"What would you know about loneliness."

"More than I wish to. For years I've been hiding behind a wall, yearning for someone to break through and find me. Love me. I grew angry when no one did, never realizing until now that it was I who pushed them away. My parents, my sisters, friends. Prince Nicholas. I was scared to let them see the brokenness inside, so I put up a wall to ensure they didn't. It's not them who didn't try, it was me."

Rose clutched the stone of her necklace so tight her hand cramped. She could be wrong, both in her revelation and decision to speak of it. She could make an already tenuous situation worse. This man before her had abused Evangeline and left her with a child, sent his own brother to murder Mykah, and potentially sent someone to kill Rose too. He held all the power in this room and they both knew it. But had anyone ever looked beyond his anger to the pain beneath?

He turned around. She dropped the stone, drawing his attention to it. He froze. Stared. She hurried to tuck the necklace back inside her gown but stopped at the choked sound from his throat. He swallowed hard.

"Lord Cavendish?"

"She gave it to you."

"My necklace? Mother g—"

Rose stopped. The look on his face. She recognized it. All too well. The steady blinking—not so fast that someone would notice but enough to hold back tears, the jump in his jaw. He was clenching his teeth together. Trying to breathe. Trying not to fall apart.

"It was from you," she said. How could Rose not have guessed? She rolled the green stone between her fingertips. Her mother had said it was a gift from someone she loved. Rose had always assumed that meant Father. But it hadn't been. It had been Lord Cavendish.

"And now I know how much it meant to her. First chance she had, she gave it away," Lord Cavendish said. His eyebrows pulled together in a frown. "Of course, why would she keep it?"

That was what he thought? "No, you're wrong. Mother wore it every day, with every gown she dressed in, no matter the color or style. She treasured this necklace more than any other jewel she owned."

"Which is why it's around your neck."

"It's mine because I begged for it. She didn't give it to me until my tenth birthday, and even then, it wasn't without sacrifice. She cried as she lifted it over my head. I almost gave it back but she wanted me to have it. She said it was special to her—that it reminded her to pray without ceasing, and never lose hope. That the hardest stones make the best altars. She must have meant you."

CHAPTER 34

Cormac stood outside his chamber and tried to stop his hands from trembling. Caralynne had kept his necklace. Even after she'd chosen Lior. It shouldn't have shaken him as much as it had.

He'd been a boy of seven when he'd found that rock. He, Lior, and Sunny had begged their nurses to let them eat by the river. Charmed as the women had always been by the three of them, the nurses had agreed. Sunny had sat on the blanket like a proper lady but he and Lior had taken their shoes off and played at the river's edge, pressing their advantage and creeping deeper and deeper as young boys were wont to do until the water raced around their knees.

A brave fish had brushed past Cormac's ankle, making him look down. The green of the rock had glinted in the sunlight, catching his attention. He'd picked it up, rolled it in his hand admiring the color and smooth surface, and put it in his pocket. A little boy's treasure. He'd put it by his bed that night, and into his pocket again the next day. Then the next. He'd carried it for the next seven years.

He'd met Caralynne when he was sixteen, fallen for her at first glance but been too afraid to say much more than a greeting. But he'd found reasons to keep seeing the young healer. He'd kept her woodpile full, offered his horse when she needed to go into the village, left a fresh bunch of flowers each day at her door. Even if he'd watched from a distance as she found them.

It had taken him a year to find the courage to instigate a real conversation. Even then, he'd fiddled with the stone the entire time. She'd asked him about it. Smiled as he mumbled his way through an explanation of where it had come from and marveled at its beauty.

He'd gone to the silversmith that same day. Asked the cost of having the rock made into a necklace. Saved his gold for the next five months until he had enough. Waited another month for his commission to be ready.

Caralynne had put a hand to her heart when he'd given it to her and told him she'd treasure it always. He'd walked away feeling like a king and made a promise to himself that the next time he saw Caralynne, he would declare his love and ask her to marry him.

Instead, he'd returned from two weeks away to find the woman he loved married to his best friend. He'd never seen the green stone again.

Until today.

Caralynne had kept it. She'd cared. More, she'd told Rose it was special. That he was. That she had hope that— What? One day they might again be friends?

Cormac shook his head. He was a fool. It was a stone. Just a stone. A young boy's useless treasure. That was all. Certainly nothing worth the amount of emotion currently coursing through his body. He should have killed Rose when he had the chance. Only, even drunk, he'd been too sober to do it in front of Maeve. And then he'd not been able to get the maid's words out of his head.

You're better than this. I know you are.

Maeve's words had followed him from the stables to the dining hall where he'd thrown back drink after drink until he passed out on the floor. The words had pounded in time with the hammer in his head when he'd woken the next morning and dragged himself upright. They'd whispered with every step he stumbled up the stairs on the way to his chamber. They'd yelled disapproval when he went to open the door and face Lady Rose, then crowed with delight when he opened another door instead, crashing onto the bed in a different room.

Better than this.

You're better than this.

For three days, they'd been both torture and hope.

He'd barged into Rose's chamber, intent on silencing the words once and for all only to see that necklace, and have the words grow all the louder.

Better than this.

Maeve was going to pay.

Cormac waited until midnight to see Maeve in the dungeon, when all but those taking the night watches slept. In part, because he refused to appear weak to his people. In part because he didn't know what to do with her.

He could kill Maeve for what she'd done, defying him like she had. Breaking Rose free. He'd be well within his rights. Were it anyone else, he would have. But Maeve was—something else. He couldn't do it, furious as he was. So he let her stew. Let her feel the coldness of the dungeon, the damp seeping into her clothing, the discomfort of hunger, the ache of regret.

Or so he'd thought.

The servant woman on her knees, hands clasped together in prayer didn't appear particularly cowed by her surroundings. She looked up when he clapped a hand on the rusty metal bars, questions on her face before she even opened her mouth.

"Is Rose—?"

"Free? No."

"But she's alive."

"I should kill her. I should kill you both."

"It would kill you."

Did she forget who he was? Grit bit into his hands as he squeezed the bars. He hadn't come here to be belittled. He was Lord Cormac Cavendish, feared wherever he went. "You forget your place, woman."

"At least I'm not a coward."

"I am not a coward."

He hated the way she smiled at him. A sad smile, as if—like Rose—Maeve saw right through his bluster to the fear and doubt he tried so hard to cover. Her acceptance sent regret like a dagger to his heart. He pushed it aside, covering the wound with bitterness before it could bleed.

"Only a coward holds on to fear when they could have freedom."

"I—"

"You can lock me up, ignore me, or even kill me as an example to the people of your power, but it won't change the fact that Lior married Caralynne. Let it go, Cormac. Please. There's so much more to you than this. So much more you could be."

"You can't change me."

Again, that sad smile. "No, but I can pray and hope and believe that one day you might."

"I'm too far gone."

"No one is too far gone. Least of all you."

CHAPTER 35

"This way."

Nicholas wanted to ask Spencer if the path he was leading them was the shorter way. Those parts of Nicholas's body that didn't ache screamed with pain. Lady Aiyana had argued against them riding through the night but been overruled. None of them were willing to waste time sleeping. Especially not when Rose's life was at risk. His mind agreed wholeheartedly. His body left him in no uncertain terms of its protest.

"We could go through the gates," Nicholas suggested. It was what King Lior, and the rest of the knights would do. He and Spencer had spoken briefly with them before continuing on. Spencer had, at least. Nicholas had been too occupied with staying upright to be an active part of the conversation. That and feeling as if he'd failed the king in not keeping Rose safe.

"And be imprisoned on sight? What use will you be to Rose then?"

Unless she was in the dungeon—which very well might be the case—very little. Nicholas turned his horse to follow Spencer and the others to the forest bordering the castle wall, thankful for the trees hiding them from view of any guards who might be watching. Their rescue mission would be short lived if an archer cut them down.

Spencer stopped. Pointed toward the wall. "See the door?" Nicholas nodded. "It leads into the stables. I don't know if it's locked or who might be on the other side—"

Nicholas tumbled off his horse in his rush to dismount, cringing as the heavy landing sent shards of fire through his middle. He clutched an arm around his ribs and ran to the door in the wall, heedless of who might be watching or what danger he might be running into. Pain chased him, making his head spin. He stopped, hand on the door, to catch his breath.

The door swung open. Nicholas lurched forward. He would have fallen again if not for the older man who caught his arm and steadied him.

"Prince Nicholas? Tell me you're Prince Nicholas."

"I am."

Nicholas was pushed aside before he could say anything else as the rest of the group filed through the door. Spencer clasped the older man's hand. "George. Thank the Almighty it's you."

"Sir Spencer. You came."

"You left the door open."

"I've been waiting. Lady Rose said you were near. We were coming to find you when Cavendish stopped us. He took Rose and Maeve. I searched and discovered your camp but no sign of you. I thought to come to Raedonleith but didn't want to leave her, not with Maeve imprisoned. I had to be here in case—" He stopped, glancing at Nicholas. "In case she needed me."

Nicholas didn't know who George was or where his loyalty lay, but he couldn't help trusting the man. Spencer did.

"You know where she is?" Nicholas asked.

"The master's chamber."

Aiyana gasped. "No."

"Lady Sunny?" George said, eyes wide.

"Hello, George."

He touched a hand to his heart and bowed his head. "Welcome home, my lady."

"Where's Rose?" Nicholas asked. The reunions going on around him were touching, to be sure, but his wife was somewhere in this monstrous castle in who knew what state. Reunions could wait.

"I'll take him," Aiyana said. "I know where it is."

George, still wide-eyed at the healer's presence, nodded. "Be careful, my lady. Your brother isn't himself. I don't know what he'd do if he saw you."

"Believe me, if I see him, I'll be the one doing the talking. He's gone too far this time and I intend to let him know it."

Rose peered out the window, wondering if this view was to be her life. The window looked out over the front gate, giving her a perfect view of every person who entered or departed Cavendish Castle. She thought her father would have come by now. He had for Evangeline, challenging Lord Cavendish for her freedom. He'd won too, bringing Evangeline and Arthur home. He hadn't come for Rose. Did he even know she was here?

No. She couldn't let herself think that. Adam had returned to Raedonleith for help. He'd gone for Nicholas, but someone would come for her too, wouldn't they?

Seven days she'd been locked in Lord Cavendish's chamber. Eight days since she'd seen Nicholas or anyone she'd consider a friend. Lord Cavendish hadn't returned, though he or someone else had sent food.

The day after his strange visit, a platter of bread and fruit had been sitting on the side table when she'd woken. A clean gown, washcloth and comb had lain on a chair near the window, along with a bowl of fresh water. The chamber pot had been emptied too. More bread and fruit had been on that same table when she woke the next day. The day after, there had been a meat dish as well with watered down ale in a jug beside it. She hadn't known what to make of any of it, grateful as she'd been.

She wandered away from the window, walking the length of the room as she played with the rock on her necklace. She hadn't known what to make of that either. All these years she'd worn and cherished the necklace never knowing how valuable it was. In sentiment, if not riches.

The hardest hearts make the best altars.

She didn't doubt now that Mother had meant Cavendish.

The door slammed open. Rose let out a yelp, skirts flaring as she spun.

"Rose."

Nicholas.

She was in his arms before she could tell whether she'd moved or he had. His tunic was warm and soft against her cheek. His embrace pressed the breath from her lungs. He was alive. And not only alive but standing. Walking. Speaking.

Kissing her. Her hair, her cheeks, her forehead. His hands trembled where they held her face.

"I thought I'd lost you," he whispered.

She'd thought the same.

"You came."

"Always, my Rose." He pressed his forehead to hers, his breathing labored. "You're well? Lord Cavendish didn't—"

Rose shook her head. "I'm well. He hasn't touched me."

Nicholas's sigh across her neck made her shiver. She lay her head on his chest, listening to his racing heartbeat as he kissed her hair.

A throat cleared. Not Nicholas's. Rose pulled back to see they weren't alone. Aiyana and Mykah stood behind Nicholas, with Spencer and Quin by their side. She was too overwhelmed to be embarrassed.

"All of you?" Tears wet her eyes. "I was watching the gate. I never saw—"

"Spencer knew another way."

She turned to thank Spencer only to see him shake his head. "I'm sorry I wasn't there, my lady. It was my job to protect you and I failed."

"You are not to blame for my choices, Sir Spencer. The choice to leave was mine and mine alone. Prince Nicholas and I are both alive, as you see. We would not be if not for you and Adam. There is no failure here."

"You've been imprisoned nigh on a week and Prince Nicholas has a concussion and more ribs broken than whole."

"Broken ribs?" She loosened her hold on Nicholas only to have him pull her straight back in.

"Dragon's wing come fairy flee. The knight overstates. 'Tis naught but a few cracks. I'm fine."

He wasn't fine, despite the rhyme which flowed with exasperation from his lips. *Dragon's wing come fairy flee?* Where had that come from? Another ballad? She'd have to ask him about it. Sometime when he wasn't so shaky.

Looking now, Rose could see it. The way Nicholas swayed slightly as he stood and leaned into her. His quick breaths. The sweat beading on his forehead. He shouldn't have been out of bed much less storming a castle to rescue her.

"You need rest."

"I needed my wife more."

Rose's mouth dropped open.

Nicholas leaned closer, his lips against her ear. "And if we didn't have four other people currently watching us, I'd show you just how much, broken ribs and all."

Heat crept up Rose's neck, burning her ears as her mind played through every mortifying thing he might mean by that. If she'd thought his ardor might wane in a week, she'd been wrong. Very wrong.

"What do we do now?" she asked.

"I could think of a few things," Nicholas said under his breath. Rose swallowed, her cheeks coloring as bright as her ears.

Mykah raised her eyebrows, amusement on her face. She couldn't hear what Nicholas was saying—*oh, please, Almighty let Mykah not be able to hear what Nicholas said!*—but she, too, was newly married.

"We wait," Spencer said. "King Lior and the rest of the knights are outside the gates."

Rose gasped. "They're here? Father came for me?"

Mykah frowned. "Of course he did. Did you think he wouldn't?"

She had. Nicholas's arm tightened around her waist, a bulwark of strength.

"Rose, he brought his whole army," Mykah said.

"No. But that's—" Foolish. Thoughtless. "He left Raedonleith vulnerable?"

"Aye, and not one of his men argued the fact. They were lined up and ready within minutes of hearing you were gone."

"But I'm—"

"Their beloved princess. Their future queen."

No. Had they not read her letter? "Broken."

"You're the only one who thinks that."

Then she was the only one accepting of the truth.

"So we wait?"

Spencer nodded. "We wait."

"Does it have to be here?" Nicholas asked.

"It's the most fortified chamber in the castle," Aiyana said. "When the fighting begins, you'll be safest here."

"Very well, but do you all have to be here?"

"Wishing us gone?" Mykah teased.

"Yes," Nicholas said without apology. The others grinned.

"As you wish."

CHAPTER 36

Baedonleith's army are at the castle gate."

"I know."

Cormac had known from the moment he sent that taunt to Lior that this would be the king's answer. He fisted his hand around the sword at his side and forced it not to shake. His captain of the guard was dressed in full armor, as were the two men who stood behind him. Cormac had no doubt the rest of his army were ready too. One word, that's all it would take to start a war.

A war he wasn't certain he wanted anymore. Certainly not today when his head pounded with the force of a thousand horses trampling it.

You're better than this. Maeve's words. Again. They were the reason he'd not slept these past three nights. The reason his head pained him now. He'd sent food and clothing to Rose and ignored the guards' taunts to ravish her every time he walked past the door to his chamber. Good deeds to allay the guilt that plagued him and purge Maeve's words from his mind. It hadn't worked.

He'd gone into his chamber that day prepared to kill Rose. The knife had been in his hand. Her plea for help had made him pause. Her necklace had made him run.

She said it was special to her—that it reminded her to pray without ceasing, and never lose hope. She must have meant you.

He couldn't kill Rose. He wasn't even sure he could fight Lior.

No. This was foolishness. One little rock did not negate twenty years of hurt. Lior would pay and Cormac would be the one to make him. But not today.

"Stay alert but don't attack," he ordered the captain.

"My lord?"

"I've waited twenty years for this war. Another day won't make a difference."

"And if they bring down our wall?"

"Then we bring them down."

The captain walked away, his men with him, leaving Cormac alone. Alone and trying to convince himself that this was for the best. He was going to wage this war, and he was going to win it. It was smart, wise, expected of him. Exactly what he'd planned, all these years.

To wait was the choice of a coward. Cormac should have ordered his men to attack, even knowing the pounding of his head meant he watched the battle from afar. He would still be the victor in the end.

Only like the key to a portal, seeing Rose's necklace had unlocked a rush of memories. His chest clenched with forgotten pain as they poured through his mind.

The time Lior had challenged Cormac to see who could climb the highest up the Raedonleith's castle walls. Cormac had won. But only because Lior had laughed so hard when Cormac put his hand in a gap in the stones only to find a wasp nest that he'd fallen off the wall.

The tree near the stables which the two of them had hidden in to watch a foal be birthed after the stable master had shooed them away.

The clearing where he'd shot his first rabbit, Lior at his side, cheering him on.

The healer's cottage where he'd first seen Caralynne. She'd been sitting on the bench outside the door, laughing at the antics of a young child trying to sneak up on a bird. Cormac had approached her only to have words fail him at her beauty. He'd mumbled something nonsensical and fled, determined to try again the next day.

The river Sunny had pushed him and Lior into after they'd teased her one too many times. The same one in which he'd found the green rock.

The branch that had struck Lior across the cheek and forced him to the healer's cottage where *he'd* met Caralynne. And lost his heart, apparently. Stolen hers too. Because within a week the two of them married. *Lior* hadn't been tongue-tied at her beauty.

He and Sunny had spent more time at Raedonleith Castle and its surrounds than they had their own home, with Father too busy serving his king to care for two rambunctious children and Mother never having fully recovered from Finnian's birth. Cavendish Castle had been a dank well of loneliness. Raedonleith had been filled with life and love and friends and adventure. Cormac had thought he'd stay forever.

Until the day his best friend and the man he'd called brother betrayed him. Ignored entirely the betrothal to Sunny that had been in place since they were children and married Caralynne. The woman Cormac loved. The fight he'd had with Lior when he heard would have been so much more satisfying if Lior had fought back. Instead, filled with equal parts fury and disgust, Cormac had thrown his sword aside, taken Sunny and left Raedonleith, never to return.

That was the day he'd determined to destroy his once friend. Slowly. Carefully. Completely. Cormac would wait until Lior had everything he ever wanted. Then Cormac would tear Lior's blissful life apart. One piece at a time.

Every year that passed, every child born to Lior and Caralynne, every event they celebrated, only intensified that longing for revenge.

But now?

Cormac rubbed his temples, cursing the persistent ache that resided there. That was what was making him weak. Making him second-guess his life's goal. He could destroy Lior, without a doubt. It was what he'd spent his whole adult life preparing for. A skirmish here, a raid there. One daughter ruined, one daughter broken, Lior's heir in Cormac's hold. Cormac could do what he wanted with Rose. Kill her. Ravish her. Thrust a knife through her chest as he'd ordered his man to do weeks ago. As he'd planned, seven days ago.

"I wish to speak with Lord Cormac Cavendish."

The king's words boomed over the gate of the castle, across the courtyard, through the walls.

Cormac closed his eyes. The time had come. Lior had no wish to wait.

Though he'd all but invited Lior with that note, and spent twenty years preparing for this day, with the moment now upon him Cormac knew.

He wasn't ready.

—◦·◦◦◦·◦—

Tension danced around King Lior, his shouted request echoing in the silence of a thousand mounted men waiting to see what would happen next. The battle was here. The war that had been brewing since the moment Lior walked through the door of the healer's cottage and saw Caralynne. He hated that it had come to this. Hated even more the years wasted when he and Cormac could have been friends.

Almighty, gird our hearts and hands for battle. Give us the strength to protect our kingdom and the wisdom to know how. Straighten our arrows and guide our swords.

Save lives today. May we live to see the sun rise on a day streaked with freedom.

Lior's armor had never felt so heavy across his shoulders.

Guide me, Almighty. Protect us all.

And if it be your will, may no blood be shed at all.

The portcullis began to rise. The heavy gates groaned as they opened. Lior sat straighter on his horse. A burst of energy coursed within him, sharpening his sight, clearing his mind. He'd prayed it wouldn't come to this. Now, he prayed with each breath that it would be over quickly. That Cormac would listen. That something would change.

"Hold your line," he called to his knights.

Whatever happened, it would be over today. No more wondering.

He touched the velvet bag at his hip, at peace with its contents. He walked his horse forward. A sound had him turning to see four others with him—Manning, Darrek, Finnian, and Edison—two at his left, two at his right. He would have told them to go away if he thought they'd listen. The fierce confidence on their faces said otherwise. He thanked the Almighty Mykah wasn't alongside them.

Lior raised his head. The flags flapped in the breeze. This was foolish. Foolhardy. He was going to get himself killed, and his best knights— and daughters' husbands—along with him. But none of them slowed.

"There, to the left," Finnian said. "There's Cormac."

Guards parted as Cormac came through, tall upon his horse. Bows dropped. Swords wavered. Whispers abounded. Lior ignored them all.

"A little late for negotiations, isn't it, my friend?" Cormac asked.

"Negotiations, yes. But not surrender."

A gasp came from beside him—Darrek?—as Lior tugged open the bag beside him, pulling forth the only thing he knew to stop the war.

A crown.

His crown.

With legs sturdier than they felt, Lior dismounted. Walked ten paces forward, knelt, and placed his crown before Cormac Cavendish.

"I surrender."

"No!" The cry from behind him was loud this time, the grass rustling as someone rushed forward. Lior held up a hand to stop them. He had no wish to give up his crown, but if the choice was his people's lives or his crown, he'd choose the people. Sometimes, the greatest way a man could care for his people was to stand down and let someone else. Cavendish wasn't going to stop until he had Lior's throne, so here it was.

Cormac, too, slid off his horse, though he kept his distance. "You'd give up your crown?"

"I will."

"Why?" Cormac's question was barely a whisper in the confusion around them.

"Because you want it."

"And you would give it to me, just like that?"

"I'd give you anything, Cormac. Don't you know that yet? I never wanted to be at war with you. If it's the crown you seek, here it is."

Cormac walked forward, his steps slow, as if expecting an ambush at any moment, or for Lior to strike. It was what Cormac would have done. But Lior wasn't Cormac. While Cormac had held on to a grudge and desire to extract revenge for over two decades, Lior had been grieving his friend.

He couldn't kill him.

So he'd done the only other thing he could. He'd surrendered.

Cormac was as silent and still as the crown that sat between them. That Lior had shocked his friend was clear. What Cormac would do from here wasn't.

He could have Lior killed on the spot.

Take Lior's wife and daughters captive.

Take Caralynne, as he'd wanted all those years ago. Force her to be his.

Cormac could destroy the very people Lior had given up his crown to save.

It was a risk. Everything about being a king was. One never knew the outcome until it happened, especially when it came to people. Rarely were people predictable. But this was right. He knew it. Though the knights muttered behind him, querying whether their king had lost his mind, Lior knew it was the right decision. A peace that passed all understanding, all logic, calmed his heart and mind. For the first time in a very long time, Lior wasn't second-guessing his decision or wracked with guilt over it. He was certain.

Cormac took a step sideways, dropped his sword, and fell to the ground.

Silence reigned as time stood still. *Cormac?*

He wasn't moving. No one was.

He wasn't moving.

Almighty, no.

Lior stumbled twice as he clambered to his feet, racing to the still prone man. No sword tore Cormac's side, no arrow protruded from his back. Lior fell to his knees again, rolling Cormac onto his side. He was breathing.

Finnian touched Cormac's shoulder, pressed a hand to his chest.

"He's alive," Finnian said.

"Aye." But not conscious. Not well. Maybe not for long.

"Get him inside. I'll find a healer."

Finnian ran through the gathering crowd of guards. Manning and Darrek lifted Cormac. Edison cleared the way. Lior stood stunned.

A hand touched his arm. Mykah. She was here after all, dressed in a deep blue gown with not one arrow in sight, though two knives hung from her belt. "Come, Father. You should be there when he wakes. Aiyana's here. Nicholas too. Rose is safe. All will be well."

He nodded, allowing himself to be pulled along by his daughter. He didn't know what happened to the crown behind him. Right now, he didn't care.

CHAPTER 37

Cormac opened his eyes to a swarm of colors and shapes. He blinked several times, trying to force them into alignment. He was...where? He didn't recognize the room, simple as it was. A table. Several wooden stools. A bed that wasn't his. Shelves filled with jars. Flowers hanging from hooks along the roof.

It reminded him of something. He closed his eyes and tugged at the memory, cajoling it into clarity. The flowers. The jars. The shelves.

Caralynne. Her cottage.

He was either hallucinating, still asleep, or crazy. He wasn't sure which he'd prefer.

"Hello?"

A woman came bustling into view, twine in her hand, relief on her face. "Cormac, you're awake."

He knew her. That face. The pale blue eyes equally piercing and comforting. The nose with its slight bump at the end. The hair was different. Lighter than he remembered. More gray than gold now, the same as his. Weariness lined her forehead and the tilt of her shoulders but there was no mistaking his sister. "Sunny? You helped me?"

"Of course. Did you expect me to let you die?"

"I would have deserved it if you did."

"I'm a healer."

That would explain why her cottage—if this was her cottage—looked like Caralynne's, but not why he was here. Or where here was. A waft of lavender made him sneeze. A waft of guilt made him weak.

"I hurt you," he said.

"I forgive you. I want you in my life."

"It's too late."

"No, it isn't. Finnian taught me that."

Finnian. Another person on the long list of people Cormac had failed.

"Where am I?"

"Raedonleith."

That couldn't be right. He'd—he'd—

Cormac frowned. Tried to make sense of the muddle of his mind. Perhaps Sunny had given him something to help him sleep. That would explain why his mind felt like a jumbled mess of ideas with no end.

He'd been at Cavendish Castle. He'd seen King Lior. He recalled that much. Then, what?

"You needed me, Lior needed Caralynne and—" She tilted her head. "—a king should be with his people."

"That doesn't explain why I'm here."

"You're their king."

"I—" No. He knew this. "Lior is the king."

"Lior surrendered his crown."

"Why would he do that?"

"Because it's what you wanted." She muttered something to herself before touching her palm to his forehead. "No fever but—headache? How's your sight?"

"Fine. No headache." He frowned at that. The pounding had been a near constant companion for months. What miracle cure had his sister given him?

"Any dizziness?"

"Not once you stop hovering above me."

She moved back, crossing her arms as she stood beside the bed. "You don't remember?"

"My head is fine. I'm tired, that's all. And wondering why I'm in a kingdom I have no memory of traveling to."

"Cormac. You collapsed. You've been unconscious for three days."

* * *

Rose was home, though it didn't feel the same. For one thing, there was a man lying in her bed. Her husband, but still a man. Nicholas had made it back to Raedonleith with the rest of the group only to succumb to fever when they arrived. Darrek and Spencer had carried him to her chamber. He'd been sleeping ever since.

Aiyana said it was fine. Good even. The fever wasn't high enough to cause worry. Nicholas's body needed the rest so was forcing it on him. All the better to heal his ribs and any other ills he still carried. Rose had been tasked with getting liquids into him whenever he was conscious enough to take them and reporting back to Aiyana should anything change.

A full day had passed. Nothing had changed.

She ran a wet cloth across Nicholas's forehead and begged the Almighty to heal him.

The journey home had been uneventful compared to the first week of their marriage. Uneventful yet full of tension. No one knew when or if Lord Cavendish might wake, and what would become of Raedonleith when he did. Father had only left Lord Cavendish's side when Aiyana had demanded it, admonishing that he'd suffer the same fate if he didn't rest.

Cavendish guards kept watch alongside Raedonleith's, neither willing to trust their fate to the other.

Most intriguing had been the way Quin's cheeks reddened each time Spencer lifted her onto his horse before climbing up behind her. Rose had thought she was imagining the maid's response until Mykah, too, commented on it. Perhaps it was nothing—Spencer, of his own admission, loved a woman he'd not yet declared himself to—but Rose had smiled at the thought that Quin might have found love. Spencer was a good man. One of the best.

Mindful of Nicholas's ribs, and her propensity for falling, Rose had ridden with Adam. It had been a long three days' ride. Though Adam had been respectful and every bit the kind friend Rose had come to appreciate, he wasn't the man Rose had wanted to be near. It was for the best, she'd reminded herself time and time again. Nicholas needed to heal. The reminders hadn't made it any easier.

And now they were home. If, indeed, this was home. Raedonleith Castle belonged to Lord Cavendish now. Or would, when he woke. Like Nicholas, Cormac lay unresponsive, though Aiyana held hope for him too. His heart beat strong, she said, and that made all the difference. Rose chose to believe as Aiyana did.

She dipped the cloth and wiped Nicholas's forehead again.

Even if Father hadn't surrendered the kingdom, and there hadn't been a man lying in her bed, the room would have felt strange. As if this was the chamber of her youth, and she'd outgrown it.

The foolish thoughts of an overtired bride.

Mother, Mykah, Evangeline, Quin, and even Spencer had offered to watch over Nicholas so Rose could sleep. She'd thanked them all but declined their offers. Though her sleep was fitful by his side, it was something. She could rest her hand atop his heart, or within the palm of his, and close her eyes, knowing she was by his side should anything change. She wouldn't have been able to sleep at all for the worrying if she'd been in another room.

Almighty, heal him. Make him well. Bring him back to strength. Bring him back to me.

They had so much life yet to share.

CHAPTER 38

It was dark when Nicholas woke. He didn't know how long he'd slept but the near-constant pounding in his head of the last few days was gone. Thank the Almighty. A large breath caught and proved his ribs were still far from healed. He should have listened to the healer and stayed at Raedonleith rather than riding to Cavendish Castle and back, but he didn't regret it. A few burning ribs were trifle to pay to have his wife by his side again.

The single lit candle on the table beside his bed showed Rose sitting on a stool, head resting on the edge of the bed he lay in. The light of the candle glinted off her hair, turning it more gold than its usual brown.

Rose.

She was safe. She was here.

Now that the night has passed away, thy glory to reveal.

In sunlight bright and hope renewed, thou land and soul is healed.

Healed. Oh how Nicholas prayed that for Rose. That she might dance with abandon and walk with freedom but, more, that she might know deep in her soul that she was whole. Not lacking, not broken, not lesser than those around her, but whole. Worthy. Cherished. Not for what she wasn't, but for who she was.

He lifted a hand to stroke her hair. She jerked and raised her head.

"Forgive me," he whispered, his voice sounding too loud in the otherwise silent room. "I didn't mean to wake you."

"I wasn't sleeping." She blinked a few times, covered a yawn. He should have known she'd not be able to sleep. "Can I get you anything? Broth? Bread?"

"No, I'm well." He touched a finger to her cheek. Even in the low light, he could see the dark circles under her eyes. "But you're not. Why don't you sleep?"

For a moment, he thought she'd deny it, but then she sighed. "I can't."

"Because of me?"

"Because of everything."

He shuffled to one side of the bed, patting the gap he'd made. "You'll sleep better on a bed."

"I couldn't. You're injured. You need rest."

"So do you."

"I haven't slept well since..." Her words tapered off. Tired? Or thinking.

"We married?" he offered.

Her mouth tipped in a wry smile. "I was going to say since I was twelve."

His heart turned over for her. What she dealt with every day with nary a complaint. One would never know to look at her how much pain she was in or how often she fought. "And here I've taken your bed." It was a guess but confirmed when she shrugged.

"It's my fault you're there in the first place."

Nicholas sincerely doubted it. "How could that be?"

"You put yourself between me and the horse that day when it stumbled. I pushed you away and you still saved me. Then you came back, when you should have been healing, and saved me again."

Was that guilt playing around the edges of her gaze? Surely she didn't think he regretted his actions. "I'd do it all over again."

"You could have died. Multiple times."

"Aye, but I didn't. And neither did you." But she'd waste away to nothing if she didn't sleep. "Sit with me on the bed at least. I'll wager it's more comfortable than that wooden stool of yours. Is there no other bed?"

"There was but I didn't want to leave you."

"Then don't."

His heart thrilled when, with a nod, she stood and carefully sat on the edge of the bed. She held herself stiff for what felt like an eternity before lifting her feet onto the bed and leaning against the headboard. He pulled himself upright enough that their shoulders aligned before taking her hand.

"Thank you," he said.

"For what?"

"For trusting me."

"You were right. The stool isn't very comfortable."

Though she brushed aside his gratitude, he had no doubt if they'd been in the same position two weeks ago, she would have stayed on the stool. If she'd found the courage to walk into the room while he slept at all. They'd come a long way in a short time. Danger had a way of doing that.

"Do you think you could sleep now?" he asked.

"Maybe." She didn't sound very certain. He wasn't tired either.

"Want to watch the stars with me?"

She frowned. "Aiyana would say you should be resting."

"I didn't ask Aiyana."

Nicholas held out a hand, the simple movement making the candle sway. Rose hesitated. He waited. Patience, Spencer had counselled. Quin too. Just when he felt his hand start to shake, she took it.

"I'd love to watch stars with you."

Rose took Nicholas to her favorite tower. She'd never taken anyone there before, not even her sisters, but she wanted to share it with Nicholas. Not only the tower but—

Everything.

Her life. Her fears. Her disappointments. Her love.

When he offered his arms, she walked into them, wrapped in his embrace as they stared out at the stars. There weren't any clouds tonight. Just an endless black sky filled with diamonds. Her mind went back to the last time they'd watched stars together.

"How does the ballad end? The one with the princess." He never had finished it.

Nicholas kissed her hair, sending a wave of warmth through her. "Where did I get to?"

"The man was searching for a gift for the woman he loved but didn't feel worthy of."

"Ah. I never thought I'd relate to such a man but here we are."

Days ago, she would have argued such a comment, sure it wasn't her he spoke of, but tonight, she felt nothing but gratitude. She snuggled in closer to his chest as he began to recite.

"Long all the kingdom's paths he searched, rough oceans did he part,
Certain nigh he'd find the gift to win his lady's heart.
But naught he found could bear the weight of expectation high,
For what to give a girl like she who owned all gold could buy?
Until by yonder stall he found a man whose wares were few,
A single pearl was all he held but seeing it, he knew.
It shone with light, its luster clear. Color stalk'd its sheen,
White, then rose, then turquoise blue, as round he'd ever seen.
'Sir, what must I pay to have that jewel? What coin, what price, what gold?
Come winter breeze and summer wind, my love that pearl must hold.'
'Ten thousand coins—'"

Rose gasped. "Ten thousand coins? For a single pearl?"

"Aye. I told you they were valuable."

"But—" So much. An amount such as that could feed a family for life. Nay, an entire village. She could only imagine what so many coins would look like, even knowing her father's treasury. "He truly thought his princess worth such a price?"

Nicholas ducked his head to kiss her shoulder. "I would."

The two words washed over Rose, smoothing the edges of doubts and fears and hurt which had been with her too long. They didn't disappear but, for the first time, she held hope that one day, they might.

I would.

"Shall I continue?" Nicholas asked. She could hear the smile in his words. She nodded. Though she suspected she knew how the ballad might end, she wanted to hear him tell it. No bard had ever before held her captive as Nicholas did.

"'Ten thousand coins, good man,' he said. 'Though few can pay the price.
I would not part with it for less. For this pearl, my son gave his life.'
The man stopped still, his heart did drop, not half so much had he,
But shone her face before his eyes, her great worth did he see.
'Time,' he asked, 'gift me but a day. My house, my horse, my land,
I'll sell it all that I might win the honor of her hand.'"

Night wound around them like the cloth from their wedding, binding the two of them together. Rose hadn't expected him, this quiet, bookish prince. Nicholas was strong, yet gentle. Confident but not arrogant. And he was hers. Here by her side despite how many times she'd pushed him away. She couldn't help but take his words to heart. *I would.* He had, giving up his crown, his family, his comfort, his sleep, that he might convince he r of his love.

"So sold he all, all that he owned, all's precious in his world,
Ten thousand coins the man he gave to buy the costly pearl.
Then knelt he there before the throne, nothing to his name,
But a single pearl, its luster bright, and a humble heart aflame.
Knelt he there in silence 'til, 'Look up,' the good king said.
There stood the man who'd sold the pearl, a crown upon his head."

Rose's breath caught. "It was the king?"

"Do you want to hear this ballad or not, my love?" Though Nicholas's words were chiding, his quiet laughter gave away his amusement.

"Forgive me. Continue."

"You're certain? You're not too cold, or too tired, or too distracted by the handsome man who holds you?"

"The last one. Most certainly." She tilted her head back to meet his gaze, smiling as she did. "But I truly do wish to hear the rest."

"Perhaps I wish to explore your answer further."

"Perhaps I might be convinced to let you."

His eyes widened and she ducked her head, blushing at her brazenness. She'd never been that kind of woman before. Nicholas made her want to be bolder, even while that same boldness made her shy. She yearned to be the person she saw in his gaze.

She also wanted to hear the rest of the ballad.

"After you finish the story. I have to know what happens. I find myself relating all too well to the princess."

Nicholas squeezed her shoulder, swallowing twice before continuing.

"Knelt he there in silence 'til, 'Look up,' the good king said.
There stood the man who'd sold the pearl, a crown upon his head."

His voice was deeper than it had been before. Rougher. As if he too struggled to contain the emotions their unexpected closeness evoked. Or was it the ballad itself? Rose's heart thudded beneath his arms.

"'Rise knight,' said the king, 'for true thou art, thine valor thou hast shown.
You gave it all, you saw true worth, more princely I've not known.

You passed the test to win her hand, though you knew not the game,
My daughter, here, I give you now and the honor of my name.
Thenceforward you shall be my son with all the riches in the world,
For you have learned to measure one's worth from the value of the pearl.'"

A tear dripped down Rose's cheek, surprising her. She let it fall, the night air cooling its trail. "He won."

"Aye, my love, he won."

"Thank you, Nicholas," she whispered, overcome.

"For the ballad?"

That certainly. She could listen to his rumbling voice recite poetry for hours. But it was more than that. So much more. "For coming here. For choosing me."

"'Twas not the burden you think, sweet Rose. I could no more let you go than cease to breathe. I only wish—"

At the catch of his breath, she turned in his arms. His left hand moved to the side of her face. His thumb stroked her cheek.

"Beautiful Rose. I wish I could give you a child. Not for myself, for you are all I need, but for you. To fill your heart. Even if the price were ten thousand coins, I'd pay it. I would give anything to see you smile."

The wave of hurt Rose knew would come didn't ache as much as usual. "Perhaps you will. One day." Standing in Nicholas's arms, staring up at a sky filled with more stars than she could ever count, hope felt close. "Perhaps the Almighty will do the impossible. He already gave me one miracle." She put a gentle hand on his chest. "He gave me you."

She kissed him then with all the gratefulness overflowing her heart. She still yearned for a child. Ached for one. A family for her and Nicholas to love together. And maybe the Almighty would give them one—through their bodies or through their hearts—but for now, in this precious moment, she was content. As if the Almighty was smiling, pointing to Nicholas as a reminder of how much he, the Almighty, loved to love her. He'd given her Nicholas. He'd look after their future too.

Nicholas pulled away and knelt, shaking his head with a smile when she bent to join him.

"Now kneel I here before you now, nothing to my name but a single hope, its luster bright, and a humble heart aflame."

His heart might be aflame but hers was going to beat out of its chest if his embrace didn't hold it in. One tug of his hand had her back in his arms. Right where she belonged.

"Rose?" Nicholas asked.

"Aye?"

"Will you marry me?"

Rose frowned. "We're already married." She wouldn't have been holding him like this if they weren't. She certainly wouldn't be kissing him.

"I know. And those vows stand." He brushed his thumb across her cheek, curling his fingers into her hair. "But marry me again. Here. Now. When it's not rushed or forced or blind or so early in the day we're still both half asleep. Choose me. Knowing who I am. A prince without a crown, who's happier with a book in his hand than a bow, who sings with all the skill of a wild boar but will dance with and quote ballads to you for as long as I live."

"You still want me?"

"More with every passing hour."

"And would you choose me, a princess without a crown, who falls off horses, couldn't name a single star, has less strength than a newborn foal, and might never bear a child, but will forever be grateful you came into my life?"

"Aye. I might fail—"

Rose laughed quietly. "I *know* I will."

"—but I will be there. Forever and always."

"Forever and always."

CHAPTER
39

Cormac leaned against the rough wood of the healer's cottage and watched a tiny but daring bird hop closer and closer to his boots. It was nice to be outside. Away from the bed his sister had confined him to. Away from the reminder of how human he truly was. Away from the two items he'd woken this morning to find sitting on the table beside him.

Lior's crown.

Rose's necklace.

The hardest hearts make the best altars.

He could be king. He could take the crown, sit on Raedonleith's throne, and rule its people. He'd be the most powerful man in the entire kingdom. He'd have everything he'd ever wanted.

"Cormac?"

Lior stood at the corner of the cottage, one hand on the wood as if he wasn't certain he was welcome. Cormac wasn't sure either but waved a hand inviting him over all the same. The bird trilled and flew away when Lior sat on the other end of the bench.

"Aiyana said you're healing well."

"Aye. I suppose."

"You never did like being sick."

He also didn't like feeling as ill at ease as he did right now. Had Lior come as a subject? A king? A friend? A murderer? Cormac was unarmed and Lior had come alone, not a guard in sight. Nor was Aiyana in the cottage behind them. Lior could pull out a knife and kill Cormac where they sat and walk away with no one the wiser if he wanted to. No one would care either. Cormac's bitterness had seen to that. He'd pushed away his sister, his brother, Maeve, Lior and Caralynne. Arthur.

He'd seen the boy from a distance yesterday as he'd stared out Sunny's—no, *Aiyana's*—window. If not for the sandy hair and the tall knight he stood beside, Cormac might not have recognized the boy. Arthur was taller and more filled out than the last time Cormac had seen him but more, he'd been laughing. *Talking.* His wooden sword had been raised high as he tried to keep up with the father who'd claimed him. Where Cormac had pushed the boy away, anger veiling his shame and fear over his tiny son's existence, Sir Darrek lavished praise and love on Arthur.

Evangeline had come to Cavendish Castle of her own accord. She'd cared for Cormac. Accepted him, faults and all. For a time, he'd considered letting the bitterness go. She was beauty and grace and wonder. The love he'd ached for.

And then he'd discovered she was expecting, and the shame of what he'd done overwhelmed him. He'd been furious with himself but taken it out on her. She'd fallen. He'd raged. Maeve had come, drawn by the scream. He'd expected anger from Maeve but seen only disappointment in her face as she'd bundled Evangeline close and her carried away. Cormac had silenced the self-loathing with drink that night and women the next, filling his bed to avoid his heart. It was easier to blame Lior for his failings than himself. Evangeline had become an extension of that. Arthur too. He hadn't been able to look at either of them without seeing how far he'd fallen and feeling his blood boil to rage.

After a while, it had been easier simply to hate. To let the rage have its way. The closer Evangeline was, the angrier Cormac grew and the more the regret burnt away in the face of it. He was owed this. Her life. Lior's pain. When Lior had taken Evangeline, Cormac had sought Mykah's life. Then Rose's.

But it had almost cost him his. Maeve had warned him. He should have listened.

He'd been gifted a second chance.

Lior clasped his hands in his lap. "Remember when you climbed that tree over there and Aiyana was so worried you'd be stuck there forever that she sent me up after you?"

"We assured her we could climb down as easily as we climbed up and laughed at her for worrying. We were stuck for hours. Aye, I remember."

"Do you remember what Father said when he rescued us?"

Strangely, Cormac did.

"'*Your hair is different, and your parents also, but I've never seen two brothers as tight. Protect this bond you have today for you'll ne'er find another like it.*'"

Lior nodded. "I want that. More than anything. I want to be brothers again."

"Why?"

"Because Father was right. I've never found another bond like it."

Twenty years of hate didn't dissolve in a single day. Cormac looked away, too ashamed to meet Lior's gaze.

"I took Evangeline." Took her. Hurt her. Got her with child. One alone would have been enough to condemn him. He'd done them all. And more. He'd seen the scars that marred her arms. Laughed at her weakness while refusing to admit he was the one who'd driven her to it. He'd broken more than her body. He'd broken her spirit.

"I forgive you."

If only that was the worst of his transgressions. "I tried to kill Mykah. I sent my own brother to do it, and when he refused, sent another."

"I forgive you."

"I wanted to kill Rose." The words were so painful they barely made it past his thickened throat. "I had her in my chamber. I went in with a knife."

"I forgive you."

A splinter bit at Cormac's hand where he gripped the wooden bench.

"I hurt your people." He'd broken families. Stolen their livelihoods. Their animals. Taken them for himself. For no reason except that he knew it would hurt Lior.

"I forgive you."

"I hurt you."

"I forgive you that as well."

"How? Is it really so easy?"

"Easy?" Lior laughed quietly. "No, it's not easy. Not at all. But it's right. I only ever wanted peace between us. If letting go of the past is what it takes, so be it. You're forgiven, brother."

Tears clogged Cormac's throat. Curse being sick. It turned him into an emotional fool. If he opened his mouth right now, he'd weep. He put a hand to his head, rubbing his temples.

"You need rest," Lior said. "I'll go. Aiyana told me you were still unwell. I should have listened. Only I wanted you to know—" His voice broke. Lior cleared his throat three times before continuing. "I wanted you to know you're welcome here. You always have been."

⁕

Cormac was still sitting outside on that same bench when Aiyana returned from her walk. He heard her moving about inside the cottage. The little bird came back with a friend, played a while, then flew away again. A white butterfly flitted past, in no hurry to get to wherever it was going. The sun reached beyond the top of the trees. His stomach grumbled its objection to not being fed for so long. The pounding in his head grew to an onslaught, pressing tears from his eyes.

I forgive you.

I forgive you.

I forgive you.

What good was Lior's forgiveness if Cormac couldn't forgive himself? It was too much. Too late. Too soon.

Footsteps sounded. Cormac growled. Enough was enough. After Lior came, it had been Darrek, then Finnian and Mykah. Then Aiyana. Rose. He didn't want to hear their welcomes or their grievances or how happy—or angry—they were that he was here. He didn't want to hear any of it. All he wanted was to be miserable in peace. No crown. No decisions. No judgment. No childish green stone that looked so innocent but held a kingdom's worth of broken dreams inside.

"Go a—" Timeworn hands wrung in front of him, a familiar white apron their backdrop. He looked up. Blinked in the sunlight. "Maeve?"

"Cormac," she said with a small smile. "You look terrible."

"What are you doing here?" He'd left her in the dungeon, like the coward he was. No food, no blankets, no compassion for the woman who'd stood by him all these years. He really was a monster.

"Sir Darrek freed me and brought me with them to Raedonleith. He and Eva asked me to be Arthur's godmother."

Of course they had. Maeve was good and noble and deserved every bit of kindness offered her. "You agreed." He'd go home without her. The pang of pain that struck his heart had him pressing a hand to his chest. Curse the weakness. Curse the pain. Curse the yearning to stay.

One day in the place he'd once thought of as home and it was like he'd never left. Like he never wanted to again.

"I didn't agree. Not yet."

Cormac frowned. "Why not?" It was a great honor. Far more than he'd ever given her. She wouldn't be a servant anymore but part of the family, with all the riches and wealth that came with it. She could burn that apron with his blood stain in the corner and never look back.

"Because you're the one I pledged my life to serve."

"I can find another maid, if that's what you wish."

"But not one who cares."

He laughed, though there was no mirth in it. "You think I'd have any trouble finding a maid to warm my bed?"

"I said cares, not fawns." She sat beside him, something she'd never have done at Cavendish Castle. He should send her away. But he didn't mind her sitting there. In truth, he liked it. Lior, Caralynne, Finnian, Aiyana, Rose—they each saw him as something different. A broken man, a potential king, the boy who'd once been a friend, the lord who'd tried to destroy them. But Maeve, she simply saw him. The good and the bad. From birth to the man he was today, she'd been there for his whole story.

"Don't fret over me. I hereby release you. Stay," he said, knowing it was the right thing to do. The cost for him would be high but Maeve had already paid so much more. "Be part of Arthur's life. No doubt you've missed him."

"I have but—" She caught his gaze before looking down at her hands. "I worry for you."

"Why? I'm going to be king."

"So I've been told. Is that what you want?"

He should say yes. It was what was expected. What he'd wanted, all these years. It was his for the taking. But—

"No." Cormac shook his head, truth settling over him in place of the crown he didn't want to accept. "I don't want to be king."

She nodded like she'd known the answer already. Perhaps she had. He'd known it from the minute he woke to see the crown sitting there beside his bed though it had taken until this moment to admit it. One didn't walk away from a throne.

"What *do* you want?" Maeve asked.

"A family."

The answer came as if it had been waiting years for its moment. Pushed aside by dreams of grandeur and power, crushed by bitterness, strangled by disillusions, it had held on. And now those things had been blown away, there it was. The hope. A spark of light.

A spark of light that dimmed as quickly as it came. A family? He'd lost that chance. He'd pushed his siblings away, destroyed any chance of friendship, and outright disowned Arthur. He could have married decades ago and had a family of his own if he'd not been so busy trying to destroy Lior's.

"You have one."

"*Had* one," he corrected.

"No. *Have.* They're here, Cormac. All around you. King Lior and Queen Caralynne, Aiyana and Finn, Rose, Mykah, Eva, and their husbands. Arthur, too. You gave up your chance to be his father but that doesn't mean you can't be part of his life."

You're welcome here.

No. Lior's words were pretty and inviting but they were just words.

"They don't want me."

I forgive you.

Words. Just words.

"Lior cared for you himself while you slept on the journey here. He'd not let anyone else help. He held your head in his lap and spooned broth into you. Wiped your face and body clean with his cloak. Gave up his own blanket to ensure you were warm.

"Darrek knelt by your side for hours, his hand on your shoulder as he beseeched the Almighty for your healing. He didn't sleep that first night and only slept the second when Finnian took his place in prayer.

"Queen Caralynne wept when you arrived and worked by Aiyana's side to see you cared for. She'd be here now except she's not certain you want to see her. The chapel has been overflowing with people beseeching the Almighty for your healing. Need you more proof?"

"Are you sure they weren't praying for my demise?"

"Cormac," Maeve admonished.

"I tried to destroy them."

"But you didn't succeed." She laid a hand over his. "It might not be the family you dreamed of, but there's a family right here in Raedonleith who care about you. Give them a second chance. Give yourself one."

"I don't deserve it."

"None of us do. That's why it's called grace."

CHAPTER 40

The tiny baby blanket spread across Rose's lap. Complete. In the early hours of the morning, when she'd not been able to sleep, she'd crept from the room she shared with Nicholas—relieved he'd not woken—and stolen to the chapel.

There, in the silence, she'd finished it. Every word. Every stitch. Every prayer.

New tear drops marred the fabric. Some would dry, never to be seen again amid the flowers and prayers. Others would stain, forever remembered.

Quin stood at the chapel's door, unwilling to let her mistress out of sight. With more Cavendish men about the castle than ever, Rose didn't blame her. Nor Spencer, who arrived not long after and took up his post by Quin's side. Sometimes they whispered. Sometimes they were silent. Always, they watched.

Rose didn't mind. She would have once, thinking their presence proof of her weakness, but now she simply felt protected.

Almighty, bless the child who sleeps beneath this blanket. May they be strong in body and mind. May they be healthy and wise. May they know your love above all.

And may they—

Her heart hitched as another tear fell. She closed her eyes to the pain and reached out to the one who held her, knowing the Almighty would never let go.

May they know their Aunt Rose loves them too.

Candles stood to attention around her, nary a breeze making them sway. The cross before her was still too, a beacon of unmoving hope. In this hallowed place she'd wept so many prayers, she offered another. Her own surrender. The blanket of hopes and dreams for a life unknown.

But not unloved.

Never unloved.

She bent forward, hands wet against the tears streaming down her face. The pain didn't go away simply because she knew the decision was right. Her heart still ached. Her body too. Here now was her surrender, but maybe it wasn't the only one. Maybe surrender, like Nicholas's patience, was a continual thing. Day by day. Moment by moment.

Almighty, I don't love my body. But I thank you for it. I thank you for my lungs that breathe and the heart that beats within my chest. I thank you for the weakness in my legs that reminds me daily to lean on your strength. I thank you for ears that hear, eyes that see, and hands to raise to you. And I thank you for—I thank you for—

A sob broke free. She couldn't do it. She couldn't thank the Almighty for her barren womb. Though it had brought her to Nicholas, the ache was still too raw.

> "Praise the Almighty from whom blessings flow,
> Praise the One who stands with us in valleys low."

Tears dripped onto the stairs as she whispered a prayer she'd learned long ago. One etched into her heart, that flowed when words ran dry.

> "Praise the One who remains when all else fails.
> Praise the One who whispers through strong and mighty gale.
> Praise the One who rides the storm, all conquering king.
> Praise the Almighty, the Lord of Everything."

The prayer carried her as she left the chapel and walked the long hall to Evangeline's chamber. Her hand trembled as she knocked on the door. It opened within seconds.

"Aunt Rose?" Bright blue eyes stared up at her. She tried to find a smile for Arthur but, like the hand he took between his child-sized ones, it trembled. "You're crying. Are you sick like Mama?"

"Arthur, don't open the door without—" Darrek walked out from behind a screen and stopped at the sight of her. "Rose. What is it?"

"Evangeline's sick?" she asked.

"Aye, but Maeve assures me it will pass soon if she carries this one like—" His eyes slid closed. There was regret in them when he met her gaze again. "Forgive me. I didn't think."

Evangeline was expecting. She and Darrek had only been married five months. Of course, Rose knew it could happen that fast and often did, but it still crushed like a blow. Rose looked down at the blanket clutched in her hand. This was why she'd come. In the chapel, she'd surrendered the blanket and the dreams that went with it and decided to give it to Evangeline for her next child. She just hadn't expected to have to see it wrapped around a babe not her own so soon.

A sob caught in her throat. *Almighty, I don't think I can do this. I know, I said I would but it's too hard.*

Adora.

I've prayed for the child who'd use this blanket for so many years. How do I let that go? How do I watch my sister grow with child, knowing my body will never carry one? It's... I can't.

Adora.

Please, Almighty.

Adora.

That word. It wouldn't leave her be. Arthur's hand squeezed hers. She looked at him, caught by his innocent blue gaze.

Evangeline's child—

Adora.

Rose gasped. It wasn't a word. It was a name. The name of the child growing under Evangeline's heart. A daughter for Darrek. A sister for Arthur.

"Rose? Please, say something. Are you ill? Let me send for your maid. Or Nicholas, if you prefer. I shouldn't have said anything. Evangeline told me not to. She planned to wait to announce the news for as long as possible." He rubbed a hand across his face. "I'm so sorry. Here, sit. I'll call for your maid."

"No." Rose fingered a purple flower stitched into the soft fabric of the blanket, the word "adore" curled in green like a leaf around it. Adore. Adora. The Almighty had named this child before she was even conceived, and, for some reason, shared that name with Rose. Not the babe's mother or father, but her aunt. Chosen. Not forgotten. Rose blinked, trying to hold back the tears of an overwhelmed heart but one escaped despite her.

Almighty, bless Adora. May she be strong in body and mind. May she be healthy and wise. May she know your love above all.

Her gold bracelet snagged the fabric as she handed the blanket to Darrek. With shaking fingers, she pulled the bracelet free. Darrek's brows pulled together in confusion.

Arthur looked from the blanket to Rose. "For the baby?"

She crouched to his height and brushed a lock of pale hair off his cheek. He brushed a tear off hers, his hand gentle against her face. Her smile was watery but real. "Aye. For your sister. She'll need it come winter."

"Sister?" Darrek asked.

"Evangeline carries your daughter."

Darrek's face—there was no word for it but wonder. His eyes widened, softened. His mouth dropped open. Questions. Wonder. Hope. Love. For his child. His wife. "How could you know?"

Adora. Almighty, bless Adora.

"Because six years ago, I started praying for her."

⁕ ⋅✤⋅ ⁕

Nicholas looked across at his wife, one hand in Arthur's, the other in Mykah's as they skipped across the Great Hall to the music of the lute and lyre. He would have joined them if not for pain in his ribs and how much he was enjoying Rose's laughter. He'd been so worried for her this morning when he'd found her sobbing near the chapel. Quin had sent Spencer for him when Rose had collapsed in the hall outside. Nicholas had carried her to their room and held her until she cried herself to sleep. It was no doubt the reason his ribs burned with each breath now, but he had no regrets.

They'd spoken when she woke. He'd asked why she cried, expecting for her to brush it off as nothing. He'd been shocked instead when she'd told him about the blanket she'd stitched, its significance, and how she'd given it to Darrek for his daughter. She'd even told him the babe's name. Adora. Adored one. Nicholas couldn't have imagined a name more fitting for Evangeline and Darrek's child, borne of the love they so clearly shared. He had no more plans to disclose the name to the couple than Rose did, but Nicholas's heart had thrilled that Rose shared it with him.

Rose laughed again, the sound mixing with the music as she joined

Mykah and Arthur's hands together in place of hers and walked toward him.

The girl whose heart rang true, her smile like hope renewed.

Something had echoed inside Nicholas the first time he'd read *The Ballad of the Pearl.* He'd spent hours committing it to memory that he might always have it with him. He'd often thought of the man in the story, wondering what it was he'd seen in the woman that he would spend so long—and sell everything he had—just for a chance at winning her heart. It was a story, Nicholas had concluded. A powerful tale of the Almighty's love and sacrifice, but a parable nonetheless.

Until he met Rose, and the ballad became his story.

You have learned to measure one's worth through the value of a pearl.

"Sire."

Nicholas startled at the voice beside him. So caught up in the way Rose's laughter danced into his thoughts, he hadn't noticed the guard bending to his ear.

"Your brother is here. He asked for Lady Rose but—"

Aldon. Here. "Yes, yes. Of course you should have come to me. Where is he?"

The question became purposeless the instant Nicholas stood. There his brother was at the edge of the Great Hall, hand gripping the doorpost as if it was all that held him upright. Nicholas ducked around servants and nobles alike to reach his brother's side.

"You're alive," Aldon said.

Nicholas frowned. "Of course I'm alive. Why wouldn't I be?"

"It's been weeks. Your guards' horses returned without you. Your ring was tucked inside one of the saddle bags."

"I sent the ring with the guards. Didn't they tell you?" He'd sent other messages with them too. His marrying Rose. His relinquishing his right to the throne. His intention to stay with Rose, even if that meant never returning to the kingdom of his birth.

"The guards never arrived. Only their horses. There was blood on the bag that held your ring."

A gasp behind Nicholas had him turning. Rose. Swaying as if she were about to faint. He swept her into his arms before she could, wincing at the searing burn to the ribs he remembered too late were healing, and carried her the few steps to a quieter room off the Great Hall. He lowered Rose to sit on a wooden bench, kneeling before her. Her hand was like ice in his, her breathing too shallow to be healthy.

"They thought you were dead. All this time? We have to send word. Right away."

He rubbed her freezing hands between his. "We will. I'll see to it. Nothing has changed."

"Your family don't know about…me and…you."

"We'll tell them. A misunderstanding, 'tis all." He touched her knee, laid his palm against her cheek, feeling it scald. Her hands were cold, her face warm. She'd stopped swaying, at least. "What do you need? I can take you to our room, call for Quin, send for Aiyana."

"No, no. I'm well. It was the shock. I can stay."

"What is this?"

Aldon's bluster made them both look up. He stood, arms crossed as he glowered down at them both. "The Nicholas I knew would never touch a woman like—"

"She was his wife?" Nicholas interrupted. A grin pleaded to be set free at the knowledge he'd done more than hold Rose's hand when they'd returned to their room last night. Yet another reason his ribs still burned.

"Lady Rose isn't a teasing servant girl throwing tokens at your feet, she's King Lior's daughter and—"

"My wife."

Nicholas leaned forward and pressed a gentle kiss to Rose's blushing cheek before bringing her to stand beside him. Aldon's face went red.

"No. She can't be."

Nicholas quirked an eyebrow. "I assure you, she is. The guards I sent were supposed to tell you but as they didn't, allow me." He wrapped an arm around her waist. "Aldon, I present to you my beloved wife, Lady Rose, heir to the throne of Raedonleith."

"You married her."

"Aye, and the feast you've interrupted is our wedding celebration. Of sorts. We were wed last month but never had the chance to celebrate until now."

The feast was smaller than it would have been, due to the impromptu nature of it. There'd been no invites sent out to neighboring kingdoms to celebrate the marriage nor a tournament to commemorate it. But Rose's family were here, and others who'd been there for their short but eventful story. Those who wouldn't usually sit at the king's table but held places of honor tonight. Quin, Aiyana, Arthur, Lord Cavendish, and Maeve.

Nicholas had already promised Rose they'd leave as soon as she was ready, no matter how early it was or that the feast was in their honor.

"She's not barren then?"

He would ignore his heartless brother. "Shall we retire?" he asked Rose instead. "Aldon and I can speak tomorrow when he learns to think before he speaks." Aldon hadn't even congratulated the two of them before bringing up Rose's greatest hurt. If Nicholas could have thrown his brother from the room without making Rose feel worse, he would have. But Rose shook her head.

"I'm still barren," she told Aldon. "Nothing has changed."

Aldon didn't even look at Rose, his frown focused entirely on Nicholas. "Why would you marry her?"

The noise of the feast nearby wasn't loud enough to quell the anger that welled at Aldon's question. Nicholas wished it had been. He wished his brother had never come. How dare Aldon insinuate in Rose's presence that she was worthless. Aldon had said the same thing all those weeks ago when he'd first come home, and indignation had filled Nicholas then at Rose's expense. He hadn't even known her then. She'd been but a name—the princess betrothed to his brother. Now, she was his wife. His heart. Forever part of him.

"Leave," he ordered.

"Nicholas." Rose said, her hand on his arm. "He's your brother."

"He's a fool."

"I—I'm sorry," Aldon said, shaking his head. "I didn't mean—" He sighed. "Forgive me. I came to Raedonleith to apologize to Rose for the way I left and ask if she or her family knew anything of your disappearance and here I've insulted you both. I never meant to hurt you. When I asked why you married her, it was because Lady Rose is her father's heir, not because of her barren state. I can see how much you love her. But what is to become of Belairisia? You cannot be in two places at once."

"Our people will have you, their next king. The throne is yours, Aldon. Take it. My place is by my wife's side."

CHAPTER
41

Rose watched as color blanched from Aldon's face. His heel tapped a beat much faster than the music still swirling about the Great Hall. He looked older than the last time she'd seen him and far more serious. The last two months had changed them all.

"No," Aldon said. "I won't do it. I have no wish to be king."

"You would have had no choice had I died as you thought."

"But you're not dead. Please, Nicholas, don't ask it of me. I've hated every moment of the past month. I'm a knight, not a king. I'll lead an army into battle and fight to the death for our kingdom but please don't make me settle disputes or placate nobles or stand before our people and instill hope. You are the one with the mind for maps and history and what's best for Belairisia. You are the one they trust to lead."

Did Aldon sway, or was that Rose? The exhaustion of the day's emotions hit her like a brick wall. The discomfort which woke her far too early this morning, the stitching by candlelight in the chapel, the wrenching of her heart as she surrendered, discovering Evangeline was expecting, falling apart all over again, finding the courage to be vulnerable with Nicholas, pushing aside fear to allow joy in at the celebration tonight, the shock of seeing Aldon.

"I won't leave Rose."

Nicholas was choosing her. Again. Putting her needs before his own. Giving up everything he'd ever known, like the man in the ballad. But this time, he didn't need to.

"Nicholas." She waited until he met her gaze. "Your people need you."

"I gave up my kingdom and right to the throne the day I married you. I didn't do so lightly. I knew what it would mean. Don't be swayed by Aldon's doubts. He'll be a great king and lead our people with strength."

"I'll come to Belairisia."

"Leave your family? No, Rose. I couldn't ask that of you."

This was who he was. Rose knew it with absolute certainty. She'd seen it in the last few weeks—the way he cared. He wasn't bluster and intimidation, as so many kings were, nor by his admission was he skilled with a sword, but he cared. Deeply. His loyalty and wisdom rang true. But more, he had the humility to lead. Nicholas knew who he was and valued the strength of others. He learned from the past and looked to the future. Like the man in the ballad, he'd learnt to judge one's worth not from riches or wealth—or health, even—but from who they were.

Yes, he would lead them well.

"You're not asking. I made promises the day we married too. Would you have me deny them for the sake of your pride?" She pulled him to the corner of the room, away from Aldon with his tapping and Quin standing to the edge the doorway. No doubt Spencer was somewhere close too. She lay her hand against the side of Nicholas's face, begging him to see the truth in her eyes. "You were made to be king, Nicholas. Your people need you. I know you gave it up for me, to prove your love, but now let me prove mine. I love you, Nicholas. And I want you to be king. I want to stand by your side as queen."

"Raedonleith—"

"Will have Mykah and Finnian to rule. Though I wrote the letter giving my crown to Mykah in haste that night, I meant every word of it. I have no wish to be queen. I want to be a helper. By your side. A support, not a leader."

Nicholas moved his head to kiss her palm.

"It's a long journey to Belairisia."

"More time to enjoy the wonders of the Almighty around us," Rose said. "Isn't that what you told me?"

His only answer was to kiss her again. This time, not on her palm.

They pulled apart when Aldon cleared his throat. "You'll return to Belairisia then?"

Rose's smile was tremulous as she called Quin closer and asked her maid to find her parents, sisters and their husbands that she might speak with them. The throne room would have been more appropriate for such a discussion but Rose didn't know if she could walk that far. Her body thrummed with borrowed strength, but she was all too aware of how fast the strength could disappear and how weak she'd be when it did.

The few minutes it took for her family to join them were a particular kind of agony. What if her father said no? What if Mykah did?

Praise the Almighty from whom blessings flow. Praise the One who stands with us in valleys low.

She waited as exclamations were made over Aldon's presence, and then all over again when he said why he'd come. A servant was sent immediately to prepare a message for the king and queen of Belairisia, confirming Nicholas still lived. Then the noise quietened, and everyone's attention turned to Rose.

She couldn't breathe.

No. She could. This was right. This was the plan the Almighty had chosen for her before she was born. It was clear. Right.

Terrifying.

Nicholas took her hand. She gripped it with a strength belying the exhaustion trying to send her to the floor.

Praise the One who remains when all else fails. Praise the One who whispers through strong and mighty gale.

A month ago, when Rose had first considered giving up her crown, it had been because she thought herself too broken for the task. Now, though she was making the same decision, it was out of strength. She was strong enough to be queen, but also strong enough to stand aside and let someone more suited take her place.

A decision based not in shame but love. For her people, her husband, and herself.

Praise the One who rides the storm, all conquering king. Praise the Almighty, the Lord of Everything.

Thank you, Almighty, for showing me the way. May I walk forward in your strength, my heart undivided that I may serve you.

And if Mykah could just accept this without arguing, I'd really appreciate it.

"Father, with your approval, I hereby relinquish my crown and any claim to the throne of Raedonleith to Mykah." Rose ignored the mix of surprise and confusion on her family's faces and continued. "She earned their respect and love as the Guardian long before they knew her identity and I cannot think of anyone more suited to lead when the sad day comes that you cannot. Mykah is the heir our people need and—" Rose took a deep breath and leaned against Nicholas's side. "My place is with my husband. In Belairisia."

In the Great Hall, the music continued. People danced, laughed and feasted. Within the circle of her family, only silence met Rose's proclamation.

"Father?"

Rose couldn't help but notice that her father, too, held his wife's hand as if she were the one keeping him standing. Enough emotion filled the room to overthrow a kingdom. Hope. Disbelief. Exhaustion. Perhaps she should have waited until tomorrow to speak with her father. Lord Cavendish had returned the king's crown today, humbly asking if he might stay at Raedonleith for a time. Having cried herself to sleep, Rose had missed the very public exchange but Quin had relayed the news when she brought an overflowing platter of food for Rose and Nicholas to share. The king had offered Lord Cavendish a room in the castle, but Lord Cavendish had chosen to accept Aiyana's offer to stay with her instead.

Father's eyes had been red-rimmed when he'd greeted Rose tonight, his voice as rough from tears as Rose's had been.

Tomorrow would have been better, but Rose knew she wouldn't sleep until this was sorted.

"Father?" she asked again.

His gaze was soft when it met hers, reminding Rose of mornings long past when as a child she'd woken before the sun and tiptoed to his study, certain to find him there with a book or a story to share.

"If that is truly your wish, then I shall honor it but are you certain? This past month has been hard on you, Rose. On us all. I can't help but think such a life-altering decision requires more time and consideration."

Rose shook her head. Time wouldn't make a difference.

"Postpone it if you must but I'll not change my mind. This past month has done nothing but prove to me how much more suited I am to support than lead. It would be my honor to step aside and allow Mykah to take up the crown and calling the Almighty has gifted her."

"Calling?" Rose heard Mykah whisper, eyes wide as she looked to her husband.

Finnian nodded, the pride on his face clear. "Aye, calling, my love. 'Tis as you heard. It seems the Almighty hasn't taken away your dream after all but grown it larger than you could have ever imagined."

Mykah's gaze swung to meet Rose's, tears in her eyes. Rose couldn't remember ever seeing her younger sister cry. "Thank you," Mykah said. "It would—would—" She shook her head with a wonder-filled smile. "Thank you."

Rose swayed, another wave of weariness washing over her. Mykah had agreed but it was of no consequence if their father didn't release Rose from the future she'd been born into. She should convince him. List all the reasons Mykah would be a better queen. All the reasons Rose didn't wish to be. She remained silent.

Almighty, let him see the wisdom of this choice.

"Forgive me. I can't. Not tonight," her father said, and fled the room.

CHAPTER
42

"Will you tell me *The Ballad of the Pearl* again?"

Rose stood in the shelter of Nicholas's arms high in the castle's tower. She hadn't even needed to ask for him to take her there. Either he'd known how much she needed it or he'd been as desperate to see the stars and feel the night air against his face as she.

"The day was bleak when first he saw the girl whose heart rang true."

They could have gone to their room. She wouldn't have argued if that's where Nicholas had led. She was grateful he hadn't. Though exhaustion made her limp, her mind raced too fast to sleep. Here in the tower, beneath the stars, it was like they were on the road again—when heirdoms and crowns faded away and they were simply Nicholas and Rose, a man and a woman falling in love.

"But who was she, this spark of light which stirred his heart to ring?"

The sky sparkled with stars. It wasn't entirely clear, a smudge of clouds painted the horizon, but Rose barely saw them as she tilted her head to lean against Nicholas's shoulder. Father would agree. He had to. She and Nicholas were married. Her allegiance was to her husband now and thereby his home.

Belairisia. What would it be like? It was nearer the coast than Raedonleith. That she knew. Would the stars be even clearer there? Would they walk the cliffs that braced it and marvel at the One who rode the storms?

"'Long all the kingdom's paths he searched, rough oceans did he part, certain nigh he'd find the gift to win his lady's heart."

Almighty, change Father's heart. Give him wisdom as he leads this kingdom. Show him Mykah is the one who should lead it.

"But naught he found could bear the weight of expectation high, for what to give a maid like she who owned all gold could buy?"

A breeze drifted past. Not strong, but enough to make Rose shiver. Nicholas pulled his cloak around them both, encasing her in his warmth. His tale didn't miss a beat. She yawned. Perhaps she could fall asleep here, wrapped in his strength, his ballad her lullaby.

"It shone with light, its luster clear. Color stalked its sheen. White, then rose, then turquoise blue. As round he'd ever seen."

His heart beat against her back, its rhythm as solid as the man it kept alive.

Thank you, Almighty, for Nicholas. For bringing him to me. For his courage the day he told one and all that he chose me. He's stronger than he thinks.

She smiled into the darkness, at peace, despite the future still unknown.

I am too.

Strong enough for the long journey to Belairisia. Strong enough to pray and hope for a child not hers. Strong enough to stand beside this man who'd one day be king and support him, believe in him, as he'd done for her.

"Then knelt he there before the throne nothing to his name but a single pearl, its luster bright, and a humble heart aflame."

"Sire."

Rose startled at Spencer's voice. She hadn't even heard him approach. The way Nicholas's arms dropped, the gasp of a breath proving his pain before he could hide it, Nicholas hadn't heard the knight either.

"Forgive us. We didn't mean to interrupt."

Spencer held out a hand inviting Quin to stand beside him.

"What is it? Is something the matter?" Nicholas asked.

"No, not at all. We heard you were to return to Belairisia and wished to ask if we might join you. Quin doesn't wish to leave her lady and"— He glanced at Quin before turning his attention back to them—"I don't wish to leave Quin."

Quin's smile was as tentative as Rose had ever seen. Rose's was not.

"You're to marry?"

"She's the one?"

Rose and Nicholas spoke over each other in their delight.

Spencer nodded. "Aye, she is that. I've admired Quin since before she was Lady Rose's maid, but I had nothing to offer her, and then days after I was knighted, the king chose me to search for Lady Evangeline. My love grew stronger in the years I was gone. When King Lior asked for knights to travel with you the day you wed, I offered my sword, knowing your maid would accompany you. Hoping I might finally find the courage to speak with her. You gave me that courage, Prince Nicholas. Watching you care for Lady Rose.

"We should like to marry, if the king grants it of us. I plan to ask him on the morrow."

"Why wait?" King Lior walked toward them. Spencer dropped to his knee. Rose's heart thudded. How long had Father been standing in the shadows of the tower's stairway? Had he come with a decision?

Almighty, please. Let him choose Mykah.

"Rise, Sir Spencer," the king said. "I hereby grant permission for you to wed. How could I do less for a man who's served me with such loyalty? You brought Evangeline home to me and protected Rose. It would be an honor to see you wed the woman you love."

"Thank you, sire."

"And they'll accompany us home to Belairisia?" Rose asked. *Home.* It felt both strange and right to Belairisia home when she'd never set foot in it. Nicholas squeezed her hand. She held her breath, waiting for her father's answer.

"You truly wish to go? To give up your right to Raedonleith's throne?" There was no question. Not anymore. "Aye. I do."

"Then go with my blessing."

"Truly, Father?"

"Aye. 'Tis your path as surely as being the next queen is Mykah's. I didn't want to accept it. I couldn't bear the thought of losing you but—"

He stopped when Rose flung herself into his arms. "You'll never lose me, Father. I will always be your daughter."

"I couldn't have asked the Almighty for a better one. Nay, a better three. I am a king truly blessed."

He left then. Spencer and Quin too, though Rose doubted they'd gone far. They too had reason to celebrate.

Nicholas wasted no time pulling Rose back into his embrace. "My precious pearl," he whispered seconds before his lips found hers.

As she thanked the Almighty again for the surprise gift of this man before her, Rose couldn't help but think that these were the moments men wrote ballads about. Perhaps hers would start like this:

'Twas bleak the day when first she saw the man who brought hope new.
His hair was brown, his shoulders strong, his eyes a brilliant blue.

She laughed quietly to herself. Balladeer she was not.

"Rose? Are you well? We can retire, if you wish."

She shook her head. No. Not yet.

"Let's stay and watch the stars."

In the early hours of the morning

K ing Lior fell to his knees before the altar. He'd been here before.
Many times.

When the message had come that Evangeline had been found.

The night he'd discovered Mykah was the Guardian he'd been searching for.

The day the healer had confirmed Rose's barrenness.

And a thousand days before and in between. To pray. To seek. To worship. To beg for wisdom and help in leading the kingdom he felt so unqualified to lead.

He hadn't come this time to beg. It wasn't fear or a torn heart that drove him to his knees but gratitude. Though tears dripped down his cheeks and caught in his beard, they came of an overwhelming sense of awe.

The Almighty had done this. Brought this family together. He and Caralynne. Rose and Nicholas. Mykah and Finnian. Evangeline and Darrek. Arthur. Aiyana. Cormac. Maeve. The Almighty had promised to care for them, to lead them, bring them love and courage and light, and he had.

He had.

There were so many things Lior could pray for—wisdom, protection over Evangeline and the babe growing inside her, his people, a child for Mykah, healing for Rose and safety as she, Nicholas and Aldon began their journey home—but today he simply wanted to praise.

The Almighty had brought them here. The Almighty had kept them safe.

And wherever their family went from this day forward, come heartbreak or famine or destruction or peace, the Almighty would lead them on.

Thank you, Almighty One. Thank you.

Acknowledgements

Tell me I'm not the only one sobbing right now. One, Rose (oh my goodness, Rose! I'm so sorry! And also, so grateful.). Two, I can't believe this series is over! Nooooo… I'm not ready. I absolutely love my first series but this one has torn my heart to pieces so many times only to heal it again with hope. Over and over again. It's been all at once humbling and terrifying and healing and an absolute honor to write.

This book in particular holds so much of my heart. Like Rose, I know what it's like to live with a chronic illness and the daily challenges that brings. Many of her prayers came from my own. What I never expected though, was how much this book I wrote to encourage others would become God's love letter to me. To remind me, just as Nicholas reminded Rose, that I'm not alone. Not forgotten. Never too broken.

I pray it reminds you of that too.

To the following people, thank you. For making this book a reality, but also for reminding me of the value of a pearl. Even when it's messy.

To my husband and kidlets. You guys are the best! Thank you just doesn't cut it when I think of all you are and all you mean to me. You're not only my favorite people but *my* people. I love our ups and downs and inside jokes and how you look out for me, but mostly, I just really love you. (PS. Sorry I had to cull the scene with the aliens.)

To Mum & Dad, who remind me time and time again that my worth doesn't come from what I can or can't do but Whose I am. I am so incredibly blessed to have you as parents and an example of what it means to love and show grace like Jesus.

To Mimi, Abbie, Abigail, Adam, Adeline, Adrianne, Allison, Anna, Annabelle, Ashley, Callie, Carter, Delanie, Dustin and Amy, Ella, Elle, Ellie, Emily M, Emily V, Evie, Grace B, Grace H, Hannah, Jake, Jayce, Jessica, Jonah, Juliana, Kiara, Lacy, Lauryn, Lucy, Lydia, Meagan, Megan, Natalie, Noelle, Olivia, Reagan, Riley, Sarah, Sorina, and the rest of the Fidele Youth Dance Company family.

In performing *Bring Her Home*, you brought these characters to life for me in a way I couldn't have imagined, and inspired me more than you'll ever know. You had me seriously questioning whether I should redeem Lord Cavendish after all (thanks Adam for being such a great bad guy!), knowing I just *had* to add more scenes with Maeve (thank you, Lacy!), and overwhelmed again at the grace of God the Father who never gives up. No matter what. Rose's story is so much deeper because of you. It was such an honor to meet you all and witness firsthand what God is doing through your faith and lives and dancing. I will never forget my week in Colorado and how incredibly special you made it. Thank you!

To Janelle. Thank you for being both my editor and friend and walking with me through all the many rewrites and changes this book has been through. It's been quite a journey (to say the least!) and I am so grateful I didn't walk it alone. Thanks for the brainstorming chats, the writing sprints, your endless patience, and for just being there. This series wouldn't be the same without you.

Eliana, all credit goes to you for suggesting this beautiful title. You'll never know how much your out-of-the-blue-but-so-perfectly-timed email meant to me after having struggled for over a year to figure out the title for this third book. Thank you! I hope you enjoy Rose's story.

To Roseanna, David and the WhiteCrown team. Thank you for your editing expertise, your answers to all my random questions, your *incredible* cover design, and for believing in this book and series. It's a privilege to work with you all. Also, I don't think I'll ever get over how stunning this cover is. I had to take the photo of it off my desktop because I kept staring at it instead of working... ha! It so perfectly fits the story. Thank you!

Above all, to the Almighty. You knew from the start that this book would be more than I imagined or could do alone, and gave me—day by day—the words to write it. When I say I couldn't have done this without you, I truly mean it. I see your fingerprints in every word and am so, so, so grateful for it. Humbled too. Thank you for the way you daily take my brokenness and, instead of running in the opposite direction, pick me up and use me to make something beautiful. I'm overwhelmed again and again by your goodness, grace, and love.

Though I wrote this prayer for Rose, it's become my battle cry too. I couldn't live a day without you.

Praise the Almighty from whom blessings flow,
Praise the One who stands with us in valleys low.
Praise the One who remains when all else fails,
Praise the One who whispers through strong and mighty gale.
Praise the One who rides the storm, all conquering king,
Praise the Almighty, the Lord of Everything.
To God be the glory.

Hannah Currie has loved royals—both real and fictional—for as long as she can remember and has always been fascinated by their lives. They started making their way into her writing somewhere around first grade, and never stopped.

While she never dreamed of being a princess for real (way too many expectations and people watching), she certainly wouldn't say no to the gorgeous gowns, endless wardrobes, chefs and cleaners that come with the job. A crown or two wouldn't go astray either. Or Belle's library. Where she'd just sit and stare at the books with a giddy smile on her face for hours.

Hannah lives with her husband and three kids in Australia, where they proudly claim Queen Elizabeth II and the royal family as their own. She is very honored to be one of the launching authors for the new WhiteCrown Publishing line with her Crown of Promise series full of faith, romance and—of course—royals.

LEARN MORE ABOUT HANNAH AND SIGN UP FOR HER NEWSLETTER
at
www.HannahCurrie.com

CROWN OF PROMISE SERIES

Sir Darrek thought the hardest part of his quest would be finding Evangeline. He had no idea how difficult it would be to get her home.

To all bar a few, the Guardian of Raedonleith is a mystery. To Lady Mykah, second daughter of King Lior, it's her calling.

ALSO BY HANNAH CURRIE

Milton Keynes UK
Ingram Content Group UK Ltd.
UKHW021512111024
2132UKWH00027BA/68/J